ELYSEN

A NOVEL

JOE COOKE

CPG

Cannon Publishing Group
Walla Walla, Washington

ELYSEN
Limited First Edition

ISBN 0-9766291-0-0

Library of Congress Control Number: 2005900933

CPG

Cannon Publishing Group
1644 Plaza Way, #231
Walla Walla, WA 99362
(509) 520-1005

Printed in the United States of America by
Morris Publishing
3212 E. Hwy 30
Kearney, NE 68847
800-650-7888

1 2 3 4 5 6 7 8 9

Cover design by Integrity Design

This book is dedicated to J.

Whose life is an example
Of the power of love
And the illusion
Of darkness

a crystal of ice sparkles
amid endless rivers of ice
a flame flickers and dies
in the barren wastelands
the burning Soel turns dark
one power
binds all
one power
tears all apart
one power
gently coaxes a flower to bloom
one power
lingers in the shadows of the keep
one power
brings forth light
returns all to night
one power
one power

The Song of Araden

Prologue

An invisible hand pressed against Aephia's nose and mouth. Soft yellow light from ancient coal lanterns reflected off red obsidian walls, and the shadows danced around her like flitting demons. Her chest would not move. She tore at her face, finding nothing but her own smooth, hot skin. Her lips moved, but her voice abandoned her.

She brought her arms down against the bed, pounding again and again, afraid that she would black out. Suddenly, something brushed against her forehead, breaking the spell. A surge of air spilled into her chest. She took another shuddering breath and then turned her head a bit. An old woman sat on the edge of the bed, touching Aephia's moist forehead with brown, withered fingers.

Shelda, Aephia realized. *The mere-dojen of the Keep. Why is she here?*

Shelda leaned close and Aephia wrinkled her nose as a sour odor washed over her. A few long, white hairs that curled outward from Shelda's chin loomed large to Aephia and she shrank back. Shelda's toothless gums and the weathered skin of her face and lips brought the taste of rotted apple into Aephia's dry mouth. Aephia pushed the sensations from her mind and turned her thoughts inward for a moment. Deep within her belly, she sensed only silence. Aephia felt a wave of fear engulf her. It dragged her into an abyss of deep water that pressed against her chest and absorbed all sounds. She grabbed Shelda's arm.

"Shelda," she said. "Something is wrong."

"You worry needlessly," Shelda said.

Shelda removed her hand from Aephia's forehead. She laced her gnarled fingers together.

"All women worry about the first born," she said.

A few strands of dark auburn hair tickled the corner of Aephia's mouth. She pulled at them with her fingers and licked her lips with a dry tongue. Shelda slowly unclasped her hands. She folded a small piece of cloth and wiped Aephia's forehead, pushing the errant hair away from the corner of her mouth.

"I couldn't breathe," Aephia said. Her voice whispered low and dusky, like wind through the pines. She placed her hands on her belly and closed her eyes. "And the baby's song is getting weaker." Aephia shivered. Shelda pulled a heavy woolen blanket up over the young woman's body.

"You have to bring Vollen," Aephia said, tossing the blanket off again. "I'm losing the baby."

"Vollen can't come right now," Shelda replied. "He is...occupied." She leaned forward and dabbed Aephia's forehead again. Aephia batted her hand away.

"You have to go get Lord Vollen now," Aephia said. Her teeth were set together and her eyes were wide. Shelda raised her eyebrows and pursed her lips. Aephia's wide eyes suddenly narrowed. "What's wrong?" she asked.

Shelda began to wipe Aephia's forehead once more, and once again Aephia brushed her hand aside.

"Tell me what's happening," Aephia demanded.

Shelda's eyes darted toward the door and then she leaned forward.

"There is panic outside the Keep," she said. "Even the guards tremble in fear. The Soel has been swallowed by some black demon. The sky has turned black as night."

Aephia grabbed Shelda's robe near the neck and pulled her down. Her dark eyes implored Shelda's.

"You have to go get Vollen," Aephia said. "This is the sign."

Shelda frowned and twisted her mouth as if she were annoyed. Aephia pulled harder. Shelda braced her arms on the bed; her face just a breath away from Aephia's.

"This baby is very important," Aephia hissed.

Shelda nodded.

"You don't understand," Aephia said. She almost snarled as she spoke, but the mere-dojen smiled.

"Oh, yes I do," Shelda said.

Aephia's eyes narrowed. Shelda pulled away from her grip and straightened out the front of her robe.

"Child of a Norgarden and a Vyr Lord. Born in the darkness of day." Shelda patted Aephia's hard, round stomach with one hand and shook her finger at Aephia with the other. "You are very presumptuous to think that you could bring forth the Shad'ya."

"You know of the legend," Aephia whispered. Her mouth hung open.

"Yes," Shelda said. "I know the legend well. And I am here for a reason. We do not let things like this pass unnoticed." She stood up and Aephia's eyes followed her.

"You are a Kaanite," Aephia said. Shelda's thin lips imitated a smile and she nodded.

"Vollen will kill you," Aephia hissed.

"He does not know. And you will not tell him either." Shelda stood up and her smile faded. "Your life, and the life of your daughter, is in my hands." She paused and smiled again. "I will summon Lord Vollen," she said.

The mere-dojen left and Aephia clutched the sheet in her hands. She glanced over at one of the fluttering pots that lit the room. A black cloud of soot covered the wall above it and fanned out across the stone ceiling. As she stared at the patterns of dark and light, she began to hear a roaring wind, and the room rocked and turned as if she were in boat on a hostile sea. She began to breathe in quick, shallow pants. A searing white light overwhelmed her.

The light faded and everything became silent, but the wind persisted, pressing against her body and blowing her through the hallways of Sunder Keep like a frightened bird. She struggled to land, to stop for a moment, but something held her arms and legs tightly and moved her relentlessly forward. She turned her head and watched as the halls turned into a cavern. Candles burned like stars in the sky, bobbing and swirling as people ran up and down the steps and leapt from one terrace to the next. No one noticed her, floating above the crowd. She reached out to touch a small, smiling girl, but a cold hand whisked her outside, into a night of stinging rain. From high above the Keep, she saw hordes of warriors swarming over the ridge that encircled the giant lake. Their weapons flashed in the darkness as if they were made of lightning, and they overwhelmed the lonely guards that held the single bridge to the island fortress. She followed the invaders into the Keep, where they began to strike people down in a bloody riot. Aephia found the girl again in the crowd and reached for her, but as their fingers touched, the warriors rushed over them like a dark tide. When the waves of hammering, hacking soldiers passed, Aephia found herself alone on a vast landscape of rolling hills, barren of all life. A cloud of brown dust swirled around her feet.

"Everyone dies," she whispered.

A soft voice brought her back to her chamber.

"Who dies?"

Aephia opened her eyes and took a trembling breath of cold air. Lord Vollen sat on the bed. Shelda stood a few paces away with her hands clasped together. Vollen leaned over. His dark eyes sparkled in the flickering yellow light.

"Vollen." Aephia breathed the name . She reached up and touched his face. He pushed a single remaining strand of hair away from her lips. Her eyes searched his. She glanced at Shelda, and the old woman's eyes narrowed for a moment. Aephia turned her attention back to Vollen.

"I had a vision," Aephia whispered. "It was terrible. The Uemn horde took the Keep. They killed everyone."

"It was just a dream," Vollen said.

Aephia's body relaxed a bit and her head dropped back onto the feather pillow.

"No. It was not a dream," she said. "It was too vivid." She closed her eyes for a moment. "What happened outside?" she asked.

"A terrible darkness passed over the Vyr. It lingered and then drifted away. It is a bad omen. The people are frightened. I have to go back and try to calm things down."

"Please don't go," she begged.

"I must," he replied. "I have a duty as Lord of the Vyr."

"But I'm afraid," she said. "I need you."

"Everything will be fine," Vollen said.

"Our baby is trying to tell me something," she whispered. "But her song is getting weaker and weaker." She stopped and took a deep breath. "In her song, I can hear her yearning for things that we can't even see yet."

"The child is a girl?" Vollen asked. "Are you certain?"

"I know it. I've always known it. It was meant to be. Our fates were carved in the channels of time before we were born."

"Maybe," Vollen said. "And maybe you're talking nonsense. The quickening of new life is on you."

She grabbed his arm, and her fingers dug into his flesh. "No, no," she said. "I'm clear. Clearer than I have ever been. And this darkening of the Soel is a sign."

Shelda stepped forward and touched Vollen on the shoulder. "If this is a girl child, we will need to perform the ritual." Her eyes glistened, wide and eager.

Vollen pushed her away and then reconsidered. He reached out and pulled the mere-dojen back.

"Prepare the way," he said. "We should be ready when the time comes."

Shelda scurried off. Aephia reached up with both hands and grabbed Vollen by the front of his tunic.

"What if we have made a mistake?" she asked. She pulled harder on his shirt and he gently peeled her hands away. She dropped back onto the wet sheets and grimaced in pain.

"The Shad'ya is just a story," Vollen whispered. "There is nothing to fear."

"Hold me," Aephia whispered. The Lord slipped his arms around her back and leaned over her so that his body rested lightly against hers. Aephia clutched at his shoulders and stared at the ceiling. Shelda returned with a small wooden barrel and set it on the ground near the center of the room. Three silent women, dojen of the keep, followed her. Water sloshed from their buckets as they hurried over and dumped the icy water into the black barrel. A fourth dojen brought a pine cradle and a folded shroud of white gossamer.

Aephia glimpsed the ceremonial casket just before her face contorted with pain again. The spasm subsided and she licked her lips.

"If only you could hear what I hear," she groaned. Tears ran from the corners of her eyes. She placed her hands onto her belly again and began to sob. Vollen tilted his head to the side, listening for the song that only Aephia could hear.

"Everything will be fine," Vollen said. He squeezed her gently.

"I'm cold," Aephia said. Vollen pulled his head away from her shoulder and glanced toward her legs. He inhaled sharply as he watched a bloody stain spread slowly across the blanket.

"Shelda, come here quickly," he said.

Shelda came over and her eyes grew wide. She pulled the sheet back and then dropped it suddenly as she screamed for help. A dojen came running with towels, but when she saw the pool of blood between Aephia's legs she fainted.

Vollen growled at the fallen servant as if he could frighten her back to consciousness. Shelda stepped over the dojen and began stripping the sheets and blankets away from Aephia.

"Owen, get in here," Vollen shouted.

He waited only a moment before he yelled again.

"Owen!"

Owen charged through the door and ran to the bed. He sucked in his breath and stood motionless for a moment.

"Get this woman out of here," Shelda hissed, pointing at the fallen dojen. "Are the boys still out there?"

"Yes," Owen said.

"Can they stand the sight of blood?" Vollen asked.

Shelda stuffed a towel between Aephia's legs.

"They're warriors," Owen said.

"Go get them," Vollen ordered.

Owen dragged the unconscious dojen out of the room and returned pulling his son Yergen by the collar. The flickering light cast deep shadows across the boy's furrowed brow and darkened the fine hair that tainted his upper lip and chin. Yergen's sparring partner, Raes, stuck his head around the corner. Raes' thin body and boyish face made Yergen seem older and meaner, even though the boys had been born during the same harvest.

Owen left the boys by the door and took a wide legged stance at the foot of the bed. The big man pulled on his beard. Shelda put both hands against his chest and pushed him out of the way.

"Stay back until I need you," she said.

He took two steps back and crossed his arms, and then tugged on his wiry beard again. His dark eyes caught Vollen's, and the brothers exchanged a worried look. The two boys, Yergen and Raes, stood just inside the door, hesitating.

"Shut the door," Vollen said.

Yergen used his shoulder to bump Raes out of the way. He pulled the door shut and then stood in front of it with his arms crossed; looking much like a smaller version of Owen with his stocky build, dark eyes and reddish-brown hair.

Aephia suddenly arched her back and screamed. Raes jumped. Yergen frowned at him. Shelda crawled onto the bed and peered between Aephia's legs. She reached up and felt for the baby, staring at the wall above Aephia's head as she searched with her fingers. She shook her head and frowned as she drew her hand back covered with blood. Aephia arched again and a long, low moan filled the chamber. Vollen and Owen exchanged worried glances.

Vollen turned his attention back to the mere-dojen.

"Do something," he hissed.

Shelda wiped her hands and arms with a towel and bit her lip with worry and apprehension.

"The baby may be in breach," she said.

"Options," Vollen said. He kept his voice low and threatening.

"We can wait," Shelda said.

Aephia screamed and kicked her legs up and down, oblivious to the conversations around her. She began a rhythmic beat with her legs and feet, kicking them high into the air and then hammering them onto the bed. She accompanied her thrashing with cries of pain. Shelda rolled off the bed and stood near Owen.

"What else?" Vollen shouted.

Shelda used an equally loud voice to reply. "My people had a way of cutting the baby out."

"Is that to save the baby or the mother?"

Shelda pressed her lips together for a moment. Aephia calmed down and began sobbing.

"I have only seen this procedure done once," she said. "And neither survived."

"Then what good is it?" Vollen asked.

"It can save both," she said. "If it is done right."

"Can you do it?"

Shelda took a deep breath. "I have done such a thing on a horse before. The foal was in breach. We saved the foal."

Vollen stood up and grabbed Shelda's robe. He picked her up off her feet and pushed her back against Owen. Vollen held the mere-dojen off the ground as he thrust his face close to hers.

"I don't care about the baby," he said.

As he spoke, tiny beads of spit sprayed Shelda in the face. She turned her head, but Vollen moved his face in front of hers again.

"Can you save the mother?" he asked.

Aephia screamed again and Shelda shook her head. "I don't know," she said. "But I do know that she is dying now. If we do nothing, we will lose both."

Vollen stared into her eyes and moments passed. Aephia whimpered and called for her Lord. Vollen let Shelda go and stepped back over to the bed. He took Aephia's hand and she squeezed his. Vollen gazed at her pale skin, stretched tightly over thin bones. He kissed her fingers.

"Who has a knife?" he asked.

Raes stepped forward and held out his knife, hilt first. The red blade glimmered like the obsidian walls of the Keep, where craftsmen forged weapons in the fires deep within the catacombs, creating sharp, fluted edges by heating the rock until it glowed and then touching it with a drop of water. In this way, flake by flake, the stone became a fine blade. Vollen grabbed the rough black leather handle and nodded at Raes.

"This is the blade you gave me," Raes said.

Vollen took the knife and handed it to Shelda.

"You will have to hold her down," Shelda said.

"Owen," Vollen said. "Grab her other arm."

Owen reached out and snared Aephia's flailing arm.

"You boys, sit on her legs," Vollen ordered. "Yergen, sit on that one. Raes, you sit on the other."

Raes moved quickly, but Yergen walked casually and crossed his arms as he sat on Aephia's naked leg.

"Hold onto it, boy," Owen snarled to his son. Yergen rolled his eyes and grabbed Aephia's leg just above her knee. Raes did the same. Shelda crawled onto the bed next to Raes and he shifted a bit to give her room. She held the knife as far away from Aephia as she could and used her other hand to check for the baby's head again. Her tight lips told the men what they needed to know.

"Do it," Vollen ordered.

Shelda pressed the point of the knife into the soft skin just below Aephia's swollen belly. She paused and glanced at Vollen. Aephia moaned. Vollen nodded and then Shelda cut. The scream pierced through every corner of the room. Raes closed his eyes tightly and hunched his shoulders as Aephia's thin leg lifted him from the bed.

Yergen kept his face as cold and stern as stone, and his bigger body stayed planted on the bed. Both Vollen and Owen brought their knees up onto the bed and used them to help pin Aephia's straining arms. Shelda sliced through an outer layer of skin, exposing the gray and pink layers underneath for just a moment before blood filled the wound and bubbled out onto the bed to join the growing pool there. Shelda dabbed the cut with a towel and cut again. Aephia screamed, then screamed again more faintly, and then her scream diminished to a soft wail. Shelda cut again and shook her head. She wiped her brow with the back of her hand, leaving a bloody trail across her forehead. She dabbed the wound once more and then peered more closely.

"I think I see the baby," she said. She dug her fingers into Aephia's belly. Aephia only whimpered.

"Raes, help me," Shelda demanded. Raes opened one eye and immediately closed it again.

"Help her," Vollen snapped.

The young boy opened his eyes and nodded, but he screwed his face into a contortion of fear and revulsion.

"I will hold this open," Shelda said. "And you must reach in and find the baby's legs."

Raes leaned forward and reached into the bloody hole in Aephia's belly. His fingers moved around, then locked on to something small and soft. He began to pull.

"Pull harder," Shelda growled. Raes tipped his head back and leaned away. For a moment, nothing happened, and then, slowly at first, he felt the tiny legs pop free, and then came the waist and chest and suddenly Raes held a bloody baby as if it were a dead fish. Shelda grabbed the leathery cord and cut it. She twisted both severed ends into a knot and rammed a towel onto Aephia's belly.

The room suddenly felt as still as an ice-covered lake.

Aephia's voice, no more than a hoarse whisper, broke the silence. "Where is my baby?"

Vollen stroked her forehead, brushing away a cold dew. He glanced at the baby. Raes still held it by the ankles. It hung, limp and bluish-white. Vollen shook his head.

"No man may ever touch the girl-child of a Lord," Owen hissed. Vollen glared at his brother.

"Is she alive?" Aephia cried.

"It was a girl," he said. "But it shows no signs of life. It is your life that is important now."

Vollen turned to Raes and spoke in a low voice. "The baby is dead, but you must perform the ritual of forbearance just the same."

"Shelda must do it," Owen said through his clenched teeth. "No man may ever touch a girl-child, especially this one."

"Quiet," Vollen snapped.

Aephia turned her head away from Owen's voice and buried her face into the blankets.

"Raes, perform the ritual," Vollen ordered.

"What do I do?" Raes said. He glanced at Yergen, who slid off the bed and stood near the corner with his arms crossed.

"Take the baby to the barrel and drop it in the water," Vollen said.

"It's already dead," Shelda said. "So you don't need to drown it. Just dunk it and then place it in the little cradle there. We will burn the body on a funeral pyre."

Raes held the dead child at arm's length as he stumbled off the bed. Yergen watched him walk over to the black wooden tub. Raes turned the baby so that he could see the face. The little arms hung limply toward the ground. The cheeks were thin and sunken. He stared at it for a moment and then he slowly lowered it into the barrel until the ice cold water covered his own wrist.

"That's enough," Shelda said. She pushed hard on the wad of cloth that did little to staunch the flow of blood from Aephia's body. Raes pulled the baby out of the water and gently turned it upright. Suddenly it squirmed and he froze. It squirmed again and its mouth gaped open. Raes opened his own mouth to speak, but no words came out. He turned toward the bed. Owen and Vollen watched Aephia's face. Shelda scrambled to sop up the flowing blood, and Yergen watched Shelda.

As Raes stood there with his mouth open, the baby arched its back, scrunched up its face, and then let loose with a tiny wail. Everyone turned and stared.

"The girl-child lives," Owen hissed.

Raes blinked and then his eyes went wide with terror. The baby sucked in a breath of air and cried again. Aephia pushed herself up and supported her upper body with her elbows. Her eyes glimmered like pools of oil and she fell back again, holding her arms in the air.

"My baby," she cried. "Bring her to me."

Vollen looked over at Owen, and then turned back toward the crying baby. Aephia waved her hands.

"Please bring her here," Aephia begged.

"Bring her," Vollen said.

"You must not," Owen snapped. "Raes, drop that baby back into that water now, and never touch that abomination again."

"I am the Lord here," Vollen roared. "Bring that baby to her mother."

Raes stepped forward and tried to hand the girl baby to Vollen. Vollen pulled his hands away and leaned back, so Raes placed the tiny, colorless child next to Aephia. She wept and stroked the child's head.

"She's so pale," Aephia said.

Owen stepped around the bed and pulled Vollen away. "You have to kill that baby," he said. He turned and pointed at Raes. "And you must cut his hands from his body and hope that we are not punished for our arrogance."

Vollen shook his head. "Don't tell me what to do," he said. He began to move away but Owen grabbed his arm. Vollen yanked his arm from Owen's grip. "Don't forget who is Lord here," Vollen said.

"That child is a violation of Thorsen's Law," Owen said. "Born under the watch of the dark ones. And look at it. It was born dead, and now it lives. It is an affront to everything that is good and natural."

Vollen clenched his teeth together and glared into his brother's eyes. He spoke slowly, carefully.

"We will stay here, quietly, and help Aephia recover. Then, when this crisis has passed, we will discuss the child. Is that understood?"

Owen rubbed his forehead and nodded. Vollen glanced around the room. Raes stood at the far corner of the bed, holding onto the short wooden upright. Yergen leaned against the other corner post with his arms crossed, his face stern. Shelda backed up against the stone wall. Her eyes glistened as she stared at the strange newborn.

Shelda's mouth formed whispered words that no one heard.

"The Shad'ya."

Her eyes were at once terrified and full of glee.

Aephia saw nothing but the baby she held in the crook of her arm.

"She is Elysen," Aephia whispered. "Like the small white flowers that grow in the northern tundra."

Vollen returned to her and knelt by the bed.

"Even the name is sacrilege," Owen hissed. "Only Lords can use the sound of Thorsen's name."

Vollen glared at him and then turned his attention back to Aephia.

"I have to take the baby now so you can rest," he said softly.

Aephia's eyes widened and her lips curled back. "You will not take this baby," she snarled.

"No harm will come to her," Vollen reassured her. He reached for the crying baby.

"Promise me," Aephia insisted. "Swear an oath to Thorsen that you will protect this child for as long as you live."

Vollen stroked Aephia's cheek and his hand brushed against the baby. He touched the child's milky white scalp.

"Her skin is so cold," he said. "And she is as white as death." He winced even as he said the words. Aephia's own skin, once tanned and freckled by the Soel, now faded to a gray-white that seemed as lifeless as the sheets around her head.

"She is just like I dreamed she would be," Aephia whispered. "Vollen, bring Owen and Yergen closer." Vollen swiveled on his knee and motioned to his brother and then to Yergen. The two men stood behind Vollen.

"Swear to me, all of you, that you will make sure that no harm comes to this child for as long as you live." Aephia glanced at Raes. "And you too young man. Swear it to me."

Owen glanced at Yergen. The boy frowned and scratched his face. Raes spoke first.

"I swear," he said.

"By the law of Thorsen," Aephia said.

"By the law of Thorsen," Raes said. "I swear."

"And I swear it as well," Vollen said. "I swear to protect her and keep her from harm."

Owen shook his head. "It is against Thorsen's Law, the law of all creation, to let the female child of a Lord live."

"I am the Lord," Vollen said. He managed a calm voice, but his tension edged into it. "I make the law. This child was dead, and came back to life. It is a sign from Thorsen that the old ways are changing. We will have a new law this day. And you and Yergen will swear by it. Now swear."

"Never," Owen snarled. Vollen grabbed his arm and pulled him to the far side of the room.

"The Vyr is dead," Vollen said. "Look around you. Where are the birds? Where is the wild game? Even the fires and the coal pots burn poorly. The harvests are poor, and we have less and less good men to fight with. The Uemn eat away at us every day." He looked into Owen's eyes, letting his words sink in. "Even Daen told of how the Vyr was dying, how the animals were becoming more and more scarce from when he was a boy. How the Uemn forced their way deeper and deeper into the Vyr. And I have seen it myself. The Vyr we swore to protect is dying under our watch."

"It is because we lose faith," Owen hissed. "When you bred with this heathen Norgarden, you doomed the Vyr even further. Our father lost faith in Thorsen, and the Vyr suffered. You openly deny Thorsen and the Vyr dies. It is obvious to me what the problem is. Once we cleanse the world of the Kaanites and the Norgarden and the Uemn and all the unbelievers, Thorsen will smile upon us again and he will restore the Vyr." Owen poked the Lord in the chest, as only a brother could do. "You are the problem here," he said. "You and that abomination that you have created."

Vollen thrust his face close to Owen's. "All of the signs are true," he said. "The darkening of the Soel, the death and rebirth of the child, everything is just as the legend predicts."

"Only because you and the Norgarden witch have forced it to be so," Owen said. The two men were poised on the balls of their feet, their chests almost touching one another. Owen's cheeks were crimson and his eyes were wide with anger.

"You are a stupid fool," Vollen said. "The Vyr dies because we are ignorant."

They stared at each other for a long time, with only the fluttering sounds of the fire disturbing the silence of the room.

"Brother," Vollen said, shaking him lightly. "I swear by my duty to the Vyr, by all that is good and just, that what Aephia and I have done here is for the good of all. You have to trust me on this."

Owen pulled at his beard for a moment. He took a deep breath and let it out slowly. "And I swear this to you, brother. My duty to the Vyr is as strong as yours. I took the same oath that you did. The same oath that our father took. The same oath that Yergen will take when he is ready. To protect the Vyr, to protect the Keep. Above all else, to keep Thorsen's Law." He poked his brother in the chest again. "And I swear now, that if any of these oaths are broken because of this child and what she may bring, I will kill her, and kill you as well."

Vollen stared at him for a moment.

"Fair enough," Vollen said. "I can ask no more of you than to do your duty."

Vollen drug his brother back to the side of the bed where the others waited. "Now," Vollen said. "Swear that you will protect this child."

"I swear," Owen said. He flashed an angry look at Vollen. The Lord nodded.

"Now you," Vollen said, turning toward Yergen. The boy looked up at his father, and Owen nodded.

"I swear," Yergen said quietly. His lips were curled into a faint snarl. No one but Raes noticed.

Vollen stood up and looked around the room. "And now you, Shelda."

All four men searched the room with their eyes. They were alone with Aephia.

"She's gone," Raes said.

"Gone where?" Vollen asked. "Did you see her go?" He glanced at Raes, and then noticed that the boy stared at the bed. Vollen followed his gaze. Aephia's face relaxed. She stared at the ceiling, a faint smile playing across her lips. The yellow light of the torches flickered off the red stone and danced in her eyes. Vollen dropped to his knees and took Aephia's hand in his own. The baby began to cry. Raes reached out for her, but Vollen struck with a quick backhand that sent the boy staggering backwards.

"Don't ever touch this child," Vollen growled. "Never again. Do you understand?"

Raes nodded and glanced at Owen.

"No man shall ever touch the female child of a Lord," Owen reminded him. "The penalty is death."

"But I only did as I was told," Raes protested.

Vollen stared into Aephia's cold eyes as he spoke.

"We will forget this time," Vollen said. "What you did, you did at my bidding. I made the mistake. But you must never touch this child again. Never."

Vollen turned and glared at the boy.

Raes nodded and backed against the wall. Yergen watched him with narrow eyes.

"What shall we do?" Owen asked.

"Go get the eunuch, Corde," Vollen said. "We will let him care for the baby for now."

Owen grabbed Raes by the arm and dragged him from the room. Yergen followed them. As they left, the wailing of the child filled the room. Vollen put his head in his arms and closed his eyes.

One

Elysen stood at the top of a lonely tower, catching the last light of day. The winds of life, endlessly twisting across the Vyr from the north, spun her white hair around her face like a shroud, and the soft evening light turned her pale, green eyes to gray. Along her cheeks and temples, faint lines, like tiny rivulets of blue water, were transformed by the dim light into etchings of black. Even her lips appeared like night against her colorless skin.

Along the western horizon, dark clouds broke open, sending shafts of light toward the jagged ridges that surrounded Turoc's Cauldron. The shadows of evening crept across the blue water of the vast crater, creeping into and across the stones of Sunder Keep.

Elysen sighed. Her leather gloves creaked softly as she flexed her fingers, and her cape billowed and then fell again, like a dark beast breathing slowly. She reached back and grasped it, pulling it around her tall, lean body. Something moved in the shadows behind her, and she paused for a moment, holding her breath, with her back stiff. She turned quickly and her knife shot forward. Her body froze and her eyes narrowed.

"Raes," she said. Her stone blade touched the fabric just below the dark mahogany chest plate that covered his ribs. Elysen relaxed a bit as Raes placed his gloved fingers against the blade and pushed it away from his belly.

Raes stepped up next to Elysen and glanced down toward the open courtyard below, where a group of boys sparred against each other with long, padded poles. He slipped his hood up over his head. A gust of wind blew it off again.

Elysen's glanced at him. Her legs strained inside her black leather leggings as she braced against the stiff wind. Elysen tossed her head, purposefully enfolding his face in a mass of blowing white hair. She let her lips twist into half a smile.

"I thought you were in the north, at the Reach," she said.

Raes waved her billowing hair away from his face as if it were cobwebs.

"I was recalled," he said.

The wind flipped Elysen's hair around again, and Raes again waved it away from his face. She reached up and ran her gloved hands along the side of her face, gathering her hair into a bundle and securing it with a golden clip in the shape of interlocking talons. She let the bundle of white hair fall over her right shoulder.

"I've missed the pleasure of your company," she said quietly.

"And I have missed you, as well," Raes said.

A gust of wind scoured the crumbling stones under their feet, hissing like an angry snake.

Below them, a mule pulled a wagon of hay toward the Keep. Even high upon the tower, surrounded by whipping winds, they heard the clip of the animal's hooves on the stone causeway that arched from the rocky slopes of the outer rim to the island fortress of Sunder Keep. The creak of the wooden wheels carried through the cold air like the call of a persistent bird. On the far shore, scattered beneath the lonely pines, the leaves of the low bushes turned to orange and yellow as the season of the Proste gripped the land.

"Raes," she said.

"Yes?"

"Do you know how many seasons I have seen now?"

Raes sucked in his lower lip and then shook his head. "No. I do not."

"I have seen eighteen harvests," she said.

Raes frowned. "Counting that far is against Thorsen's Law."

"Counting is as natural as the rhythms of the seasons. It is a violation of my very nature not to count."

"Thorsen's Law imposes discipline upon us. We don't do things just because they feel natural."

Elysen pulled away from him and stared out across the darkness of the cauldron. "Thorsen's Law, Thorsen's Law," she said, mocking Raes' litany. "Sometimes I think that everything is against Thorsen's Law."

Raes took a deep breath and exhaled slowly. The wind tore the plume of vapor from his lips.

"Thorsen has set these laws in place to protect us," he said. You would do well to be more mindful of your place as a keeper of the law."

"You can be a keeper of the law," she said. "I am a maker of the law."

Raes' mouth opened as he prepared a retort, but Elysen continued.

"I am Thorsen's heir," she reminded him. "I am the daughter of Lord Vollen, who is in turn the eldest son of Lord Daen. I hold the lineage before Yergen or any of his brothers."

"But you were…" he paused.

"I was a mistake," she said. "No. I am a mistake."

"That was not what I was going to say," Raes said.

Elysen lowered her head and pulled her cloak around her body.

"Nevertheless," she said. "The law of the Lords bequeaths the Vyr to the first born. Vollen is eldest; therefore he is Lord during his life. Owen is next in line as the last living son of Daen. When he is gone, I am Lord. That is Thorsen's Law. The law of the Vyr."

Raes frowned and shook his head. "The law is not clear there. The Vyr passes to the eldest born, but no woman should be in line. You have cheated the law by surviving the ritual of forbearance." He rubbed his forehead. "Owen and Vollen argued this point when you were born."

Elysen's eyes opened wide and her lips parted. "You were there that night?"

Raes nodded. "But it was a long time ago." He ran both hands through his hair and then crossed his arms and shuddered.

"And you remember it?"

"Some." He looked away from her.

Elysen stepped close to him and tipped her head back slightly so that she could see his face. "Why haven't you told me before this? You were there the night I was born? The night my mother died?"

He nodded but avoided looking into her eyes. Elysen turned away.

"I can't believe that you have never told me this before."

She put her hands on her hips and stared at the high walls of the Caldera, the great circular theater where the Lord kept his council and debated strategies of war. A soft glow filtered from within through tall, slotted windows and the wind blew a flat plume of smoke toward the eastern rim of the Cauldron. Beyond the Keep, and all around it, black water stretched wide and cold like a mirror of the dark sky above.

"You taught me to fight, taught me to ride, and we fought the Uemn side by side at the Rift, and in all that time, you have never once mentioned my mother or my birth."

She sighed and placed her hands on top of her head with her fingers laced together. "You were there when my mother died," she remarked. He nodded, even though she stared at the horizon, hardly noticing his presence next to her.

"I'll gladly tell you what I remember," he said. "But let's wait until after the council meeting. We'll have more time then."

"I am not interested in the war with the Uemn anymore," Elysen said. "Besides, the Uemn are beasts. They'll never advance beyond the marshes of the south."

Elysen closed her eyes and pressed her lips together, breathing slowly through her nose. As she inhaled, her nostrils flared slightly. The faint smell of roasting meat mixed with that of burning cedar and mesquite. The smoky aroma wafted up along the battlements.

"You can not refuse Owen's invitation. His word is law."

Elysen blew a puff of air from between her lips.

"Owen's law does not bind me," she said.

Raes shook his head slowly. "In all time since Thorsen created this world, there has never been one who so flaunts and questions the law like you do."

"And in all the time since Thorsen there has never been one so set in the law as you."

"Thorsen's Law protects us. It is by his grace and his power that we exist at all."

"And yet he left the Uemn to torment us," Elysen said.

Raes placed his hands over his ears. "Why do you do this to me?"

"What?" she asked.

"Question the law. Question Thorsen. Question everything." He shook his head and closed his eyes. "I do remember one thing about your mother. She was stubborn and questioned everything. There is a lot of that part of her in you."

Elysen touched his cheek. "There," she said. "Now you have given me a compliment."

Raes took a step away from her with his eyes wide.

"You know that your touch condemns me to death," he said.

"We have touched before," she reminded him. She tossed her head back and laughed. "You can not keep that one law, hard as you try."

Raes swallowed hard and bit his lip.

"After council, come and dine with me," she said. "You can tell me everything about that night."

The red sky turned his face into a golden mask, crossed with weathered lines from his years in the north. He suddenly looked old and tired.

"On second thought, let's skip the council," she said. "I'm hungry now. Besides, I'm not welcome there."

"You can skip the council if you dare," he said. "But I have to go. It's my place as Sire of the Keep." He paused for a moment, and then continued with a quiet urging in his voice. "Owen commands your presence. It would be very rude if you did not go."

"Owen commands my presence? And why should I come running like a dojen when my uncle beckons me. My father is Lord of the Vyr. Not Owen."

"Regardless, it is Owen that requests your presence. You would do well to attend."

A gust of cold wind embraced Elysen and a shiver passed through the fine white hair on the back of her neck. She hunched her shoulders and shook it off.

"Why is Owen calling a council on such short notice?" she asked.

"He didn't tell me anything more than I have told you," Raes said. The wind lifted her cape and he glanced at the tight, black bodysuit that she wore underneath. "You should change into full battle gear," he said.

"Why?" she asked.

"It is a council of war," he reminded her. "You must come in battle gear. And braid your hair and tie it back. The others will not take your council seriously if you come dressed like a lark."

She spread her arms out, holding her cape our like giant wings. "I am not dressed as a lark," she said. "I am a raven."

"You are too skinny to be a raven. Maybe you are a bat."

She pulled her cloak tight around her body again and her lips showed the hint of a smile. "Maybe I am a black beetle. Like a scarab or a fire chub."

Raes' smile faded, and he closed his eyes. Elysen frowned and stepped closer to him.

"What is it? What troubles you so?"

"Forgive me," he said. "Our friendly banter usually pleases me, but tonight I am lost in my thoughts." He sighed and opened his eyes.

"You're in a melancholy mood," she said. She took his hand, but as he stepped away their hands parted. Raes took a deep breath and opened his mouth to speak. He closed it again and bit his upper lip.

"Speak, Raes," Elysen said, noting his discomfort. "You look like you want to say something."

"I do," he said. "But I'm not sure that you'll understand."

"Try me," she suggested.

He pressed his lips together and considered her offer for a moment. He finally closed his eyes and blew the last of his breath from his nose.

"While I was gone, I had a dream," he said. "In my dream, the Uemn overran the Keep and you were killed."

"Dreams are nothing," Elysen said. "The night was just playing with you."

"It was so vivid," he said, "that when I woke up, I had a terrible feeling in the pit of my stomach. I thought that I might never see you again."

Raes swallowed and cleared his throat softly. He turned his head so that he looked straight into her eyes.

"Do you remember when we vowed to always be friends?" he asked.

She nodded. "We can be no more than that."

Raes closed his eyes and took a breath through his nose.

"In my heart, that vow is broken," he said.

Elysen's eyes searched his face as she tried to discern his meaning.

"I want to be more than just friends," he said.

Elysen shut her eyes slowly and hid her arms under her cloak. She turned away from Raes and opened her eyes. She gazed out toward broken clouds on the horizon.

"You know that can never be," she said.

Raes put his arm around her and she settled in against his side and let her head drop against his shoulder.

"Someone will see us," Elysen said.

"No they won't."

"You take a foolish risk."

As the shafts of light began to wane, the clouds became edged with gold and red, and the winds of life that tugged and slapped at their cloaks lost its vigor. It sighed and relaxed, and then settled into a light breeze. They stood waiting, motionless, until the Soel turned from orange to red and finally dropped below the edge of the world.

"All I ever wanted was just to be touched," Elysen said.

"You've been touched," Raes reminded her.

"I've been hit, beaten, whacked and pummeled with sticks and jubos and all kinds of weapons. That's not what I mean." She pushed her body in closer against his. "I want to feel a human touch. Skin against skin."

Raes pulled away from her. "I have to go," he said. "If I'm late for council, I'll be punished."

Elysen smiled. "You could be killed for touching me. Yet you worry about being late for council."

Raes opened his mouth but Elysen stepped away and waved him away with the back of her hand. "Go on. I'll be there in a moment."

Raes hesitated for just a moment before he turned and slipped away. Elysen watched the last red tendrils of light from the Soel before she too turned and descended from the tower.

Two

The soft scuffle of Elysen's boots echoed off the stone walls and the hem of her cloak swept along the floor as she strode through the halls. She stayed away from the sputtering torches that threw circles of dim light across the black stone, slipping in and out of the shadows between. When she came to a group of dojen fussing over a torch that would not light, she ducked into an unlit side tunnel. She continued to walk quickly, even in the almost complete darkness. She emerged into another dimly lit hallway and turned without hesitation. As she did, she ran directly into her servant, Corde. His tray tipped, and a goblet of wine fell against him. A bowl rocked on the edge of the tray, then slipped and fell. The contents landed in a steaming heap on the cold stones at their feet. Corde stood with his mouth open, wine trickling down his chest like blood.

"May leeches consume you," he said as he whisked his shirt and pants with the backs of his fingers. The wine left a red stain across the front of his white tunic. Elysen reached out and picked a small green onion off his shoulder.

"I don't think that leeches would want me," she said.

Corde stooped over and set the tray on the ground. He scooped the steaming pile of stew into one half of the clay bowl. The other half sat nearby, rocking gently on the stone floor. Elysen squatted down next to him and twisted the onion between her fingers. Corde set the broken bowl on the tray and then stopped to stare at Elysen's fingers as they worried the onion into a limp green string.

"What is that?" he asked her.

"What is what?"

"That. In your hand."

She shrugged. "It appears to be an onion."

Corde carefully snatched it from her fingers and leaned forward. "Leek," he said. He slapped her on top of the head with the weary tuber. She tucked her chin against her chest and frowned.

"Why did you do that?" she asked. They both stood up at the same time.

Corde shook the vegetable in front of her face as he held the tray with his other hand.

"This is a leek," he said. He raised his eyebrows and held the leek in front of his face. "Much like an onion, I admit. But a leek nonetheless."

Elysen frowned and shook her head. "What does it matter, old man? What do I care if it is a leek or an onion or a tulip?" She waved him off and began to walk away. He followed her.

"It matters," he said, "because you don't listen to me. I teach and teach and teach, and you ask so many questions that my head hurts, and yet you don't listen." He shook the leek at her back. "This is a leek. Not an onion."

"I listen," Elysen said. "When it matters."

"How do you know what matters? You listen to what you want to hear." He threw the leek and it landed on the back of her head. She brushed it away and it fell to the floor. Corde stepped over it as if it were a snake.

"What possible difference could it make if I knew an onion from a leek?" she asked. Corde still trailed behind her. He took a few quick steps and came up beside her. For every other step Elysen took, Corde added a skipping step to keep up.

"That is not the point," he said. They passed by a dojen and Corde stopped just long enough to thrust the tray of broken pottery into her hands. She kept her eyes on the floor as Elysen passed. Corde ran to catch up again.

"How many seasons have you seen?" Elysen asked.

Corde touched her arm. "Can we slow down?" he asked between gasps. Elysen stopped suddenly and Corde took another step before he caught his balance. "Why are we rushing so?" he asked.

"Owen has called a council of war. He insists that I attend the council, and I am running very late."

"Ah," Corde said. "And you have missed your supper, which, I am afraid, is in the hands of the dojen that we just passed."

"I will dine later with Raes in my quarters. You can bring us bread and stew and as much wine as you can carry. Now, tell me, how many seasons have you seen?"

Corde scratched his chin. "I have seen the snow of the Proste settle on Thorsen's Watch more than thirty times. And before that, I spent at least thirty dark seasons in my homeland, beyond the reach of the Soel, where we worked and played in the nights that did not end."

Elysen folded her hands together and closed her eyes. "Thirty and thirty would be sixty."

Corde slapped her on the arm and she opened her eyes. "Ha," he said. "You do listen to some things."

"Sixty seems like a very long life," she said.

"Oh, yes indeed," Corde replied.

"How old is Lord Vollen then?" They began to walk again.

Corde took a deep breath and exhaled slowly, then shook his head. "He was a boy, perhaps Yergen's age, when I first saw him."

"Yergen is hardly a boy," Elysen reminded him. Corde waved his hand and turned his head.

"To me, everyone appears young." He rubbed his chin with his fingers. "Yergen was just a child when I first met him." He nudged Elysen with his elbow. "And he was a tempestuous lad, even back then. Now, let me see." Corde spread his fingers out and began to mutter quietly as he used them to count. "Your father and mother were together for a few years before you were born. Lord Vollen was maybe twenty then, so perhaps he is now forty." He nodded sharply. "Yes. Forty seasons of the Proste."

"My father seems older than you. His life seems to be waning in his body." She shook her head and began to ascend the stairs two at a time. Corde lagged behind. She stopped and waited for him to catch up. He stopped and gasped for breath again.

"How is it that you live so long, old man?" Elysen asked.

"I don't hurry where I go," he said. "Nor do I treat people poorly. This is the secret to long life."

Elysen turned and began to climb again, more slowly this time. Corde followed her.

"Be serious for a moment," Elysen said. "Most of the people of the Vyr are lucky to live as long as Vollen." She stopped and Corde nearly ran into her again. He put one foot on the next step up and placed both hands on his knee. "If I have now seen eighteen harvests, my life is nearly half over."

"Nonsense," Corde said. "The Norgarden blood of the icelanders runs through your body, as it does in mine. You will most likely live to see a hundred harvests, or more."

"I don't think so," she said. "I fear that I will see very few more."

Corde waved his hand at her. "No one knows how long they will live."

"Why not?"

"Because," Corde said. "That is myst."

Elysen bounded up the stairs again and paused at the top, waiting for Corde to catch up. At the upper landing, she stood next to the arched entry to her sleeping quarters and let him enter first. Corde collapsed into a stocky, wooden chair. His arms draped over the sides and he stretched his legs out toward the middle of the room. A dojen lit a fire in the central pit and then scurried from the room. Elysen walked into a smaller room off the main one and pulled her ebony body armor from a shelf. She brought it out and dumped it on the bed.

"I can't believe they're making me wear this tonight." She slipped her arm between the carved breastplate and the back. "Corde, come help me."

He tucked his chin against his chest. "M'lady," he said. "You know that I can not."

"Oh, nonsense. No one is about. The dojen are all gone, and they would never say anything anyway."

"The law forbids us to touch."

"Poop on the law," Elysen said. Corde laughed. Elysen continued. "You and I have been together for too long to worry about that."

Corde struggled to his feet and walked over to her.

"You are in a light mood tonight," Corde remarked.

"I have a wicked plan in my head," she said.

He pulled the leather laces tight under her arms, doing his best to avoid her body. His fingers brushed against her side and she squirmed a bit.

"The counting that you teach me," Elysen asked as she tried to nudge the heavy armor into a more comfortable position. "Is that myst or science?"

"Counting would be science, if science was not forbidden, but since science is not allowed, it must not be that."

Elysen turned and held the old man by his shoulders.

"The reason that I don't know the difference between a leek and an onion is because you always speak in riddles, old man."

She let go of him and he helped her strap hard, black wooden plates over her upper arms and forearms. She closed her eyes as his fingers danced and flitted along the buckles and laces.

"I'm going to ask you a question, old man, and I want you to answer as clearly as you can." Corde placed heavy shoulder guards over her head, and she slipped her fingers back into her black leather gloves.

"Promise me," she said.

"Ack, I'm too old to promise." he replied.

Elysen shook her head, letting her long, white hair fall around her shoulders. "Just tell me," she said. "Do the Norgarden follow Thorsen's Laws?"

"Of course they do."

"You talk about the Norgarden as if you weren't one yourself." she said.

He puffed up his chest with pride. "I am Norgarden," he said. His shoulders slumped a bit. "And yet, I have been in the service of the Vyr for so long, I may have forgotten from whence I came."

"Do the Norgarden follow the law as blindly as we do?" Elysen asked.

She put her leg up on the chair and strapped on her upper leg plates. Corde stood by, holding her shin guards in his hands as he waited. He turned them back and forth, examining the polished wooden surface.

"Of course they do." He paused and thought for a moment. "I mean, no, of course not. We Norgarden have our own laws."

Elysen grabbed him and pulled him close. "I met a Norgarden once," she whispered. "A real one. And he told me that the Norgarden don't believe that Thorsen created all the world."

Corde pulled away and smoothed out the front of his tunic. "I need not remind you that we don't speak of such things," Corde said. "And I am a real Norgarden."

Elysen took her shin plates from his hands and laced them around the backs of her calves as Corde scratched his chin again. She took her foot off the chair and walked over to the bed, where a headband of rare silver hung on the corner post. She put her hand on the simple crown and paused there.

"What about the one power?" she asked. "It is myst, or science?"

"If there was such a thing, it would be myst," he said.

"Why?" she asked.

"Because it can not be explained," Corde said. "Science is an attempt to explain things. Myst is that which can not be explained by science. If there was only one power, it would be myst by its very nature."

"You still make no sense, old man," Elysen said.

Corde put his hands on his hips. "If there was one power that came before all things, that created all things, then it must necessarily be the explanation of all things, and therefore, it can not be explained. Therefore, it must be myst."

Elysen turned her back to him and shook her hair so that it all fell down her back. Corde ran his fingers through the fine, white strands, separating it into three bundles. Elysen glanced over her shoulder at him and looked at his weathered face.

"Be still," Corde said gently. Elysen clasped her hands together and faced forward again. She closed her eyes and took a deep breath.

"You are the only person in the world who can braid my hair," she said.

"It is like trying to weave smoke," Corde responded. His brown, knobby fingers flipped the three bundles over and across each other exactly seven times, ending with just a small tuft of loose hair. Elysen handed him a golden clasp and he used it to secure the braid.

"If my father ever saw you touching me like you do," Elysen said. "Your life would be forfeit."

"We do forget the law," Corde said. "It will be the death of us someday."

"Ah well," Elysen said. "We've nothing much to live for except to fight and die."

Elysen placed the ring of silver on her head and dismissed Corde with a flick of her hands and a smile.

"I'm late," she said. "And you have to prepare supper for Raes and me." She paused for a moment, and her eyes sparkled. "I take it that cooking is science, and that it is therefore forbidden, but that such a triviality of the law will not stop you from preparing this one last meal before you and all others who prepared meals in this land are thrown into the frigid waters of Turoc's Cauldron."

Corde bowed as he backed out of the room. "Cooking is myst, m'lady, as you would well know if you ever tried it, as is the classification of vegetables, as you also well know, since you are unable to tell a leek from a common onion."

Elysen stepped quickly forward and caught Corde at the door. She touched him lightly on the shoulder. "I would like to talk more of the one power," she said.

"Perhaps it is best left alone," Corde said.

"Of all people, you should be most curious about the possibility of one power," Elysen said. "It could explain much."

Corde shook his head. "Or it may explain nothing."

"What are you afraid of?"

Corde bit his lower lip. "I am afraid of what I don't know."

"Then let us know more, and we will be less afraid."

Corde's face became less stern as he considered her statement. "I may know a little bit of the legend," he said.

"How much is a little bit?" she asked.

He shrugged. "Not much. A little bit is not much."

"Then we must find someone who knows more than we do."

Corde's eyes searched hers. "Many have thought to uncover the secrets of the time before Thorsen. None have succeeded."

"Well, maybe I am the one," Elysen said.

Corde scratched his head. Elysen stepped past him into the hall and disappeared down the steps.

Three

As she entered the Caldera of the central Keep, Elysen paused just inside the door. Two dojen moved slowly, placing coal lamps along the wide stone stairways that descended through the terraces of stone benches circling the cavern. Along the steps, the cup-shaped torches threw clouds of yellow light and sputtered black smoke into the emptiness above, creating dim paths from each entrance high along the top of the Caldera toward the open floor of the Pithe far below. In the middle of the Pithe, four men waited while a dojen cleared dishes away.

Elysen stepped into the open space of the great hall and a small flock of starlings fluttered out of the darkness above her head. They swirled and dived as if they shared one purpose, and then split apart and spread out, circling around a nearby pillar and losing themselves again in the black night of the domed ceiling. Elysen listened for a moment, and then picked her way down toward the Pithe, stepping lightly from one terrace to another. She stopped at a low wall that separated the last row of the empty spectator seating from the meeting area below. A narrow ramp led downward, through an archway and into darkness before it emerged onto the black floor of the Pithe. Elysen slipped almost silently through the arch, but as she stepped into the Pithe, her foot ground against a pile of loose rock and she stopped like a cautious animal.

Owen pushed his chair back from the table and looked toward Elysen. He nodded at her and motioned for her to enter. Owen's youngest son, Brenden, sat alone at the far side of the table with his head resting on his arms. He scratched a scar in the dark wood with the end of his gloved finger. A long roll of dark burlap sat just beyond his reach. On the far side of the Pithe, at the base of a giant stone column that towered into the darkness above, a fire blazed in a large open cooking hearth. Light from the flames threw dancing shadows across the floor. Even though most of the smoke drifted up through the hollow center of the column, a thin haze hung throughout the Pithe, stinging Elysen's eyes. Raes stood away from the table, near the edge of the lit area, stationed halfway between Brenden and Owen.

Yergen propped his broad back against the stone fireplace. He held a clay goblet in his hand. His polished battle armor of hard ebony showed chips and dents, but it still reflected the flames as if they were serpent's tongues. As he stood staring into the fire, a stone dropped from the flue and bounced off one of the logs. It rolled out of the fire and came to rest against the toe of Yergen's boot. He kicked the stone and it left a black mark of soot on the floor as it skipped toward Lord Owen's chair.

"Look at this," Yergen said. "Another stone. This place is falling apart."

"Then maybe we should just let the Uemn have it," Elysen said.

Yergen took a step toward her and waved his goblet, spilling amber liquid onto the black stones under his feet. It glistened there like fresh blood.

"We took an oath," he growled. "We will never abandon our home to the heathen Uemn. Ever." He turned his back to Elysen and faced the table. Elysen took the last few steps into the Pithe, staying near the wall with her arms at her sides and her lips pressed tightly together.

"Stop it," Owen snapped. "You two still fight like children." He waved his hands toward the guards and the dojen and they slipped away through doors and up stairs.

"It looks like your council is poorly attended," Elysen said as the room cleared, leaving her with only the four men. Brenden's head came up and his eyes narrowed.

Owen put up his hand.

"She does not know," he said.

She pushed away from the wall and stepped over the stone that Yergen had kicked across the floor. She stopped and placed her fingers on the back of an empty chair to Owen's left. Five more chairs sat empty around the table between her and Brenden, who now sat staring into the fire. Beyond him, six more vacant chairs completed the circle.

"What don't I know?" Elysen asked. She felt her heart fluttering in her chest and shrugged off the sensation of some small insect crawling on the back of her neck.

"My brothers are dead," Brenden said. The words gushed out of his mouth as if they were brackish water. He dropped his head down and his forehead landed on the hard oak planks. He rolled his face back and forth and clutched at the wooden table.

"Dead how?" Elysen asked. She felt a prickling sensation at the back of her neck again. Suddenly she took a quick breath. "Where is my father?"

Yergen walked around behind her, moving slowly, like a stalking tiger. He stopped on the other side of Owen and dragged one of the heavy, wooden chairs back from the table. It screeched against the cold stone floor as Elysen stared at Brenden. The boy opened his mouth, but Yergen turned to Owen and glared.

"Father, it is time to exclude this witch from our council. We have put up with her for long enough. You are Lord of the Vyr now. Send her away."

The burning logs of alder sputtered quietly. Elysen ran the words through her mind. The sounds were familiar, but she could not put the meanings together. Lord of the Vyr. Owen. Vollen's younger brother. *How could he be Lord of the Vyr?* Vollen ruled the Vyr. To Vollen, the Vyr stood for everything. The plains, the deserts, the ice, the Sud de Mer, the mountains at the edge of darkness, the sky, the fire and the dirt and the rain. Vollen encompassed all of it. Lord of life. Lord of death. Death. Elysen felt something inside her chest turn hot, like a kettle boiling over. A deep ache grabbed her stomach and wrapped it into a knot. She sat down hard, her legs no longer able to support her body. Her hands shook and she could not take her eyes off the top of Brenden's head. She found the ache and sent it away, into a dark cavern in her chest. The ache left a numbing pain that she found easier to ignore.

"Tell me what happened," she asked. She tried to swallow, but her lips and throat were dry. A faint aroma wafted from the cup of wine in front of her and joined with the stinging smoke. "How could Vyr Lords have been killed? That's not possible. You're wrong."

Yergen slammed his goblet on the table and wiped his lips with the back of his hand.

"We engaged the Uemn in the swamps of the Southern Wash," he said. "The conscripted men abandoned their posts and the enemy killed brave Eoth, Clint and Justin. They cut off their heads and placed them on pikes. The Uemn now control the forests and swamps of the south." Yergen spit on the floor and made a face as if his wine had turned to vinegar. "Your father ran as well, but the Uemn caught him and tore him to pieces."

"That isn't possible," Elysen said. Her gaze wandered along the cracks in the stone floor.

"It's true," Brenden said.

Elysen shook her head.

"Tell her the rest," Owen said.

"The Uemn had knives. Long knives. Made of hard metal."

Elysen looked at them, studied their faces, and then turned toward Owen. "Is this some kind of nightmare?" she asked.

Owen shook his head. Elysen turned to Raes.

"Did you know of this?" she snapped.

He shook his head. His eyes drifted toward the floor. Elysen stood up. She turned around and grabbed the heavy wooden chair by the armrests. She struggled with the weight of it as she heaved it into the air. It flew a very short distance before it cracked against the stone floor. Her shoulders hunched forward as she stared at the toppled chair.

"Everything you say is a lie," she said. "Vollen cannot be dead. Abundant hard metals are a myth. They are a violation of Thorsen's Law. They can not exist."

"You, of all people, should know that Thorsen's Law can be violated," Yergen said. He sat down and took a long drink of wine. "The Uemn have hard metal. They have killed your father. They have killed my brothers. And now they must pay."

"This is simply not possible," Elysen said. She looked around the Pithe as if she expected her father to come striding in at any moment. She slid into the next empty chair and stared at the fire. She could feel the weight of the metal band on her head – the only thing her mother left for her. She wore it in defiance of the law, in defiance of the very nature of the Vyr. For so long it had been nothing more than a curiosity. Now it served as a stark reminder that hard metals existed, and that the law could be broken. Still, Elysen refused to accept Yergen's claim.

"There is no hard metal in this world that is plentiful enough to make a blade," she said. "And there is no Uemn brave enough to kill a lord."

"Then explain this," Yergen said. He stood up and leaned across the table so that he could reach the burlap bundle. He yanked on it shaking out the contents. A long, hard blade clattered onto the wooden table and the air filled with a ringing that made Elysen grab her ears. She jumped back and hit her head against the back of the chair. Yergen reached out and slid the blade across the table. It skidded to a stop in front of Elysen and she slowly leaned forward to examine it. Her fingers clutched the edge of the worn table as she peered at the long knife. The handle accommodated two fists, hand over hand. A small cross-shaped guard separated the handle from the pointed blade – long enough to impale three grown men with one thrust. The light from the fire reflected off the smooth, silver surface. The blade itself, only as wide as four of Elysen's slender fingers, tapered to an edge so thin that it seemed almost invisible. Blood stained the surface of the blade, and the coppery taste of death tainted the air.

"This is the blade that killed your father," Yergen said. "I took it from the Uemn that cut him down." Yergen banged his fist on his chest. "I did this. As Vollen ran from battle, I took my knife and slit the demon's throat."

Elysen put her hands over her ears and closed her eyes tightly.

"Vollen was not fit to be Lord," Yergen said. "He was soft and full of doubt and fear." Yergen placed his knuckles on the table and leaned forward. "I am a proper Lord. I am true to the law of Thorsen and to the Vyr."

Owen glared at him. Elysen put her elbows on the table and pressed her fists into her eyes to keep the tears from rolling down her cheeks.

A warrior does not weep. A warrior takes revenge.

"How many Uemn have these?" Raes asked quietly, unable to remove his eyes from the blade.

"We saw dozens," Brenden said. His face turned pale and his eyes became rimmed with red. Elysen could see his knuckles turning white. "Many of them were riding horses," Brenden added through clenched teeth.

Owen sat with his hands clasped together, his lips pursed, eyes locked on some point in space in front of him.

"There's more," Brenden said.

He paused. Yergen and Owen were both lost in thought. Brenden glanced at each of them in turn, and then spoke again.

"The Uemn on horseback had armor of hard metal as well. Our stone-tipped arrows and obsidian knives bounced off them. Worthless."

"How could this be?" Elysen asked.

"They have enlisted the aid of an ancient dark lord," Brenden said quietly.

The room grew quiet, disturbed only by the logs in the fire as they shifted and sent a shower of sparks drifting up the chimney.

Owen spoke sternly. "We will gather the army tomorrow and I will lead them myself."

"There is no army left, father," Brenden said. "Once we lost Vollen, the conscripts lost their will to fight. The Uemn butchered our bravest soldiers. The cowards fled back to their homes to hide like sheep." Brenden's voice shook.

Owen turned to Yergen. "You claim that Vollen ran like a coward, and yet here you are, and there he lies fallen on the field of battle."

Yergen glared at his father and clenched his teeth. Owen continued. "For uncountable years, since the beginning of time, we have held back the Uemn, and no Vyr Lord has ever been lost. The swamps and marshes and forests of the south have always been our sporting grounds." He paused for a moment and gripped the edge of the table. "We kill the Uemn for sport. They are not warriors. They are an infestation. They are like ants that we squash with our boots. Never, since time began, have the Uemn ever killed a Lord. Never." He leaned back again, still glaring at Yergen. "I can not believe that Vollen ran like a mouse," he said. "It was more likely you that ran."

Yergen came to his feet and slammed his fist on the table.

"There was no one left to command," he growled. "Haven't you been listening to us?"

"We showered them with arrows, father," Brenden said. "They fought on, with our arrows hanging on their tunics like quills porcupine quills. Our knives cut their clothes, but we could not make them bleed. If they fell, they rose again like the walking dead. Only the crossbows could penetrate their armor, and they were too slow to reload. The Uemn marched into our lines, walking over us and hacking us to pieces."

Owen put his hands up. "I don't want to hear excuses," he said. He turned his eyes toward the table in front of him and pulled on his beard.

"I will gather a new army," Yergen hissed. "I will enlist every farmer, every rancher, every shepherd, every man and woman that can carry a weapon, and I will take the battle to them in the swamps. I will arm everyone with heavy crossbows and fire-hardened bolts, and once I have pushed them out of the swamps, I will chase them into the high desert where they live and I will kill them and their women and their children until there are none left to scourge this world." Yergen slammed his fist on the table again. "We have been patient, and tolerant and temperate long enough."

"Sit down," Owen said. "We are not thinking clearly tonight. I have lost my sons and my brother and we have lost a great Lord. We need time to calm down and regroup."

Raes stopped behind Brenden. He looked into Owen's eyes. "If the Uemn control the swamps and marshes of the Southern Wash," he said. "They will soon advance into the plains. We may not have time to grieve yet."

"We will discuss this later," Owen said.

"No," Yergen blurted. "We have to decide now."

Elysen glanced at Brenden and Raes, and then spoke. Her upper lip curled away from her teeth. "I agree," she said. Her voice came out low and hoarse. "We have to do something now. Our reaction must be swift and sure. These Uemn will pay. There is no reason to wait."

"No one asked for your opinion," Yergen said. "Or your help."

"I will be at the front of the charge," Elysen said. "Just as I was at the Rift."

Yergen sneered at her. "If we get lucky this time, they will cut your head off and set it on a pike next to your father's, and then the Vyr will be as it was before Vollen spoiled it."

Elysen stood up.

"The Vyr was dying long before Vollen was Lord," she said, growling low and soft like a threatened animal.

Owen motioned for Elysen and Yergen to back down, and they both sat.

"Raes, you are the only one here tonight with a cool head," Owen said. "Tell me what you would propose."

Yergen glared first at his father and then at Raes. He crossed his arms and closed his lips so tightly that they turned white.

"I agree with Yergen," he said. "We need to make some kind of plan right now. Our dages reported to me that there are very few men left to fight. We have taken most of the strongest men and lost them to the Uemn. Our Gennissaries are down to old men and children. We may have to start conscripting women."

"If we do," Owen said. "The Uemn will surely know that they have us beaten."

"That is why we must move quickly," Raes said. He glanced at Yergen. Owen's oldest son slumped down in his chair with his arms crossed and a frown on his face, paying attention to no one. Raes stepped around Brenden and poured the boy's wine across the oak planks.

"Here are the southern swamps that mark the boundary between the Vyr and the endless sea," Raes said as he spread the dark liquid out with the palm of his hand. He turned the empty goblet upside down and slammed it on the table in front of Brenden.

"The Uemn," Raes said, pushing the goblet slightly toward Owen. Raes walked back toward the side of the table. He touched the back of one empty chair after another. "In the west, the end of the world, protected by the Mountains of Oken and the devils that live there." He continued toward Yergen and Owen, but his eyes were fixed on Elysen. He reached out and pushed Yergen's cup toward the middle of the table. "Turoc's Cauldron, in the northern Vyr, at the foot of BlackBonne." He walked around behind Elysen and stopped at her left. "In the far north, beyond the Reach, the lands of ice." He continued along the far side of the wooden table. "The Great Rift in the east," he said, running his hands along the edge of the oak planks.

"We don't need a lecture in the lay of the land," Yergen said. Raes circled around until he stood by Brenden again. He pushed the upended goblet an arm's length further toward Yergen.

"The Uemn have tried to attack us before, from the Rift, but we stopped them easily," Raes said.

"They were stupid," Elysen said. "We butchered them as they climbed."

"The Rift is wide open, little cover, and we were in an elevated position," Raes added.

"They hide in the forests of the southern Vyr now," Brenden said. "They are advancing slowly, carefully. They learned their lesson in the battle of the Rift."

"What is your point, Master Raes," Elysen said. Her eyes drifted from his hands to his face and then back to the upended dishes on the table. Her heart hammered again and something welled up inside her. She pushed it back down, into the darkness.

"We have to draw them west," he said. He pulled the goblet further toward Yergen as he spoke, walking along the side of the table again. "Between the Three Sisters and Thane's Peak. There, we can trap them and destroy them without sacrificing too many Gennissaries."

"And how do you propose to lure them into such an obvious trap?" Yergen asked.

"We stage our troops in such a way to make the Uemn believe that we protect the western passage. We make it look like a weakness. When they move that direction, we strike."

"Meanwhile, we leave the approach to Sunder Keep relatively unguarded," Owen said.

Raes nodded. "We must use misdirection."

Brenden raised his head. His eyes were sunken and tired. "What if they are not misdirected?" he asked.

"They are stupid beasts," Elysen said. "We need only herd them like cattle into Raes' trap." She turned her attention back to the fire and tried to pull her legs up against her chest, but the arms of the oak chair and her bulky armor prevented it. She slumped down and turned sideways a bit.

"These stupid beasts have learned to make weapons of hard metal," Brenden reminded her.

Elysen raised her hand, palm toward the boy, as if to brush his comment away. She stopped in mid motion and instead reached up and slowly removed the silver band from her head. She set it on the table and pushed it away, towards the steel blade that taunted her with the thought of her father's head, rolling in the mud, vacant eyes staring toward the sky. She could see his smile. She could see the lines across his forehead as he raised his eyebrows when something roused his curiosity. She could see his hands running through his tangled brown hair. The thought brought her back to his dead, vacant eyes and she squeezed her own eyes shut.

Owen waved his arm in the air. "We can not leave the eastern approach to the Keep unguarded. We need another option."

"Approach from the north," Elysen said. She felt tired and far away. Her voice lost its edge. "Attack them in the desert where they live. It is the only way to wipe them out."

"The north," Yergen roared. "Only you would suggest the north. The ice fields are impassable, and we would have to fight our way through the

Norgarden as well as the desert people. You are as crazy as you are grotesque."

"Enough," Owen said, raising his hand. "We can't go north. Yergen is right. With Vollen and Aephia both dead, our alliance with the Norgarden is broken, and even if that was not the case, we can't take an army across the ice."

"But the Norgarden travel back and forth across the ice somehow," Elysen persisted.

"No one knows that for sure," Owen said.

"But you have told me that yourself," she said.

"It is all just rumor," Owen insisted. "Even if it is possible for a few Norgarden to travel back and forth between the desert and the plains, we could never take an army across the great ice mass."

Elysen felt her anger and fear sapping her strength, but she would not give up. "Give me a division," she said. "Yergen can clear the southern lands and advance northward across the desert. Brenden and I will lead an army from the north, and we will box them in."

"Your obsession with the ice shows your true alliance, half-breed," Yergen snarled. "Like your mother, you are a Norgarden spy." Yergen stood. "She must be expelled from this meeting immediately. She will give away our plans to the Norgarden and they will warn the Uemn."

"Sit down," Owen said. "Elysen is every bit as loyal as you are, Yergen. If I ever doubt her loyalty to me, I will deal with it myself. Do you understand?"

The coal lamps around the perimeter of the Pithe began to run out of fuel. They sputtered and fumed, and Elysen stirred in her chair, leaning closer to the blade. She peered more closely, squinting at it. The steel shimmered with subtle hues of ice blue.

"How could they have forged such a thing?" she whispered. She could taste her father's blood in her mouth.

"The dark lords," Owen said. "Ancient enemies of Thorsen. Only they could know how to make weapons like this."

"What can we do against such a thing?" Elysen asked. Owen shook his head slowly, but Yergen slammed his fist on the table.

"Vollen was weak and stupid," he said. "He led us to our deaths. Send me south, father. I'll roust the devils myself."

"With what?" Owen asked. "Sticks and rocks?"

"If that is what it takes. I'll crush them with my bare hands if I have to." Yergen's dark eyes were lit with fierce intensity. Owen studied his face for a few moments and then smiled.

"Yes, I believe that you would," he said.

"They will strike you down," Elysen said, still staring at the blade.

Yergen jumped out of his chair and clenched his fists, leaning over Owen toward Elysen with his teeth bared. "You are the cause of all of this. You are an abomination to nature and all the laws of the Lords, cursed offspring of Vyr Lord and Norgarden. Before you were born, the Vyr Lords were masters of everything. It is your presence that spoils this world."

Raes stood with his knees slightly bent and his hand on the grip of the red knife that lay sheathed at his waist.

"Enough," Owen said. He waved his arm again. "I will consider these options, and more. We have to wait and consider."

"Enough waiting, father," Yergen said. "We wait and wait and plan and plan. We need action, not more planning."

Owen stood up and glared at Yergen. "You lead our armies into poorly planned battles and your brothers, my sons, pay the price with their lives."

The two men stood frozen, face to face, snarling at each other. Yergen broke away, stomping back to the fireplace to stare at the flames.

"I will make my decision in my private quarters," Owen said. "Yergen, bring the blade and join me. But give me a few moments first. I wish to be alone for a time." He pointed toward Raes. "I will call for you later. As of this moment, you are relieved from any duties that you may still have in the north. Your services are required here."

Owen gathered his cloak in his arms and walked through the arched doorway reserved for the Lord of the Vyr. The door slammed behind him.

Raes faced Elysen. "M'lady," he said. His eyes searched hers. She turned her head slowly away from his gaze and stared into the fire.

"Leave me," she said. "I need to be alone."

Raes stood for a moment, poised on the balls of his feet as if his body yearned to move toward her. He stared at her for a moment, and then bowed and left.

Yergen watched Raes leave and then came over to Elysen and leaned over her. He grabbed both of her arms and pulled her to her feet. Elysen's wooden breastplate clattered against Yergen's, and she turned her head as his hot breath washed over her face.

"Stay away from Raes," he said.

Brenden's eyes were wide and his mouth hung open. He stammered as he spoke.

"Brother, you must not touch her," Brenden said.

Yergen let go of Elysen with one hand and pointed a gloved finger at the boy.

"You stay out of this, little brother," he said.

Elysen yanked her arm from his grip and pushed him away with a blow from the palm of her hand. She wanted to protest, to scream, to hammer on Yergen's chest with her fists, to curse him for bothering her with such a stupid and trivial fear because Vollen mattered more than the Vyr and the Keep and the law and then it hit her again that Vollen was gone and the fire inside her chest died like a candle snuffed out in a bowl of water.

"You are violating the very base of the law," Brenden said.

Yergen picked up the closest goblet and threw it at Brenden. It bounced off the table and Brenden ducked sideways as it flew past his shoulder.

"She is the violation," Yergen screamed. "She is the cause of all our grief."

Yergen turned back toward Elysen and pointed at her chest with his finger. "You are nothing to me," he said. "You are like trash to be thrown out to the pigs. And when I am Lord I will take the greatest pleasure in feeding you to the hogs and swine, and then I will eat them in turn and with them, you."

Elysen frowned at Yergen, shaking her head slightly as he raved. In her mind, Yergen's words kept repeating – *stay away from Raes, stay away from Raes. Why did he care about Raes?* In her mind, she saw him, tall and sweaty on a summer afternoon, parrying her blows as she swung her jubo again and again, never getting in a blow against his naked chest, and she saw him laugh with glee as she staggered forward, exhausted. His eyes suddenly hardened, and his bronze skin glistened like ice in the afternoon light. She could smell the sweet grass, and she could see the tiny flecks of wheat chaff that stuck to his jaw and cheek. Even as Yergen stood glaring with hate, something inside her stirred, and she felt a moment of calm as she realized Yergen's fear.

"You are not Lord yet," she said, musing aloud. "And my claim is stronger than even your father's. And my son's claim will be stronger still."

"You will not live to have a son," he said.

Yergen picked up the long blade and pointed it at her. It shook slightly as he spoke.

"And you will not live to ever be touched by a man in any way," he said. He brought his face close to hers. "When Owen is gone, and I am Lord, your life will be forfeit to me." He pointed at his chest with his free hand. "I will decide whether you live or die. I will decide how you will live or die." He lowered his voice to a whisper. "And if you are to have a child, it will be my child. Do you understand?"

"You," she hissed. "You who are so full of the law. You threaten to break the deepest of the laws. You dream of inbreeding, and the dream itself is a violation of your precious laws." She glared at him and then spit on the floor in front of his boots. Yergen stood, red-faced, with his fists clenched and his arms straight down.

"You are too full of yourself, Yergen," she said. "I would never be with you unless it was to slip a knife between your ribs."

Yergen threw the blade on the table and took two steps forward, ripping his glove from his hand as he moved. He struck her across the cheek with his bare palm. She staggered sideways and touched her lip with her glove. Blood glistened a darker black against the leather. She stared at her fingers, and then touched her cheek again.

"Your skin touched mine," she said.

Brenden's mouth dropped open and he stared at Yergen with wide eyes.

Yergen licked his lips and took a few steps back. "Your blood may be as red as mine," he said. "But it is not the blood of a true lord. Never forget that."

He took a few more steps back and then snarled at his brother.

"You saw nothing," Yergen said. "And you heard nothing."

He grabbed the blade and burlap off the table and bounded up the steps toward the door that Owen had used, disappearing into the gloom. Brenden followed his brother slowly, glancing at Elysen as he left.

After they were all gone, she sat for a long time just staring at the flames. Nothing moved in the Pithe as the torches went out one by one, and eventually the only light came from the fire. Elysen stood up and the silence overwhelmed her. She grabbed a chair and threw it to the floor, and then another and another. She worked her way around the table, pushing and shoving at the chairs as if they were somehow to blame. She tipped every chair and then kicked the last one before she turned her rage on the table. She grabbed the edge of the giant oak planks and screamed with rage and anger and pain as she tried to lift it. The table remained solidly on the ground. She collapsed forward and rested for a moment, squeezing her eyes shut. When she opened them, she stared at the goblet that Raes had used to represent Turoc's Cauldron. She stood up and straightened her back, and then reached out and struck the goblet with the back of her hand. The dark wine swept across the oak like fire across an open prairie.

Four

Elysen heard a voice and stirred. She opened her eyes and pushed herself into a sitting position. Corde's lamp threw a circle of light around the hearth.

"M'lady," he said.

Elysen grabbed his arm. Corde stared at her fingers for a moment, and then looked around to make sure no one else watched. He held his arm rigid as she pulled herself up.

"Did you hear?" she asked. Her voice rustled like dry leaves.

"I did," he said. "News travels fast among the dojen and the servants. My heart is heavy. I was worried. I came to find you."

"Thank you," she said. She let go of his arm and he took a deep breath.

"Come to your quarters now," he said. "There is nothing more you can do here."

"No," she said. "I have to see Owen."

Corde sighed. "All you have ever known is fighting and hardship and cold. There is more to this life than just the darkness. Come eat some food and sleep in your bed, and tomorrow when you wake you can grieve some more."

"I don't want to grieve," she said. "My father was a warrior. So am I. I will avenge him, and grieve later, if at all. Now walk with me."

The light from Corde's torch bobbed behind Elysen as she walked the long, dark hallways of the Keep. She came to a large door, guarded by two of the dage of the Keep. The dage held stout jubos, pointed on one end and affixed with four rows of sharp, tooth-like stones on the other. The guards stared straight ahead as Elysen knocked. Owen's voice came from within.

"Come in," he said. Elysen turned to Corde.

"Go to the stables at BlackBonne and see if my father's horse came back. I will need it."

Corde nodded and slipped away into the darkness. Elysen stepped into Owen's chamber.

Yergen leaned over the table, bracing his arms against the wooden surface. Owen stood next to him with his arms crossed. They were staring at the silver blade that sat uncovered on top of the rough, oily burlap. The light from the torches mounted along the four walls gleamed on the polished steel.

"Where have you been?" Owen asked.

Elysen rubbed her cheeks and said nothing.

"The Lord asked you a question," Yergen snapped.

"I was considering options," she snarled back.

"More likely you were crying in the arms of poor, lonely Raes," Yergen said, taunting her.

"Yergen," Owen barked. "She has just lost her father. Have some compassion."

Yergen whirled around to face the Lord.

"You speak of compassion just like your weak brother did," Yergen said. He grabbed his own head and pulled on his long tangle of dark hair. He snarled through his teeth. "I am surrounded by weakness." He turned back to face Elysen. "And you, abomination, are the source of all this. When you have been wiped from this world, then everything will be all right again."

"Leave her alone," Owen warned. "Remember the oath we made to her mother."

Yergen let go of his hair and shook his head violently. "I made no oath," he said. He stepped toward Elysen and she shifted on the balls of her feet. Her legs braced against the floor and her fingers flexed. Yergen reached out, almost casually, as if greeting and old friend with a gentle tap on the shoulder. At the very last moment, he twisted his torso and balled his hand into a fist. His short swing caught Elysen on the edge of her jaw and sent her staggering backwards into a heavy chair.

Owen grabbed Yergen from behind and spun him around. The Lord's face filled with fury as he slapped his son across a ruddy cheek. Yergen's head turned, and his face went blank. He rolled his head in a circle as if to clear the kinks and strains from his neck, and then he licked his lips with the tip of his tongue. He smiled at his father, but his smile turned to a sneer as his fingers shot forward into Owen's throat. The Lord grabbed his neck and gagged as he stepped away from his son. The two men stared at each other for a moment. Owen began to sag forward, about to fall, but as Yergen stepped toward him, Owen came up swinging his fist.

The blow came close, but the younger man reared back just out of reach. As Owen's arm shot through empty space, his weight shifted away from his target. Yergen slipped in sideways and used his elbow to strike Owen across the bridge of the nose. Elysen heard the sharp crack of bone against bone, and the force of the blow snapped Owen's head backwards. He caught his balance and regained his poise as Yergen stepped away. Owen reached up and touched the bridge of his nose gingerly. His eyes went wide. Owen looked at the blood on his hand and then reached out and slapped Yergen across the cheek.

"You stupid fool," Owen snarled.

Yergen stood for a moment with a look of shock on his face, and then he roared in anger and swung his fist up from his waist, bringing it across Owen's jaw like the kick of a mule. Elysen tasted her own blood in her mouth as Owen's head snapped back again. The sound of Owen's jaw breaking and popping out of its socket filled the room. Owen reeled sideways and fell across the oak table. Yergen stepped back. He chest heaved hard and fast, and his eyes held a wild, far away look.

The Lord kept his back toward Yergen as he regained his footing, his head hanging forward. Suddenly, he swung around, his knife in hand, and thrust the stone blade directly at Yergen's throat. Yergen moved quickly, but the edge of the blade caught his cheek as he dodged. He grabbed his own blade from his belt and swung it upward, slipping it under the bottom edge of Owen's chest plate and planting it deep into the Lord's belly. Elysen heard Owen inhale sharply, then his eyes widened and his breathing stopped, as if he had been thrown into an icy, frozen lake. He sat down on the edge of the table and stared at Yergen, who backed away, gazing curiously at the bloody blade in his hand.

They stood in a death-like silence. Owen still held his blade in front of his body, his fingers loosening moment by moment. Yergen stared at his knife, and then turned and glared at Elysen. Her breath came in quick, shallow pants as she stared at Yergen. Their eyes locked together. The silence of the council chamber descended like a shroud.

Owen touched his stomach, now covered with blood. He raised his head slowly, glaring at his son. He lunged, taking Yergen by surprise, but despite his courage, the Lord's grip weakened and his injuries impaired his aim. Owen tried to thrust his knife into the unplated area under Yergen's right arm, where it might puncture his heart and end the battle, but the blow glanced off Yergen's armor. Yergen caught his father in his arms and staggered backwards. His back hit the rock wall, and both father and son dropped their knives to the floor. Owen snapped his head upward, catching Yergen's chin. As Yergen's head snapped back, it hit the stone wall. Yergen's knees sagged, and then he recovered and slammed one knee upward into Owen's exposed stomach. The Lord doubled over, and Yergen grabbed him, spun him around and tossed him like a broken doll. The Lord crashed into the council table.

Elysen took a step backward as Yergen picked up a heavy wooden chair and lifted it above his head, ready to smash it down on the disabled lord. She found the strange metal weapon in her hand and stared at it, as if unaware that she had picked it up.

Yergen's eyes were full of fierce anger, and his teeth showed between his parted lips. His brow gleamed with sweat. Owen pulled himself across the table, slowly, with great effort. Elysen grabbed the handle of the blade with both hands and held it in front of her body. Her eyes were wide, and her nostrils flared as she breathed. She hesitated only a moment more before she stepped forward with her right foot and brought the blade around from her left to her right in a great arc that struck the chair above Yergen's head with tremendous force. The blade cut through one of the wooden legs and the cross-bracing and knocked the chair from Yergen's grip. He stood there, dazed, staring at Elysen as she recovered from the blow, staggering backwards and dragging the tip of the blade across the floor where it left a trail of sparks.

They stood for a few moments, breathing hard, Owen bleeding from his mouth and nose, laying face up on the table, Yergen, standing with his hands held limply in the air as if they still held some ghostly vestige of the shattered chair, and Elysen, holding the blade at her left side, both hands on the hilt, the tip of the blade pointing backwards, away from her cousin, but poised to strike an arc from left to right that would sever him at the waist.

He moved backwards as she took a sideways step toward Owen. She swung the point of the blade toward Yergen and they circled, Yergen moving away from the table and toward the door, and Elysen moving to protect Owen. Yergen backed up the steps, holding his hands in front of him, his face contorted with anger. He stepped out the door. Elysen heard him shout for help as she stood there, gripping the handle of the blade with both hands. The weight of the thing overcame her and the tip fell against the flagstones again. She let go of it, and it clattered noisily to the floor. Owen gasped. Elysen helped him up. His head bobbed up and down, as if the muscles in his neck were no longer working, and blood and saliva were dripping freely from his dislocated jaw. His eyes wandered aimlessly around the room. Elysen yelled for help. Owen reached up and touched her face. His voice escaped as barely a whisper. Blood trickled from his lips as he spoke, and the pain of his injury malformed and slurred his words.

"There is so much I wanted to tell you," he said. She hugged him tightly as his eyes closed.

Raes and a regiment of the Lord's Guard rushed in, led by Yergen, their ebony armor clattering, wood against stone, wood against wood.

Owen whispered to Elysen, ignoring the chaos around them.

"Your mother and father broke the law," he said. "They thought that they could bring the Shad'ya."

Three guards formed a loose circle around Elysen and held her between them with the pointed ends of their jubos. Yergen rushed over to Owen and picked him up, cradling him in his arms.

"The witch picked up the blade and attacked us," he said. "Look at the chair I used to protect our Lord; she cut it into pieces in her fit of rage."

Brenden stood near the door as two more guards helped Yergen gently lift Owen. The guards created a sling out of their intertwined arms and Yergen let them carry the fallen Lord away. Owen's head hung back, and his eyes were wild with pain and confusion.

Yergen addressed two of the men that surrounded Elysen. "Seleste, Portis," he said. "Take her to the tunnels and lock her in storage until I decide what to do with her." He paced for a moment, shaking his hands as if they were burning. He grabbed a chair and threw it against the wall. "Post yourselves at the nearest junction," he said, catching his breath. "Let no one past, and stay away from the witch. She will deceive you with lies." He turned toward Raes and poked him in the chest with a finger. "And you," he said. "Stay away from her, or I will have you killed."

The two guards prodded Elysen and she stepped backwards, away from Yergen. One of the guards turned his jubo around and struck her in the chest with the blunt end. She tripped over the steps and fell on her back, striking her elbows on the floor. The men jabbed at her bare neck with their long weapons, forcing her to her feet, and then pushing her from the room. As she backed away, she saw Yergen picking up the blade from the floor where she had dropped it. He turned and called after the two dages.

"Be careful," he said. "She can disappear in the darkness. She is as dangerous as a viper. And do not touch her in any way."

Raes stood, useless, watching Elysen as the guards dragged her away.

"I should have killed you," she hissed at Yergen.

He nodded, his face expressionless.

Five

The guards looped ropes around Elysen's forearms to avoid touching her directly as they dragged her down the long, empty hallway. She turned toward the dage that held her left arm in a trap-like knot. She recognized him from his service to her father.

"Seleste," she pleaded. "Let me go. If you check Lord Owen's wounds you will find that they are not of my doing."

"Shut up, heathen," Seleste said. His teeth were clenched together. He and the other guard fell into a fast march.

"Seleste," she said. She kept her voice low. "We fought the Uemn together at the edge of the Great Rift. You and me and Raes, and my father."

"Those were different times," Seleste reminded her.

As they passed by a torch, Elysen could see that Seleste's chest plate had taken at least glancing blows from a sharp instrument, leaving deep scrapes and gouges in the hard wood. The thick rope dug deep into the muscles of Elysen's arm. She winced as Seleste yanked her off her feet. She scrambled to regain her footing. Seleste glared at her with dark brown eyes that were almost black in the dim light of the corridor.

Elysen turned toward the guard that clutched the other rope.

"Dage Portis, please listen to me," Elysen said.

Portis' eyes matched the mahogany of his armor, and they held a far away, almost sad look. She let her eyes plead with his as she spoke to him.

"Examine Lord Owen's wounds when you..."

Seleste stopped without warning, pulling hard on the rope around Elysen's arm. The sudden halt took Portis by surprise. He staggered one step ahead before his grip on Elysen's other binding caused him to stop as well. The sudden separation of her two captors rattled her wooden armor and caused a wash of pain to pass across her face. Seleste placed his face close to Elysen's.

"We have suffered and lost much since you last saw us, witch," he hissed. His hot breath smelled of meat and beer and onions, and a spray of moisture punctuated the final sound. She closed her eyes and turned her face from his.

"Calm down," Portis said. "Both of you."

Elysen glanced at the taller, calmer dage. His brow furrowed and he turned to stare off down the darkened tunnel.

"Yergen struck Lord Owen," Elysen insisted. "Check his wounds when you get back. Do with me what you will, just promise me that you will protect our Lord."

"Blasphemy," Seleste hissed. "Yergen would not harm our Lord, his father."

"Come on," Portis said. He pulled on the rope, treating Elysen like a stray dog. The group walked again.

"Promise me," Elysen pleaded.

Seleste growled a warning to her. "Shut up, child."

This time Portis brought the group to a halt. The torches that lined the walls stopped abruptly here, leaving only darkness beyond. Portis swung around and put his hand on Seleste's chest plate.

"We have all felt pain tonight, Dage Seleste," he said. "You are not yourself, neither am I. Leave this one to me, I'll lock her up, you wait here for me. We will stand guard together."

Seleste bared his teeth and leaned against Portis' outstretched arm.

"I can handle this grotesque," Portis said quietly. He kept his voice calm and clear.

Seleste took one step back, and then turned toward Elysen.

"I'll come down and check on you later," he said. The unfriendly undertones echoed through the caverns like the whispers of unseen devils, hiding in the shadows.

Portis grabbed the last torch and stepped away from Seleste, pulling Elysen with him. They left Seleste standing in the middle of the hallway, his fists clenched, arms held straight down.

Portis led her into a dead-end enclosed with a sturdy wooden gate made of horizontal hardwood timbers as thick as a man's arm, contained between two giant vertical posts that were three times as thick as the cross beams. The horizontal poles were spaced evenly, just far enough apart so that a small, skinny child could slip through, but no more. Portis used the ropes like a whip and swung her inside as if she were no more than a handful of rags. He set his shoulder against the gate, dropped his head and pushed. The outer post scraped against the rock floor as the gate swung on its large, wooden hinge pins. When it squared up with the wooden beam that ran along the wall from floor to ceiling, the upright post dropped into a depression in the floor with a heavy thud. Elysen came forward and touched the cold, bare wood that imprisoned her.

"Thank you, Portis," she said.

"For what?" he asked.

"For helping me."

"Don't mistake me, child," he said. "I am not helping you."

"Portis, please listen to me," she said. He shook his head and stepped backwards, into the darkness, taking the torch with him.

"It is not my place to listen to you," he said.

As he turned and walked away, all light went with him.

In the utter blackness of the deep reaches below the Keep, Elysen could not track the passing of the night or the coming of the day. She sat and receded into thoughts that spun in circles. She tried to sleep, but her eyes would not close. She stared into an emptiness blacker and darker than any sleep. At some point, she drifted away, to a snow covered field, pure and white and silent. She walked through the field, felt the snow crunch under her bare feet. A small child hugged her neck tightly. She felt his warm naked body against hers. A sense of peace came over her for a moment, but as she watched gray clouds roll overhead, the snow began to turn red, and shouts and screams mixed with laughter and murmuring voices broke the silence. She woke with a start and found amber light surrounding her.

"Elysen?" Brenden's soft voice floated through the haze in her mind. He held a lamp up and peered into her prison.

She stood and placed her hands on the bars that held her in.

"Brenden?" she asked.

He came up to the gate and held the torch so that they could see each other's faces.

"You should not be here," she said.

"Lord Owen is dead," Brenden said. His eyes searched hers.

Elysen sat down on a cask, just at the edge of Brenden's light. Her fingers gripped the edge of the barrel as if she were perched far above the world, tilting precariously toward the edge of nothingness.

"My brother claims that you killed Owen. That you killed him with the heathen blade." Brenden paused for a moment, and then continued. "Did you?"

Elysen shook her head and stared at the stone floor as shadows flickered and danced in the smoky light.

"I could no more kill Lord Owen than I could kill you, sweet cousin," she said. "Yergen killed him. Not me."

"Yergen now claims the spirit of the Vyr Lord, and vows to lead the armies of the Vyr against the Uemn to cleanse them from this world once and for all." Brenden said.

"Then we are doomed," Elysen said.

"Don't talk like that," Brenden said. "Yergen is the Lord now."

"Yergen is a fool," she replied.

Brenden began to back up. Elysen stood up and grabbed the wooden rails again.

"Don't leave me," she said.

"I can't stay," he said.

"Please," Elysen pleaded, reaching out to him through the bars.

He shook his head.

"Help me," she said.

He turned around, putting his back toward her, but he did not walk away.

"Please, tell them I did not kill Lord Owen," she said.

He hung his head and shook it. "I can't stand against Yergen's will," he said.

"You have to," she said. "You know I didn't do this terrible thing. I cared for my uncle, as much as he cared for me."

Brenden spun around to face her again.

"His care for you was false," Brenden said. His voice sounded as dry as the leaves that blew on the winter wind outside.

"You're wrong," she protested.

Brenden shook his head again. There were tears in his eyes.

"You were a mistake," Brenden said. "He regretted the unholy union that created you, but was too embarrassed to admit it, didn't want our people to see that your father had been wrong."

"That's a lie," she said. "Lord Owen and I were as close as a father and daughter would ever be. He told me so, in his own voice, his own words. He looked me in the eye and told me."

Brenden just shook his head again. "He felt sorry for you. Nothing else. Just pity."

"Why are you telling me these lies?" she cried. "Why are you saying these terrible things to me?"

He turned away again, but still did not walk away.

Her voice became quiet, resolved.

"Owen told you these things himself?" she asked.

He hesitated before he responded. "Yes."

"Why?"

"Why what?"

"Why did he tell you this?"

"He told me everything."

"What do you mean, everything?"

Brenden shook his head again. "Never mind. It doesn't matter anymore."

Elysen reached out through the horizontal bars again.

"Brenden, help me get out of here," she said.

"I can't."

"Please."

"No."

"Brenden, if you care for me at all, you will at least tell me why you crept all the way down here, risking your life."

Brenden touched the wooden bars that separated them.

"I just wanted to look in your eyes. To hear you say that you did not kill him."

"And now that you have seen my eyes, do you believe me?"

He shook his head. Elysen grabbed the bars and shook them.

"Brenden, how could you believe that I would do such a thing?"

"You have every reason to."

"What reasons?"

Brenden turned his head away as he spoke. "You made it clear that you believe you are rightful heir to the lordship of the Vyr."

Elysen's eyes narrowed. Brenden glanced at her and then looked away again.

"I have never spoken ill against Lord Owen," Elysen said. "Yergen is the only one who ever expressed ambition to rule the Vyr before his time. You heard him tonight at council, strutting like an angry cock."

Brenden turned his back to her and walked away, taking the light with him. Elysen sat down and wrapped her arms around her body, listening to the darkness that held her again in its black grip. Water dripped somewhere. A small animal scurried across the floor, its tiny claws clicking rapidly against the hard stones, and then it too was gone.

Six

Elysen paced like a trapped animal, too angry and afraid to sleep. She finally sat down on the floor with her legs crossed over each other. She placed her hands on her knees and took a deep breath.

"Father," she whispered. "My emptiness consumes me more and more as each hour passes."

She sat up suddenly as two lights broke the darkness, first dim, far away, then moving closer, hurriedly, like anxious fireflies. Two men appeared at the gate, faces illuminated by the red and yellow sputtering of the torches.

"So, here is the traitor," Yergen said. He wore a sleeveless leather jerkin, still stained with blood. His skin glistened in the light of the coal lamps. A smear of crusted blood ran along his forearm.

"Lord Owen is dead," Portis muttered.

"I know," Elysen said. "Brenden told me."

Yergen and Portis exchanged disapproving looks. "Brenden exceeds his authority," Yergen said. "I will have to have a chat with him." He shoved his torch into a holder along the wall. Portis did the same.

"Leave Brenden alone," Elysen snarled.

Yergen grabbed the bars and shook them.

"Don't ever raise your voice to me, wretched creature," he screamed. "My father's spirit has passed to me now, I am the Lord, and you will bow to me." His eyes were wild and a drop of saliva dripped from his lip. Elysen stared at the white, foamy drip and suddenly smiled.

"You sputter like an old tallow candle," she said.

Yergen howled and heaved the gate upward with his legs and arms, his muscles bulging and shining in the torchlight. Portis stepped back as Yergen swung the gate outward and stepped into the makeshift cage with Elysen. She moved away from him, glancing at Portis for support. The guard turned his eyes away.

"Stay away from me," she said as Yergen stalked forward. "You've already made one mistake today. Don't make another."

He put his hands on his hips and laughed.

"Now you scare me," he said. He peered at her, tipping his head slightly. "There is no caring for you in this world, witch. I should do us all a favor and snuff out your pitiful life right now."

"Then do it," she said.

He reached out and slapped her, almost lethargically. It looked like an easy, almost comfortable swing, but his hand hit the side of her face like the hoof of a bucking stallion, knocking her sideways. She stumbled and fell against a stack of casks, gasping for breath.

"I now have the power and knowledge of all Lords," he said as he ambled over to her. He picked her up by grabbing her chest plate. She felt like a rag doll in his grip. He glared at her fine wooden armor, holding it as if there were no person inside of it.

"You are not to touch me, Yergen," Elysen said.

He peered into her eyes and curled his upper lip.

"I will do as I please with you," he said. He tossed her toward the gate and she landed on her side, rolling to a stop at Portis' feet.

"Help me get that off her," Yergen commanded him.

Portis turned his head away.

"I can't touch her," he said.

Yergen flew forward and grabbed Portis by the shoulders, slamming him against the wall. Portis regained his balance and turned his face away from Yergen's hot breath.

"What is this rebellion?" Yergen snarled. "Is it contagious? Does everyone question my authority?" He spun Portis around and threw him toward Elysen, who pushed herself up to a half-sitting position.

"Hold her," Yergen said.

Portis moved too slowly.

"Hold her," Yergen yelled. He picked Elysen off the floor like a father picks up a naughty child and he shoved her into Portis' arms. The guard pinned her arms behind her back and Yergen planted his feet in front of her. He grabbed her chest plate and reached around behind it, under her arm. She twisted away to keep Yergen from grabbing the leather bindings that held her armor to her body, but Yergen backhanded her across the jaw. Her head rocked and she blinked several times to regain her focus. Portis held her up while Yergen took his knife and slashed the leather ties that held her ebony chest plate to the plates that protected her back and shoulder blades. The armor fell to the floor. Yergen continued to cut, carefully at first, and then more and more recklessly, drawing blood along her arms and legs as he first pried and cut away all the ebony plates, and then cut through the thick, black leather underneath, revealing her stark, white skin. He pulled the gloves off her hands and wrestled the boots off her feet, leaving her naked. Her long, thin legs braced against the cold stone floor as she struggled against Portis' grip. Yergen finished by hacking off her long, white hair close to her scalp, leaving only a few tattered remnants.

"Let her go," Yergen said, panting.

Portis released her with a push toward the storeroom. Yergen wiped the sweat from his upper lip and stared at the back of his hand. Elysen stood, unprotected, blood trickling down her legs onto the floor beneath her ankles, and dripping along the insides of her arms, down her long, narrow fingers. Every sinew and rib showed in stark relief as the lamp light both revealed her with light and concealed her with shadow.

She stood on the balls of her feet with her hands away from her hips, poised in the air in a defensive position. Yergen stared at her. He licked his lips.

"There now," he said. "You look like the mangy dog that you are."

Yergen moved forward slightly. Portis watched him carefully. Yergen came closer. Elysen followed him with her eyes as he paced around her slowly, examining her white body in the dim light.

"I would have taken you myself, long ago, if you weren't such an abomination," he said.

Elysen stepped backwards and bumped against one of the wooden casks. She braced her arms against it. The top slid open and her fingers touched grit inside. She brought her hands into the light and glanced at them. They were covered with the coal black that the dojen used in the lanterns. She quickly put her hands behind her back again.

Yergen continued to pace. He stopped suddenly.

"Leave a lamp," he said to Portis. "And go back to your post."

"I can't leave you alone here," Portis said.

Yergen whirled around and struck him with an open palm. Portis' head twisted sideways and the slapping sound echoed off the walls.

"You will obey me," Yergen snarled. His teeth showed between his open lips, and a tiny drop of spit hung from his chin. Portis stared at him for a moment with rage in his eyes. He rubbed his cheek, glanced at Elysen, and then stepped backward, taking one of the lamps with him. The light receded slowly and then disappeared. Yergen turned back to face Elysen.

"Shall we finish what we started earlier?" he asked.

A strange smile crossed his face, and he winked. Elysen's back stiffened. Yergen moved forward, slowly, cautiously.

"You've already seen that I am far stronger than you," he said. Elysen's heels left the ground and her fingers clutched at the rim of the barrel.

"I'll kill you if you touch me again," she said.

Yergen struck as quick as a snake. His fist darted forward, hitting her just below the ribs. She grabbed at him and felt her fingers slide across the wet, oily skin of his arms as she doubled over. He locked her head under his arm and brought his knee up into her stomach. Without breath, the sound of her cry stayed trapped deep inside her belly. Yergen spun her around and pressed her chest against the open barrel. He kicked her legs apart and as she reached back, flailing with her arms, he grabbed them and pinned them behind her back with one hand. With the other he reached down and tore at the bindings and straps that held his armor to his legs and thighs. Elysen kicked and thrashed, arching her lean, muscular body, but Yergen just pressed harder against her and laughed.

"You took an oath to uphold Thorsen's Law," Elysen hissed. Her breath stuck in her lungs as something hard and hot rammed into her belly. She screamed.

"Here is the touch you've always wanted," he whispered.

Yergen pounded her against the cask until his body arched and a deep moan echoed off the rock walls. Every muscle in Elysen's body went rigid, and she pressed her eyes tightly closed.

Yergen pulled out and then grabbed the back of her head and pounded it against the edge of the barrel. She slipped to the floor as he stepped back. He stared for a moment, and then adjusted his clothing and picked up the loose pieces of armor that lay scattered across the floor. He stopped for a moment and stared at Elysen with greedy eyes.

"There's the touch you so longed for," he said.

He moved away slowly, out of the cage and into the hallway. The muscles in his arms rippled and gleamed in the dim light as he pushed the gate back into position. Elysen turned her head toward him and stared at the black streaks of coal dust along his biceps as he picked up his lantern and turned to go. He stared at her for a moment longer and then clumsily replaced his armor. He left quickly, without a word, without a sound. Once again the darkness became complete.

Elysen shuddered as she pulled a breath of damp air into her burning lungs. She dropped forward, onto her knees. Her palms slapped the cold, wet floor and her stomach rolled and heaved, throwing hot liquid onto her forearms and the floor and the backs of her hands.

She waited for some time before she stood up, using the wooden barrel for support. She thrust her hands deep inside and rubbed the fine dust between her fingers. She brought her hands close to her face and touched her fingers to her nose. Then she began to rub the gritty dust into her scalp and face, down her neck and shoulders, across her chest and belly. She rubbed hard, her breath coming in ragged gasps. She dug deeper into the barrel and threw the powder against her body as if it were water. She rubbed it into the fronts of her legs and her feet. Her gasps turned to sobs as the rough dust abraded her skin. She moved her hands up the insides of her legs and she touched a slick wetness that crawled down her leg. She dropped to her knees again and her stomach heaved, but nothing came out. She hung her head for a while, sobbing, until the sobs turned to a heavy, angry pant. She ground her teeth together and slowly stood up again. She went back to the coal dust, this time slower, more methodical. She covered her calves and the backs of her legs. She drizzled it down her back and scrubbed herself with it over and over, rubbing it into her ears and under her arms, slowly at first, and then more and more frantically, like a mad woman, until her skin and hair turned black and not even a sliver of white showed.

She stood for a long time with her legs spread wide and her arms stretched out, just breathing and feeling nothing. Then she crawled up onto the pile of casks and wedged her blackened body between the ceiling and the wall, in a small, cramped space far in the corner of the room.

Seven

Yergen returned followed by Seleste and Portis. They stood outside the gate and peered inside, waving their torches back and forth. Elysen watched from her perch with her eyes closed to a slit.

"Where is she?" Yergen hissed. "Open this gate."

Seleste handed his torch to Portis and heaved the gate open. The three men entered the small storage area and poked their torches into the corners.

"Impossible," Portis said. "She could not have escaped. The gate was too heavy for her to move."

"Someone helped her," Yergen said. His eyes gleamed in the torchlight.

Portis scowled at him. "No one passed us after your..." Yergen spun and pushed the guard's head against the stone wall, slicing his throat with a cross stroke so quick that the cut gaped gray before it filled with blood. Portis grabbed his neck with both hands and fell to his knees. Seleste stood with his mouth hanging open. Yergen turned and pointed his blade toward the remaining dage, shaking it at him.

"I told you both to guard this witch carefully," he growled. "Now you have let her escape." He waved his knife toward Portis again. "This is discipline," he said. "Do you understand discipline?"

Seleste raised his hands in front of his body and took a step backwards.

"I swear, Lord Yergen, she did not pass by us in the corridor."

"Then did she simply melt into these walls, like water?" he asked.

He backed Seleste against the wall and then grabbed the front of his armor and slung him toward the gate.

"Post guards at every exit from the tunnels. Then we will begin a sweep." He peered around the room. "She's still down here," he said. "I can smell her. We will chase her out like a rabbit, or we will drown her in the lower tunnels." He sheathed his knife and picked up Portis' lamp. He waved it at Seleste. "Go," he snarled. "Go now. And if you see the witch, kill her. Tell everyone that she is to be killed on sight. She should be easy to find. Now go."

Seleste broke into a fast walk. Yergen followed him slowly, walking backwards down the tunnel for a time before he turned and walked more quickly. Elysen waited before she unwound her long legs from under her body and slipped from her hiding place. The blackness of the tunnel consumed even the white of her teeth as she grinned.

She followed the lights like a rat, sliding through the darkness on silent feet, keeping to the wall. She drifted like a shadow, with only the whites of her eyes to give her away. Her soft footfalls were masked by the voices that echoed off the walls of the tunnels. She stopped as a group of torches passed near her. She turned and fled down a side tunnel, descending a flight of steps. Her bare foot touched water and she stopped. She waited for a moment, and then took a step upward. Voices and dim light above her stopped her again. The light came closer.

"Check all the way down."

"These tunnels are flooded."

"Just go to the water, fool."

Elysen backed into the water. It closed around her calf, then her thighs, and her hips. Still the light came closer.

"No one down here."

"Are you all the way down?"

Elysen took another step backwards. The stairs dropped off and she fell backwards, plunging into the black water. The cold hit her like a clap of thunder. She thrashed her arms and surfaced. Her mouth opened, but her lungs took no breath. As she tried to swim toward the steps again, a man stood just above the waterline waving his torch and yelling.

"She's here, she's here."

Elysen lifted her head from the water and gasped. Her feet touched the broken stairway but she pushed away as more torches joined the first. She arched her back, facing upward in the water, and she kicked her legs as she reached back above her head and pulled her arms through the water. She did not go far before her head hit rock and she cried out in pain. As she glanced toward the steps, more torches gleamed in the darkness.

"Go in and get her."

"The water is like ice. It will kill us."

Yergen's voice cut through the shadows.

"Get in there," He said. Someone grunted, followed by a splash and then a scream.

"Get him out," someone yelled. The sound of arms and legs flailing against the black water filled the cavern. Elysen gasped for another breath of air. The water washed some of the coal black from her skin, and her face glowed white in the darkness. She dropped below the surface, scrambled up again and sucked in more air. Something snicked through the air and rattled against the stones above her head. Another bolt struck the water next to her with a sucking sound. Elysen turned and tried to grab onto the slippery stone wall, but her hands found no purchase.

Yergen's voice rang out against the hard walls. "Give me that."

Elysen reached upward and felt her way along the rough ceiling until she found an open space above her. She reached into the blackness and touched a small outcropping of rock. She turned toward the light just as something struck the surface of the water in front of her, parting it like the whisper of wind in trees. Elysen frowned. The cold dulled and slowed her senses. It took a few moments for the piercing pain to reach deep inside her, but once it did it raced through her bones like fire.

Yergen's voice drifted through the darkness. "Reload, reload."

Elysen's fingers relaxed and she dropped back into the water. She frowned, touched her stomach, low down, near her pelvic bone. Her frown deepened as her fingers closed around the haft of a small arrow. She pulled on it and winced. The broadhead moved inside her like an animal burrowing deeper. The pain blew out the last of her air. She struggled to the surface again, sucked in cold, moist air, and then she relaxed and let her body fall below the surface again, into the blackness of the deep water, kicking gently, feeling the wall with her hands. She closed her eyes and then opened them again. Tiny bubbles drifted from her mouth and across her face and eyes, and she tipped her head to the side. She looked up, into blackness, then down, into a faint blue light. She pushed her hands against the wall, forcing her body, toward the light. She grimaced, held her nose and blew air into her ears, and then continued. Her eyes grew wider and wider as she went deeper into the cavern. She followed the brilliant light, going faster and faster toward it. She rounded a corner, unable to tell up from down, and the tiny bubbles streaming from between her lips stopped. Her hands grabbed wildly at the water. Her eyes rolled back and her lips parted, and the pale, blue light filled her mouth.

Eight

Inside a silent chamber, flooded and undisturbed since the beginning of time, a naked white body erupted from the glassy surface of the water. Elysen gagged, and then coughed, and a flood of liquid spewed from her mouth as she dropped under the surface again. She bobbed to the top and gagged, this time arching and splashing. She slapped her arms against the surface of the water and opened her eyes for a moment, then gagged and coughed once more. Somehow she found solid rock under her feet and pushed her body forward. She fell to her hands and knees, and then crawled up onto a ledge of shallow water, where she cowered on all fours like a whipped animal. A long string of thick, wet liquid hung from her lips. She coughed again and spit a cold, frothy mouthful of water into the clear pool that stretched around her. She tipped her head to the side and opened her eyes slowly. She closed them again for a moment as her chest heaved. She spit into the water again and then wrapped her arms around her chest and staggered to her feet. She stood slightly hunched over, gazing at her surroundings. Then she looked down at her body. A thin, watery trail of blood, bright red against the stark white of her skin, streamed down her leg from the shaft that protruded from the flat, soft area between her belly and her hip. She reached down and touched it gently with her fingers, gasping as it moved slightly. She fell to her knees in the shallow water and moaned. She closed her eyes and threw her head back.

"Oh father," she whispered. "Just let me die here."

She looked again at the wooden shaft. Touched it. Then grabbed it and tugged. She screamed and fell backwards with her legs still folded under her body. She grabbed the shaft again and pulled again, letting loose with another scream that echoed off the cavern walls like a hundred tormented devils. She put the fingers of one hand over the wound, grabbed the arrow with the other hand, and pulled hard again and again. It finally slipped free, almost easily. Elysen gripped it in her hand as the pain brought tears to her eyes. She brought the broken shaft in front of her face and then threw it toward the deeper blue water. Without the large stone broadhead, it made only a small splash and floated aimlessly on the still surface. Elysen curled her head up toward her chest and touched the wound lightly. She winced as the tips of her fingers brushed against a piece of the broken stone tip. She again used one hand to push against the wound as she gently picked at the stone shard with the other. She gasped as a rush of blood and less than half of the weapon's cutting edge came sliding out of her body.

Elysen pressed her hand over the ragged gash and staggered into a standing position. She took a step, tipped slightly, and then steadied herself. Blood continued to trickle from between her fingers and she could feel the rest of the stone blade working its way deeper into her belly.

Somehow, through the pain, the warrior in her took stock of her surroundings. She stood near the ceiling of a large, flooded room, illuminated from somewhere below by a pale blue light. Rows and rows of colored bricks lined the walls, looking close enough to touch. Elysen settled back onto her knees and reached into the water. Her fingers rippled the surface, destroying the illusion. She hung her head and coughed again. This time a small dribble of blood hung from the corner of her mouth and dripped into the water next to her hand. She shook her head and coughed again, wincing as her stomach contracted.

"This is a strange place indeed," she said.

Her voice echoed hoarse and small in the vastness of the cavern above her.

"A strange tomb for a strange person," she mused out loud. She called out, yelling at the silent walls. "Why have you brought me here? To die? What is this place?"

She slogged forward a few steps and then slid into the water, gasping for breath again. She pushed her way over to one wall and grabbed at the shelf in front of her. Her fingers touched one of the strange objects, and she pried it loose. As it slipped free, she realized that she had only been able to see the edge before. It appeared more like a thick tile, but as it slipped from her stiff fingers and dropped slowly through the water, it opened. Inside, white leaves covered with black markings fluttered as the tile drifted toward the bottom, spinning and turning like a wounded bird. Elysen grabbed the wall above the shelf to keep from following the strange artifact, but she turned her upper body so that she could watch it slide toward the center of the large room. It settled on the bottom and stirred up a small plume of debris.

Elysen stared into the water for a time and then pulled her way toward the other side of the room. She found another ledge, covered with a shallow layer of water. She crawled onto it and curled into a ball.

"So," she said. "Here I am. Now what? Do I die here?" She glanced around again, then shivered and spoke quietly to herself. "So cold here. So cold."

As she stared into the clear water a thin glimmer along the bottom caught her eye. She brought her head closer to the surface, and then pushed her face into the water. Below her, a large fish, silver with diamond markings along its back, snaked along the gray stone floor. It's long, narrow body curled and rolled like silk in a gentle wind. It prowled along, moving steadily. Then it turned suddenly and shot upward, its mouth open, gaping, full of sharp teeth that pointed straight toward Elysen. She pulled her face out of the water and cried out. The sudden movement brought more blood from her wound and she curled up in pain again.

She waited for a few moments, resting, before she peered into the water again. Nothing moved. She examined her wound, touching it gently. She took a deep, shuddering breath and then dipped her fingers into the water and flicked them back and forth. As she did, a flash of silver appeared. She jerked her hand back toward her body and peered through the rippled surface.

"Where did you come from?" she mused.

She watched the beast slide around a corner. Elysen touched her belly again and flicked more blood into the water. She crouched and watched. The snake-like fish appeared again, rose to the surface, and then descended again, rounding the same corner. Elysen's teeth chattered together and she rubbed her arms. Her breath filled the air around her with a frosty mist. She glanced again at her wound. When she looked up again, the monster shot from somewhere beneath her feet and then turned and moved straight toward her.

Another one lurked just below, circling slowly. The first one broke the surface next to the ledge where Elysen's toes gripped the cold, wet stone. It tossed its head and dove again with a flick of its great body. Elysen watched it descend and round the corner, followed by another one. Her face relaxed and her eyes stared into the water. She sat that way, watching. The two fish were joined by a third before they slid around a corner far below. She blinked, took a breath, and slid into the water after them.

Elysen used her hands and feet to pull her body down along the towering shelves as if she were climbing a wall in some topsy-turvy world. As she neared the bottom, she pressed her body against the wall as the giant fish snaked by her. Its spiny back rubbed against her chest, and then it curled into a ball and lashed out. It darted as quick as an arrow, and its small, sharp teeth tore into Elysen's hip. She screamed and a burst of bubbles erupted from her mouth as the monster pulled her away from the shelves with a single ripple of its muscular body. She kicked her legs, dislodging more of the tiles. The beast let go of her and she watched the strange objects flip open and fall slowly to the bottom.

She swam back to the surface and rested against the ledge for a moment, laughing hysterically as she tried to catch her breath. She calmed down a bit and then took a long, slow breath and slipped back under the water. This time the serpents left her alone. She followed them around the corner and through a dark opening that led away from the light. She pulled relentlessly against the water, feeling her way along as best she could. The blue light receded behind her, and she became enveloped again in complete darkness. She began to kick harder, her eyes opening wider and wider. Her hands lost the wall. She thrashed against the pull of the cold, lost in some wide open space, kicking, struggling, flailing.

Her head filled with white light and a noise like a hundred people talking. She smiled and stopped fighting. The water caressed her and carried her gently along. She spread her arms wide and opened her mouth, but just as she did, her head broke the surface and she gasped, fell under again, threw her arms frantically, broke again and took another gasping breath.

The light of Turoc, hanging above her head, colored her breath silver-white. She waved her arms in the water, sucking in air. Above her, the bridge across the Channel of the Skell loomed dark and ominous. Voices drifted across the water, and torches flickered on the shoreline at the base of Sunder

Keep. Elysen turned away from the island and pulled her way through the frigid water toward the base of the nearest pillar. She crawled onto the smooth block and closed her eyes.

"By all curses," she whispered. She coughed and spit water. "Why can't I just die?"

Her frown turned into a smile, and then she laughed quietly. She rolled over onto her back and stared into the sky, filling her eyes with the light from Turoc. A cold, thin mist drifted from between her lips. Slowly, she pushed her gaunt, naked body into a sitting position. Her white skin glowed like a candle in the silver light.

"There is some higher purpose in this," she said. She expelled the last of her breath and then inhaled deeply before she slipped back into the freezing water.

Her arms slipped through the water with slow but rhythmic strokes. She managed to get from one platform to the next, resting longer at each one. When she finally reached the far shore, she dragged her body onto the jagged rocks and collapsed. Her chest heaved and she coughed, muffling the sound in the crook of her arm. She crawled and lurched over the boulders near the water line until she reached the wiry brush and sparse pines that dotted the inner slopes of the Cauldron. Above her, lights appeared as a group of soldiers patrolled the switchbacks that wound their way toward the top of the ridge. She crouched down and waited for them to pass. As the lights of their torches faded, she slipped upward and to the north, away from the road. The Cauldron wall turned steep here. She pulled herself from one foothold to the next using roots and small branches.

She finally crested the rise and stopped to look back. She stood on the ridge like a white ghost staring down at the Keep that jutted out of the black water of Turoc's Cauldron.

"I will be back for you, dear Yergen," she whispered.

As she spoke, a wisp of icy mist seeped from her mouth. She turned and jumped onto a large rock, but as she landed, her knees buckled under her and she bent over at the waist, groaning and clutching her side. Her hand came away bloody. She glanced down. Blood still seeped from the gash in her belly. She placed her hand against the wound and proceeded more carefully down the slope.

By the time she made it to the bottom, Turoc had settled below the horizon and, from somewhere in the east, the Soel began casting its first wash of pale blue across the sky. She stumbled forward and leaned against a tree. The dages and servants of the Keep had cleared the land here and had built stables for the working animals of the Keep. She gazed across the meadow at the row of short, squat buildings and staggered forward. She crossed nearly half of the empty space before she fell down. Her face pressed against the wiry grass. As she gasped for breath, a hand reached down and touched her. She rolled over.

"Corde," she whispered.

He knelt beside her. He placed a large, woolen blanket over her body and wrapped it around her as he helped her sit up.

"You are in a very bad way," he said. "And my instincts tell me that we are in terrible trouble. We need to get out of the open. Can you move?"

She shook her head. "I don't think so. I am tired. So tired. Can't I just sleep for a moment?"

Corde placed his arms under hers and pulled her to her feet, but she slipped from his grasp like limp fish. He gathered the blanket around her again and shook her.

"We have to get moving," he urged, using a hissing whisper.

"I can't," she said. She laughed. "Look, even my breath does not have life in it now." She pointed at the clouds of mist that came from Corde's mouth as he struggled to get Elysen to her feet. Corde glanced at her and nodded.

"It is true. You are near death. Your breath is as cold as the air around us."

She blew air into his face and laughed again. "Look," she said. "There is nothing. I am truly dead now."

"You are not dead yet, m'lady. And you won't die as long as I live, now get up." He gave her one last heave and she came to her feet, tottering like a small child.

"Owen is dead," she said.

Corde tried to lift her but they almost landed in a heap on the ground. He pulled her arm around his neck and she staggered along beside him.

"I know," he said. "I was in the stable, tending to your father's horse, as you instructed, when I heard the boys talking of the events from the Keep. There was much that was hushed, but I gathered that things had gone badly."

They stepped into the protection of the sparse pine trees and Corde let Elysen slip to the ground. He leaned against a stump, speaking between each deep, gasping breath.

"The soldiers came, looking for me. Not finding me, because I had climbed into the rafters above Temper, they left again. I saddled your horse, slipped out into the night, and then waited over here, hoping that you would appear."

Elysen closed her eyes. Corde pushed himself back to his feet and sighed as he reached down and grabbed her. Her eyes fluttered open for a moment, and she heard her father's big, black horse clearing his lungs.

"Good Corde," she said. Her words came thick and slow. "I would not do well without you."

"I know m'lady, now come on. Wake up. We have to leave this place in a hurry."

He helped her up onto the back of the horse. Temper snorted and Corde waved his hand up and down.

"Quiet now," he said.

Elysen rode hunched forward, over the pommel, her face contorted with pain. They walked through the night and all the next day, and then Corde pulled Elysen from the saddle and pushed and shoved on Temper's flanks, forcing him into a line of thick brush. Inside the tangle of vines and small trees, a maze of game trails led to an open space. They rested there. Corde held Elysen in his arms to keep her warm. As dusk fell, he settled her onto the ground and removed Temper's saddle. He tossed the saddle into the tall grass and led the horse back into the more open woods. He went back for Elysen and woke her gently.

"We have to keep moving," he said.

Elysen's eyes were rimmed with red and her arms and legs were like feathers. Corde tugged and pulled on her until they found Temper, and then he helped her onto the horse's bare back. Elysen leaned forward again and hugged Temper's neck. Corde threw a blanket over her and wrapped a leather strap around both horse and rider. He took the reins and they began their slow, rocking walk again.

Days and nights passed much the same. Corde made soup from what he could find in the brush and dig from the thin soil. Elysen drifted into a long sleep.

She woke in a small cabin, next to a blazing fire, covered with a thick brown blanket. Corde touched a cup to her lips. She sipped, coughed it out, and then collapsed again. She woke again, much later, as Corde washed her with warm water and a cloth.

"What are you doing?" she asked.

His eyes became bright and his mouth hung open. He stammered for a moment.

"M'lady," he said.

"How long have I been sleeping?" she asked.

Corde closed his mouth. "Well," he said. "Turoc is full again."

"Impossible," she said. She collapsed back onto the soft padding and stared at the ceiling.

"You were so close to death, that I thought I was tending to a corpse," Corde said.

She glanced toward the door. It hung open, and the light from the Soel streamed in, along with a draft of cold air. A bowl on the floor next to her caught her eye.

"Is that soup?" she asked.

Corde nodded.

"Have you been feeding me?"

He nodded again.

"For an entire cycle?"

He tipped his head. "You seem wide awake now."

"Must be myst," Elysen said.

"Definitely myst," Corde replied.

She glanced down at her belly. The arrow had left a small wound that still oozed a yellow-brown liquid. Corde reached over and placed a clean cloth over the open wound.

"Is it bad?" she asked.

Corde shrugged.

"It hasn't killed you yet," he said. "But you need a healer." He shook his head. "It's not a good wound."

"Ah," Elysen said. "Not like my other good wounds." She paused. "I would have more good wounds if it were not for you."

Corde smiled. "Your sense of humor returns."

She closed her eyes and a long sigh slipped from her lips.

Her mind drifted into a swirling eddy of noise and movement. She stood in a field of blood-stained snow. She tried to run, clutching a child in her arms. The child pushed away from her and reared back like an animal with Yergen's face. Elysen woke with a start and a sharp cry.

The charred remains of the fire smoldered and a shaft of dusty light lay across the room. She pushed into a sitting position.

"Corde?" she asked. Silence answered her. She glanced around. A bed took up one corner facing the hearth in front of where she sat. A small table occupied the center of the room. These meager furnishings crowded the cabin. The light came from the open door. Elysen rolled forward, into a crouching position, and then stood. Her legs immediately collapsed again and she cried out and clutched her stomach. Her fingers explored a long cloth wrapped around and around her belly. A small yellow and red spot marked her unhealed wound. Corde came running inside.

"You are too weak to stand," he said.

"I'm like a baby," she moaned.

"And look, your wound has reopened." He took a deep breath. "You need help that is beyond me."

"Help me up," she said. Corde pushed her gently back onto the blanket.

"You need to rest," he said.

She waved both arms in the air. "Help me up I say."

Corde slipped his arm around her shoulders and she struggled to her feet, wrapping the blanket around her body.

"I want to go outside and sit in the light," she said. "And I am frightfully hungry."

Corde's eyes brightened. "That's a good sign," he said.

He helped her to the door. She stood on a small porch of rotting logs and stared into the clear blue sky. The cabin sat nestled among a pile of boulders along the side of a rugged valley. A small stream coursed through the bottom of the valley, lined with the skeletons of trees that dropped their leaves in brown piles on the ground. All around them, the Mountains of Oken slept under blankets of white; their steep sides covered with a light frosting of new snow. Even the ground in front of her lay dusted with ice.

"This place seems to be abandoned," Corde said. "No one has bothered us. No one has come by. We have been alone since we left Sunder Keep."

"Why would someone leave this place?" she wondered aloud.

Corde shrugged. "Probably recruited for the southern wars. Died at the hands of the Uemn. That is the fate of most men of the Vyr it seems."

"The Soel is low on the horizon," Elysen said.

"The days are very short now," Corde replied. "The season of the Proste approaches." His voice trailed off. He stared into the valley, frowning.

Elysen glanced at the sky. Turoc hovered above them, a white shadow against the brilliant blue sky.

"We can't stay here forever," Elysen said. She looked at Corde, and then followed his gaze into the valley. A lone horse and rider stood at the edge of the woods, staring back at them. He put his hand in the air, palm facing toward them. Corde responded with a similar gesture. Elysen pulled her blanket around her shoulders and took a step back, into the doorway.

Nine

Elysen slipped all the way back into the cabin, leaving Corde alone on the porch as the visitor rode up the hill. She glanced around the small hut for a weapon. She grabbed a piece of firewood and hid just behind the frame of the door. She could hear the frosty ground crunch under the heavy hooves of the horse as it approached.

"Ho there," a gruff voice called out. "We need shelter for the night."

Corde paused as he searched for a response. Elysen set the log down and pulled her robe around her head. She peered around the corner. The man rode with bare arms, bronzed by fire and wind, heedless of the cold. His blue eyes caught her, and she ducked back around the corner.

"We won't stay long," the man said. "My daughter is cold, and she needs food and shelter."

Elysen looked again. A small child hung onto the man's waist, riding behind him, looking like a bundle of blankets. Elysen stepped out onto the porch and let her hood down. The man's eyes narrowed and his horse took a step back.

"They said you were dead," the man said.

"I am," Elysen replied. "Who are you?"

His horse turned in a circle, favoring its right foreleg. The rider spent a moment settling it down.

"My name is Petyr," he said. "And this is my daughter, Joli."

Elysen studied him for a moment. The lines in his face deepened as he peered back at her. A wisp of gray hair separated from the wavy dark tangles tied behind his head, and it drifted across his face. He pushed the stray lock back with his fingers.

"You may stay one night," Elysen said. "And then be on your way again."

He remained in the saddle, staring at Elysen. Joli squeezed his waist and her head came up.

"I'm so hungry," she said.

Petyr swung his leg off the horse and landed on the ground like a cat. He reached up and whisked his daughter from the saddle and held her in his arms. He waited for a moment, watching Elysen. She stood aside and Petyr stepped onto the porch, passing between Elysen and Corde as he entered the cabin.

"What are you doing?" Corde hissed. "You are hunted now. You can't let strangers bunk with us."

"We are the strangers here," Elysen said. "These people have as much right to shelter as we do."

Corde clenched his teeth together and grunted.

"Take care of his horse," she said. "And then prepare some of that marvelous potato soup for our guests. We will dine with company tonight."

She stopped and a smile crept across her face, erasing some of the lines of pain.

"Get out the finest dishes," she said. "And a cask of our best wine."

She stepped up close to Corde and lowered her voice. "And get me some clothes," she said. She held him there with her eyes until he smiled, and then she let her smile broaden as well before she backed away. Corde shook his head and grabbed the horse by the bridle. Elysen took a look around the valley and then followed Petyr into the cabin.

Petyr and Joli stood by the fireplace, waiting. Elysen picked up the stick she had intended to use for a club. She threw it on the smoldering fire along with a few smaller branches. She knelt down and blew on the coal until they erupted in flame. She stood up and wiped her hands together. Joli smiled at her. Petyr shuffled uncomfortably.

Corde returned from the corral and Elysen stepped away from the fire.

"Your horse has been ridden hard," Corde said.

Petyr nodded.

"How long will you stay?" Corde asked.

"Not long," Petyr said.

Corde slipped between Petyr and Elysen, forcing them both to take a step backwards. The small cabin barely contained them all. Corde slipped a small kettle of water over a hook above the fire and threw in some potatoes and leeks. Elysen scrunched up her face.

Corde shook his head.

"I saw that," he said.

They sat at the small table and waited while Corde finished his simple vegetable broth. Petyr sat with his back to the fire, across from Elysen. Corde served them, but stood up to eat his own soup. Joli ate only a tiny bit before she crawled into Petyr's lap. She wrapped her tiny arms around his neck and put her head against his shoulder, but did not take her eyes off of Elysen.

Elysen avoided the little girl's dark brown eyes, looking toward the fire instead.

"Look," Joli said to Elysen.

The little girl pulled a small object from under her shirt.

"I have a toy," she said.

She held it up for Elysen to see. A wooden ball, perfectly carved and polished by a loving hand, hung from a thin leather string attached to a stick with a small bone cup affixed to the top. Joli showed Elysen how to swing the ball into the air and to catch it in the cup.

"My papa made this for me," she said. "Here, you try."

Joli reached across the table and held the toy in front of Elysen. She took it and stared at it, realizing that she had never been given a toy as a child, only a bow and a knife.

"Time for you to go to bed," Petyr said to the girl.

Elysen started to hand the toy back to Joli, but the little girl gave her a serious look.

"I want you to have it," she said. "It is my best toy."

"Why would you give me your best toy?" Elysen asked, still trying to get Joli to take it back. "You should keep it for yourself."

Joli smiled at her and wrapped her tiny hands around Elysen's delicate white fingers, closing them on the toy.

"Oh no," she said. "I am giving it to you because it is special to me."

Elysen glanced at Petyr. He nodded.

"You should accept the gift," he said.

"Why?" Elysen asked.

Petyr smiled.

"That's the way she gets to know you," he said. He wrinkled his brow slightly. "You haven't been around children much, have you?"

She shook her head. Petyr picked Joli up and carried her over to the small bed in the corner. He laid her down and covered her with a rough woolen blanket, kissing her gently on the forehead before returning. As he settled back onto the bench, he turned his head and checked on the little girl. When he turned back toward Elysen, she noticed that his face had softened into a small, sad smile.

"What is it that brings you out in the wilderness with this small child?" Elysen asked.

He stared into her green eyes and sat quietly for a moment before responding. He tapped the table with his fingers.

"I'm from the south," he said. "I was a wheat farmer down there. Do you know the village of Werth?"

Elysen shook her head.

Petyr continued. "My town, Werth, was a trading town," he said. "A good town. The main village had a hostel for travelers, a trading post, a garrison and a livery stable. We lived a full day's north in a cottage along a wooded brook. My family farmed that land for generations, tending those same fields, sowing and harvesting, year in, year out. When my grandfather was still alive, he would tell stories of his grandfather and his grandfather's grandfather, all stories of that same land, that same house, same village. Always serving the Vyr Lord. Most of the grain went to the lord's granary. In exchange, we were allowed to keep a small share for ourselves, as well as most of the meat from our hunts and some fruits and vegetables from our small garden. The weather was always moderate there, warm in summer, cool in winter, but not cold, not like it is here."

He glanced at Joli, curled into a tight ball under her blankets.

"We grew wheat all year 'round, rotating the crops so that the soil could rest between seasons."

"Why did you leave your family?" Elysen asked.

"I had five boys. Strong boys. And smart too. They were good farmers, good hunters, good fishermen. And good workers too. Every one of us, even my wife, worked for the Lords, for you, from the first light of the Soel to the last."

Elysen nodded and glanced at Corde. His eyes caught hers for a moment before she turned her attention back to their guest.

"We were working in the fields one afternoon," Petyr said. "Preparing the land and planting. Seems like a long time ago now," he mused. "The army came through, gathering people for a campaign in the deep south. They took us all. All my boys and me. Left my wife at home, alone, pregnant." He paused and frowned. "Of course, that was your father's right; I don't need to tell you that."

Elysen nodded. Petyr continued.

"We traveled for a long time, marching southward through the hottest days of the growing season. We picked up more and more men as we went, conscripting all of the best workers from each town we passed, leaving just women and children to bring in the harvests. We marched out of the dry, warm plains into the sticky air of the southern swamplands, where we saw lizards as big as cattle. We lost men to venomous snake bites, to crippling disease and to silent predators that came in the night and dragged our men away. But the worst of it was the fighting. We met the enemy one evening and our division was wiped out by morning." He looked into her eyes, ignoring Corde's tight-lipped glare.

"My boys were farmhands, Lady Elysen," he said. "Not warriors. We served your father well, but we were taken into the swamps and marshes where we were told to chase the enemy hordes out of their hiding places in the tangled roots of the Banyan. While Yergen watched from the hills above us, we slogged through soupy water up to our waists, and the Uemn hordes dropped out of the trees onto our backs, drowning us, stabbing us, choking us. We were slaughtered like spring chickens, defenseless, stupid, disorganized, weak. I was wounded, pinned against the base of a tree by the body of my youngest son, torn and pierced from a dozen wounds, drowning in the bloody, brackish water of a land that was far from my home, and that I cared nothing about. I could see your cousin, Yergen, riding high on his horse, a look of disgust and disdain on his face, as if we were trash to be thrown out, and he was yelling at us, calling us worthless imbeciles, as if he thought we could hear him through our dead ears." Petyr paused and took a deep breath.

"The Uemn cleared out of the Banyan as soon as Lord Yergen left. I struggled free and buried my boys there in the dead, sandy soil of a far away land. When I came home again, I found my wife hanging in the town square along with anyone else who had protested the drafting of their sons and husbands and fathers. The town was deserted, the buildings burned. Maybe by the Uemn, but I have never seen them that far north. More likely by the retreating Gennissaries. And I can almost understand why they would do something so, so horrible. War does that to us. It turns us into monsters. We forget who we really are."

He shrugged, as if making the pain go away was as easy as brushing a grasshopper off his shoulder.

"Anyway, the farmhouse that my family had lived in for generations was nothing but a smoldering pile of rubble. I found this little girl hiding in our potato shed, which had been left untouched for some reason. Her life is myst."

Elysen glanced toward the bundle of blankets in the corner where Joli huddled, away from the cold.

"So, we traveled north until we found this cabin," Petyr said.

He glanced at Corde before returning his gaze to Elysen.

"We had no plan, no destination in mind. We just began riding. It seemed as if north was the only way. West was the end of the world, east was the great Rift, and I had already seen all of the south that I needed to see. North was all that was left."

"How do you know the child is yours?" Corde asked.

Petyr shrugged.

"I just know. A father knows those things. Besides, it doesn't matter. We're both survivors, and that's all that counts."

"You're a deserter from the Lord's Gennissaries," Elysen said.

"What Gennissaries?" Petyr countered. "There was no one left except for the Lord's Guard, cowards riding on horseback while the conscripted men fought on foot in the swamps."

"You took a pledge," Elysen reminded him. "The Gennissaries fight to the death."

"I fought till everyone was dead," he said. "I've done my time."

"Still, the law does not release you. The Guard will be searching for you."

Petyr looked deep into Elysen's eyes.

"The Uemn foray deeper and deeper into our lands, and they get braver and stronger, while we grow weaker and more timid. Lord Yergen wastes good men and boys in useless follies into the Banyan and the swamps of the

Southern Wash, leaving the villages and towns unguarded and unsafe. The people of the Vyr are torn by civil strife as the Kaanites recruit more and more people to their cause. The soil grows thinner and thinner, and our crops wither. The Vyr is dying. And you can do nothing. Yergen can do nothing."

He paused to catch his breath, relaxed a bit, and then continued.

"The lords and ladies of the Keep, tucked away up there in a decaying fortress surrounded by high walls and water, have lost touch with the common people. I will tell you this because I can. Because I am not afraid. We don't believe in Thorsen's Law any more. Yergen is a ghost. A pitiful, sad little man who rules nothing but a dying land."

She studied him for a moment.

"You mentioned the Kaanites," she said. "What do you know about them?"

Petyr considered for a moment before answering.

"They claim to be followers of an ancient prophet," he said. "They long for the return of the Shad'ya. The one power that ushers in the end of our world."

Elysen touched her wound. The skin felt hot.

"Some say that you are the Shad'ya," Petyr said.

"Then you were most unlucky to find me here," she said. She could taste her own blood in her mouth. She forced herself to ignore it.

Petyr chuckled. "You don't look like you are bringing in the end of the world," he said.

"The Shad'ya is just a story, made up by the Kaanites to scare the ignorant." She paused for a moment.

I am a warrior. I do not feel pain.

"The Kaanites want to bring an end to the reign of the Vyr Lords," she said. "Maybe they were the ones that destroyed your village."

Petyr was lost in his thoughts for a moment, and in the silence, Elysen felt the pain welling up inside her like a fever. Her father, dead. Owen, dead. She tried to push her thoughts back into the darkness, but they refused to obey her.

Joli moaned in her sleep and Petyr glanced at the pile of blankets on the bed. She had kicked them off, and her little body twisted around as she tried to get warm again.

"A child shouldn't have to witness so much violence," he said.

"We live in an age of violence," Elysen said. "I was learning to fight when I was a child like that."

Petyr stood up and tucked a blanket around Joli. She pulled her legs up and placed her palms together and slipped them under her cheek. She squirmed deeper into the covers and then settled down.

Elysen glanced down at the binding around her waist, and noticed blood soaking through again. She stood up, but her legs buckled and the world turned white.

Elysen woke up in a pile of blankets on the floor. Joli pushed a small bowl of broth towards her mouth.

"Here," the little girl said. "Take some."

Elysen took a sip and made a face.

"What is that?" she asked.

"Soup," Petyr said.

"It's worse than Corde's," Elysen said. She pushed the cup away from her mouth.

Petyr dumped the last of his own soup into the pot that hung over the fire and set his cup on the mantle above the fireplace.

"It tastes awful, but it's nourishing."

Joli clasped her hands behind her back. The look of concern in the little girl's eyes moved Elysen to sip again. Acting satisfied with the progress, Joli sat down in front of Elysen and crossed her legs. Elysen drank a few more times then placed the bowl on the stone floor in front of Joli before she curled back up into a ball and pulled the blankets back around her body. Petyr sat down at the table and watched Elysen.

"Where is Corde?" Elysen asked.

"He went to get food, and to find a healer," Petyr said.

"I can be your healer," Joli said.

"Leave her alone now," Petyr said to Joli. "Come crawl into your own bed."

"But I want to sleep here," she said.

"No. Leave her alone now."

"Is she going to die?"

"I don't know," Petyr said. "Now it's time for bed. Crawl in there and close your eyes."

Petyr helped the little girl into her bed and tucked the rough woolen blanket around her tiny body. He kissed her on the forehead and she closed her eyes. Petyr propped himself up against the wall next to the fire and pulled his coat closed around his body.

Elysen drifted off to sleep again and awoke in the cold. She watched Petyr toss a few more sticks into the hearth. As the flames took hold, Elysen sat up.

"Are you warm enough?" Petyr asked.

She nodded.

"Are you hungry?"

She shook her head.

Petyr poked the fire with a stick. A spray of embers fell from the older, charred logs, and the light flared. Petyr glanced at Elysen, and saw that her eyes glistened in the firelight.

"I know how you feel," he said, staring into the fire.

No one knows how I feel, she thought.

She stood up slowly and stepped over to where Petyr crouched, dragging her robe along like a shroud. She sat down next to him and stared into the flames with him. Petyr sat cross legged on the ground and placed his hands on his knees.

"I miss my father," she said. She surprised herself with her own bluntness.

Petyr watched the flames dance among the small logs as they searched for untouched wood to consume.

"He was a good Lord," Petyr said. "The people respected him." The fire popped softly as they watched it burn. He looked over at his sleeping child and his jaw tightened.

"Yergen will not rest until he finds you," he said. He turned back toward the fire.

Elysen pulled her cloak around her shoulders and shivered.

"Are you cold?" Petyr asked.

"I don't feel the cold," she said. "My mother was Norgarden."

"Then why are you shivering?"

"I don't know."

Petyr reached over and touched her forehead with his fingers, then drew them back.

"Your skin is ice cold," he said.

She sat, staring into the fire, no expression on her face. Petyr stood up and threw more wood on the fire. It gained momentum slowly, turning from a handful of flickering red fingers into dozens of angry, snapping snakes that roared as they engulfed the dry logs and threw tongues of orange and amber across the room. Close to the hearth the heat grew intense. Petyr moved back, but Elysen sat, sulking. Petyr gently reached around her and pulled her back toward him, away from the harsh heat, back into the bearable warmth. He pulled her against his side, and she curled up into a ball, sinking as deep as she could into the embrace of his arm. Her face peered out from the dark depths of her robe. Petyr touched her forehead again.

"I think you're ill," he said.

She sat silently, motionless. Petyr leaned forward to see into her eyes. In the firelight, the milky, gray-green, so much like the icy rivers that ran through the tundra, appeared to be a dull brown, as if they had been muddied by a torrential rain.

"I'm fine," Elysen said.

"You are as cold as death," Petyr said.

"I am a ghost," she said. "Ghosts are supposed to be cold."

"You live and breathe as surely as I do," he replied.

"Against my own will," she said.

She shivered again. Petyr pulled the robe off her shoulders and pulled her closer, closing his blanket around their combined bodies to contain the warmth.

The fire crackled and sputtered, dying down so slowly that its progress could not be tracked. As the fire consumed itself, Elysen's body warmed and she relaxed into Petyr's arms. She fell into a deep sleep and Petyr stroked the tattered remains of her fine white hair as he gazed at her in the firelight. Finally, he dozed.

When he awoke, Petyr wrapped Elysen in his own rough blanket and carried her to the straw mat in the corner, tucking her in like a father tucks in a child. He threw some more sticks on the fire to fight the cold air of the gray dawn that drifted in under the door.

Petyr made a strong tea out of a potpourri that he kept in a special wooden container, and then sat at the table. As he sipped and stared at the fire, Elysen stirred, sat up, blinked. She sat for a long time, watching the fire. Neither one spoke. Finally, almost as if against her own will, Elysen rose, wrapping her robe around her shoulders again. She sat across from Petyr.

"Would you like some tea?" he asked. "The herbs and other things that I use help the body heal."

"What is it?" she asked.

"Pine bark, dried crushed grape seeds, bilberry, zythium."

He got up and made some for her. She cradled the warm stone cup between her hands, the blackness of it in stark contrast to the pale, colorless white of her fingers.

"How are you feeling this morning?" Petyr asked her.

She folded her legs up against her chest and put her feet on the bench, ankles crossed, toes hanging over the wooden edge. She held her arms close to her sides.

"Still cold," she said. She paused and stared into the shimmering brown liquid. "Thank you."

He nodded.

"Drink it all," he said. "The tea will help you regain your strength."

"Why are you helping me?" she asked.

He smiled, very slightly, but a sad twist sat on the edge of his lips.

"When I came here, I became part of a chain of events. I must now play that chain out to its conclusion."

"Is that what you believe? That there is some chain that binds you?"

Petyr shrugged.

"Like I said, I don't believe anything."

"That's a lie," she said.

"No."

"If say that you don't believe anything, then you are lying to yourself. Everybody believes in something."

"I believe in what I can see and touch," he said.

Elysen pursed her lips.

"I have seen and touched the spells of Thorsen," she said. "In a cavern, under the Keep." She had no idea why that memory popped into her mind and out of her mouth.

Petyr furrowed his brow.

"In a dream," he said.

"No. It was real."

"That makes no sense."

"I did see it."

"You saw spells?"

"I think so. I saw something."

Petyr closed his lips tightly.

"All the power in the world is there," Elysen said. "Right under Yergen's nose."

Petyr tipped his head. "Maybe," he said. "Maybe not."

"I know it," she said. "I can feel it in my bones. The spells of Thorsen. The spells that created the Vyr, the fire, even the people." Her eyes sparkled. "If we could unleash that power again..."

Petyr stood up quickly and pressed a finger to his lips. He sat frozen like that for a minute. Elysen felt the skin on the back of her neck tingle. Petyr glanced over at Joli, sleeping peacefully. He stood up slowly and cracked the door open just a bit so that he could peer outside. He watched for a moment, and then slipped out. Just as he did, Joli sat up and rubbed her eyes.

"Where is papa going?" she asked.

Her voice rang loud in the cold air. Elysen hurried over to the bed and hushed her. Joli's lower lip began to quiver. Elysen hushed her again with a warning frown, and Joli broke into a wail. Elysen grabbed her, holding her close.

"Quiet now," Elysen whispered. She rocked back and forth. "Your papa is just outside."

Joli tipped her head back and her mouth opened wide as tears filled her eyes, but only a soft cry escaped her lips. Elysen clutched her even more tightly and stroked her hair. Outside, nothing moved. Elysen picked up Joli and moved toward the door.

Ten

Elysen stood just inside the threshold, protecting Joli. She tipped her head just enough to see through the wide crack between the door and the frame.

A man crouched in the corral. Petyr walked up to him and he stood up. The two men slapped each other's shoulders. They talked for a while, Petyr motioning toward the cabin. They glanced at the open door and nodded. After some more conversation, they came inside.

Petyr took the visitor's coat and introduced him to Elysen.

"Lady Elysen, this is Tell. A friend of mine."

Elysen studied him for a moment.

"We've met before," she said, remembering him even as she spoke. "At the Keep. You were in the service of my father."

"Yes," Tell said.

Wiry brown whiskers and bushy, wild eyebrows hid most of Tell's face. He studied Elysen with his dark eyes. Joli slipped out of her arms and took up a position behind Elysen's legs, peeking around at the hairy giant, watching him warily. Tell never took his eyes off Elysen.

"You stare at me as if I were a ghost," she said.

"We were told that you were dead. That you killed Owen, and were then killed by Yergen and drowned in the catacombs. Rumors fly of how you walk the Vyr at night, undead, eating flesh and sucking marrow from bones."

Elysen smiled. "I grow more fearsome every day."

Petyr brought a tray of white cheese and smoked venison and placed it on the table. Tell sat down and grabbed a piece of the oily meat. He bit into it hungrily. Elysen sat across from him.

"Petyr's horse has gone lame," Tell said.

"And I must tend to it," Petyr said. "Please pardon me."

Petyr stepped outside. Joli crept over to her bed and wrapped a blanket around her body, leaving only her face exposed.

"What brings you out here?" Elysen asked. "Surely not just Petyr's horse."

Tell shifted and the wooden bench groaned. "I came to warn friend Petyr that the Lord's Guard is active in the hills around here. They have been especially vicious. Killing everyone they find."

"Except you."

"They haven't found me yet," Tell said. He smiled and winked at her. She smiled back for a moment, and then poked at a piece of meat.

"You are becoming legend," Tell said.

Elysen glanced over at Joli. The little girl sat quietly in the corner, singing softly to herself and winding a piece of thick yarn around a stick.

"Ah, to be young and careless again," Tell said as he watched her play.

"She has seen her share of troubles," Elysen said.

"Haven't we all," Tell remarked. "And yet, she still knows how to find the simple pleasures in life."

Elysen glanced at the door. A cold wind blew in. The trees stirred green against the blue sky. Elysen turned her attention back to Tell.

"Tell me of your time with my father," she said. She tasted a piece of the cheese and made a face.

"I only met your father once," he said. "I actually served under your cousin Yergen, during a campaign against the Kaanites."

"Then you've been to the far north," she said. "Past the Northern Reach?"

He shook his head. "No. We marched into the Mountains of Oken, at the edge of the world. Mostly west of the Keep. We chased a group of them northward, but we never went as far north as the Reach."

"You went into the forbidden mountains? With Yergen?"

Tell nodded.

"Did you see the end of the world?"

He shook his head. "No, m'lady. We did not venture that far. Not even Yergen's great powers could have protected us from certain death had we tried to cross the mountains."

"Did you find the Kaanites?"

He nodded. "We engaged in a few skirmishes. Even managed to capture a few of them. But they escaped. Disappeared. Maybe they tried to escape to the ends of the world and died there."

His lips tightened and he shook his head.

"How did we start talking about such things as this?" he asked. "We should converse about happier things."

"There are no happy things," Elysen said. "Tell me more about the Kaanites."

Tell sighed. "What is it that I could tell you?" he asked.

"Tell me what they believe," she said.

He shrugged. "I'm not sure what they believe," he said. "They worship the Shad'ya, a being from before time. They say that the Shad'ya is gong to return to destroy all that Thorsen created."

Elysen leaned forward slightly as she listened.

"Do the Kaanites believe that the time of the Shad'ya is near?"

Tell nodded.

"Why?"

He sighed and returned his gaze from the floor to her eyes.

"They say they know the time is near, because of you."

"Why me?"

"For centuries, they have been waiting for a sign, a white storm that signals the end of the Vyr Lord's reign, and the beginning of darkness. Ever since you were born, they have watched you, spied upon you. They are most likely watching you now. Waiting for their prophecy to be fulfilled."

He paused for a moment and ate a piece of cheese. Elysen watched his whiskers rise and fall as his jaw moved. He finally spoke again, even though he still chewed.

"They think that you are the Shad'ya," he said. "They believe you bringer of the destruction of the world."

Elysen sat quietly for a moment.

"That would be a heavy burden for a person as small as me," she said. She picked up a piece of jerked venison and stuck it in her mouth. Tell did not break away from her gaze.

"You served under my cousin, Yergen," she said.

Tell nodded.

"Did you get to know him well?"

Tell nodded again. "I was his captain. I was at his side through most of the campaign."

"Did he speak of me?"

"Often."

"Why?"

Tell shrugged again. "Mostly because the Kaanites insisted that you were the harbinger of the end of the world as we know it. It made Yergen angry, almost crazy at times. He swore against you and impaled our prisoners every time they mentioned your name. At one time, we had a dozen or so men tied to trees, all in a row, and one called out your name 'Elysen, the White Queen, queen of blackness and destruction.' Yergen transfixed him in the eye with an arrow, but the man continued to cry out your name as if he were in ecstasy, so Yergen ran up to him and drove the arrow deeper by grabbing on to it with both hands and twisting it like this."

Tell's eyes were wild and full of fear as he recounted the story and acted out Yergen's violent behavior with his own hands.

"As the first man's cries died away, the next man began shouting your name, and then the next, and Yergen killed them, one by one, stabbing them over and over with the same bloody arrow until it broke and then he took another and he killed each of them in turn. His arms and face were covered with blood and his eyes were wild with hate."

As Tell finished speaking, he let his arms hang in the air, and he stared at the wall above Elysen's head. He lowered his arms slowly, and then lowered his head.

"M'lady, forgive me," he said.

"A terrible sight to behold," Elysen said.

"I lost my will to fight after that," he said. "We finished our campaign, but I never took another life after that. My fighting days were done. Yergen released me and sent me home." His voice trailed off.

"And where is home?" Elysen asked softly.

He shook his head. "Like Petyr, I returned to nothing. I make my home now in these hills." Tell stood up. "I must go now." He put his hands on the table and leaned forward. He stared into Elysen's eyes.

"Yergen is out there," he said. "Searching for you. You should go north.

Toward the ice. I don't think he will follow you there."

"He's out there?" Elysen asked. She felt her heart pound.

Tell nodded.

"Where. Exactly."

"His troops are scouring the foothills right now. Toward the east. You could slip by them if you hurry."

Elysen nodded. She had no intention of slipping by Yergen.

"Thank you," she said.

Tell sighed and stood up again.

"Farewell, Lady Elysen."

Tell walked away. Elysen turned and stared at Joli.

Running from death, like me, she thought.

She wondered if there was a little girl somewhere, playing with her toys, in the bright, warm light of the Soel, surrounded by a laughing, running crowd of other children, with smiling parents watching.

Elysen shivered, recalling her own childhood. Fighting. Bloodshed. The cold, dark halls of the Keep. The ever-present threat of the Uemn hordes. Her lip curled back into a snarl as hate filled her heart.

This is a terrible world for a child.

Eleven

As Tell stepped out the door, Corde returned on Temper with one bag of grain and one bag of corn. He dismounted by the corral where Petyr brushed his horse. Corde let Temper loose to search the frozen ground for grass and gave the feed to Petyr. Elysen came out and met Corde on the porch.

"The Soel is low on the horizon," Elysen said to Corde as they watched Tell fit a bridle on Petyr's horse.

"The days are very short now," Corde replied. "The season of the Proste approaches."

Elysen glanced at the sky. Turoc hovered above them like a white shadow against the brilliant blue sky. Petyr slapped his horse on the flank and it lurched forward, pulling Tell along. Tell waved without turning around.

"I found some food," Corde said. "I stopped in a small village, called Juro, and begged."

"What about a healer?" Elysen asked. Her wound burned like fire.

Corde shook his head.

"They didn't have a healer. But they did say that there was a woman in the mountains, near Lake Orman. They pressed me with questions about who needed to be healed, what kind of wound, that sort of thing. I think they were becoming suspicious when I avoided the answers."

Elysen watched him for a moment. Corde did not return her gaze. Instead, he fiddled with the sleeve of his coat.

"What else?" she asked.

"The Lord's Guard," he said. "They are combing the hills and the northern prairie. I don't think it will be long before they find us."

Elysen stared out across the valley.

"I saw Yergen himself," Corde said. "And Raes."

Elysen glared at him.

Raes.

"Did he see you?" she asked. Corde shook his head.

"They passed through Juro though, just after I left. I watched them from the hills. They burned the town to the ground."

Elysen stared at him. Corde rubbed his cheeks and shook his head.

"I did nothing," he said. "I just turned Temper around and rode away as fast as I could."

They stood on the porch and watched the shadows creep across the valley as the Soel dropped behind the ridge above them.

"What will we do now?" Corde asked.

Elysen shook her head slowly. "My anger seethes inside me, festering like my wound."

"Your anger will consume you."

"Let it," she said.

She glanced down at her wound and her chest constricted as she remembered the feel of Yergen's hard pelvis pounding against her thighs. She fell to her hands and knees and heaved a sour mouthful of hot soup onto the dark wood of the porch.

Corde knelt down and put his arm over her back. "You can not go up against Yergen. He is Lord of the Vyr now."

"I will kill him," she said.

Corde sighed. "We could wait here through the Proste and then go north, to the ice. Return to the land of the Norgarden. You could live unnoticed. I think they would shelter you. They are a peaceful people."

"I don't want to be sheltered by a peaceful people," Elysen snapped. "I want to kill Yergen. I will let him find me, and when he leans close to me, gloating, I will plunge my fist into his belly and pull his heart from his chest."

She wiped her mouth with the back of her sleeve. The rough fabric grated against her skin. She put her hand back on the ground to support her. "Corde," she said. Her mouth filled with liquid again and she spit it out. The spreading wet stain steamed in the cold air.

"Yes, m'lady?"

She took a deep, shuddering breath.

"It is time for you to go home," she said.

"I can't leave you," he said.

"You can't stay."

Corde frowned. "My place is here," he said. "With you."

Elysen shook her head. "I don't want you here. We have come to a parting of the ways."

"Your wound has not healed."

"Don't argue with me, old man," she said. "I want you to go." She hung her head forward and then held out one arm. Corde took it and helped her stand. She leaned against the outer wall of the shack.

"I don't understand," Corde said.

"That's right, you don't."

"I have been with you all your life," he said. "I took you from Raes' arms the night you were born and I have cared for you ever since."

Elysen stared at him. "What do you mean? When did you take me from Raes' arms?"

"The night you were born. It was young Master Raes who held you that night, as your mother was dying. He performed the ritual of forbearance on your body. They thought you were born dead, but the shock of the ice water revived you and you were re-born. It was Raes who revived you."

She brought her head up slowly.

"That's right," she said. "Raes was there." Her eyes looked tired, but she struggled to stay awake. "Who else was there?" she asked.

Corde pursed his lips and thought for a moment. "Vollen, Owen and Yergen. And a mere-dojen. I don't remember her name. No matter though."

"And where were you?"

"I was outside. I was not called in until after."

Elysen slumped down into a sitting position with her arms extended forward and her wrists limp. Her chin touched her chest.

"It doesn't matter," she said. "You need to go now."

"M'lady," Corde said, bowing his head. "I have no home to go to. Other than this."

He raised his head and opened his arms.

"This is not our home," she said.

She felt her forceful resolve melting. She closed her eyes and focused on the agony in her belly.

"You have to go now," she said.

"I can't leave you," he insisted.

Elysen pushed her back against the wall and used the palms of her hands against the stones to steady herself as she gathered her legs under her body and struggled upright. Corde moved forward to help her, but she shook her head.

"You have to go. I won't argue with you anymore, Corde. I want you gone. Out of my life. Forever. Get out."

She raised her voice and let her anger at Yergen seep into her words. "Get out," she snapped. She let more rage surface. Her snarl turned into a yell. "Go away." She stomped her feet and tore at her robe. "Go away." The force of the last scream echoed through the valley and returned to the cabin from the steep cliffs around them.

Petyr stood in the corral, watching.

Corde closed his eyes and sat down on the edge of the porch. Elysen stormed inside and slammed the flimsy door.

The next morning, Elysen got up and stepped past Corde and Petyr without waking them. She wrapped a blanket around her shoulders slipped outside just as the Soel cleared the peaks of the mountains. Darkness still covered the bottom of the valley. Elysen walked to a high meadow and sat down in the damp grass.

Corde set out walking a short time later with a small pack slung across his shoulder. He stopped at the bottom of the valley and gazed back at the cabin. From her perch higher on the hillside, she watched him step into the woods.

Elysen closed her eyes and let a long, slow breath pass from her lips.

"Good-bye, old friend," she said.

Twelve

For the rest of that whole day, not a single word passed between Petyr and Elysen.

The next morning, they ate a silent breakfast of hard biscuits and drank an herbal tea made of dried flowers and brown and green leaves, and then packed a few small bags of dried rice and beans and as much smoked venison as they could carry. Joli sipped from a bowl of cold soup.

"I know where Lake Orman is," Petyr said. "We will go there and hide, and you can see the healer."

Elysen took another bite of her biscuit. Petyr waited, hoping that she would break her silence. After a moment, she did.

"Do you have any weapons?" she asked.

"I have this." Petyr handed her his hunting bow – a long recurve, made with strips of willow bound together with hide glue and horsehair. Elysen cocked the bow without an arrow and then carefully returned it to its neutral position, knowing far better than to ever dry fire such a fine weapon. She nodded in approval.

"This is a good bow," she said. "How many arrows do we have?"

"Only these," he said.

He handed her a quiver with five arrows. She checked them by sighting down the shafts and touching her finger against the tips.

"And I have this," he said, pulling a knife from a sheath hidden against the small of his back. Elysen examined it carefully. In the dim light of morning, the smooth black blade took on a red cast. Holding it made her heart pound. She could feel Raes near her, his arm around her waist, his face close to hers.

"This is a good knife," she said.

"It was issued to me in the service of your Lord," he said.

She looked closer. Other than the color, it felt similar to the knife Raes carried. She held it out to Petyr, but her fingers did not want to let go.

"We should get going," Petyr said, putting the blade back in its sheath.

Joli came to Elysen and tugged at her hem.

"You forgot your toy," Joli said. She held the ball and cup in her hand, offering it. Elysen took it and tucked it into her belt.

"Thank you, Joli," she said. She stroked the little girl's hair, and Joli reached up with both arms. Elysen picked her up and carried her to the horse. The strain of lifting the little girl shot pain through Elysen's side.

A warrior does not feel pain, she told herself. The words came into her mind in the voice of her teacher, Raes. She shook the thought of him out of her head.

Elsyen put Joli on the ground and mounted Temper. Petyr handed the little girl up to Elysen and then took Temper's reins in his hand. Petyr walked along side Temper. Elysen held Joli in front of her between her legs.

"Will the soldiers kill us?" she asked.

Petyr glanced at Elysen.

"No," Elysen said. "The soldiers are far away. Besides, you have Petyr and me to protect you."

"How?" the little girl asked. Her voice held the soft, incredulous timber of youth and innocence, despite the horrors she had survived.

Elysen opened her mouth, but Petyr glared at her and shook his head.

"Don't lie to her," he said. "She deserves more than that."

"She deserves to be happy, not terrified for her life," Elysen said.

Joli craned her head around so that she could see Elysen's face.

"Are you fighting?" she asked.

"We are disagreeing," Elysen told her.

"Why?" she asked.

Elysen frowned.

"You haven't been around children much, have you?" Petyr asked. Elysen shook her head.

The gravel along the bank of the river became hard for Temper to negotiate, so Elysen dismounted and walked along side Petyr, leaving tiny Joli perched on Temper's back by herself. She rocked back and forth atop the huge black horse, her head nodding and her eyes drooping.

They continued for a while in silence.

"We should stop here for the night," Elysen said. "Joli is about to fall off. She's exhausted."

Petyr came to a slow stop. Elysen reached up and put her arms around the child. Joli slipped her arms around Elysen's neck and buried her face against her rough goatskin cloak.

Petyr led Temper up the bank, away from the noisy river, toward a small grove of alders that grew along a rocky moraine of higher ground. Elysen followed him, carrying Joli in her arms. Petyr led the horse into the grove and left him a few feet away from where Elysen stood waiting. He returned and threw his blanket on the ground at Elysen's feet and placed Joli gently on the rough, woolen padding. Petyr wandered off collecting firewood while Elysen sat cross-legged next to the sleeping child, covering her with the flare of her cloak.

Petyr built a small fire and cooked a simple stew of smoked venison and spicy white tubers. Joli slept through dinner, leaving her father alone with Elysen. They stared at each other across the fire, sipping their stew from wooden cups, listening to the sticks of hemlock and alder crack and pop as the fire consumed them.

"Thank you for dinner and the warm fire," Elysen said as she set her cup on the ground.

Petyr nodded. They sat in an awkward silence. Elysen picked up a long, thin straight branch and poked the fire. A shower of sparks lifted into the air and drifted across her robe. She fanned them away with her hand, and brushed them from the blanket around Joli.

The babbling of the nearby river sounded like a chorus of eerie voices, almost human, like the murmur of a large group of people just out of sight, just beyond the range where words could be heard distinctly. Petyr sat listening, staring toward the river. Elysen's gaze followed his. They stayed that way, tense and still in the darkness, their faces lit by the gloomy fire. A light drizzle of rain began to fall, and Petyr turned his face toward the sky.

"We may need to find shelter against this rain," he said, keeping his voice quiet.

Elysen tilted her head toward the sleeping Joli, who had burrowed down under the heavy cloak, covering her head against the cold and damp.

"We can't go anywhere tonight," Elysen said. "Joli is safe and warm under my cloak. I'll watch over her."

Petyr pulled his own cloak up around his head.

"Tomorrow we will go as far as we can, but we should keep our eyes open for shelter. Joli and I are not as immune to the cold as you are."

He moved closer to the fire and lay on his side, curling up in a ball. He rested his head on his arm and closed his eyes. Elysen sat staring at the fire as it cracked and sputtered in the light rain.

"I will be a threat to the people at Lake Orman," Elysen said.

"I think not," Petyr said. He yawned.

"I am hunted," she reminded him. "I will draw the Lord's Guard down on them."

"They don't fear Yergen or his guard."

"They should," Elysen said.

A long period of silence passed. Elysen listened to Petyr's slow breathing. She did her best to get comfortable. She woke up in the gray light just before dawn. Petyr was fanning the fire and tossing small sticks into the flames.

"How long have you been awake?" Elysen asked.

"For a while," he said.

Elysen felt her body relaxing as the fire sputtered to life. For just a moment, she let herself imagine that these were her people, a husband and a child. The thought took hold, surging within her, growing like the fire that Petyr tended. She allowed herself the luxury of enjoying the feeling, and in that moment, she felt safe. She almost said something to Petyr, but just as she opened her mouth, not sure of what she would say, a small branch cracked and a horse exhaled. Elysen froze.

"That was not Temper," she said.

Petyr's hand slipped under his cloak. He pulled out his knife. The obsidian blade glinted in the firelight. Elysen pulled her hood over her head and tilted her head forward, hiding her face in the deep shadow. With his boots, Petyr scuffed the thin soil over the fire as gently as he could. When that did not work, he kicked and scattered it sideways so that the cinders did not spray Elysen and Joli too badly. They sat, muscles tensed, eyes wide, hearts pounding. Nothing moved around them.

When the sky began to turn light blue and they could discern the shape of the trees around them, Elysen gathered Joli into her arms.

"Shall we wake her?" he asked.

"She'll be hungry. We're out of food." Elysen wrapped her into her cloak and held her tight against her body.

"I'll carry her," Petyr said, holding out his arms.

"No," Elysen said. "I've got her. I'll carry her until I get tired."

Petyr dropped his arms to his side.

"You're stronger that you look," he said.

They stared at each other for a moment, just watching each other's eyes, as if they were staring into a pool of reflecting water. Elysen felt a faint stirring in the pit of her stomach. She wanted to reach out to Petyr, to reassure him, to tell him that Joli would be fine, that no one would harm her. The stirring in her belly turned to a sickness that made her legs tremble.

Petyr reached out and touched Joli's head. He pressed his lips together and then turned and looked down river, back along the way they had come.

"You go on," he said. "I'm going to backtrack a bit, maybe circle around. See who might be following us."

He put his gloved hand under Elysen's chin and lifted her head. The touch of his hand scared her.

"Just stay along the river and keep moving," he said. "Don't stop and wait for me. Just keep going."

"I don't know the way."

"Just follow the river. I'll catch up. I promise."

"Take the bow, and the arrows," Elysen urged.

"No. I have my knife. I won't even need that. I'm not going to get close enough to anyone to fight."

"Be careful," Elysen said.

Petyr crouched down. He laced his fingers together and Elysen placed her foot in his hands. She held Joli tightly against her chest as she swung her leg over Temper's back. Petyr handed the reins to her and she stared straight ahead. He turned the horse upstream and slapped him on the flank. The big steed lurched into a stiff walk, still troubled by the uneven, rocky ground. Elysen craned her neck so that she could see Petyr. He watched them ride away, and then turned and began to circle slowly around the camp, examining the ground. Elysen lost sight of him as Temper rounded a bend in the river.

Joli woke up some time later.

"Where is my father?" she asked, gazing up into Elysen's eyes.

"He's hunting," Elysen said.

"Oh, good. I'm so hungry."

"So am I," Elysen said. "If you go back to sleep, time will pass more quickly."

Joli clutched Elysen with her tiny hands and they rode through the day. By evening, Elysen's pain made riding too difficult, so she walked and helped Joli balance on Temper's back. They stopped and found some wild onions and Elysen smiled as she thought of Corde. The next day they made a broth from a morgred fungus that Elysen found on an ailing alder. As evening fell, they startled a small deer that had been standing in the brush watching them, but it bounded away before Elysen could get to Petyr's bow.

Another cold night passed. They ate light in the morning and broke camp early. The ground finally became more solid. They rode on the bank through short grass that covered fine soil, along a well-worn trail. A few feet away, the Ryn Gladde swept by, undercutting the bank.

Further on, the terrain flattened and the river became wide and slow. Scrub brush gave way to lodge pole pine and large, spider-like rhododendrons adorned only with broad, waxy leaves that waved gently in the life-giving wind. A thick pall of clouds covered the sky and a light dusting of fine snow blew and swirled across the trail.

"When will I see my papa again?" Joli asked.

It took Elsyen a moment to awaken enough to answer. Joli sat nestled between Elysen's legs.

"Soon," she said.

"I miss him so much," Joli said.

"Yes. I know you do. He'll be here soon."

The little girl shivered.

"How are you feeling?" Elysen asked.

"I'm very tired. Can we stop and rest for a while?"

Elysen surveyed the terrain. The plateau stretched out before them, promising an easy ride before they hit the steep slopes in the distance, where the Mountains of Oken rose from the meadows in rocky crags. She stopped in a small grove of pine trees. Temper nuzzled the cold ground and began pulling tufts of wiry grass from the loosely packed dirt, munching noisily as he ate.

"I'm so hungry," Joli said. Her chin trembled.

Elysen built a small fire and huddled together with the shivering girl.

"I want my papa," Joli said, whimpering softly.

Elysen rocked her in her lap and stared into the smoky fire. The sticks were frosty and did not burn well. Very little heat radiated from the tiny flames.

Elysen dozed, but something disturbed her sleep. She felt Joli asleep in her lap. It was late afternoon. She struggled to wake up. As her eyes focused, she realized that a face peered at her from the other side of the smoldering fire.

Elysen's back stiffened. Her eyes went wide, and then narrow. She bared her teeth and snarled, but did not move. The young man that squatted across from her placed a few sticks on the fire and smiled. He bowed his head and clasped his hands together in front of his body as if he were holding a fragile butterfly close to his chest.

"Peace be with you," he said quietly.

"Who are you?" Elysen asked.

"My name is Arador. I was out hunting and saw you here."

Arador's blue eyes and a bright, quick smile did nothing to disarm Elysen. He put more sticks on the fire, and then blew on it lightly, bringing it to life. The flames licked hungrily along the black wood.

"This small child is sick and hungry. She needs shelter and warmth and food. Do you have a settlement nearby?"

He poked at the fire and smiled again. "Yes."

"Can you take us there?"

"Yes."

"When?"

"As soon as you are ready," he said.

"I'm waiting for a companion," she said.

"I know," he said, suddenly serious. "We've been watching you for a few days now."

Elysen frowned. "You've been watching us, letting us freeze to death out here?"

"We were in no position to help."

"And what do you know of my traveling companion?"

"He has been captured."

Elysen's heart jumped. "By whom?"

"By those you seek to escape from," Arador said.

"How do you know this?" Elysen asked. She felt a fluttering in her chest. She clenched her teeth together and forced her mind to concentrate.

"We saw him taken."

"How long ago?" she asked.

"Two days. Right after you split up. You were being followed by armed men, mounted on horses."

Elysen's concentration slipped and her shoulders sagged. She rubbed her forehead and glanced at the sleeping Joli.

"Take this child to safety," Elysen demanded.

Arador raised his eyebrows.

"You take her," he said. "There is a village. Up on that next plateau."

They sat for a while, staring at each other. She noticed that Arador studied her face carefully. He finally stood up.

"Come on," he said. "I'll show you the way."

Arador kicked dirt over the fire and scattered the dying embers with his foot. His actions reminded her of Petyr.

"I have to go find my friend," she said.

Arador pointed at Joli.

"First things first," he said. "Let's get her to Lake Orman, and then you can go get your friend."

Arador led Temper along the path. Elysen carried Joli in her arms as she followed. The big steed kept his head down and snorted occasionally as if to voice his discomfort at being led by the fair-haired stranger.

"I can carry her if you would rather ride," Arador said. "We'll make better time."

"No," Elysen replied. "I'll carry her."

Elysen gazed at the child and held her tightly. Her arms ached, but she refused to place Petyr's child in the arms of a stranger. She tried to take her mind off her pain.

"Where are you from?" she asked.

"The far south," he said.

"You are a farmer?"

He nodded. "My father was. Once."

"What are you doing here?" she asked.

He shrugged. "My father was called."

"Called by whom?"

"Just called. Like you. To show up here."

"I didn't get a calling. I am being chased."

"Same thing," he said.

"No, it isn't." She glanced back the way they had come. "You say you saw Petyr captured?"

"I saw a man being taken by a small company of armed men. He fought bravely."

Elysen hesitated, only for a moment, a heartbeat. "Did they kill him?"

Arador shook his head. "No. I don't think so. I think they were plenty mad though." His wry smile showed respect for Petyr's resistance.

"Why didn't you help him?"

"M'lady, I don't know why they wanted him, but I'm pretty sure they didn't want me. They would have killed me for sure."

They walked for quite some time, until they came to the base of a black cliff. The rock rose in tall, irregular columns. Between two of the largest pillars, a pile of loose debris fanned out into the valley. They stood at the bottom of this slope of impossibly sharp, loose and dangerous rocks, some the size of a horse, some as small as a person's thumb.

"Where do we go now?" Elysen asked.

"You follow," Arador said. "Carefully."

They circled around the leftmost column and ascended a steep, packed dirt trail that hugged the base of the giant monolith. The trail turned back upon itself and snaked behind another column. Then it became wider and more defined. It wound back and forth under gnarled trees and between shattered columns, rising quickly along the side of the steep plateau. Unable to carry the sleeping girl, and unwilling to place her into Arador's unfamiliar arms, Elysen woke Joli so that she could ride on Temper's back. She did not complain or ask questions as she clutched the coarse mane. Her eyes held a sad, sleeping look, as if she did not care anymore.

The last stretch ascended a steep pile of boulders, black and wet from a running creek that scattered a fine mist as it tumbled its way along the rubble.

"We have to climb from here on," Arador said. "Give me the girl. I'll carry her on my back."

Elysen took Joli off Temper's back and held her.

"I'm not leaving my horse," she said.

"You'll have to. There is no other way."

"You must have another way to get up there."

"No. This is the only way."

"I won't leave my horse," Elysen repeated.

Arador began to unhitch the harness. Elysen reached out. She grabbed Arador's arm and pulled it away from Temper's mouth.

"Don't touch him," she snarled.

"You don't have a choice," Arador said. "He can't make it up this cliff. You have to let him go."

"*I* don't have to do anything," Elysen protested. "This is my horse and I am taking him with me, or I am not going at all. Got it?"

Arador smiled again, and then chuckled. He looked up the cliff and put his hands on his hips.

"I'm not saying it hasn't been done before," he said. "We have hauled some goats and sheep up there. Just never anything as big as him."

He turned toward Temper and assessed the job with his eyes.

"We're going to need some rope," he sighed. "You'll have to wait here while I go get help." He began to climb up the embankment of boulders.

"How long will you be?" Elysen asked. He stopped and looked back down at her.

"Not long," he said. "I should be back before nightfall."

Elysen glanced down at Joli. "Can you take the girl with you?" Elysen asked. "She needs food and warmth."

Arador hesitated, and then shook his head.

"I'm sorry. I need to move quickly. She'll be better off with you. A girl needs to stay with her mother."

Elysen began to protest, but Arador disappeared into the rocks, bounding away like a wild deer. Elysen settled down into a sheltered spot and wrapped her cloak around Joli's shoulders, clutching the little girl against her chest.

Time passed and the day grew old. Elysen watched Temper chew on a piece of wood, saliva dripping from his lips. She sighed, and then gently slipped her cloak off her shoulders and wrapped it around Joli's little body. Elysen stood up slowly and placed her hands on her knees as she stretched out her legs. She stood up and flexed her arms to get the circulation going again. She stood over Joli's still body and listened carefully to the little girl's slow, shallow breath. After a moment, she sighed and took Temper's reins in her hands.

"Come on, boy," she said.

She led Temper down the path to a small, flat meadow. A pond glistened on the far side of the meadow, well away from the path. Tufts of green grass poked through the snow. Elysen released the bridle and placed it on a stump just within the tree line. She tapped Temper on the flank and he wandered off toward the pond. Elysen walked away. The snow whispered softly under her feet.

Back at the base of the cliffs, Joli still slept. Elysen sat down and waited. Arador returned just before night fell. He called down from the top of the cliff.

"Lady Elysen, are you there?"

"Yes," she called back.

"I've brought back ropes and five strong men," he shouted. "I'm coming down."

Arador showed up a few minutes later, scampering down the last few feet of talus slope with a small cascade of sharp stones.

"We'll take him up over there." Arador pointed to the south. "It's steeper. Less chance of him getting snagged up in the rocks."

"I sent him off," Elysen said.

Arador gaped at her, and then smiled and shook his head.

"You are precious," he said. He reached out his hand and motioned to her.

"Come on then," he said. "Let's get going. We still have half a day's walk ahead of us. It will be dark by the time we get home."

Arador bent over and scooped Joli up in his arms.

"She's light as a feather," he said.

"I'm sorry that I sent you back for nothing," Elysen said.

"No need to apologize," Arador replied. "All things have a purpose in their own way."

"What do you mean?"

Arador slung the girl over his shoulder, creating a makeshift pack out of her blanket. She woke up.

"Where are we?" Joli asked.

She arched her back so that she could see Elysen. Joli's eyes were tired and rimmed with red. Elysen reached out and touched the child's gray face with her bare hand. Joli's skin felt cold.

"We're going someplace warm and dry," Elysen said.

"Will papa be there?" Joli asked.

"Maybe," Elysen said. "Maybe he'll come tomorrow. I don't know. Try to relax now. We'll have you in a nice soft bed soon."

"Don't promise too much," Arador said as they climbed the steep trail. "You haven't seen it yet."

He glanced back at her with a broad smile on his face, but creases of underlying worry. Elysen followed him, barely able to keep up even though she used both hands to steady herself. Arador carried the girl over one shoulder and used his free hand to negotiate the path. They did not climb straight up, but it was steep nonetheless. Much too steep for Temper.

Five rugged men waited for them at the top with ropes slung across their shoulders. They stood close to the edge of the cliffs, watching Elysen and Arador climb.

At the top, Elysen stopped to catch her breath. Arador and his friends stepped back to give her room. As she gazed out across the lands of the Vyr, her shoulders relaxed and her mind cleared.

A broad vista opened up in front of and below her as if she were an eagle, soaring above the landscape. Her eyes followed the valley of the Ryn Gladde as it cut through ancient ridges covered with snow-laden pines. The ridges fanned out before her like razorback hogs sleeping side by side, packed together in a pen. Further out, the ridges became more and more rounded, and less and less wooded, until they were lost in the distant, gray horizon.

Elysen turned around. The immensity of the mountains loomed above her, their snow-covered tops lost in the clouds. She did not even notice the men standing there, watching her, as her mind marveled at the sheer grandeur of the Mountains of Oken, the land of devils and ghosts. She took an involuntary step backwards. A hand touched her shoulder and she stopped. A weathered man with a thick coat and sad, slow voice held onto her robe.

"Easy now, m'lady," he said. "You don't want to be walking backwards just there."

Elysen looked back and saw that her heels were just touching the edge of the cliff. She nodded and took two steps forward toward the mountains.

"Thank you," she said.

Arador interceded. "This is Jaramis," he said, patting the old man on the back. Jaramis clasped his hands together in front of his chest and bowed his head slightly. The light gleamed off the top of his bare head.

"Peace be with you," he said.

The other four men introduced themselves in turn. Shelby, gray bearded with sinewy arms and a twinkle in his eye as he smiled; Raymond, a giant of a man with the innocent face of a child, whose breadth made Arador's thin frame seem like a wisp of smoke; Chans, with short legs and big hands; and Jacobi, thin and wiry, his face weathered and wrinkled like dry leather. Each in turn clasped their hands and bowed to her, saying "Peace be with you" as they lowered their eyes to the ground.

"Come on," Jaramis said to Elysen. "We need to get this little girl to shelter, and we need to get you to Mother Rachael." He took little Joli and held her gently against his giant chest.

"Who is Mother Rachael?" Elysen asked as they began to walk away from the cliff. She looked back over her shoulder, taking a last glance toward the valley below.

"She is our prophetess," Arador said. "She's been waiting for you for as long as I can remember. This is going to be very exciting for her."

"Waiting for me?" Elsyen asked.

Arador nodded.

"Does she know me?" Elsyen asked.

"Everyone knows you," Jaramis said.

Elysen grunted quietly. They walked for a while in silence before Elysen spoke again.

"What does a prophetess do?" she asked.

"She is our leader," Arador said. "She knows the future. And the past. She knows all the secrets of the world!"

"Arador," Jaramis scolded. "Enough."

Arador scuffed his feet in the thin snow.

The boyish Raymond pointed out across the plateau toward a distant lake and another cliff of high columns.

"There is Lake Orman," he said.

Chans put his hand on Elysen's arm. She rocked a bit as she walked.

"Maybe you should slow down a bit," he said.

"She's going to pass out," Jaramis said. He stepped toward her.

Elysen staggered backwards and her legs crumpled under her. She went from one knee to two, and then fell to all fours before her face hit the ground.

She woke in a small wooden hut, lying on a grass mat on the floor, looking up at the ceiling. Rough blankets covered her naked skin. An old woman sat cross-legged on the floor next to her. The woman's eyes closed, and she whispered, chanting under her breath, so softly that Elysen could not hear the words, just a hint of the sounds, like cloth rubbing against cloth. Her whispers mixed with the hissing murmur of a fire that burned in the center of the hut. Smoke drifted upward and escaped out of a small hole in the center of the roof.

"So, you awaken," the woman said. She opened her eyes.

Elysen turned her head slightly so that she could see the woman better.

"I'm Rachael," the woman said.

Elysen turned her head and scanned the room.

"Where is Joli?" she asked. "How is she?"

"She is drifting away from us," Rachael said.

"What do you mean? She's dying?"

"Her purpose here on the Vyr is fulfilled."

"I don't understand," Elysen said.

"All things will be revealed to you in their proper time," Rachael said.

"What do you mean? What things will be revealed to me?"

"We see only the tiniest portion of this life, this world, Elysen. We are like ants crawling along the flagstones of your Keep. We see only the paths that we need to see at the time. Our minds and our vision are too limited to see any more than that, even though there is so much more. Only time will reveal more to you."

"Arador said you were a prophetess," Elysen said.

Rachael leaned back a bit and a glimmer of a smile crossed her lips.

"My gift is that of a guide," she said.

"Can you see the future?"

She shook her head.

"Arador said you could," Elysen said.

"Are you curious about what the future holds?" Rachael asked.

Elysen turned her head away from Rachael's gaze.

"Let me see Joli now," Elysen said.

"I'll have the girl brought here. We will lay her next to you."

Elysen sat up and held the blanket against her breasts, leaving her naked back exposed. Rachael rose gracefully, easily, and slipped out of a thick, hide flap that served as a door for the round hut. Soon after, Arador returned, carrying Joli in his arms, swaddled like a baby. Arador settled Joli in next to Elysen. The little girl slept with her mouth slightly open. The dark circles around her eyes made her face seem even more pale and gaunt. Elysen sat up again, holding the blanket over her chest with one hand. Arador struggled to avoid staring at her.

Elysen noticed that he averted his eyes.

"Do I disgust you?" she asked.

He blushed and shook his head.

"You are absolutely beautiful," he said.

Elysen felt a smile creep across her face, suppressed it, and instead leaned over slightly, so that she could see Joli's face in the flickering fire light.

"How is she?" Elysen asked. She reached over and touched the girl's forehead.

Cold. Too cold.

"She's dying."

Elysen clenched her teeth.

"We will pray for her tonight," Arador said. "Her journey here on the Vyr is almost over. Soon, we will all meet her again in J'halla."

"What is J'halla?" Elysen asked.

"J'halla is the land of the dead," Arador said.

Elysen looked at Arador with a puzzled look on her face, and then turned back to Joli.

"Leave us alone, please," Elysen said. She kept her voice low and quiet. Arador nodded and left. Elysen lay down next to the tiny girl and pulled Joli's body close to her own. Joli looked at Elysen for a moment, but her puffy, heavy eyelids did not want to stay open.

"Is my papa here?" Joli asked. Her voice barely registered. Elysen frowned. It took her a moment to understand the question.

"No," she said. "He's just off on an errand." Elysen held her tight, squeezing her thin, bony body as firmly as she dared. She stroked Joli's hair.

"No, he isn't." Joli sobbed as she struggled with her words. "He's not on an errand."

Too weak to cry, her sobs were devoid of tears, and her body shuddered as she took deep breaths between her almost silent wails.

"Please try to rest," Elysen whispered.

"I want you to get him for me," Joli whimpered.

Elysen bundled her own blanket around the sobbing girl and rocked back and forth. Joli grew quiet. Her sobs subsided. Elysen kept rocking, her eyes staring straight ahead. She thought about Petyr. Her mind drifted to her own father. All of the knowledge of Thorsen, locked deep within the Keep of the Vyr. The power to create. The power to destroy. The power to heal. The power to bring back the dead.

Elysen leaned over and placed Joli gently on the bedding. She rose to her feet and began to look for clothing. As she scanned the one room hut, her back to the door, Arador yanked the heavy hide away from the doorway and ducked through the opening. Elysen turned sharply so that she faced him.

"I need some clothes," she said.

Arador nodded and quickly peeled off his own cloak and handed it to her. She flung it around her shoulders and held it closed across her body with both hands.

"Stay right here," he said. "I'll get you something."

She waited, listening to Joli's ragged breathing. Arador came back with black leather pants, boots and a soft, woolen shirt. Elysen slipped one arm out from under the cloak and he handed the clothes to her.

"Where is my bow?"

"Jaramis has it. Why do you need a weapon?"

"I'm going to get her father," Elysen said.

She let the cloak drop to the floor and Arador turned his back. She slipped into the pants. They were slightly large. She sat on the ground to pull on the tall, black boots. The loose, thick shirt felt tough and warm. Elysen pulled the cloak around her shoulders again and fastened the loop to hold it closed.

"I can't go with you," Arador said.

"I didn't ask you to," Elysen said. She frowned at him. "Why can't you go with me?"

"It is against the law," he said.

"Against what law?"

"The law."

"What law? I know of no law that says that we can't go searching for someone who may be in trouble."

"We can't do violence to another human being," Arador said.

"Who told you that? Rachael?"

Arador nodded.

"Is she the law-maker here then? Not my father? Not my brothers? Not me?"

Arador nodded again.

Elysen reached around behind his neck and grabbed his long, tangled hair in her hand. She pulled hard. Arador's head tilted back slightly and the tendons in his neck stood out like ropes.

"Are you just going to leave this girl's father out there to die?"

"You are strong for your size," Arador said through his clenched teeth. The intensity of Elysen's grip came through in his voice. "He is most likely dead already. And, as I said, our law does not allow us to fight."

"What is this law of which you speak?" she snarled. "Who makes these laws?"

"Our prophetess," he replied.

Elysen released her hold on his hair abruptly. She shook her head and closed her eyes. "Forgive me father. I have fallen in with cowards who hide like mice."

"I guess it all depends on your point of view," Arador said, rubbing his neck. "We think it takes more courage to stand in peace than it does to fight."

Elysen stared blankly at the wall. She stood that way for a moment before turning back to face Arador.

"I'm going to find Petyr," she said. "Then I'm coming back for this girl. Make sure no harm comes to her while I'm gone. When I get back, I'll take her from here and we'll be done with you." She stepped toward the opening, but Arador stopped her with a gentle grip on her arm.

"I can't do that," he said.

"Can't do what?" Elysen snapped.

"I can't stay here," he said. "I have to go with you."

"I thought that you said it was against your law."

"It is against the law. The law. Not my law. The law. Anyway, I have to go with you. It is my place to walk with you."

"What are you then? My bodyguard?"

He shook his head. "No. More like your student I think."

"I don't need a student. I'm not a teacher. I need a warrior, a tracker and a whole lot of fighters. Can you be any of those?"

He shook his head again, sadly, staring at the ground in front of his feet. He still had a hand on Elysen's arm. She stood poised to leave, held in stasis by Arador's soft touch.

"My name is taken from our most sacred and ancient stories. In long ago times, Arador wandered the desert until he came across a prophet who saved him. Arador followed the prophet everywhere, even through the flaming gates of eternal punishment."

"Sounds like a nice story," Elysen said, pulling her arm out of his grip. "But I'm not your prophet."

"Even so," Arador said, shrugging his shoulders in resignation. "My duty is to follow you and to help you. I can do at least that much. I can't fight though, under any circumstances. If I break our law, I will burn in eternal fire."

"Your law sounds awful," Elysen replied. "I think I'll follow my own law."

He shrugged. "The law is what it is. We don't choose it. It just is."

"This talk of laws irritates me," she said. "Where can I find fighters?"

"No one here will help you harm another. It is against our way."

"What will you do when the Lord's Guard comes here hunting for me? They don't share your code. They will pierce your women and children with arrows and hang their bodies on the crosses of the Northern Reach."

"Rachael has told us that this village will most likely be destroyed."

"You don't seem too broken up about it."

Arador smiled. "Everything has its time," he said. "Perhaps our time is over. Maybe there is something better coming."

Elysen pulled her arm away from Arador's light touch. "Or something worse," she said. She turned away. "Well, student," she said. "Are you coming?"

Arador followed her out of the light and into the dark night.

Thirteen

The thin clouds parted slightly. Turoc hung above them like a serpent's eye, glowing white in the center, surrounded by a light, round haze rimmed with reddish orange.

"Can you get us down the cliffs?" Elysen asked as they walked.

"It will be tricky in the dark," Arador said. "And the red ring around Turoc is a bad sign."

"Nonsense," Elysen replied. "A red ring around Turoc means good hunting."

Arador looked unconvinced.

As they traveled, their eyes grew accustomed to the dim, colorless world around them. By the time they came to the cliffs, Turoc had grown tired of their trek. It slid behind the trees, shrouding the mountains in complete darkness.

"Turoc abandons us," Arador said. "We should wait here until morning, so that we have light to navigate by."

"No. Every moment we leave Petyr in the hands of the enemy is a moment too long. We go now."

"In the dark? Without even Turoc to guide us?"

"Yes. In the dark. You will guide us."

Arador clasped his hands together and whispered something, then sighed.

"If we can find the trail, we can feel our way down the mountain," he said.

"But you will have to hold onto me so that we don't get separated."

Elysen nodded in the darkness and put her hand on Arador's shoulder.

"Lead the way," she said.

They inched along, feeling their way along the tiny trail cut into the steep slope, sometimes sitting and scuffing along the ground, sometimes crawling. After a long time of this, the slope became more gradual and Arador stopped with his hand against a large, round boulder.

"This is the bottom of the cliff, the spot where I left you before. The worst is over."

"How long until first light?" Elysen asked.

She could barely see the boy in the dim starlight. His voice and her hand touching his shoulder were the only signs that he was still with her.

"Not long. Maybe we should wait here."

"We've come this far in the darkness," Elysen said. "If we can find Temper, he will lead us to Petyr. I'm sure of it."

"How will we find Temper?"

"I left him in a meadow beside one of the small lakes below us. If we're lucky, he'll still be there, waiting."

"If he is, he's a loyal friend indeed."

"He is."

"Well, let's go then. As you say, we've made it this far."

They crept along in the darkness, wandering among the pine trees, feeling their way from one tree to the next.

"This is kind of crazy," Arador said. "We have no idea where we are going."

"Trust me," Elysen said.

After a while, she whistled softly. They continued on, Elysen's hand on Arador's shoulder, her soft whistle piercing the night every now and again. For a while, the only answer was an occasional hoot of an owl or the startling flutter of a blue forest grouse as it sprung from under their feet. Then, suddenly, they heard the crunching snap of twigs under heavy feet, and they froze, waiting silently. The heavy footsteps were irregular, noisy, and then they heard the reassuring snort of a horse clearing his nostrils.

"It's a beast, not a man," Arador whispered.

Elysen whistled again, and the horse snorted in reply.

"It's Temper," Elysen said.

"If the Lord's Guard found him, it could be a trap."

"If the army had found him, he wouldn't be wandering around out here in the woods looking for us."

They carefully picked their way through the dry undergrowth and over fallen logs. Elysen kept whistling softly. She jumped when Temper's hot breath touched the back of her neck.

"It's getting light," Elysen said.

Above them, through the trees, they could see that the black sky that had been dotted with stars had turned a light, bluish-gray, and they saw shapes and forms in the woods around them – tall, narrow trees with straight trunks that towered above them before the first whorls of branches began, forming a high canopy of conical evergreen boughs high above their heads, and a maze of downed branches and fallen trees along the ground, along with scattered bushes sparsely adorned with broad leaves.

Elysen grabbed Temper's mane and stepped on a nearby log for leverage. She launched herself onto his broad back and offered her hand to Arador, who stood peering into the darkness, unable to see her invitation.

"Take my hand," Elysen said quietly.

Arador reached out, into the indistinct grayness, and Elysen took his hand. As he stepped toward her, she leaned back and pulled hard on his arm. Arador instinctively stepped on the log in front of him and swung his leg high. In one fluid motion, he slipped onto Temper's back behind Elysen and slipped his arms around her waist. The sensation both thrilled and frightened Elysen. She felt her shoulders tighten.

"Hang on," she said.

Temper eased them through the forest and into a meadow where they dismounted. The dawn of the Soel approached, and they could see a fine mist hanging over the large, flat open space into which they had emerged.

"There is an encampment on the other side of this meadow," Elysen said. She kept her voice quiet, just above a whisper.

"How do you know that?" Arador asked.

"I can see it." She pointed with a long, white finger. She frowned slightly, her jaw tight with anger.

"Your eyesight must be a whole lot better than mine," Arador said.

"It is," Elysen replied. "You stay here with Temper."

Elysen set off across the meadow, heading southward to the southern side of the encampment. The light became more and more favorable for travel, but less and less friendly for Elysen's task. She circled the camp, noting the smoldering fires and the lack of guards. She saw four small tents and a larger one sporting a black banner with the crest of the Vyr Lord upon it – a red shield adorned with four white stars in quadrants. The camp had been set up along the edge of the meadow. Elysen slipped along the open side of the encampment by staying low in the tall grass. When she came to the woods, she passed from tree to tree, using them for cover as she went, moving silently like a wild animal, waiting, watching, and then flowing toward the next hiding spot like the shadow of a cloud passing overhead. She continued on this way, seeing no one stir, until she came to the far side of the camp. There, between two small trees, a man sat, his arms tied with stout ropes to the tops of the young, tough birch trees that now bent inward like the ends of Elysen's bow, pulling on the man's arms like a pair of angry lovers.

"Petyr," Elysen whispered.

She approached him carefully, watching everything around her as she crept slowly through the low grass that grew along the edge of the forest. She found little cover here, so she moved rapidly, almost carelessly toward the prisoner. She came close and touched his leg. His head hung forward. Blood seeped through his tattered clothes.

"Petyr," she whispered again.

He groaned. Elysen glanced at the taut ropes that held him and touched one. Petyr stirred and the trees above him swayed and shuddered as his body tugged at the stiff, rough bindings that connected them.

"Easy," Elysen said, touching his leg again. "I'll be back. Just hold on."

She slipped back into the relative darkness of the woods and crawled into the cradle formed by the roots of an upturned deadfall. Time passed. A few men came out of one of the smaller tents. They fanned their fires back to life and roasted their breakfast of wild rabbit on long wooden skewers. The smell of cooking meat wafted to where Elysen crouched, and her stomach growled loudly. One man roasted two small rabbits or birds in addition to his own, and took them on their sticks, smoking and steaming, into the larger tent. Elysen watched a soldier tether a mangy, blue-gray hound to a post near the other edge of the small camp. It barked for a few moments and then stopped abruptly, but it kept sniffing the light breeze as if trying to catch a scent again.

The day turned out lightly overcast as sheets of thin clouds drifted overhead. Even so, the Soel peered through every now and then, baking the wet ground for just a moment, just long enough to shake the chill from Elysen's bones, even though she stayed hidden in the shade. After the men had eaten their fill, they tossed their sticks into the fire and gathered their horses from a makeshift corral just beyond where Petyr sat, still hunched forward. Eight men rode off, leaving two horses behind. Elysen's eyes narrowed as she recognized the chestnut mare that Temper loved so fondly.

Roan, she said to herself.

She knew the lean, auburn colored horse almost as well as her own.

Raes is here.

The other horse pranced around angrily, already saddled and ready to go. Roan kept to the far side of the corral. Soon, three men emerged from the tent. Elysen snarled as she recognized her cousin.

"Yergen," she said, under her breath.

Raes and another soldier followed Yergen. Raes turned toward her hiding place and scanned the woods. Elysen held her breath. In the thin, cold air, she could hear Yergen's voice.

"We're running out of time here," he said. He motioned toward Petyr's body. "As soon as you find the witch, get rid of that pile of rubbish. And make sure you scour out every last one of the faithless living up there."

Yergen glanced toward the mountains above them. He turned away from his companions and walked toward the horses. Yergen stopped suddenly and turned back toward Raes.

"Kill them all," he said. "Hang every last one of them on the crossed pikes at the Northern Reach. I want to see bodies hanging from the mountains to the Rift. I want a line of blood from here to the great river. And Raes," he said.

"Yes, my Lord."

"Make sure that you bring Elysen to me. Unharmed. Untouched. Do you understand me?"

Raes hesitated.

"Yes, my Lord."

"I will kill her myself," Yergen said. "Hang her from Thorsen's Watch next to all other traitors to the Vyr."

Yergen turned away, his cloak swirled, sweeping the ground behind him.

"We will bring order back to this land, Master Raes," he said as he walked away.

"Yes, my Lord," Raes said.

Yergen mounted his horse and rode away. Raes walked over to Petyr and grabbed his hair. Petyr's head snapped back and Elysen gasped when she saw the bloody rag tied around his face. Raes paused, cocked his head to the side and stood very still. He waited for a moment, and then looked down at Petyr again.

"You aren't doing your job very well," Raes mused aloud.

Petyr's head fell forward. Elysen held her hand over her mouth and sat very still, hunkered down in her hiding place like a mother bear protecting her cubs. Her breath came in shallow, quick pants. She fixed her ice-green eyes on Raes. She bit her lip and scowled as he walked slowly back to the tent.

Raes, she pleaded. *What are you doing?*

He suddenly stopped and began a slow survey of the woods, as if he sensed Elysen's presence. He circled slowly, and then waited for a moment before he went inside.

Elysen crept forward, across the fallen logs that separated her from the camp. Under her hand, a dry twig snapped, and she froze. After a moment of waiting, she continued her stalking, staying low to the ground, close to the trees. As she came to the edge of the woods, she paused, surveying the encampment again for signs of movement. Nothing stirred, other than the wisps of white smoke from the unattended fires. She crouched next to the last towering pine tree and braced against it with her left shoulder. She slipped her bow from around her arm and pulled an arrow from the quiver on her back. She placed the nock of the arrow against the string and drew the bow. Under her loose sleeve, the muscles of her arm locked into hard knots, strengthened by years of patient practice. She stayed that way, motionless, tensed, poised to strike. The smoke wafted through the trees. A bird sent a lonely cry across the meadow. The tall grass between Elysen and the small group of tents bent in ripples with the breeze as it came and went in no regular rhythm.

A twig snapped somewhere behind her. Her eyes darted sideways but her head did not move. Again the crunching sound of a boot on the dry, thick bed of needles and twigs that carpeted the woods, this time from her left. Still she did not move. She kept her eyes fixed straight ahead, at the large tent where Raes waited. Around her, lurking in the trees and deadfalls like deer, her pursuers moved, one step, then a pause, then another step and another. But, unlike deer, these moving bodies were converging, moving steadily toward the spot where Elysen crouched, the sounds not quite random enough for wild animals.

Elysen closed her eyes and waited. Despite the coldness around her, a bead of moisture appeared on her brow. Her forehead locked in a frown of concentration. A snap from her left. A shuffle from behind. Closer now.

Like a pouncing cat, she spun and released the arrow that she had held so patiently for so long. It traced a gradual, silent arc, spinning lazily. Before it even struck its mark, burying itself deep in the exposed throat of the guardsman who had just stepped from behind a tree to her left, she spun around and had reached behind her head and had drawn another arrow from the quiver with a practiced grace, her delicate fingers wrapping around the nock of the arrow and placing it on the string in one graceful movement. This second arrow, released in haste, hit its mark just as well as the first. The guardsman reached up with both hands and grasped the shaft of the arrow with a surprised look on his face as he gagged and coughed blood from his ruined throat. Elysen's hand went for a third arrow, but a blow to the side of her head sent her spinning dizzily across the ground and out into the open. Her bow fell from her hand, and the last few arrows that she had flew from the quiver and scattered across the grass. She rolled over just in time to see her assailant, a large and angry guardsman holding a heavy jubo. He struck her again across the side of her head with the blunt end of the big spear and she lay still, flopped onto her back like a rag doll.

A shot of cold water brought stinging light back to her eyes. She found herself in a tent, her back against the central pole, hands tied behind her. A haze of light smoke filled the air.

"I knew you would find us," Raes said.

He crouched in front of Elysen, studying her. He motioned to the guardsman that stood on the other side of Elysen.

"Leave us," he said. "She won't do any more harm."

The guardsman turned and left. Raes leaned forward and stared into her eyes.

Elysen tried to speak, but no sound emerged. Raes stripped off his glove and touched the side of her face with his fingers. Elysen winced as Raes' fingers gently traced a ragged tear that ran from her cheekbone to her jaw.

"I'm sorry about your face," Raes said.

He touched her swollen jaw.

"And it looks like they broke your jaw as well."

His eyes looked sad and tired.

"So delicate, and yet so deadly," he mused.

He stood up and stepped back.

"This is what you brought us to," he said. "You made us enemies."

"We cared about each other once," Elysen said. Her voice rasped from her dry throat.

"And yet you were stationed out there in the edge of the woods with an arrow pointed toward my heart," he said. She turned her head away.

He stood for a moment, with his arms crossed, glaring at her.

"Did you sleep with him too?" Raes asked.

Elysen ground her teeth together.

"Yergen tortured him," Raes said. "Gouged out his eyes, beat him nearly to death. That's no man out there. Just an empty shell."

Elysen closed her eyes and she felt something inside slipping away. No cares, no worries. Death brought peace. Death brought release.

"Kill me now," she said. Her voice barely rose above a whisper. "Just let me die."

"I won't do you the favor," he said. "I'll let Yergen take care of your fate from here on."

"I'd rather die by your hand than by his."

Raes closed his eyes and clenched his teeth, listening to the silence. In an instant, they both froze, eyes open wide to the sickening snick of an arrow punching through soft skin and the gurgling thud of a human body in a futile struggle to regain a stolen life. All fell silent again. Elysen pulled at the thongs around her wrists, but could not move them. Raes pulled his knife from his belt. Elysen watched him as he held the red-orange blade lightly in his fingers, facing toward the door of the hide covered tent.

Moments passed by slowly. Nothing moved. Elysen barely breathed. She focused on the long, straight poles above her that supported the thin, tightly stretched hide roof. She blinked away the tears and the pain.

"Pain is just weakness leaving the body," she whispered.

Suddenly she realized that the pain in her chest came from watching Raes stand there with his knife drawn, an ally of Yergen.

Raes chose the law of the Vyr over me.

The thought felt like death.

The flap opened, and Petyr staggered in. The ragged, dirty, bloody cloth still hung around his face, leaving only his mouth visible. Raes lunged, but even blind Petyr managed to avoid the thrusting blade. He wrapped his arms around Raes, pulling him to the ground. As they fell, Arador slipped into the tent and ran to Elysen. He severed the leather bindings with his skinning knife and Elysen rolled to the floor. Raes scrambled up, on his feet again. He kicked Petyr in the ribs and spun around to face Arador and Elysen. Arador held his small knife out in front of his body. His face turned solemn, as if he knew he looked at death. Raes glanced down at Petyr, who struggled to get back to his feet. As Raes delivered another swift kick to Petyr's ribs, Arador lunged forward with Elysen no more than a step behind him, but Raes recovered and caught the boy in mid stride, jamming his knife in just below Arador's ribs in an upward thrust. Arador's back arched. Petyr lurched to his feet just as Elysen threw her arm around Raes' throat and kicked her feet up in the air and around his back. The momentum of her body pulled Raes away from the boy and tipped him backwards over a small bench. Raes landed hard on his back and lost his grip on the bloody knife. Petyr dove for the noisy scuffle and landed on Raes' chest. Elysen rolled away. Petyr reared back and cocked his arm back with his fist balled up, letting it loose like a man hammering a post into the hard ground. He struck again and again, first with one fist and then with the other until Elysen grabbed him from behind and pulled him away.

"Enough," she said.

Petyr struggled for a moment longer and then relaxed a bit. Raes lay still on the ground, his face bloody and his eyes closed. Arador had pulled himself into a sitting position against the center post. Elysen left Petyr and staggered over to where Raes' knife lay. She picked it up and then she crawled back to Raes' body on her hands and knees. She placed the knife against his throat and pushed.

"No," Arador said softly. He coughed, and blood trickled down his chin. "Don't do it, my lady."

Petyr sat down, panting. His body trembled.

Elysen looked down at Raes. She stared at him, her eyes bright and her lips parted in a snarl. She pressed the knife against his throat hard enough that a trickle of blood ran from under the stone blade.

I used to dream about you, she screamed inside her mind.

"Please don't," Arador said. "There has been enough killing today."

Elysen looked at Arador, then back to Raes. She pressed harder on his throat.

"Please," Arador said. "Leave him be. You have to ride away now."

"Why?" she asked.

She glanced at Petyr. His bandage hung loose around his neck, ripped from his face during the struggle. He fell backwards onto his back. His empty eye sockets stared toward the ceiling, rimmed with crusted blood, but his chest rose and fell with the breath of life.

"Look at us," she said. "We're all dead anyway. What reason is there to let any one of us live? If any of us should have lived past this day, it should have been you. Raes deserves to die."

"No one deserves to die at our hands," Arador said.

Elysen glared at him. "Didn't you kill the guards outside?"

He shook his head and his face turned into a mask of pain.

"Elysen, I am dying. Please come here."

She hesitated, her hand still pressing the blade against Raes' bare throat. She pulled it away and held it above him. She stared at him, watching his chest as it moved slowly up and down under his leather coat.

"I have little life left," Arador said softly.

His breath came in ragged shudders now, and bubbles of blood oozed from his lips. Elysen reached down and ripped the leather sheath from Raes' waist. She hesitated for a moment as she glimpsed a small, brown leather pouch tied close to where the sheath had been. Almost by instinct, she reached down and tore it off his belt. She sheathed the knife and crawled over to Arador so that she could sit next to him and put her arms around his shoulders. He tipped into her arms and rested there.

"Tell Rachael that I'm sorry," he said.

Elysen stroked his hair. "You have nothing to be sorry for," she said.

"There was a man in the woods," Arador said. "He helped."

Elysen frowned and wanted to ask him more, but he coughed up blood and she held him as he trembled and sobbed. He calmed down a bit and she ran her hand through his hair again.

"I killed," he said.

"How many men did you kill?" she asked.

"Just one outside the tent. Then I released Petyr and we came for you."

He paused. His eyes closed and his chest barely moved.

"It hurts to breathe," he whispered.

Elysen stroked his forehead.

"I know," she said. "Try to lay still."

"Plenty of time for that," he said. "Please, forgive me. I took human lives. I lost my faith."

"No, you didn't," Elysen said.

"Yes. In the very last, I lost my faith. I made a terrible mistake."

"You saved Petyr and me."

He smiled briefly.

"It's wrong to kill humans," he said. "I will burn forever in a terrible place for what I have done."

"Please don't believe that," she said.

He shook his head.

"If you believe in a great power, then at least believe in a good power, one that forgives you for your mistakes. If there is some existence after this one, then I pray that you will find happiness and peace there. If anyone deserves such a place, you do. It's Raes and Petyr and I that will suffer forever in some fiery pit. Not you. You are a good person, Arador of Lake Orman. What was the name of your place in the sky? J'Halla?"

Arador smiled and managed a small nod. He took a slow, ragged breath, and spoke softly.

"Please tell my father that I love him, and that I'm sorry that I disappointed him."

"Do I know your father?" Elysen asked.

Arador smiled. "Jaramis is my father here on the Vyr," he said. "Please tell him."

"I'll tell him," she said.

"You must learn to forgive," Arador whispered.

A grimace of pain suddenly replaced Arador's smile. His eyes closed and Elysen could feel the tension in his body relaxing as he lay in her arms.

"Peace be with you, Arador," she said. "May your light shine brightly in the sky."

His body went limp, and the sucking sound that had accompanied his last few breaths stopped. She rocked back and forth for a time, as if unaware of her surroundings.

Petyr coughed, and Elysen awoke from her reverie. She let Arador's body slide to the ground, carefully, like a mother placing a child in a crib to sleep, and then she stood up. Her legs wavered slightly before she regained a steady pose. She walked over to where Petyr lay and dropped to her knees. She shrugged off her heavy cloak and tore off her wool shirt, wrapping it around Petyr's face. She leaned close to him and spoke softly as she pulled her cloak back around her naked shoulders.

"Can you rise?" she asked quietly.

He groaned. Elysen shot a glance at Raes, who lay still and unconscious on the floor just a step away.

"We have to go," Elysen whispered. "We have to go now."

She pulled on Petyr's arm. He groaned again.

"Get up," she growled.

Petyr groaned again, and then rolled to his side. He pushed upward with his arms. His head hung forward, dark wet hair falling toward the ground like tangled moss hanging from the trees. Elysen reached around his chest and together they brought him to his feet.

"I'm no good to you anymore," he said. Pain and sadness filled his voice. "Leave me and get out of here."

"I can't do that. I promised a little girl that I would bring her father home to her."

"You can't."

"I have to."

"They'll follow us."

Elysen looked back toward Raes' fallen body. She could not help but take one last look at Arador, his boyish face stained with blood, the life and energy drained from it.

"We have no choice. I made a promise."

She pulled on his arm and dragged him to the doorway. She peered outside. She glanced around and then pulled Petyr out into the hazy afternoon.

"If there is some greater power than Thorsen," she said quietly, "I pray that it may protect us now."

Petyr stumbled and staggered as Elysen drug him across the open meadow, ignoring the safety and cover of the trees in favor of a straight route across the meadow.

"Where are we going?" Petyr asked. He tripped and fell, and Elysen helped him to his feet again.

"We hid my horse in the trees beyond the camp," she said.

"How do you know he's still there?" Petyr asked.

"I don't. I'm just...hoping."

They came to the woods without running into any guards. Elysen found Temper tethered where they had left him.

"Thank you, Arador," she whispered.

She helped Petyr mount and then led the horse away from the meadow, away from the encampment. They picked their way through the sparse pine forest, traveling uphill, until they came to a high ridge where Elysen could see the valley of the Ryn Gladde below. To the west, she could make out the towering cliffs that led to the high plateau of Lake Orman.

They traveled along the ridge, staying away from the river, and came to the cliffs as evening fell. Petyr rocked unsteadily on Temper's back. When they stopped, he nearly crushed Elysen as she helped him dismount. They both landed on the ground and lay there, exhausted. Temper snorted and shook his head. He pawed the dusty ground with his front hooves and waited impatiently for Elysen. She sighed, rolled over and checked on Petyr, who groaned but still breathed. She staggered back to her feet. She had been walking all day, and could barely stand now. She unhitched Temper's bridle and dropped it on the ground.

"This is where we say good-bye, I think," she said between ragged breaths. "I don't expect to ever come this way again, old boy."

She patted the big black stallion on the neck and then hugged him.

"Go free now, old friend," she said. "Maybe we'll meet in the sky one day, or in J'Halla."

Somewhere better than this, she thought.

She laughed and placed her hands just below his ears. She let her head fall forward against his, butting her forehead against his broad face. She winced, laughing and crying at the same time.

"Go boy, go," she said. "Before I lose my mind along with everything else. Go."

She rocked her face back and forth against his, holding him close to her. Then she stroked his neck and let her hands find their way along his back to his flanks. She pushed him, and then slapped him.

"Get," she snapped. She hit his flank again with the palm of her hand. "Get going. Get out of here. Go home."

She picked up a stick and whipped him with it. He snorted and snarled and pranced away, stopping just a few paces away. Elysen picked up a few small sticks and threw them at him. They hit his flanks, but he just quivered and swished at them with his tail as if they were annoying little flies. Elysen finally stood with her arms hanging limply at her sides. Temper turned and walked slowly away, stepping between the trees, the sounds of his footsteps becoming more and more indistinct, yet still audible long after she lost sight of him. Then, almost in a single moment, as if he had paused somewhere off in the distance, the sounds of snapping twigs stopped, and in that same moment, a final dash of heavy hooves on hard soil crept through the ground like a drumbeat. Then the quiet of the forest settled in again, with only a lonely bird whistling in the treetops. Elysen stood listening for a long time.

"Good-bye, old friend," she said.

A warrior feels no pain.

She watched the trees until the darkness of the forest turned into the gloom of night, and then she dropped onto the ground next to Petyr. She wrapped her arms around him and pulled her cloak over their bodies. An owl settled into a tree above them and cooed softly as they slept.

Fourteen

Elysen woke slowly. She struggled into a sitting position, and then fell back again. The gray light of dawn filtered through the trees, and the damp air left a chilling dew on Elysen's scalp. She retched, tried to throw up, but her empty stomach revolted and threw her into a series of heaving cramps. As they passed, she rolled over and pushed on Petyr's heavy body. He groaned. She fell back again and stared at the sky. She rested for a moment and then rolled onto her stomach and pushed up onto all fours.

"We have to get moving," she said.

"Just leave me here to die," he pleaded. "I can't go on."

"Get up," she said. She pushed again. "Your daughter is waiting for you. She needs you. Alive."

"I'm of no use to her now," he said.

"Yes, you are. Now get up. You're acting like a child yourself. Get up."

Elysen staggered to her feet and continued to tug on Petyr's arm. He pulled himself to his feet, hanging on Elysen for support. She nearly tipped over, but regained her footing. As she brought her head up, she nearly ran into a burly giant of a man with his hands on his hips. It took her a moment to realize who he was.

"Tell," she said.

"You look like you could use some help there," he said. "Where is your young friend?"

Elysen gave him a puzzled look.

"Air-door?" he said. "Or Air-dale? I didn't quite get his name, he was shaking so badly."

"Arador," she said. "He's dead."

Tell put his arm around Petyr and lifted him off Elysen's shoulders.

"It was you who helped him then," Elysen said. "What happened?"

They began to walk slowly toward the cliffs. Petyr's feet dragged and he stumbled as Tell carried him along.

"I have been tracking the Lord's Guard through the hills here ever since they burned Juro," Tell said.

"I heard about that," Elysen said.

Tell nodded. "They burned Juro and Metting. And Illenbrand." Tell paused for a moment and shuddered. "Anyway, I found your young friend standing in the woods with your horse, and just about scared the skin off him."

"He was alone when he found us," Elysen said.

"I took out two of the Guard and drew two more off into the woods. That was our plan."

"And what happened to the two you drew off?"

"No one will be going back to the Keep," Tell said, smiling. In her mind, Elysen saw Raes laying there on the floor, breathing heavily, and her heart sank in her chest. She closed her eyes for just a moment and spoke to her memory of him.

I'll never forgive you, she said.

"We're going to have to climb here," Elysen said as they reached the steepest part of the trail. She led the way with Petyr groping and clawing his way behind her and Tell pushing him from behind. The ground gradually became less steep, finally leveling out.

They walked until Petyr's stumbling brought him to the ground, then rested where he fell until with Elysen's urging and Tell's support, he found his feet again. They continued in this way, stopping more and more often, until they came to the edge of Lake Orman. Elysen splashed water on her face and drank deeply. Petyr rested on the ground as Tell stood over him. As they sat there on the rocky shore of the clear, calm lake, two men approached. Petyr heard them coming.

"I hope these are friends," he said. "I have no strength or heart left to fight."

"I know these men," Elysen said. "The old one is Jaramis. The other is a friend as well. I can't remember his name."

"The big boy is Raymond," Tell said.

Gravel crunched under the men's boots as they stopped a few paces from where Elysen sat. Petyr sprawled on the ground next to her, his bloody face still wrapped in the fabric of her blouse, turned upward toward the overcast sky.

"Tell," Jaramis said, nodding. The lines in his face held deep concern as he knelt to the ground. He placed his hand on Elysen's back and put a goatskin flask to her lips. She took a sip of something that burned her throat like fire.

"What happened," Jaramis asked.

"I have Joli's father," Elysen said. The words caught in her throat and felt false and empty as she realized the stark reality, that she had traded Jaramis' son for Petyr. She wanted to pull the sounds from the air and throw them away.

"You have brought destruction upon us all," Raymond said. His voice growled in his chest, and his eyes were bright and hot.

"Enough," Jaramis snapped. He stepped forward and offered his hand to Tell. "Peace be with you, Tell."

Tell took his arm and gripped it. He gave Jaramis a sad smile.

"Peace will not be with us in this lifetime, old man," he said. "But may we find it in J'Halla."

"Come," Jaramis said. He pulled Elysen to her feet. "We will help you the rest of the way. Where is young Arador? Was he with you? We have not seen him today."

Elysen shook her head. "I'm sorry Jaramis, he's dead. He died in the fight to free Petyr."

"He died a warrior's death," Petyr whispered.

Jaramis sat down on a nearby log. His body landed as if his legs had been cut off.

"Arador," he said. He stared at the ground. His hands hung limp in his lap and his shoulders slumped forward. "He was my only child," he said.

"I'm sorry," Elysen said. "I should never have let him come with me." She reached out toward him, wanting to touch him, to comfort him, but her hand paused in mid-air.

A warrior feels no pain, she thought. And yet, her heart felt ready to burst.

Jaramis raised his head slowly and looked up at Elysen. His eyes filled with tears, but his voice held steady.

"He followed you of his own accord. You say he died as a fighter?"

"Yes. He took human life, against his own beliefs, in order to save me."

Jaramis bit his lower lip and hung his head again, shaking it slowly back and forth.

"The dark times begin already, when our boys become fighters and kill people and then are killed themselves."

Raymond's face softened. He knelt down and put his hand on Jaramis' shoulder.

"We can grieve together my friend. But our time is short here, we have to return to the village, and then to the lower lands, where we can mourn Arador's passing in safer surroundings."

Jaramis put his hand in the air. It hung there in front of him for a moment and then dropped back to his lap.

"I will mourn here," Jaramis said. "Leave me."

Elysen dropped to her knees in front of Jaramis.

"I knew Arador for only a short time," she whispered. "But I had already grown to love him like a brother. He was kind and gentle. A good boy. I will miss him too."

Jaramis put his hands on Elysen's cheeks and tipped her head back so that he could look into her eyes. His brow furrowed with concern and pain, but a softness surrounded his mouth, almost like a smile. His gentle touch stirred something deep within her, and she felt tears forming in her eyes.

"How can you ever forgive me for the death of your son?" she asked.

Jaramis sighed. "Life and death are part of our existence here, m'lady. Please don't take responsibility for Arador's death. You don't yet know all there is to know about his life. There is a greater purpose in all things, even in death."

Tell touched Elysen on the shoulder and then helped her to her feet. She staggered, so he picked her up and held her in his arms like a baby. She wiped her eyes with the back of her hand and squeezed them shut. Tell looked away, pretending not to notice her tears.

"You are as light as a feather," he said. "I can carry you, but your friend must walk. He is much too big for either of us to carry."

Raymond leaned over and put his hand out to Petyr.

"How is my daughter?" Petyr asked.

"She calls for you," Raymond said. With that, Petyr took the big man's hand and pulled himself to his feet. Raymond staggered under Petyr's weight.

"Jaramis," Raymond said. "I need your help."

Jaramis looked up. He stood slowly, reluctantly, but took his place next to Raymond. They carried Petyr between them, his arms slung over their backs.

As they came within sight of the encampment, Elysen arched her back and squirmed out of Tell's arms.

"Let me walk," she said.

Tell helped her get her feet back on the ground. She leaned against him as she walked. She watched the ground pass by under her feet, moving slowly, a procession of brown pine needles, strewn about in a thick, pungent carpet, covered with sticks, punctuated by an occasional straggling bush, most with broad, dark-green waxy leaves. She walked in silence, unable to speak.

Jaramis and Raymond led them to the hut where Joli slept. Rachael joined them and dismissed the woman that had been caring for Joli. The men parted company with Elysen in silence, Jaramis looking back once, his face a sad reflection of Elysen's. Rachael touched Petyr's arm lightly.

"Wake her," she urged quietly. "She needs to hear your voice."

Petyr leaned over the child and touched her forehead with his rough fingers. The girl stirred, and then sighed.

"Papa?" she asked. Her voice lilted soft and quiet, as if it floated on a breeze from some remote part of the Vyr.

"Yes, Joli," Petyr said. "I'm here."

"Oh, papa," she said. "I am so happy to see you." Her lashes fluttered like the wings of tiny butterflies as she tried to open her eyes. "Where is Lady'lysen?"

"She is here as well."

Joli's tired eyes opened a bit wider. She reached up and touched the dirty bandage around Petyr's face.

"What happened to you?" she asked. "Are you hurt?"

"Just a bit," he said.

Elysen came over and knelt by the girl's makeshift bed.

"Oh," Joli said. "You are hurt too."

She reached out to touch Elysen's bloody cheek. Elysen stopped Joli's hand, but touched her cheek with her own hand and winced as her fingers traced the ragged tear that ran from just below her eye to the back of her jaw. The side of her face felt swollen and soft except for a hard lump along her jaw line.

"I must look a fright," Elysen said.

"Yes," Joli replied.

She reached up for Petyr and he slipped his arms around her neck. She clung to him and squeezed her eyes shut.

"Thank you for coming home," she said. "I missed you so much."

"I missed you too," he said. They hugged as Rachael and Elysen sat watching and waiting in patient silence.

"Will you sleep here next to me?" Joli asked.

"Of course I will," Petyr said.

Rachael came over. She leaned over the little girl and stroked her hair.

"Your father will be back shortly," she said. "First we will have someone tend to his wounds, and then he can return here and we'll let him sleep next to you."

"Please don't go," Joli said. Tears welled up in her eyes, and she reached for her father again.

"Just for a few moments," he said. A small, withered woman wrapped in a thick fur cloak slipped into the tent and helped Petyr to his feet.

"Joryn is our village healer," Rachael said, motioning toward the elderly woman that pulled Petyr away from them. "She will help your man as best she can, then she will return for you."

Rachael sat watching Joli, stroking the little girl's hair, wiping the tears from her cheek with the back of her finger. Elysen wrapped a blanket around her shoulder and sat nearby. Her eyes slowly closed. A voice woke her. Joryn squatted on the floor next to Elysen, speaking to Rachael.

"His wounds are deep," she said. She turned to Elysen. "Ah, you're alive. Let me have a look at you."

She pushed on Elysen, gently forcing her onto a woolen mat. Joryn touched the jagged tear in Elysen's face with her tiny, knobby fingers.

"This will have to be cleaned out," Joryn said. "And we will have to lace it up."

Elysen tried to sit up to protest, but Joryn and Rachael both placed their hands on her chest and gently pushed her back down. Joryn began examining Elysen's body inch by inch, beginning with her scalp.

"Curious," she said. "So many scars for such a beautiful young woman. You've done some fighting."

Elysen nodded. Joryn closed her eyes and continued her examination. Her fingers traced lightly across Elysen's temples, down each side of her cheeks, along her neck to her shoulders, and down her arms. She then returned her hands to Elysen's shoulders and let them follow the edges of her cloak to the small wooden button that held it closed. Joryn released the clasp and let the cloak fall open, revealing Elysen's chest. Joryn touched each rib lightly, nodding and humming as she progressed downward. Elysen shuddered as the old woman's fingers danced across her belly. Joryn pulled away suddenly, a look of surprise and confusion on her face.

"What is it?" Rachael asked. Elysen's eyes watched the women's faces.

"A wound." Joryn paused for a moment, and then touched Elysen's skin again. "And a new life."

Elysen tried to close her cloak and sit up again, but Rachael and Joryn held her back.

"Lay still, child," Joryn chided.

"A baby?" Rachael asked.

Joryn nodded. "This life is very new. Unformed. Faint, but strong." Joryn smiled and nodded. "A boy, I think."

"Impossible," Elysen said.

"Not at all," Joryn replied. "A boy is just as likely as a girl."

"No, neither is likely. It is forbidden."

Elysen's mind raced with thoughts, none of them making any sense. Yergen, the law, and surprisingly, she thought of Raes.

"Forbidden or not, you are with child," Joryn said.

"It can't be," Elysen insisted.

Her gut tightened and every fiber of her body burned with rage. She could still feel the trap-like grip of Yergen's hands on her arms and she could taste the coal dust and the oak and feel the cold, damp stones of the Keep under her feet. She felt fear and hate and anger welling up inside her throat, and something even worse. A sense of being cheated.

I was never meant to be happy, she realized. The thought left her empty and hollow.

Joryn sensed her distress and put her hand on Elysen's forehead. She spoke softly.

"Be at peace for a while. This is a time for rest." Elysen took a deep breath and clenched her fists.

The healer turned to Rachael. "There is a problem," she said.

Rachael's face became serious and her eyes searched Joryn's.

Joryn went on. "The wound. It threatens the child's ability to thrive. There is some kind of foreign object. We have to exorcise it."

"Will we have time?" Rachael asked.

Joryn shrugged. "Time is not my specialty," she said. "I am a healer. I cannot tell if it will take a day or a season to heal. I do know that if we don't remove this object, the baby will die."

Elysen's arms relaxed slightly. "Maybe it is the baby's fate to die," she said.

Joryn shrugged.

"Your baby's fate is not for us to know. I think that our task at hand is to heal your wounds." She tilted her head and smiled. "I have no worries about this baby. I feel his song. It is very strong. He will be a strong boy."

"You cannot know he is a boy," Elysen said.

"I know it as well as you do, young lady. You have seen this boy in your dreams."

"How do you know that?"

"Dreams are part of healing. I sense your dreams as I help you heal."

Elysen lay quietly for a while. At first, she boiled like a pot of water on the fire and her head filled with voices, chattering senselessly. She shook them away and decided to focus on something else.

A boy, she thought.

"What else do you know about this baby?" Elysen asked.

"I know he will bring you great joy, and that you will endure much for him."

"Are you a prophetess now, too?" Rachael asked.

Joryn laughed.

"No, Rachael," she said. "I just know mothers and children. Mothers suffer greatly for their children. And children always bring their mothers great joy."

Joryn touched Elysen's forehead and smiled.

"Now tell me of your dreams," she said. "And then tell me how you got your wound. You must be in great pain."

"Yes."

"You bear it like a warrior."

"Thank you," Elysen said.

"It was not meant as a compliment, m'lady," Joryn said. "You hide your pain, instead of facing it."

"There is nothing I can do about my pain. I bear it silently so that others will not have to listen to me complain."

Joryn smiled at her and stroked the top of her head.

"You're avoiding my request by bantering like this. Let me hear about your dream now."

With that, Joryn became silent, waiting patiently for Elysen to speak next.

"I try not to dream anymore," Elysen said.

Joryn touched her again.

"You're among friends here," she said. "Your dreams are welcomed here. They are a treasure to us. No good to you alone unless you share them with those who love you."

"Love? What is that?" Elysen asked.

Joryn smiled at Rachael, and Rachael nodded.

"Love is how one spirit talks to another," Rachael said. "Dreams are one way that we hear love. Not the dreams of sleep, but the dreams that tug at your chest, the dreams that drive you forward, the dreams that bring peace to you in the waking hours."

Elysen frowned, unable to make any sense of what Rachael said.

Waking dreams, she thought. She reached down and touched her belly.

"I used to dream about a child," she said. "I would stand on the towers of the keep, holding him. I could feel him in my arms. It was that real."

"You don't dream of this child any more?" Joryn asked.

"The dream became a nightmare, torturing me."

"How was it torture?" Rachael asked.

"It is forbidden for me to have a child."

"Why?" Joryn asked.

Elysen frowned again.

"It is Thorsen's Law," she said. "Any female child of a Lord must be drowned in the icy waters of Turoc's Cauldron."

"And yet you were spared," Joryn said.

"I was still born," Elysen said. "The ritual of forbearance revived me. And they say that an evil spirit consumed the Soel just before I was born."

"And they let you live?"

Elysen nodded. "My father was the Lord of all things. His will was stronger than the Law. He decided that I would live, and so I did. He protected me. So did Owen."

"We were told that you killed your uncle," Rachael said.

"I would never do that," Elysen replied.

"And yet, there is a dangerous and violent place in you," Joryn said.

Elysen locked her green eyes onto Joryn.

"There is a place in me that survives," she said.

"Perhaps you have some great purpose in this world," Rachael said.

Joryn leaned back against the pile of pillows. She allowed a moment of silence before she spoke again.

"And so you dreamed of a child," she said. "A boy."

Elysen nodded. Joryn pressed on.

"And you found yourself smiling, your pain momentarily forgotten."

"Yes. Sometimes the dream is so vivid that I can feel his tiny hand in mine. Then I remember that it cannot be for me, and I turn my mind away from such thoughts. Yet they torture me every day."

"So," Joryn said. "The dream persists, even in your darkness."

Elysen ignored the comment.

"My dream now is to kill Yergen," she said. "I have devised ways to kill him, slowly, quickly, too many to count."

"You have a baby to think of now," Joryn reminded her.

Elysen closed her eyes.

"If there is a baby, it is Yergen's," she said. Her hands still rested gently on her bare abdomen. She glanced down at them and then closed her eyes again.

Joryn did not appear to be surprised.

"In any case," she said. "We have to remove the shard from your belly without harming the baby. That is our task now."

"How?" Elysen asked.

Joryn reached over and touched Elysen just above her hip.

"We will have to cut here," she said. "Then extract the object as gently as possible." She paused. "The pain will be great."

"And what if this cutting kills me?"

Joryn closed her eyes and pursed her lips.

"Your fate, like ours, is in the hands of a power greater than us." She opened her eyes and smiled as she patted Elysen's belly. "Some higher power has been watching over you for a long time my girl. I'm not worried."

"The power of Thorsen," Elysen said.

Joryn shook her head. "Thorsen was just a man, with no more power than any other."

"But I saw his power," Elysen said. "Spells hidden deep beneath Sunder Keep. The spells he used to create the Vyr, and the mountains and the Rift, and the ice and the southern seas."

Joryn and Rachael exchanged worried glances.

"You saw the spells of Thorsen?" Rachael asked. "What did these spells look like?"

Elysen made a shape with her hands. "About this size," she said. "Many colors. They were filled with white leaves that fluttered in the water like sheets in the wind. On the leaves were spells. Too many to even imagine."

Rachael stood up. Joryn nodded. Rachael slipped out the door and returned a few moments later with a small bundle in her arms. She placed the greasy cloth in Elysen's lap. Elysen peeled back the folds of fabric and gasped.

"Were the objects like this one?" Rachael asked.

Elysen picked it up and opened it. "Similar," she said. She gently touched the pages.

"This is very ancient," Rachael said. "It is called a tome."

"It looks as if it is falling apart," Elysen said. "Yet the ones I saw in the labyrinth were fresh, and solid, not like this one."

"Time has decayed this spell, as it does all things," Joryn said. She reached over and closed the tome before she wrapped it again in the cloth. "We have to be very careful with this," she said.

"All the knowledge that our people possessed in the time before Thorsen is in those tomes," Rachael said.

"Can you understand the spells?" Elysen asked.

Rachael shook her head and her eyes shifted toward Joryn again.

Elysen whispered to herself. "All of the knowledge and power of Thorsen."

"There is knowledge there that can heal, as well as destroy," Joryn said.

Elysen's eyes were blank, as if she were staring inside her own mind.

"We have spoken of many things this night," Joryn said. "And our heads are full. We must meditate on these things. But first, we have to stitch up that tear on your face."

Joryn pulled out a thin bone needle and threaded it with a thread of rare silk. Rachael brought a cup of hot water and a clean cloth and Joryn dipped the cloth in the water.

"This will hurt," she said.

Elysen nodded. "Just do it," she said.

Joryn cleaned the jagged wound on Elysen's face and stitched it closed, stabbing and pulling, shooting pain through her jaw. She occupied her mind with thoughts of the spells of the Keep.

The power to heal, or destroy.

"Time is short now," Joryn said as she finished. "Rachael, gather together your things. We will go out in the woods, away from Lake Orman. An attack from the Lord's Guard is imminent."

Joryn placed a clean cloth over Elysen's wound and then placed Elysen's hand on the cloth to hold it against her jaw.

"Yergen is searching for her," Joryn said.

The voices in Elysen's head all spoke clearly, all at once, as if they suddenly shared one common thought. Elysen's eyes opened wide.

"My child will be the true Lord," she said.

Rachael nodded.

"That is all the more reason for him to kill both of you," she said.

Fifteen

Rachael filled two packs with smoked meat, hard cheese and bread. Raymond came in leading Petyr. He looked a bit better, and seemed solid on his feet. He picked up his daughter. Joli draped her head over her father's shoulder, clinging to him tightly.

"Where is Tell?" Elysen asked. "And Jaramis?"

"Tell left in the night," Raymond said. "And Jaramis is nowhere to be found." He paused for a moment, looking lost and concerned. "Where will you go?" he asked.

"There's a cave that hunters use for shelter at the base of Broken Top," Joryn said. "We'll go there."

She picked up a pack that appeared far too heavy for her slight frame.

"Let me take that," Elysen said.

"Your burdens are heavy enough," Rachael said. She hugged Raymond and held him at arm's length, staring into his eyes. "Get as many as you can to safety," she told him. "And get yourself away from here as well. Don't stay and wait for the Lord's Guard to find you. Let them instead find empty homes with cold hearths."

Raymond walked with them to the edge of camp. Dark clouds rolled in overhead, bringing a cold mist with them. Joryn and Rachael took turns hugging him before they began hiking northward, away from the camp. Elysen followed, leading Petyr who still carried Joli. Raymond stood and watched them go until they crested a hill that led into the forest.

After a short time, Petyr's pace slowed, as if great weights chained his legs, and his head hung forward. Joryn stopped and wrapped a clean bandage around his face. She pulled his hood over the top of his head so that only his chin and mouth showed from under the brown cloth that concealed his head.

"Does it hurt much?" Elysen asked.

Petyr shook his head. "Joryn gave me herbs to chew on. They seem to ease the pain."

"Have you been able to sleep? You seem so tired."

Petyr shook his head. His mouth twisted with pain.

They plodded onward along a game trail that rose steadily. The trees grew scrawny and twisted as they neared the timberline, and then became no more than gnarled bushes, and then they passed one last pine, bent and twisted by the ever-present wind.

Once above the tree line, they traversed along a high slope, picking their way along a rocky path. Far below, they could see the village, nestled against the shore of the serene black waters of Lake Orman. The clouds became a high haze, and the afternoon emerged crisp and clear of rain. They could see out beyond the lake, to the rolling, forested hills and ridges that spread out from below the cliffs to the far horizon.

"It's hard to believe that we've come this far," Elysen said quietly.

"Look," Joryn said, pointing out across the plateau toward the other side of the lake. A group of men followed the shoreline, moving quickly, approaching the encampment like a column of marching ants.

"They haven't had time to escape," Rachael said.

"Keep moving," Rachael said. "If they see us, they might follow."

Elysen pressed her lips tightly together and balled up her fists. Petyr stood with his head hanging down. Joli stared at Elysen. Rachael and Joryn began walking again. Elysen followed, looking back over her shoulder each time she took a few steps. They crested a small rise and dropped into a rocky draw. The walls of the ravine hid them from view.

"We follow this now," Rachael said. "Above us, there is a cave that cuts through a wall of rock. Then we will be at the base of Broken Top. We will camp there, and hopefully we will be safe enough there to perform our healing ritual for you."

"After that, then what?" Elysen asked.

"Then we'll see. One day at a time is all we can do right now."

They followed the ravine for most of the morning, emerging along a game trail onto a rocky slope. Under the overhangs of some of the larger rocks, patches of ice still clung tenaciously to the ground, waiting for the renewal soon to come. The winds of life, cold and harsh, blew across the open ground, swirling particles of grainy dust into their faces. Elysen felt the dirt on her tongue and teeth.

Further on, the slope above them turned into a cliff. They followed the game trail toward an opening in the cliff face where a dark pit, like an empty eye socket, stared down at them. Joli shivered and clung even more tightly to her father, who walked slowly, powered by some weary force that defied death but did not rise to the level of life. Elysen kept her face hidden under her hood. Tears streamed from her eyes and coursed down her cheeks. She clenched her fists and tucked them deep within the folds of her sleeves. Her dry, chapped lips would not close against the wind, and she could taste the grit of the mountain as it ground between her teeth.

The base of the cliff forced them to climb a treacherous slope. Petyr shifted Joli onto his back so that he could feel his way along with his hands. She clung there weakly, slipping often. Petyr stopped, reached back with one hand, and pushed her up higher onto his back. Rachael and Elysen steadied Petyr as best they could from behind. Elysen tried to keep her head low and her face covered, but the dirty wind blew her hood back. Rachael glanced at her, saw the anguish in her face, and closed her eyes for a moment, muttering a prayer. Then they pushed on, up, over the lip of the cave floor, and came to rest in the mouth of the hole. A trickle of moisture wept over the edge of the cave and soaked into the dusty gravel below. Behind them, the darkness smelled wet and stale. Rachael and Joryn dropped their packs and sat down. Petyr put Joli in his lap and cradled her there. Elysen sat with her back against the wall, panting.

"This is it," Joryn said, gasping. "We will pass through here and camp on the other side." Her chest heaved and her eyes almost closed.

"We're running out of breath," Elysen said. "Can you feel it? We must be nearing the end of the world."

Joryn and Rachael both nodded.

"The hunters tell us that we will get used to it soon," Rachael said. "They see wapiti and large deer up here, as well as goats and eagles. Where the game goes, so can we."

They gathered up their gear and entered the darkness. After several paces, their eyes adjusted to the lack of light. Rocks and boulders littered the tunnel. It rose and fell slightly, but maintained a fairly straight course toward the light at the other side.

They emerged into a sheltered ravine that led toward Broken Top's craggy peak. The old mountain towered into the shifting clouds, allowing them only an occasional glance at sharp spires and towers of snow-crusted rock. Between the spikes and peaks, great sheets of ice had gouged horseshoe canyons, and now ground slowly toward the base of the giant mountain, carrying bits of it away as they crawled forward on their heavy bellies. Elysen stared upward, unable to pull away from the sight so frozen in time and yet so alive and full of movement.

"You can see it, can't you?" Rachael asked. Joryn unrolled several woolen blankets. She placed one around Petyr's shoulders.

"See what?" Elysen asked, still staring upward.

"The mountain. The way it moves. The life within it."

Elysen nodded.

"Can we risk a fire?" Joryn asked. "The girl and her father are in need of warmth." She fed Petyr a bit of jerky. He chewed solemnly. Joli was invisible, draped within his blanket, held tight against his body.

Rachael shook her head.

"No," she said. "We dare not."

Joryn came over to where they stood and glanced at Elysen, then sighed and breathed deeply through her nose.

"Petyr has no life left in him," she said. She took another quick glance at Elysen, but continued. "I don't know what it is that keeps him going."

"The little girl," Rachael said.

Joryn nodded in agreement.

"His love for her is so great, that it defies death. His body died days ago, yet his heart goes on as long as she does. It is hope that keeps him alive now."

"And his love for Elysen," Rachael said.

Elysen turned away from them and wandered off a few steps.

His love for me?

She knelt down and placed her hands on her knees. She dropped her chin against her chest and stared at the barren ground. Between her legs, struggling for purchase on rocky ground devoid of soil, a tiny white wildflower bloomed. Elysen stared at it as Rachael and Joryn talked softly together.

"We need to tend to Elysen," Rachael said.

"I know," Joryn said. She sighed again, and then looked at Elysen. "I am trying to avoid what must be done."

"Can we do anything for Petyr?" Rachael asked.

Joryn shook her head. Elysen pretended not to listen, concentrating on the strange flower that bloomed against all logic.

"We should do it now," Rachael said. "While we still have some light. We'll be safe here for tonight. If we don't freeze to death."

Joryn closed her eyes and took Rachael's hands.

"There is power in this mountain," she said. "It will give us strength and guidance in this task we do here today."

"And so it is," Rachael added.

"A fire would be helpful," Joryn said.

"Very well then," Rachael said. "We'll have a fire."

Joryn unbundled the sticks she had collected along the way and struck a fire with her flint. The gnarled, stringy sticks ignited well, and the fire produced very little smoke. Joryn put a blanket on the ground next to the fire for Elysen. Rachael moved Petyr and Joli closer to the flames and peeked under the blanket.

"She's asleep," Rachael said. "Now is the time."

"Give me your knife," Joryn said.

Elysen slipped Raes' knife from its sheath. She turned it around, holding the stone blade between her fingers. Joryn grasped the hilt and Elysen let go slowly. Rachael took the sheath and Elysen settled down onto the blanket with her arms at her sides. Above her, a small cloud of ice twisted in the wind.

"Arms up," Joryn said.

Elysen obeyed, stretching her long, thin arms above her head. Rachael crouched down and bound her wrists together. Elysen began to struggle, but Joryn touched her forehead and soothed her.

"Everything will be fine," she said. "I know this is frightening. Just try to focus on the baby inside you. We will take care of the rest."

"Just what is it that you intend to do?" Elysen asked.

"There is a piece of the broadhead still lodged within your belly," Joryn said. "I think it is close to your womb. But your body is strong, and it repels the object."

Joryn opened Elysen's cloak and unlaced the front of her leather breeches, exposing her white belly to the cold air. Joryn closed her eyes and touched Elysen just above the pelvic bone. Elysen shivered.

"Left alone, this object might come out on its own. But it endangers the life within you. We have to remove it now."

Joryn's fingers explored Elysen's skin. Her fingers wandered, moving like spiders, and then they stopped. She pushed down lightly. Elysen sucked in air.

"Does that hurt?" Joryn asked.

"Yes," Elysen whispered.

Rachael slipped the hard leather sheath between Elysen's teeth. Joryn hefted Raes' knife in her hand.

"This blade has seen much use," she said. She closed her eyes. "It has done much harm in the hands of man. But some healing too. Let us use it now for healing, and hope that it never takes a human life again."

Joryn sat astride Elysen's legs and sliced her belly with a single, deft stroke. Elysen sucked in air, her eyes wide. She bit down on the hard leather. Joryn waited for a moment, staring into the wound, still fresh and gray. Within moments, the red blood began to bubble out. Joryn set the blade on the ground beside Elysen and poised her hand above Elysen's pelvis, then reached down quickly, slipping two fingers into the gaping wound. Elysen screamed, the sheath lying useless in her open mouth. The sound echoed off the rock walls and bounded among the boulders and outcroppings. An eagle screamed back at her and flew away, cursing them. Just as quickly as her hand had descended, Joryn pulled her fingers away. She opened her hand, revealing a thin, sharp shard of obsidian that dripped with wet blood. Elysen gasped with pain. Joryn dropped the shard on the ground and pressed a folded cloth against the wound.

"She will not be able to travel for many days," Joryn announced. "The object was bigger than I thought. She will need to rest now."

Elysen fell into a silent agony. Petyr hugged Joli's still form and rocked back and forth.

Joryn tended to Elysen through the night and all the next day. Rachael descended back to the tree line several times, each time bringing back a large bundle of twisted sticks tied to her back. She kept the fire fed with the driest wood, and left the rest near the flames to dry. The fire smelled pungent, but the smoke dissipated rapidly.

"I can smell it sometimes from the other side," Rachael told Joryn between forays. "But the smoke clears before it reaches the top of the ravine. I think we are safe enough."

"Even so," Joryn reminded her. "Keep a watchful eye for the guardsmen. They will be hunting Elysen. I doubt if they will just give up and go home empty handed."

"How is she?" Rachael asked.

"She has a fever," Joryn replied. "And she is weak. Very weak."

Joryn wiped Elysen's lips with a small chunk of snow that had long ago frozen into a granular piece of white ice. Rachael gathered several large chunks of such ice from patches that lay all around them, and melted them one by one in a clay pot. She added the last few leeks, small potatoes and jerked beef from her pack. It made a weak stew. Petyr ate very little. Joryn made Joli drink broth.

That night, it became bitterly cold. Elysen awoke with a shriek. Joryn calmed her. Joli cried again, but it was a weak, sobbing cry, without hope, without strength.

"Save them," Elysen whispered to Joryn. "It will be my greatest grief if they should die up here on this cold mountain. Let it take me, but spare them."

Joryn shushed her and stroked her forehead. Elysen dozed for a while, and then awoke again, calling out for Petyr. Joryn tried to calm her again, but she tossed her head back and forth like an angry child.

"Rachael," Joryn said, shaking her friend to wakefulness. "Help me."

Together, they managed to get Petyr moved over next to Elysen. He had been sitting up holding Joli for two days, and laying down now clearly caused him discomfort, but even without his sight, he could sense the calming effect his presence had on Elysen. The two women placed Joli between Petyr and Elysen. Rachael stoked the fire while Joryn rocked back and forth and sang softly. She sang sounds, rather than words, in a haunting tune that carried rhythms of sadness and courage. Rachel listened with her eyes closed, rocking in cadence with Joryn.

Elysen stirred, hearing the song.

"What is that song?" she asked.

"Go back to sleep," Joryn said softly, with a gentle voice.

"Please tell me," Elysen mumbled.

Joryn continued to sing for a moment, and then paused.

"I am singing to the baby, singing for him to be strong and patient, to help you heal, to be resilient while your body mends."

"I feel it," Elysen said.

"The baby?"

"No, the song."

"Ah, yes," Joryn said. "The song of the baby's spirit. We believe that every person has a song. Before we come to this world, we know that song perfectly. It is the song of our spirit. It sings of our strengths, our gifts, and our goodness. By singing the spirit's song, we remember its strength, and it is brought into harmony with the world."

"Do you know my song?" Elysen asked.

"I'm sorry," Joryn said. "I am not a spirit-singer. But this one is strong. Even I can hear it and can sing it. He brings a special gift to our world."

She smiled, but an underlying sadness in her expression tainted the joyful outward appearance.

"You have to sleep now," she said.

Elysen refused to fall back asleep.

"Tell me more of the songs," she insisted.

Joryn smiled and glanced at Rachael. Rachael smiled back and nodded.

Joryn leaned forward slightly.

"Your mother was the greatest spirit singer we ever met," she said. "She came to us from the lands of never-ending ice. She could sense the giftedness of every child in the village. She was a wonderful blessing to us all."

"I never knew my mother," Elysen said. "Do you think she knew my song?"

"She knew of your song long before you were born," Rachael said.

"Did she share it with you?" Elysen asked.

"No. I wish she had. We could use it now, and please know that we would be singing it with all of our hearts for you right now if we knew it."

A tear rolled down Rachael's cheek. Elysen reached up and touched it. She studied the end of her finger as it glistened in the firelight.

"I am happy now," Elysen said, but she frowned. "I'm ready to die. This place. This is the last place I will ever be."

Rachael shook her head.

"You have to go on," she said. "No matter what. Remember the child that grows within you."

"What kind of world is this to bring a child into?" she asked. "What right do I have to bring a child into this world?"

"Your child's spirit cries out to you, to come into the world. What right do you have to deny him?"

"But I am so tired," Elysen mumbled. Her eyes closed. Neither woman answered her, and she did not speak again that night.

Another day and night passed. Petyr stayed next to Elysen and several times during the night she woke and stroked his head, reaching across Joli who barely stirred. During the blackest part of the night, with only the dying embers of the fire giving light, Elysen found her breath coming in ragged gasps. She touched Petyr again. The rhythm of his breathing calmed her, even though it sounded ragged and shallow.

The next morning, she awoke to a light, dry snow that floated into the ravine like finely ground flour. A gust of wind swept through, swirling the powdery ice into a frenzied dance. Joryn sat huddled in a blanket with only her arms sticking out, trying to coax the fire back to life.

Elysen reached over to touch Petyr. She stopped when she heard his breath and saw the frosty plume of his exhalation, but her arm brushed against Joli and she gasped, and then cried out for Joryn. Joryn pulled the little girl's body from under the blanket.

"She's dead," Joryn said. "There was nothing we could do. She would not eat. She was tired of living."

"But you're a healer," Elysen cried. "You healed me. Why does she die while I live? What kind of great power would let a little girl die while a monster like me lives?"

Joryn stroked Elysen's hair and tried to calm her down. In her other arm she held the stiff, cold body of the child.

"Your time on the Vyr is not done. This one's was. Her sweet spirit lives on in J'Halla."

Petyr moaned and struggled to sit up. Elysen helped him.

"Where is Joli?" he asked in a voice as quiet as the patter of mice in a tomb.

Joryn reluctantly placed the girl's body in his lap and wrapped a blanket around her. He rocked the dead child in his arms, his head tilted forward as if he could gaze at her once more.

"All is lost," Elysen mourned.

Rachael slipped into camp, landing like a cat next to the smoldering fire in a crouch. She threw rocks and dirt over the coals and looked up with wild, fearful eyes.

"The Lord's Guard is nearly upon us," she said. "I saw them marching along the tree line below us."

"Did they see you?" Joryn asked, glancing at Elysen.

"I don't think so," Rachael said. "But it's only a matter of time before they explore the cave."

Rachael glanced at Petyr and then her eyes dropped to the small bundle in his lap.

"Joli is dead," Joryn said.

Rachael closed her eyes and clasped her hands in silent prayer.

"You have to go with Elysen," Joryn said. "I will stay here with Petyr. He is in no condition to move."

"Neither is Elysen," Rachael reminded her.

"The guard is searching for Elysen. Petyr and I will just have to take our chances. As will Elysen."

"I won't leave Petyr," Elysen said.

"And I won't leave you," Rachael said to Joryn.

Joryn stood and so did Rachael. They faced each other squarely and Joryn took hold of Rachael's arms.

"You have to get Elysen to safety, somehow," Joryn said.

"Come with us then," Rachael begged. Joryn gazed at Petyr.

"I can't." she said. "Petyr and I have played our parts." She looked back into Rachael's eyes and hugged her. "Go now. And may a higher power watch over you."

Together, they helped Elysen to her feet. She staggered and swayed and then steadied herself on Rachael's shoulder. Joryn pressed Raes' knife, sheathed in its leather scabbard, into her hand. Elysen stared at the object for a moment, as if she did not remember it. She frowned and tucked it into her belt, behind her back. She found Raes' pouch, still tied there to her belt. She loosened it with her fingers and held it in her hand, frowning at it. She opened it. Inside, she found a twisted strand of snow-white hair. She stared at it for a moment, and then stooped down and picked up the shard that still lay on the rocky ground next to her feet. She placed the shard in the pouch, and then took the small toy that Joli had given her and placed that in the pouch as well.

Rachael pulled on Elysen's arm.

"We have to go now," she said.

"Get up, Petyr," Elysen said. She tried to make it a demand, but her voice came out weak and awkward.

He shook his head slowly.

"I can't," he whispered. "Please go now."

"I won't leave you here," she said.

Joryn reached over and cut a handful of Petyr's hair with her own knife. She pushed the dark brown locks into Elysen's hand.

"Take this to remember him by. Add this to your things. But you have to go now, and go quickly, or all that we did is for nothing."

Elysen cried and reached out for Petyr, but Rachael pulled her away, along the ravine, away from the mouth of the canyon, upward into the snow. Elysen struggled, but Rachael prevailed. Elysen cried as she stumbled along, wincing in pain with every staggering step.

"You have to be strong now," Rachael said. "Your journey is just beginning."

"My journey, my life," she panted, "feels as if it just ended."

"I know," Rachael said. "I know."

Elysen tugged hard against the older woman's grip and tore free for a moment.

"I have to go back," she said.

"No," Rachael said. "We can't go back there. We have to keep moving."

Rachael grabbed her and hugged her. Elysen sobbed. They stood that way, with the snow now pelting against them like tiny spears of ice, while the world around them turned as white as Elysen's fine skin. She clutched Petyr's hair in her fist as if she were afraid that the cold wind would take it away. Rachael helped her pry the fine locks from her fingers and place them safely in the pouch with her other keepsakes.

"We must think of the future," Rachael said.

She paused for a moment.

"What will you name your baby?" she asked as they closed up the small bag and put their arms around each other. The wind almost screamed now, and Rachael's spoken words were just a whisper in Elysen's ear. Elysen shook her head and took Rachael's hand. Together, they began to feel their way along, blindly following an upward path with nothing but hope to guide them.

I have a baby, Elysen realized.

Suddenly, the cold became her enemy.

Sixteen

They hiked up and away from the hidden ravine, circling around the lower part of the peak. Just before dark, they found an outcropping of rock that provided a small amount of shelter from the wind that howled around them. Rachael shivered and her teeth chattered.

"I can't stop shivering," she said.

Elysen wrapped her arms around the older woman and hugged her close. They crouched behind the big, overhanging rock and waited.

"Where will we go?" Elysen asked.

Rachael shook her head.

"Maybe we made a mistake," she said. "Maybe we should have stayed in the ravine with Joryn and Petyr. What if they need us now?"

"You're delirious," Elysen told her. "We would have been captured or killed there. Your decision was the right one."

"Why do you say that now?" Rachael said. "You were the one against leaving."

Elysen shrugged. Her mind searched for the song within her.

"So, where will we go?" Rachael asked.

Her jaw quivered as she tried in vain to control the shivering that overtook her body. Elysen tried to cover Rachael even more, hug her even closer. The wind bit through their clothes, snaking through every tiny opening, sifting between layers of wool and leather until it found their bodies and sucked the heat away.

Elysen watched the swirling wind for a while and then spoke.

"We're nearly at the end of the world here," she said. "Maybe I'll go to the edge and throw myself off."

"No, no," Rachael begged. "Remember your child."

"I do my child no greater service than to spare him from this life of pain."

"Your child deserves his own chance at happiness, his own time to experience life. Don't take that away from him." Rachael struggled to talk. Her jaw trembled and her teeth clicked together frantically as her body fought to create warmth.

Elysen just stared out at the white storm.

"I'll throw myself into the void of nothingness. If some higher power wants this baby to live, it will deliver me from death and will place me on solid ground. If not, then I will fall forever into the darkness beyond the Vyr." She turned back to face Rachael. "You should go back to Joryn and Petyr. I'll take the rest of this journey alone."

"My love for you keeps me here with you," Rachael said.

"All this talk of love," Elysen said. "I don't understand it. To me, love is nothing but a black hole in my heart. Everyone I have ever loved has been taken from me."

"That black hole is not love. Your love for your mother, and your father, and Petyr and his daughter, and for Arador and for all the other people that have come into your life, even your cousin Yergen, that is the love that keeps you going. That gives you purpose."

Elysen shook her head.

"This love you talk about only gives me pain."

"Your pain and emptiness comes from your lack of faith." Rachael reached up and stroked Elysen's cheek. Her bare fingers were as cold as the icy air that swirled around them. "If you believe in nothing, then when your love seems to slip away from you, that is all that you have left, nothing."

"I believe in Thorsen," Elysen said.

"Do you believe that Thorsen is all there is?"

"I don't know. I guess I don't what to believe."

Rachael sighed and closed her eyes.

"You have to get back to the others now," Elysen urged.

"I have to rest first," Rachael said, closing her eyes. Her shivering had almost stopped.

"You can't rest, Rachael," Elysen whispered. "If you fall asleep, you'll die."

Rachael's lips parted in a slight smile.

"Everyone dies," she said. Her voice melted into the wind around them. "I've lived my life well," she whispered. "I'm ready to die."

Elysen held her close, but Rachael's body offered no warmth, and Elysen's offered little more. They rested for a while. The storm subsided. The snow stopped, and the clouds broke above them. Flowing white mists separated and merged, leaving holes of piercing blue. Crystals of frost formed on Elysen's cowl around her neck and mouth. She looked down at Rachael's face, pale, almost blue, her eyes closed. No breath came from her slightly parted lips. Elysen released the old woman, setting her rigid body gently on the ground.

"What do you say to one who has passed on?" Elysen asked her. "I know you must have some kind of song or chant."

She knelt next to Rachael's body and pondered for a while. Then she closed her eyes.

"Whatever is out there, whatever kind of power, please look after this woman. She was goodness in a world of darkness. To whatever afterlife she believed in and aspired to, I now commend her. May she rest now, forever, in peace."

She crouched for a moment longer, then stood and backed away for a few steps. The cold wind whipped. She sighed and stepped away, following nothing. Just walking, threading her way among the boulders, climbing ever upward.

Darkness came quickly. Elysen found a small cave and huddled under her cloak. Although she did not sleep, with the darkness, the cold seemed less bitter, the wind less painful. She felt as if the dark world waited for her to finish some task.

The darkness finally ended, as it always did. She began to walk again as soon as the Soel broke over the edge of the endless piles of cotton clouds that covered the world below. The piercing light chased the wispy, blowing mountain mists around Elysen's body like shrieking ghosts, waiting gleefully for her to join them; impatient, dancing around her, then gone, suddenly back again. Soon, gusts of wind filled the air with stinging whips of ice and sand. Elysen clambered among the boulders and rocky outcroppings, moving forward blindly. She shielded her eyes from the white glare around her by hiding under her hood. She stared only at the ground in front of her. High upon the rocky, unsheltered slopes of the mountain, even the snow could not stay put. It drifted in powdery, sloping piles on the leeward sides of the larger rocks, resting for a moment before the ever-changing wind grabbed it away again.

The air cleared and Elysen kept the bright light of the Soel to her back as she wandered along the rocky slopes, her black cloak barely warming even under the watchful glare of the white orb above her.

As time passed, the Soel moved west and then came to a point where she began to follow it as it proceeded toward the far side of the mountain, where the very end of the world awaited. Elysen clambered hand over hand over a steep slope and then walked upright along a plateau.

As she traveled further westward, the Soel stole behind the mountain, leaving her alone at the edge of a large glacial expanse of dirty ice. Behind her, Turoc rose, and she climbed the rolling frozen slope in front of her. As the light of day faded, the light from Turoc shone brilliant, silver and ghostly, and the mountain turned from rock to ice. Elysen kept moving slowly, jumping small crevasses that appeared before her as silent black rivers in the endless expanse of white. She headed as close to west as possible, following the vagaries of the ice, skirting around holes and larger cracks, glancing at Turoc every now and then as it moved from one end of the night sky to the other.

When Turoc slipped behind the shield of clouds below her, it left a brilliant blanket of stars against a sky of utter blackness. She sat down and ate the last of her bread and smoked venison. She left her pack on the ground and rested her head against it, feeling the prickly cold of the ice under her back. She slept fitfully.

At dawn, she stood slowly, stiffness filling her joints. She spent the day alternating between walking and climbing until the mists burned away and the Soel hovered above a white blanket of clouds that stretched out in front of her. She realized that she stood on the western edge of the world, where the Soel dropped into darkness. She spoke to the winds that whipped around her.

"The end of the world."

Her lips were cracked and dry, and the sound of her voice came out as nothing more than a hoarse whisper. She began to scramble down the ice, toward the clouds. She tripped and fell, skidded forward, tumbled against a pile of rocks, and lay still for a time. Finally, she pulled herself up and huddled for another cold night under her cloak.

Morning came again, this time with a long period of deep blue, followed by gray and then pale blue. The Soel hid behind the mountain for a long time. When it finally warmed the western slope, Elysen staggered forward, moving downward for the first time in days. Her path led across more rocky slopes and into the mists. Mists became clouds, and the clouds became thicker and thicker, until she could only see the ground just before her. Dampness crept into her clothes, chilled her skin, and matted her short hair into dirty white straggles. Still she descended, finding a game trail that made the way easier. She frowned, puzzled by the idea that some wild animal had made a habit of traveling toward the edge of the world. She proceeded more quickly. Even so, the light of day ended, and darkness cloaked her again. She found a single, stray tree, twisted and curled, holding tenaciously to the frigid slope high above the edge of the world. The clouds enclosed her, swirled about her.

"Tomorrow, we go to the edge," she whispered to her baby. "Maybe beyond the edge."

During the night, a warm wind cleared away the clouds and Elysen stared upward into a sky of stars again. Turoc glowed brilliant and bright and loomed so close that she could see the faint outline of his face. Ever so slowly, the night began to give way to day. Elysen sat back against the trunk of the ancient tree, gnarled like an old woman's fingers. She squinted out at the vista before her, expecting blackness. She stared into the grayness for a while, and then shook her head and wiped her hands across her eyes.

Instead of an endless void she saw barren hills, frosted white with a dusting of new snow. To the south, another mountain loomed, streaked white with snow amid the patches of brown and gray rock. The hills cascaded away from her; the more distant hills below the snow line were brown and dry. As far as she could see, in all directions, a world beyond the Vyr stretched endlessly. Above her, the blue sky radiated outward forever. She pulled her hood off her matted hair and loosened the clasp on her cloak, letting the cool mountain air touch her skin.

Elysen sat with her jaw slack. She stared at the world that unrolled before her. She touched her stomach and a tear coursed down her cheek. She sat, trance-like, for the entire morning. Morning turned to midday. The Soel shone hot against the back of her black garb, coaxing courses of wispy steam from her damp clothes. She sat, resting, holding her belly, staring out at the breathtaking vista before her and cried. She wiped her eyes, and then cried again. For the first time in her life, she felt something powerful within her. In her tears, she found strength instead of weakness. For the first time in her life, she allowed herself to cry.

Eventually she stood. She picked up a small rock and threw it at the world below her. She screamed into the vast, blue sky.

"A dead world," she shouted. "Is this what you bring me to see? Is that all there is? The Vyr is dying, my father is dead, Owen, Petyr, little Joli, and Arador and Rachael. Everyone dies. Is that it? Everyone dies but me?"

The wind whispered a cryptic answer that only the ice could understand.

Elysen tore her clothes off, throwing them on the icy ground around her. She stood with her arms outstretched, legs spread wide, bare feet planted on the snow.

"Whatever you are out there, take me now," she screamed.

She picked up another stone and threw it. Then another. And another. Soon, she threw stone after stone, frantically, almost hysterically. She began screaming again. She tore at the tattered remains of her hair. She stomped her feet and screamed again.

Exhausted, she sat down in the snow and stared at the frosted hills. Silence enfolded her. She laughed. Suddenly, the dead world beyond beckoned to her like a long lost lover, tugging at her heart, but as she stared out across the vast, frozen landscape, she thought of Yergen, and a numbing cold began to harden her, as if she were water, freezing into a solid, unbreakable mass. She clenched her teeth together and breathed deeply, relishing the frigid air. Clouds of vapor drifted from her mouth and nose.

"Yergen, I am coming for you now," she said.

She buried her fists in the snow. Her legs jutted straight out in front of her. Tiny crystals of ice sparkled on her white skin.

"I will chase you through the very fires of the Perde. I will never rest until you are dead and the world is mine again. I will be the Shad'ya. And I will bring death to you all."

She took one last, long look at the empty wastelands of the far side, and then picked up her clothes and turned back toward the east.

I am coming.

Seventeen

Elysen crossed the summit of Broken Top and descended the eastern slopes through a misty rain into a sparse forest of lodge pole pine. Her thoughts wandered into the dark reaches of the Keep and so she barely noticed time passing.

Her heart jumped into her throat as she scared up a large buck. It bounded away from her, leaping over a deadfall. The sounds of its flight lasted a few moments longer than her vision of it as it bounded away, stiff legged, flashing an instinctive warning with its cream colored tail. She listened as the misty forest calmed again, and then she slid into a small ravine. She stopped to drink from a clear running brook. The alders and birch that grew along the banks stood naked of leaves, and Elysen found a plague of morgred fungus infecting several of the trees. She pulled a handful of the spongy brown material from where it clung to the bark, paused, then stuffed it into her mouth and chewed hungrily. She gagged, spit some of it out, and then swallowed.

"Enough of that," she said.

She wandered along the ravine, following the flow of the stream, until she came to a rocky outcropping. The stream fell along the face of the cliff, forming a pool far below. She felt as if she could reach out and touch the hills below her, and suddenly the Vyr seemed very small. She studied the view for a long time as her thoughts swirled.

If Thorsen made all this, why did he abandon us?

The sky cleared near the middle of the day but the Soel crept along the southern horizon, moving toward the west. She put the pale white orb to her back and walked along the top of the cliff, heading northward. She found wild berries, small and blue. They tasted both sweet and tart, and she ate until her stomach ached. Near dark, she managed to creep up on a mountain grouse, close enough to stun it with a well-thrown rock. She sliced open the breast and dug out the choicest pieces of meat with her fingers, deciding to eat it raw rather than to try a fire. She ate in darkness, and then huddled under her cloak and rested fitfully until dawn.

She traveled for two more days before she found the valley of the Ryn Gladde. She stayed high above the thicker forests and rolling hills of the river valley, keeping along the tops of the cliffs and ridges, traveling carefully, until she came to the shore of Lake Orman. She crouched in the edge of the trees, peering out at the still water. The large rocks that formed the bottom of the lake showed clearly below the calm surface until a breeze blew riffles across the water. On the other side, the village smoldered in ruins. Nothing moved. She waited, patiently, watching.

The day grew old and the Soel began to set. At dusk, she ventured forth, circling the lake at a respectful distance, staying inside the forest edge. As she neared the village, she stopped again and crouched down. The Soel dropped behind the treetops, casting a chilling shadow on the world. A cracking twig startled her. Her back stiffened and her hand moved toward her knife.

"Lady Elysen," said a familiar voice, speaking in a soft whisper. "What are you doing here? Where are the others?"

Tell knelt down beside her. She glanced at him, and then returned her stare to the burned village.

"If they didn't return here, then they're probably dead," she said.

Tell stared at the ground.

"The Lord's Guard marched in and burned the village. Most everyone got out before they came though."

"Why are you still here?" she asked.

He shook his head and drew a line in the dirt with a stick.

"I have nowhere to go. I simply follow the guard around and wait for a chance to strike."

Elysen stared out at the smoldering village. The smoke hung across the lake like a funeral veil.

"They all extended graciousness and generosity to me," she said. "And this is what they received in return."

"It was not your fault," Tell said.

"I knew that Yergen was after me."

"Where will you go now?" Tell asked.

"I'll stay in the mountains."

"Yergen will find you."

She chewed on her lip for a moment, and then she looked into Tell's eyes and decided to trust him.

"I am going to find the Kaanites," she said. "I think that there may be enough of them to protect me long enough for me to bear my son into this ugly world."

She withheld part of the truth from him.

"The Kaanites are dangerous, m'lady."

"The world is dangerous," she said. "I'm looking for dangerous people." She glanced at the remains of the village by the lake. "Look what happens to nice people. They're murdered and their lives are destroyed."

They sat for a while, watching the darkness of night as it settled between them like a wall.

"How can I find them?" she asked.

He paused for a moment.

"M'lady," he said. "Just because they worship you, don't be misled into thinking that they will help you or protect you. They believe that there is no greater honor in life than to die in battle. They may see your death at their hands as a great sign."

"I don't fear death anymore," she said.

"Why don't you go north?" Tell suggested.

"The ice lands?" she asked.

"Perhaps your mother's people will protect you."

She shook her head in the darkness.

"The Norgarden are a peaceful people," she said. "Like I said, I'm looking for warriors."

"The Kaanites may not be as easily recruited for your task as you think."

"I will persuade them."

"Or, they may persuade you to their task."

"Not likely," Elysen said.

Tell sighed and stared at the smoldering ruins.

"I wish you well in this journey that you choose. But I'm afraid that it won't turn out the way you intend."

"Perhaps not," she said.

She stared out into the darkness. The soft snowflakes touched her eyelashes and cheeks like tiny butterflies of ice. She pondered for a moment before she spoke again.

"Tell," she said. "Can you return to Yergen's service without suspicion?"

He shrugged.

"Perhaps. Why would I do that?"

Elysen transfixed him with her eyes.

"The bulk of the army is Gennissaries, conscripted men with no real stomach for fighting. If you could circulate through their ranks, in secret, as you serve Yergen in form only, we could weaken the army, weaken their resolve."

Tell's expression darkened.

"And you would have to fight as if you were loyal to Yergen," Elysen said.

"Again," he said. "Why would I do such a terrible thing?"

"Because," she said. She held his eyes with hers. "I intend to take my place as Lord."

Tell swallowed and licked his lips.

"This is a dangerous game you play," he said.

"This is no game."

"Yergen will never let you," Tell said.

"That's why I need your help," she said.

He shook his head and looked down at the table. "I can't," he said.

"Then you are stuck with Yergen," she reminded him.

Tell shook his head. "I can't believe that you will be able to rally anyone to your cause."

She stood up and grabbed his arms.

"You're right, if you don't help me. But with or without your help, I will return to the Keep and take it back in the name of Lord Vollen. And we will throw out Thorsen's Law and start anew."

Tell scratched his face.

Elysen winced and grabbed her stomach. She sat down and Tell knelt down next to her.

"You are not well, m'lady," he said.

She tipped her head up and glared into his eyes.

"Tell, before I die, I will cut Yergen's head from his body and place it on a pike at the top of Thorsen's Watch."

Tell's concerned look did not waver. He nodded as he looked through her pain and into her spirit.

"Yes," he said. "I believe that you will."

"Nothing will stand in my way."

"Do you know the legend of the Shad'ya?" Tell asked.

Elysen shook her head. She heard Tell sigh.

"In the legend," he said. "Everyone dies"

Sometime during the night, she slept. She woke up to a blanket of thick, white snow across the plateau, a blanket that covered everything, as if there had never been a settlement. The snow edged into the lake on a shelf of ice, making the water like a black hole in the white world. Elysen stretched and sat up.

On the ground next to her, Tell had left a light crossbow and a quiver with five hunting bolts, good for small game, but too fragile for effective defense. Tracks led away, into the forest, disappearing into the bare ground of the undergrowth.

"May a greater power be with you," Elysen said.

She stood and shook the snow off her shoulders. She picked up the weapon and strapped the quiver to her arm, then stepped into the dark depths of the pine forest. She took one look backwards before she walked away, avoiding the faint trail left by Tell. He appeared to be moving north, so Elysen turned south and headed upward, into the mountains again.

That afternoon she came upon a trail of chewed up snow and mud left by the boots and horses of the Lord's Guard. Elysen crouched for a while, studying their tracks, and then moved away from them, toward the east. Along the way, she pinned a fat rabbit with a well-placed shot from her crossbow and chanced a small fire. She skinned the animal with Raes' knife and cooked it quickly. She kicked dirt over the remains of the fire before she continued east toward the black cliffs. She slept in the high country that night. In the morning, before the Soel lit the sky, Elysen climbed down the long, steep slope to the valley of the Ryn Gladde.

The day turned dark and cloudy, and an icy sleet fell during the middle of the day. She moved south along the Ryn Gladde for another day before she came upon the remains of an encampment. There were only footprints, no horses or pack animals. She followed the trail for three days. It wandered higher into the mountains, into a heavily forested area where large rhododendron bushes and fields of thick salal made travel difficult. In places, the mossy trunks of vine maple laced together like a giant thicket, forcing Elysen to follow a narrow but well-defined trail closely, with no room to observe at a distance.

On the fourth day, the sleet turned to snow and a heavy, white blanket accumulated on the ground. Every now and then Elysen stepped off the path, leaping across the fresh snow to land on the roots of a deadfall or on a pile of composted leaves under the branches of a large evergreen bush, so that she could crouch in silence, watching the trail behind her for signs of pursuit. She saw no one. That afternoon the snow stopped and she stepped into a clearing and froze in her tracks.

A dozen tents filled the clearing. They were made of animal hide, stretched tightly across a frame of eight sticks that leaned together at a single, central point. Smoke drifted from the openings. A black design painted in large, blocky strokes emblazoned the side of each tent. Four men crouched in the center of the circle, tending a fire, unconcerned with the possible presence of the Lord's Guard in the high woods. Elysen stepped backwards slowly and slipped off the path. She watched them for a while from the safety of a thicket of giant rhododendrons. Soon, two more men joined the four by the fire. They talked loudly, but only bits and snatches of their conversation were audible in the damp air.

As the air began to grow dark with the oncoming night, several women joined the men. Two small boys came out of a tent to play by the fire, and then another woman carrying a baby swaddled up in a rough bundle of woolen blankets. They were roasting something that smelled like venison. Talking. Sometimes laughing. Elysen checked her quiver out of habit. Only five bolts. She would be no match for the entire tribe in a battle.

Elysen chewed on her lower lip for a while, then sighed and stood slowly, carefully. She let her arms hang at her sides, holding her weapon, unloaded, pointed at the ground.

These are the people I wanted to see, she told herself.

She walked into the circle of tents.

Eighteen

As she approached, everyone stood up at once. All movement halted except for one boy in mid-motion as he threw a snowball at another child. His arm slowed as he saw Elysen walking into the camp. The snowball lobbed in a high arc and landed silently in the ankle-deep snow. Elysen moved into the circle of tents, toward the warmth of the fire. Suddenly the entire village crossed their arms and dropped to their knees, bowing their heads. They remained that way until an older man came forth to address her.

"I am Sethe," he said. "Of the clan of Rige Dreven. We have been waiting for you to join us."

His eyes glistened in the firelight. Black runes, carved into the side of his face and neck, ran from his temple to his shoulder.

As he spoke, five more men emerged from the forest from behind Elysen, appearing with nothing more than a whisper. Elysen watched them as they circled her, bowing their heads slightly, but never taking their eyes off her. She stood as still as the trees that surrounded them.

Sethe motioned toward the fire with his hand.

"Please join us," he said. "We have waited many days for you to come to us."

Elysen approached the fire, and the clan members moved away from her, leaving a clear space for her to sit. She sat cross-legged on the ground and placed her crossbow next to her leg. Sethe sat down not more than an arm's length away from her.

"You were not hard to find," she said.

Sethe smiled.

"This small group of devoted clan members was chosen for you to find. It was a dangerous calling. We don't normally crash about in the brush, taking such obvious trails. Now that you have joined us, we will have to disband quickly."

The people of the clan stared at her. The five men that had been hiding in the forest still stood behind her with arrows nocked but not drawn.

"You must be hungry," Sethe said. He handed her a stick with a steaming piece of meat skewered on the end. Elysen ate in silence, ignoring the statue-like warriors behind her.

"Why are you painted like that?" she asked as she wiped her mouth on her sleeve.

"These tattoos are ancient runes that speak of our purpose." He pointed at his face. "This identifies me as a guide." He stripped his shirt off. The tattoo that began on his cheek and chin continued down his neck and onto his shoulder.

"I recognize the shape of those runes," she said.

"Impossible," he replied.

"I have seen a tome, held by the people of Lake Orman, filled with symbols such as those. We call them spells."

Sethe frowned. The air filled with a soft muttering. Sethe held up his hand and the group fell silent.

"We are the keepers of the runes," Sethe said. "Not the peasants of Lake Orman."

Elysen shrugged. "Maybe you don't keep all the runes."

Sethe leaned toward her. His lips took on an expression that looked like a sneer. "There are those among us who can cite the spell of the runes."

Elysen froze in mid-bite.

Sethe leaned back and smiled.

"We will talk of that another day," he said. "For now, all you need to know is that the world belongs to dark lords. They come to reclaim their lands from the arrogance of the Vyr Lords. And you are the instrument of destruction. Your coming marks the beginning of the reign of darkness." He leaned forward, his eyes wild. "We have waited so long."

"Hail the white lord, bringer of the realm of death," one of the women said from the far side of the fire. An eerie murmuring of agreement arose from the rest of the group. One of the little boys approached her carefully, then spat at her and ran away.

Her body suddenly tensed. The men behind her raised their bows into a more ready position.

"Why did he do that?" Elysen asked.

"They hate you. Fear you," Sethe said.

Again, the group nodded and there were whispers and quiet hand motions.

"I thought your people would be friendly toward me."

"Oh no," Sethe said. "You are the bringer of the destruction of the world. They revere you only because they know that they cannot hide. They cannot escape the final judgment."

Elysen glanced around at the group, at the darkness beyond them, at the five men, poised around the clan like a secondary line of defense.

"You are all insane," she said. "Like mad dogs, frothing at the mouth."

"You came to us," Sethe reminded her.

"I was mistaken," she said.

She began to uncross her legs. The movement caused the guards to come to full readiness, their arrows suddenly drawn back and pointed at Elysen's head. Sethe motioned with his hand for them to stay their weapons, and they lowered them slightly.

"I am not going to bring death and destruction down on anyone but myself," she said. She considered her own words for a moment. "I can't even seem to do that right," she added.

Sethe smiled. "Your fate has been locked into place since the beginning of time. You can't escape it. You can't change it."

"Well," Elysen said. "Thank you for the food. I thought I might find sanctuary with your people for a while."

She picked up her crossbow and stood to go. Sethe sent a glance toward one of the men behind her. He lowered his bow and reached toward her. He managed to grab onto the loose fabric of her sleeve, but Elysen turned quickly and tore her garment from the young man's grasp. As she ran toward the darkness that loomed outside the ring of the fire and into the deep black of the woods, she drew the cord of the crossbow and fitted a bolt into the breech. She turned and fired at a shadow, heard the thud of the short arrow as it penetrated chest and lung, heard the gurgle of blood, and could sense the shocked look on the young boy's face as he fell forward, gasping for breath. She reloaded, still running, but her feet tangled in the brush, or perhaps someone's arms wrapped around her ankles, throwing her to the ground. She fell hard, gasping for her own breath, and a foot kicked her in the stomach. Another struck her forehead.

"Enough," Sethe's voice roared in the darkness. Rough hands picked Elysen up off the ground, stripped her crossbow from her hand, and wrestled her back to the fire.

"Standgar is dead," one of the young men growled.

"See?" Sethe said. "She is the bringer of death and destruction. She is the one."

From behind her, someone forced her jaw open and stuffed a wad of rank leather into her mouth, securing it with a piece of prickly hemp. Her arms were pinned behind her back and tied with more of the rough rope, as were her feet. Someone pushed her to the ground and then Sethe loomed over her, leering at her with wild, hungry eyes.

"You will resist," he said. "But your fate is inevitable. We have read the runes, and from them we know that you are the one. You will plunge the world into darkness."

He took a moment to touch her white hair with his thick, short fingers, his eyes wide and greedy in the flickering firelight. She clenched her teeth tightly together. Sethe spoke to the group, but did not take his eyes from Elysen.

"She is the one," he said. "Bring her."

Two men stripped Elysen's outer garments and bound her wrists and ankles. They carried her on a long stick as if she were a dead animal, dressed only in thin woolen pants and a shirt with no sleeves. The bindings around her wrists, strained by the weight of her upper body, cut into her skin. Tiny rivulets of blood ran down her naked forearms and onto her shoulders, leaving a trail of red dots in the snow. Her head hung back, giving her a wildly upside-down view of the forest. The pole bounced and jerked with every step, grinding against her bones, and the rough hemp cut and chaffed at her skin.

As her captors walked, their feet kicked up bits of icy mud that struck Elysen in the face and arms. She kept her eyes closed and her lips pressed together, wincing occasionally as her captors shifted the weight of the pole on their shoulders, making the bindings cut deeper.

The tribe stopped at a more permanent camp high in the hills next to a small lake covered with bluish ice around the edges. Smoke from small fires trickled from the tops of countless spire-shaped tents. Several tall trees that stood around the lake like silent sentinels cast long cold, shadows across the camp.

The men dropped Elysen onto the ground and slid the pole from between her arms and legs. She rolled over in the snow and buried her burned wrists under the ice. The feel of snow against her body sucked her breath from her lungs. Sethe came to her and helped her stand.

"Time is short," he said. "And we have much to do. And a long way to go."

Elysen staggered. A man grabbed her other arm and held her up while Sethe spoke.

"Our tribe has never before come together like this," he said. He wore a weary smile across his leathery face. "This is a great and glorious time, but it is very dangerous for us," he said. "The Lord's Guard could easily find us here."

"I hope they do," Elysen said. She nearly choked on the words.

"They will not," Sethe said. "We track them. Follow them. Lead them astray. They are no problem for us. They are like stupid little children, running back and forth. We play hide and seek with them." He grinned. "Sometimes we kill them. Sometimes we just keep them off balance." He waved his arms. "Never mind the Lord's Guard. Let us proceed."

The Soel set, leaving the dark gloom of night to shroud the clearing. The men of the camp began to build two large fires in the center of the group of tents. The Kaanites gathered as Sethe and his companion half led, half-carried Elysen into the orange light. Some were gnawing tattered bits of meat off bones, others were just sitting, staring at Elysen, their hands in their laps, or their arms wrapped around small children.

Two posts stood in the very middle of the clearing, between the fires. Sethe led Elysen to a spot between the posts and pulled her arms up. Elysen twisted her body and yanked at his grip, but her arms were weak from being bound all day. Sethe and another man tied one wrist to each post at a spot just higher than her head.

"What about her legs?" the other one asked Sethe.

"Leave them loose," he said. He paused and pondered for a moment, then shook his head. "On second thought, we should tie them too."

The other man kicked Elysen's foot out from underneath her body and she fell, dangling from her wrists like a broken puppet. They tied her legs and then the other man backed away. Sethe pulled Raes' knife from under his coat and used it to cut away Elysen's remaining garments, leaving her naked in the cold night, her white body glowing orange in the firelight.

"That is my knife," Elysen hissed.

Sethe ignored her and spoke to the assembled tribe.

"The time of great reckoning is upon us," he said. "Behold the white devil."

He reached skyward with his arms, and the Kaanites gazed upward with him, some of them swaying back and forth as if in a trance. Some held their hands aloft, or simply turned their palms upward. Sethe chanted.

"Oh great spirit of Kaan, we beg of you to deliver us to your womb of darkness. We await your punishment, oh Lord." He turned and pointed toward Elysen. "Behold the mother of our doom, the evil white one, from whose loins spring the birth of our destruction." He held the knife out, pointing the chiseled tip toward Elysen's abdomen. She glared at him.

"Go ahead and kill me," she whispered.

He shook his head. "That is not the will of Kaan."

"Your dark power is nothing," she said.

Sethe laughed. "No, m'lady. Take a look at yourself now. It is your Vyr Lord who is nothing. He is just a man. His time on this world is over. We serve his master, the new master, the master as old as time. He rises from the darkness again to claim what is rightfully his. His time of exile is over."

Sethe reached skyward again in triumph, and the group began chanting softly around Elysen, their words filling the night like ghosts.

"Let us prepare her body for the journey," Sethe said.

He took Raes' knife and began to slice off what was left of her matted hair. As he cut, he threw handfuls into the snow behind him. A young boy came forward, handed Sethe a small bowl, and then ran away. Sethe took a salve from the jar with two fingers and rubbed it on Elysen's head. He used the edge of the knife to scrape away the paste and along with it the stubble that was all that remained of Elysen's hair, wiping the knife on his trousers as he proceeded.

"You do not know what an honor this is," he whispered to her as he shaved her head. He finished and stepped away. Someone hit her in the head from behind and Elysen's knees buckled. She took the weight of her body on her arms.

Two women scurried forward, avoiding Elysen's dazed glare by keeping their eyes focused on the wooden bowls they carried in their gnarled hands. They placed their bowls on the ground in front of Elysen and bowed, mumbling some incoherent prayer. Then they each produced a thin, sharp bone needle from some hidden pocket inside their sleeves. Almost as if one were the reflection of the other, they dipped their needles into the thick, black liquid that swirled within the shallow containers. Each one paused with the now blackened needle poised above a foot, mumbled another prayer, and with a single movement, they began. At the first pricks of the needles along the sides of her frozen feet, Elysen's muscles tensed and she arched her back.

Sethe took a seat with the tribe and began to speak as the women scribed.

"In the beginning, there was only darkness," he said. "And that is how it will be in the end."

He sat silently, patiently, as the women worked across the tops of Elysen's feet with delicate movements, dipping, pricking, dipping and pricking.

After a long period of silence, broken only by Elysen's gasps, Sethe continued his chant. "And the dark lords cherished the darkness, and their happiness was pain and suffering. There was only emptiness."

Slowly, methodically, the scribes moved their needles up along the skin that stretched tightly across the bones and muscles of Elysen's lower leg. Sethe and the tribe waited patiently while they drew. When they paused, he began to speak again.

"But there came into the darkness a pin prick of light. The dark lords did not notice the light at first. It was weak, and they tolerated it. But as time went by, the light grew, and other lights joined it. And one day the light created land and water, and put animals and humans on the land, and the dark lords saw this and were angered."

Elysen cried out as the needles bit deep into the soft skin behind her knees.

"And so the lords of darkness came to destroy the land and the water. They brought fire and ice, and they threw them at the light, but the light resisted."

The needles danced across Elysen's thighs, winding ever higher, touching, pricking, leaving a trail of black runes, an indecipherable tome of pain and suffering, past, present and future. Below her feet, now covered with the markings of the Kaanites, tiny droplets of blood showed red against the white snow.

"And the lords of darkness, the true lords, the first lords, came to destroy the pitiful creatures that the light had created. The lords of darkness toyed with the people, taught them dark sciences, and the people came to worship the darkness. But one of the lights came to resist, and he called himself Thorsen. Thorsen disguised himself as one of the dark lords, and led them to the edge of the world, where he stole their powers. He locked them in a pit of their own fire, and he buried their secrets deep within the far desert."

As they finished their grisly task around her hips and thighs, the scribes paused to rub cold snow over their work so far. Elysen shivered and moaned, throwing her head back. As the women carved lines across her belly and lower back, Elysen bit her tongue and blood trickled from the corner of her mouth. She saw a dark shadow rising up, engulfing her.

"Please stop," she whispered. The women ignored her. Sethe glared at her, and then crossed his arms and closed his eyes, concentrating on his words.

The shadow caressed her, whispered to her.

"But there were those who knew the power of the dark lords, and who served them well, and they pushed Thorsen from the edge of the world, into the darkness beyond. And then they waited."

The shadow moved away, as if it was studying her. It poised there for a moment and then shot forward, piercing her body, filling it with a cold deeper than anything she had ever known.

Elysen threw her head back and screamed.

Nineteen

The tribe sat and listened quietly, knowing the finality of this simple ritual. For them, the entire world stood transfixed at that moment, in that place. Even the children sat as quiet as statues. They were no more than ghosts and shadows, as if they themselves were the runes that coursed black across Elysen's naked body. Sethe continued his litany.

"Kaan, the destroyer of Thorsen, was a deserter from the light. He embraced the darkness. But he was weak, and Thorsen wounded him in battle. Before he died, he created a storm, a white storm, that would purge the world of light. That would return everything to darkness. And all would be as it was. And he told his disciples to wait for the storm, to watch for the child of Genis, the child of death, who would rise to power and destroy the world. The Shad'ya."

Sethe sat silently for a while as the scribes drew more markings across Elysen's ribs and her breasts, and then moved across her shoulders and onto her back.

Sethe stood up and circled around Elysen, examining the dark spells.

"You are the Shad'ya," he said. "We have waited so long for your coming." He clasped his hands together. Elysen moaned and squeezed her eyes shut.

"What is this shadow around me?" she whispered.

Sethe frowned.

"You are having a vision," he said. "This is the end of the world. There are but a few seasons left before the darkness consumes all of us."

The runes converged at the small of her back, and the women paused for a moment to rub her body with snow again before they continued at the base of her neck, across her scalp, diverging again, cryptic shapes flowing in perfect symmetry down her forehead, across the bridge of her nose and onto her cheeks. Exhausted, Elysen had no strength left to fight. The women held her head upright so that they could draw the final chapter. They covered her eyes, mouth, cheeks, and even her lips with the black runes, working around the wounds on her face.

Sethe came forward and touched her torn and broken jaw with the tips of his fingers, running them down her neck to the straight bone across the top of her chest. He let his fingers drift down, tracing the gentle curve of her breast, before he pulled his hand away and made a fist.

The women glanced up at Sethe and then stood up. They stepped back, bowing as they retreated into the crowd. A fog blew in off the lake and the sky turned light gray above them.

As morning broke, the tribe broke into smaller fragments that melted into the woods, leaving only the remains of two large fires and scuffed snow for the white hand of the Proste to conceal.

Sethe cut Elysen down and let her body fall onto a thick robe of mildewed bearskin. Two men tied the robe to the same long pole they had used to transport Elysen to the camp. She now hung in a more comfortable bundle, swinging back and forth gently as they carried her through the woods.

Elysen slept fitfully. She stirred on the third day, took some soup, and then slept again, curled into a ball with her knees against her arms and her arms against her naked chest. On the fourth day, she woke as they dropped her to the ground, and she struggled into a sitting position. An old woman placed a warm blanket over her shoulders, and Elysen pulled it tight around her body.

They sat in front of a small fire and the woman offered her more broth. Elysen drank it and fell asleep again, unable to keep her eyes open. She curled into a ball again, retaining as much warmth as she could.

The fifth night she stayed awake after drinking a cup of broth. She ate some stringy, tough meat and boiled onions. She glanced around the fire. Sethe sat on a log across from her, staring into the flames. A pair of crossbows leaned against the log on either side of him.

Two men sat on the ground close to the fire, huddled under heavy fur cloaks that looked like a mixture of wolf and coyote and bear and smaller animals like badger and raccoon. Tiny embers from the fire drifted toward them like fireflies.

"Rejoined the world," Sethe said.

Elysen let her eyes drift toward the flames. The old woman walked into the ring of light and sat nearby.

"I am Shelda," she said. Elysen's eyes strained to see into the darkness around the camp. She counted only the five.

"Shelda is the one that prepared us for your coming," Sethe said.

"I was there the day you were born," Shelda whispered.

Her face reminded Elysen of a dried apple, deeply wrinkled and brown. Her white, wispy hair made Elysen reach up to touch her own scalp. She frowned as her fingers touched the soft, downy stubble that remained there.

"I thought that I was a believer," Shelda said. "I watched your mother as she struggled with your birth. She was so arrogant, thinking that she could be mother of the Shad'ya. And then, when I saw you, and when I witnessed all the events that came to pass, I knew. My faith before that was but a wisp of what it is now."

Elysen barely listened. Her eyes focused on the strange spells that covered her arm. The runes traced wild lines from her fingers along the backs of her hands and arms and up to her shoulders. Heedless of the two men that sat on either side of Sethe, Elysen peeled back the blanket and stared at her chest and stomach and legs, and finally her feet, once as pure and white as the snow around them, now covered with a myriad of markings, as black and dark as the night sky.

"What have you done to me?" she asked. She pulled the blanket closed around her body. Sethe's companions stared at her from under their hoods.

"We have marked you according to the teachings of Kaan," Sethe said. "These spells are your brand. Your body now tells our story. When you die, we will claim your body again, and we will embalm your skin in the ancient traditions, so that you may rise again from the dead someday."

"Why would you do this?"

Sethe leaned forward and spoke to her, the fire crackling between them.

"Because, this is what we are told to do," Sethe said.

"Told by whom?"

"By Kaan."

"Kaan was a traitor," Elysen said.

"Oh, no," Sethe said. "Kaan was against Thorsen, but it was Thorsen who was the traitor."

Elysen shook her head.

"In the time before Thorsen, the world was full of spells and knowledge," Sethe said. "The dark lords ruled, but they taught people to dance and to study science, to build, to create. There were wonders we can not even imagine."

"Like hard metal?" Elysen asked.

"And things even more wondrous. But Thorsen defied the dark lords and threw them out of the Vyr. He took all knowledge and power and buried it deep within the Keep, and set the Vyr Lords to defend it, to keep it hidden."

Elysen hunched her shoulders and exhaled slowly.

"You sense the truth of it," Sethe said.

"What is the role of the Kaanites in all this?" Elysen asked.

"Those of us in the tribe are the descendents of Kaan," he said. "There are many others who have joined us from the Vyr."

"How many?" Elysen asked.

Sethe smiled but his eyes were narrow. "The law of the Vyr forbids us to count."

"You don't seem to be bound by the laws of the Vyr," Elysen reminded him.

"There are many," he said. "That is all I can tell you."

Elysen looked at him with some suspicion.

"Enough of this chatter," Shelda said. "We shall all sleep now. Grayson and Hauking will stand guard tonight. The Lord's Guard will be out and about. We are nearing the Northern Reach. Tomorrow we have to cross it quickly. We will need our rest."

"We're traveling north?" Elysen asked.

"Yes," Shelda said. "And tomorrow you have to learn to walk again. These boys are tired of carrying you."

"I'm too weak to walk," Elysen said. "These black spells have poisoned me."

"Nonsense," Shelda said. "Your weakness is all in your head. You will find the strength you need."

Elysen stared into the fire as Sethe and Shelda settled down and pulled their cloaks over their shoulders. The two younger men sat glaring at Elysen for a moment, then stood and slipped into the darkness, making no sound as they went. Elysen pulled her blanket over her head to keep the chill off her naked scalp. She drifted off to sleep but woke with a start to a dead fire and a gray sky. A cold dampness soaked into her blanket. The others were moving about, breaking up the camp.

Sethe helped pack their few belongings into heavy leather packs. The two younger men shouldered the big packs, while Shelda and Sethe carried lighter ones made of brown fabric. Before they left, Shelda kicked dirt over the dead fire.

"You'll walk on your own from here on," one of the men said as he helped her to her feet. His nose hooked over like a beak, and his small eyes held a predatory look.

"Tell me your name," Elysen said.

"Hauking," he said.

"That's a strange name," she said. "Not like any Vyr name I've ever heard before."

"My friends call me Hawk," he said.

"I'll call you that also."

"You haven't earned the right," he said.

"Nevertheless," Elysen said. "I'll call you that." She turned toward the other man.

"And your name must be Grayson," she said, recalling Shelda's comments the night before. His hair bristled short along the sides, only slightly longer on top. He nodded curtly and then pulled his hood over his head. The shadows from his hood gave his face a sullen, sunken look, but the light reflected from his bright blue eyes.

"What do your friends call you?" Elysen asked.

"Just Grayson," he said.

"You're not of the Vyr either," Elysen noted.

"Quiet now," Shelda snapped. "It's time for us to get moving."

"May I have a pair of boots?" Elysen asked as they began walking.

"No," Sethe said. "You will not get boots or gloves or clothes."

"That is insane," she said. "How can you expect me to survive the cold of the ice lands with nothing but this sheet?"

Sethe shrugged. "You will survive. It is your destiny to survive."

"I don't understand why you test the fates by treating me like a troublesome dog."

Sethe smiled. "Your trials have only just begun. You will learn to be patient and to accept your fate willingly."

"Perhaps some night when you are sleeping I will creep over to your bedside and slit your throat," Elysen said. "Then we'll see if you can just accept your fate willingly."

"Hush now," Shelda hissed. "We will travel in silence."

Sethe squared his shoulders and held his head high. He moved a few paces ahead, leading the way. Elysen tipped her head slightly and glanced at Shelda, who walked slightly behind the others, and then she caught Hawk's eye.

"Does she always boss you around like this?" she asked.

"We are just tolerating her," he said quietly.

"You are Uemn," Elysen said.

Hawk ignored her, but out of the corner of her eye she saw Grayson's eyes narrow as he regarded her.

They walked all morning without rest. Elysen's feet burned from the cold. The snow crunched as she stepped on it and it lodged between her toes, melting and then refreezing. Her blanket became damp and cold, and where her hands held it closed, her fingers glistened with ice. She finally dropped to her knees. The morning's broth came up her throat like fire, staining the white snow. Her stomach cramped and she fell on her side in the snow. Hawk scooped her up in his arms and slung her over his shoulder like a rolled up tent, her bare legs forward, her toes pointing down at the icy ground. He held her tight around her waist with his hard shoulder pressed into her stomach. He carried her for most of the day until she finally pounded on his back with her fists.

"Put me down here," she said.

"Gladly," he responded. She slid off his shoulder and landed in a heap in the snow. Sethe helped her stand. A row of thick posts, each with a stout crossbeam tied high above the ground, stood like silent sentinels as far as they could see in both directions.

"I want to walk across the Reach on my own two feet," she said. She held her cloak closed over one shoulder with one hand and steadied herself with the other on Sethe's shoulder.

The northern boundary, she thought. *I'm about to leave the lands of the Vyr.*

She crossed over the line in silence. The group walked steadily north for the rest of the day, making slow progress as Elysen's frozen feet refused to hold her body upright. That night they chanced a small fire. Elysen warmed her feet in the melting snow near the flames.

Hawk sat up during the night watch and cut swatches of leather from his coat, expertly sewing them into a pair of soft boots. He rubbed them with globs of noxious smelling grease that he carried in a small leather pouch under his coat. Elysen thawed her feet in front of the fire as Hawk worked. When he finished, he pulled the boots up over her feet while she huddled under her blanket.

"Thank you," she said.

"My back and arms are tired from carrying you. You have your boots now. Tomorrow you will walk. All day."

"Clothes would be helpful," she said. Hawk tossed her a short piece of hemp.

"Give me your blanket for a moment," he said. She hesitated, and then slipped it from around her shoulders and handed it to Hawk. She sat, naked except for her boots, waiting, with her hands pressed between her legs. Hawk cut a hole in the middle of the blanket and then handed it back to her.

"Put your head through the hole," he said. "And tie the cord around your waist."

The edges of the blanket overlapped around her waist and hung down over her shoulders, long enough to reach her knees. She kept the small piece of rope clenched tightly in her hand as she pulled her legs up inside her newly made outfit and wrapped her arms around her knees.

Hawk settled down and fell asleep at the edge of the firelight. A cold wind snaked down Elysen's back and she shivered.

Sethe glared at her the next day.

"Who did this?" he snarled.

Hawk ran into the small camp breathing heavily.

"The Lord's Guard is close," he said. His breath clouded the air around him with frosty plumes.

"They have followed us north of the Reach?" Sethe asked.

"Don't underestimate their desperation," Shelda said.

They picked up their things hurriedly. Elysen tied her robe shut and Hawk dragged her away at a pace that caused her to stumble and fall. Grayson picked her up by the rope around her waist and dragged her. She struggled free of his grasp, stumbled again, and then regained her footing.

"I will walk myself," she said. "No more carrying."

Grayson snorted and took the lead. Shelda and Sethe followed him. Hawk took the rear position, behind Elysen. They abandoned the more open terrain for the thicker forests where they were forced to crawl over tangled deadfalls covered with ice and snow.

"We leave a trail in the snow that an idiot could follow," Elysen said.

"Just keep moving," Hawk said.

"Is this how you normally escape from the patrols of the Lord's Guard? Traveling through the snow where your tracks are as easy to follow as wagon ruts?"

"Keep quiet now," Sethe hissed. "We travel this way because of you."

"I can travel anywhere that you can," Elysen snapped.

"You are weak and clumsy," he snapped back.

Elysen fell further and further behind the other three, breathing hard. Hawk pushed her and prodded her, but she could not keep up. Grayson led the group up a small stream that ran through a rocky ravine, leaping from rock to boulder, from boulder to log, sometimes wading, sometimes crawling over logs that had tipped into the small canyon from the banks above. They came to a giant deadfall that stopped Elysen in her tracks. It blocked a steep incline leading to a tall stand of trees high above them. She leaned forward and braced her hands on her legs to catch her breath.

Hawk grabbed her from behind and hoisted her onto his shoulder. He glared at the twisted mass of tree trunks in front of him. With one arm wrapped around Elysen and only one hand to steady his climb, he managed to get a leg over one trunk before he slipped and fell between two others, dropping Elysen. She grabbed a branch and clung there while Hawk pulled himself up. He sat on the ice-covered log and glared at Elysen.

"We can't go this way," she said.

"You are trouble," he said.

She laughed quietly. "Then let me go," she said. "I would be of no trouble at all if you and your Kaanite friends hadn't kidnapped me and tortured me."

He grunted. "You are being purposefully difficult," he said.

She looked up at the pile of logs piled above her. Then she looked back at Hawk. He rubbed his leg and grimaced.

"How much longer can we run?" she asked.

Hawk shook his head and looked back along the ravine.

"We need to keep moving until we get a snowfall heavy enough to cover our tracks," he said.

"Why don't we stand and fight?" she asked.

"Too many of them."

"How many?"

"Six that I saw. Maybe more."

"There are five of us."

"Only three that can fight."

"Four."

"Shelda is no fighter."

"I am."

"Sethe will never allow you to have a weapon. You would turn against us."

She shrugged. "I'm doomed either way. At least let me die fighting, instead of being hauled around like a child."

"You are just a child though, look at yourself."

"I am no child," she said. She crossed her arms and glared at the woods through which they had come.

"See?" Hawk said. "You even act like a child."

He stood, teetering, and tested his leg. It would not take his weight, and he almost fell again. Grayson's face appeared above them.

"What are you doing down there?" he asked. His quiet voice carried an urgent tone.

"Hawk is hurt," Elysen said.

Hawk glared at her, but said nothing. Grayson scrambled down the wreckage of trees and branches and squatted next to Hawk.

"What is it?" he asked.

"I've twisted my leg. Maybe broken it."

"How?"

Hawk glanced at Elysen, and then looked back at Grayson. "Just clumsiness," he said.

Grayson's eyes shifted toward Elysen.

"Can you climb?" Grayson asked.

Hawk looked up. "I can try," he said.

"What about her?" Grayson asked, tipping his head slightly toward their prisoner.

"I can't carry her and climb," Hawk said.

Grayson glared at him. "Then I'll carry her," he said.

He took a step toward Elysen. Hawk reached out and grabbed his arm.

"No, sir," he said. They stood that way for a moment, staring at each other.

Grayson put his hand on Hawk's arm and spoke softly. "We don't have time to stay here and argue about it, Hawk. We have to keep moving."

"Sir," he said. "It's my task to carry her. I will do it."

Elysen bit her lower lip and looked upward, then placed her hand on the log in front of her and clambered onto it. She stopped for a moment to look at Grayson and Hawk, and they turned to watch her. She pulled herself, slowly, from log to log, finding her own way up the giant tangle of dead trees, stripped of their leaves, their branches, their bark. The two men followed her.

"Go faster," Grayson hissed.

Elysen glared at him, and then continued to climb as slowly as before. Hawk clambered along behind them, obviously in pain. His brow furrowed with every movement of his leg. They climbed for a long time, finally arriving at a narrow draw that led them up to a higher position along a small rise. Below them, the forest stretched out into rolling ridges of white.

"Do we know where we are going?" Elysen asked as she leaned against a tree, gasping for breath. She watched the vapor stream from her mouth with every exhalation. The canopy above them here grew denser. The snow piled on the branches, but barely penetrated to the ground below. Shelda and Sethe were crouched on a patch of bare soil under a nearby tree, waiting.

"We need a place to stand and fight," Hawk said.

"Looks like it will be here," Grayson said.

"Not here," Sethe said. "This is not defensible."

"No choice," Grayson said. "They are upon us."

Shelda came to the edge of the deadfall and peered down.

"I can't see…" An arrow sliced through her throat, cutting off her words. She grabbed the exposed shaft and stood up with a surprised look on her face. She stepped backwards and fell, still holding the now bloody arrow with both hands.

Grayson and Hawk reacted instantly, each nocking an arrow and drawing it partway. They swiveled so that their backs were toward Elysen and Shelda. Sethe drew one of his crossbows and used both hands to cock it. He loaded it with a heavy bolt tipped with a cruel stone blade and crouched in front of Shelda's fallen body, facing the top of the deadfall that they had just climbed. Elysen knelt over Shelda and touched the arrow lightly with her fingers. Shelda's eyes were wide with fright and they pleaded with Elysen. She stared into Shelda's brown eyes. Touched her wrinkled cheek. Blood pumped from the wound.

"Can you remove the arrow?" Hawk whispered. He did not take his eyes from the woods around them.

Elysen shook her head, even though no one looked at her.

"No," she said. "The head of the arrow is lodged deep in her neck."

Elysen watched blood gush from the wound, bright red against the white snow beneath Shelda's head. Elysen stroked Shelda's gray hair.

"Take this," Shelda croaked, pushing a small pouch into Elysen's hand. Elysen recognized it instantly. She could sense the shape of Joli's small toy inside, along with the slippery feel of locks of her own white hair twisted with Petyr's brown hair and the small, sharp shard that Joryn had excised.

"Thank you," Elysen said.

Shelda's eyes closed and she lay still. The wound bubbled now, frothing slightly, and the old woman coughed, spraying blood into the air. Droplets of the hot liquid struck Elysen's face. She watched as Shelda's chest stopped moving. Elysen tucked the pouch inside her makeshift tunic.

"We need to find cover," Sethe said.

"This way," Grayson said.

Sethe backed up and grabbed Elysen with his free hand, keeping his crossbow trained on the deadfall.

"Give me your other crossbow," Elysen said. "I'll fight with you."

"You will kill us," Sethe said.

"I should kill you," she said.

"Give it to her," Grayson said. "We're probably going to die anyway."

They moved deeper into the thick stand of fir trees, much larger and closer together than the pines of the lower lands. They stopped with their backs against the stump of a tree that had split and fallen, a monstrous corpse stretched out into the forest, strewn with dead branches and sticks and the bodies of smaller trees that fell victim to its demise. Sethe released the second crossbow from behind his back and handed it to Elysen. She cocked it and held out her hand. He gave her one of his quivers. Far too big for her narrow arm, she strapped it to her thigh, trapping the hem of her sackcloth robe under the quiver so that she could easily reach the bolts. She loaded a bolt onto the crossbow and put her back to Sethe. Hawk and Grayson faced outward as well.

"We should go on the offensive," Elysen said.

"Don't trust her," Sethe replied.

"No," Grayson said. "She's right. If we wait here, they will creep up on us and kill us as surely as we stand here. We need to take the battle to them."

A twig snapped somewhere behind them. A squirrel chattered in the trees above them, angry at being awakened from a peaceful hibernation.

Grayson turned and grabbed Elysen's arm.

"Don't try to run away," he said. "Hawk, go." He motioned with one hand and Hawk disappeared.

Elysen yanked her arm from Grayson's grip and slipped away into the forest, creeping from tree to tree, stalking as silently as a deer. From somewhere behind her, she heard the snick of an arrow leaving a bow. Sounds of a scuffle. The hollow, grunting sound of a life being taken. She stopped, crouched down with her back against a tree and waited. The brush of fabric against a branch. The crunch of a soft boot on dead needles and twigs. She stood still. Frozen. Waiting. A movement in the trees in front of her, careful, watchful. She glanced down at her body, covered in black, her once pure white skin now covered with strange black shapes that swirled and flowed in odd patterns. In the shadows, she existed as specks of white against a background of night. The hunter before her searched for a human. She was a ghost. She raised her crossbow and waited. The stalker moved again. He stayed in the shadows, moving slowly, carefully. He drew nearer and then stopped, his face lost in the gloom of the forest. Elysen's eyes narrowed and the crossbow aimed of its own accord, years of practice making action an instinct. Her finger tightened on the release. The man's head came into view. She fired. Heard the thud as the arrow penetrated the skull. Something hit her in the shoulder. She reached down to reload, and found herself pinned to the tree behind her by an arrow. She gasped, put her foot through the stirrup of the crossbow and tried to pull the string back with one hand. Failing that, she dropped the crossbow and grabbed the shaft of the arrow where it protruded from her chest, just below her collarbone. She tried to break it, but the pain stopped her. She gasped for breath. As she crouched there, trapped, a man landed in front of her, as if from nowhere. She glared at him.

"Raes," she said through gritted teeth.

His menacing snarl turned into a puzzled expression and then horror. "What have they done to you?" he asked. He reached out and touched her face. She jerked her head away from his fingers and then turned back abruptly and spat in his face.

"Like a stupid child, you keep missing your mark," she said. "This is the second time you have tried to kill me. When are you going to get it right?"

"I'm not trying to kill you," he said. "I'm trying to save you."

"Well then," she said. "Why is this arrow sticking out of my body? Is this your idea of saving me?"

"You killed my man over there."

"And just what was he up to?"

"Same as me. Find you. Bring you home."

"To Yergen?"

Raes nodded.

"What if I don't want to go home?"

He shook his head. "You have no choice."

"Yes I do," she said. She brought her hand up quickly and tried to ram the crossbow bolt into Raes' side. He deflected it with his arm, but as he did, an arrow struck him, piercing his armor, snaking in just below his shoulder plate. As he tried to scramble away, another arrow split his back plate.

"Stop," Elysen said. Her cry came out half shout, half whisper. Her own desperation surprised her.

I should let them kill him, she thought. But something else, deep inside, told her no.

Raes dropped his bow and then scrambled in the snow to recover it. Grayson stepped from the shelter of a tree within forty paces of where Elysen sat pinned. A few moments later, Hawk appeared, crouched on a log above Raes' head.

"A dage of the Keep," Hawk said.

Sethe slipped from behind the tree and used both hands to snap the arrow close to Elysen's shoulder.

"All of your men are dead," Sethe said.

He pulled Elysen forward, leaving a short piece of arrow protruding from the tree, dripping blood. Sethe picked up the crossbow from the ground and unstrapped the quiver from Elysen's leg. He holstered both crossbows on his back again and pulled Elysen's robe off her shoulders, ripping the neck open to do so. Hawk and Grayson stood over Raes with their bows drawn, arrows aimed at his face. He snarled at them. The first arrow stuck awkwardly out of his shoulder, dripping blood. The second arrow had broken his armor but had not penetrated his skin.

"Don't kill him," Elysen said.

She winced as Sethe rubbed a spicy smelling powder into her wound, both front and back. He ripped a piece from the bottom of her robe, exposing even more of her flesh to the cold, and used the ragged piece of cloth to bind the injury, looping it over her shoulder and under her arm. The cloth became soaked with blood almost immediately. Sethe pulled her robe back around her shoulders and Elysen held it closed with her uninjured arm.

"We should kill him," Hawk said as he stared down the shaft of the arrow.

"No," Elysen said.

She staggered forward. Sethe caught her. She slumped down next to Raes and leaned close to him. His teeth showed between his lips and his eyes were angry.

"Go home, Raes," she said. "And tell Yergen that I'm coming for him."

Sethe pulled Elysen to her feet and then put his arm around her back to help steady her. Hawk backed away from Raes, but kept his arrow cocked and aimed. Grayson picked up Raes' bow and ripped the quiver from Raes' back. Raes rolled over and groaned as the strap of the quiver yanked on the arrow. They all stepped away slowly.

Elysen planted her feet wide, bringing Sethe to a stop. She took a ragged breath, and then spoke to Raes again. His face showed pain; wincing, frowning, snarling through clenched teeth.

"Tell my dear cousin one more thing for me," she said. "Tell him that I am the Shad'ya, and that he is Lord of nothing. She spat at the ground. "Nothing. Lord of nothing."

Twenty

That night they set up camp under a rocky outcropping at the base of a steep cliff. Grayson tended to Hawk's leg, binding it with cloth, using two short but stout sticks for splints. Elysen could hear Hawk's teeth grinding together.

"We should have killed him," Grayson said. "He'll bring more of the guard, and they'll be all over us."

"It'll take him a week to find reinforcements," Elysen said. She looked out into the swirling snow and added softly, "If he lives."

"What do we have in the way of weapons," Grayson asked. He checked his belt, touching an empty sheath where his knife should have been.

"I have a bow," Hawk said. "And three arrows."

"Two crossbows, three bolts," Sethe said. "And a knife I took from the dage."

"I have my bow as well," Grayson said. "And a few arrows." He paused for a moment. "We can't face another attack."

Sethe sat staring into the fire, chewing on a piece of dried meat. "Tomorrow, we will reach the end of the forests."

"Then we will be in the lands of ice?" Elysen asked.

Sethe nodded.

"Why did you let him go?" Sethe asked. He glanced at Elysen.

"We all let him go," she said.

"We followed her orders as if she was the leader," Grayson said with disgust in his voice.

"It's too late to worry about it now," Sethe said.

Grayson finished his work on Hawk's leg. Elysen checked her own wound. There were still some fluids seeping from under the bloody patch in front. She pulled her robe back over her shoulder. Grayson stood up and threw Shelda's deer hide coat and fur boot covers into Elysen's lap. She tucked herself into the coat like a fox into a hole, pulling the big hood up over her bare head.

"You went back and got Shelda's clothes?" she asked.

He nodded. Hawk ignored them and curled up close to the fire. Sethe lay on his side and sighed. Grayson stayed awake with his back to the fire so that his eyes could adjust to the darkness. Elysen watched them with narrowed eyes.

"Why did you let him go?" Grayson asked quietly. Elysen took a moment to listen to the steady, soft breathing from Hawk and Sethe.

"Raes was my friend once," she said.

"Some friend," Grayson said.

"Things change," Elysen responded.

"How so?"

She sighed and turned her face away.

"Is he the father of the child?" Grayson asked.

She shook her head. "No."

Grayson sat quietly and listened to the night. A light snow fell, blanketing everything in silence. The fire sputtered and steamed, but its heat kept it going.

"When we were children we used to sneak out of the Keep at night and ride into the hills," Elysen said. "We would lie on our backs all night, staring into the sky, watching the spirits of all the past Lords as they watched us." She paused. "This is the second time I could have killed him."

"When someone harms us we pray to the dark lords that misfortune will befall them," Grayson said.

"Then I will pray that blessings fall upon Raes."

"Why would you do that?" Grayson turned to look at her. Deep within her hood, her eyes shone in the firelight.

"Just to spite you," she said.

"You are crazy," he said.

She grinned and Grayson turned away.

"Do you know what these markings on my body mean?" she asked.

Grayson shrugged. "You'd have to ask Sethe. He is a spellcaster and a keeper of the word. Or maybe you will find out when we deliver you to the dark lords."

Elysen's breath came quicker. "I thought we were going to the lands of ice," she said.

"We will pass through the lands of the ice people. The southern path is too dangerous. We will take the northern path to the high desert. It is harsh and cold, but the ice people are peaceful and will not interfere with our journey."

Sethe's hoarse whisper broke the silence around them.

"Quiet now," he said. "It's time to sleep."

Hawk pulled his blanket around his shoulders and curled into a ball. Elysen stared into the fire and let the long night pass by. At some point, she nodded off to sleep, but slept sitting up. In the morning, she awoke to the gray dawn and groaned. She touched her shoulder and winced. Her wounded arm barely moved. She checked her belly as well. She scratched the jagged red scar where Joryn had cut into her. She winced in pain, but then scratched it again.

Hawk sat on the ground, stirring the remains of the fire. The snow stopped. Sethe sat with his hands in his lap. Hawk poured a cup of steaming black liquid and handed it to Elysen. It tasted bitter and pungent.

"This will help you heal," he said.

She stared into the concoction, startled at the reflection of her tattooed face. She sipped and almost spit it out.

"I am almost as tired of these healing potions as I am of being wounded," she said.

"You do seem to have your share of wounds and scars," Hawk said.

"More than you know."

Grayson appeared from out of the woods.

"The nights grow longer and longer, and the days grow shorter and shorter," he said. "It is as if the dark lords have hastened the Proste along our way."

"He's right," Hawk said. "The days grow short. And the Soel barely rises above the southern horizon."

Sethe stood up. "Well then," he said. "If the daylight is scarce, let's make good use of it."

Elysen stopped to rest often. At midday, they stopped to eat hard biscuits and cheese under a sky of dark, twisted clouds. An icy wind blew through the sparse stand of trees. Elysen drifted off to sleep. Hawk sat with her while Grayson paced and Sethe sulked.

Elysen woke after a while and struggled to a sitting position.

"Is the day over?" she asked.

"You only slept for a short time," Hawk said.

"This is the land of eternal evening," Sethe said. "It is no wonder that the ice never melts."

"How do you know we are traveling in the right direction?" Elysen asked. "I can't get my bearings. The Soel never quite rises before it sets, and the sky is always covered with clouds."

"The winds of life come off the great rivers of ice," Hawk said. "We follow the wind now."

"These are the winds of death," Elysen muttered.

As they traveled, the forest thinned out to a few straggling trees. At the last dim light of day, they finally stepped onto a wide sloping field of undisturbed snow. A cold wind blew off distant white cliffs, stinging their faces with bits of ice. The cliffs reached upward into the clouds.

"They say the ice is alive," Hawk whispered. "It moves and crawls so slowly that generations of our people pass by and the ice moves only a few paces. The spirit of the ice does not know the seasons as we do. It does not know youth or old age or even the passing of time. Our seasons are but the blink of an eye for the ice lord, exiled to these high slopes where nothing can live."

"Yet the Norgarden live here somehow," Elysen reminded him.

She gazed in wonder at the frozen world around them, musing, more to herself than to her companions.

"How can you look at all the majesty and grandeur and beauty in this world and believe that it is ruled by a lord of darkness? There is far more light in the world than there is darkness."

"Enough," said Grayson. "We camp here tonight. Tomorrow we head east. The next few weeks will be…" he paused. "Difficult."

They built a fire from gnarled twigs but the heat barely reached beyond the flames. Hawk shivered. His teeth chattered as he forced his chest to suck in and expel the frigid air. At first light, they walked away from the sparse forest and onto a giant sheet of endless white.

"We have to get him warm," Elysen said. "I have seen this before. He is dying of the cold."

"Nonsense," Sethe said. The older man's face had turned pale, and his lips were a bluish-purple. Grayson did not look much better.

"You are all succumbing to the cold," she said. "We have to get off this blanket of ice and get you somewhere warm."

"No," Sethe said. "We keep moving."

"Hawk is dying," Elysen said. "We have to warm him up."

"How is it that you don't feel the cold?" Grayson asked.

His teeth chattered as well. Sethe tried to be strong, tried to hide his shivering, but he could not. They hiked far onto the face of the glacier, higher and higher, avoiding the breaks and crevasses that were the only landmarks on an endless landscape of monotonous ice. All around them, as far as they could see, the ice stretched into a white and gray imitation of the flat, grassy plains of the Vyr. Above them, clouds rolled across the ice like misty apparitions waiting to claim their bodies when they fell.

"I need to rest," Hawk said. He dropped to his knees.

"No," Elysen cried, pulling him back to his feet. "You have to keep moving."

"Moving to where?" he said.

"Down," Elysen said. "We have to get off the ice. You can't survive this journey. It was insane to try."

Sethe pulled out a knife, familiar to Elysen with its orange-red blade and sharp edges, scalloped and sculpted in the dark reaches of Sunder Keep by her father's finest artisans and cutlers. He waved it at her, his tired eyes fixed on her face.

"That is my knife," she reminded him.

Why do I want that knife so badly? Why can't I just let Raes go? She wanted to hate him. She tried to imagine killing him with his own knife, but even as she poised, about to strike, his eyes stopped her and her resolve melted.

Sethe's voice broke her train of thought.

"We travel on the ice for three more days," he said. "Then we will pass the headwaters of the Mortain, where we will be warmed by the very fires of the Perde, the dark lord's place of torture and agony."

"I don't know about the Perde," she said. "But I do know that none of you will last on the ice for even one more day. You will all die tonight if you don't find warmth."

"The Mortain is the dark lord's river," Sethe said. His words were slow and slurred. "The dark lord is the creator and master of the Mortain, and of the Rift through which it runs. He melts the ice with great furnaces of fire and steam." Sethe waved his arm wildly as he spoke. "Now march onward," he said. He motioned with the knife, flicking it like the tongue of a serpent.

"No," she said.

Sethe lunged forward and grabbed her arm. Elysen remained calm, almost relaxed, as he touched the tip of the knife to her throat.

"You won't kill me," she said. "That isn't part of your plan."

"I might just make it part of my plan," he said.

Hawk came to life.

"No you won't," he said.

He grabbed Sethe from behind and peeled him away from Elysen. He looped his arms under Sethe's and pressed the older man's head forward and down.

"Do it," Grayson said.

Hawk put more pressure on Sethe's neck. The old man's face turned red, even in the cold, and he moaned. Grayson stood like a man mostly asleep.

"Let him go," Elysen warned.

Hawk ignored her and Sethe cried out. Elysen stepped in quickly and hammered Hawk in the lower back with a balled up fist. Hawk arched and gritted his teeth, but did not release Sethe. Elysen hit him again with the same result, and again, alternating fists each time. With the fourth hit, Hawk let go and staggered backwards. Sethe spun around, his face full of anger and fear. He surged forward, his cold, tired body moving slowly. Hawk looked ready, but even so, the sharp blade of Raes' stolen knife slipped neatly into Hawk's chest, and out again. Hawk's look of surprise was the only indication that the blade had even struck. Grayson stood frozen, uncertain. Hawk staggered backwards, and then sat heavily. His eyes closed and he lay down as if he were simply going to sleep. Grayson blinked. Sethe turned. He stared first at Elysen, then at Grayson.

"He was going to kill me," Sethe said. "The white witch has cursed us. She wants us to kill each other."

Grayson glared at Elysen. He pulled his bow from its perch on his back and nocked an arrow all in one movement. He pulled the cord back, and Elysen found herself staring at a glistening broadhead made of hard metal. She stood breathless. The wind whipped around her, flapping her coat around her legs. In one moment, she stared at death, in the next, Grayson turned and released the arrow. It struck Sethe in the chest and buried itself deep inside his body. He dropped to his knees and gasped. Blood trickled from his mouth.

"I will finish this task myself," Grayson said. "In the name of my brother Uemn, dead at your hands, I will finish this."

He repositioned his bow on his back and walked over to where Sethe knelt with his hands clutching the shaft of the arrow. Grayson picked up Raes' knife and tucked it into his own empty sheath.

He stepped over to Hawk and knelt down. Hawk's body sprawled at an awkward angle, his arms splayed out in unnatural anguish.

"Good-bye to you, brave soldier" he said. "May we meet again in the fires of the Perde."

Grayson stood up and glared at Elysen. "Hawk was fond of you," he said.

She waited for him to go on.

"I am not fond of you. Don't expect me to coddle you as he did."

"I don't," she said.

"We'll go on," he said.

She looked down at Hawk's body and then back into Grayson's sleepy eyes.

"You will be joining the others soon enough," she said. "And then I will be free anyway. You should run for the lowlands now, while you still have the strength."

"No," he said. "I will finish this."

"You are dying of the cold even now," she said.

He moved closer to her, his eyes fixed on hers. She stepped back. He lunged, grabbed her. Even cold and tired, Grayson still overpowered her. He tore her clothes from her body and threw them on the ground, then threw her down on top of the makeshift bedding. She scrambled to her hands and knees but he grabbed her and threw her down again. She rolled onto the ice, gasped for breath, and then he picked her up and dumped her on the small pile of fur once more. She moved slowly, crawling away, but he stripped and wrapped himself around her before she could stagger to her feet. He pulled her down and covered their bodies with his clothing. She struggled and tried to bite him, but he turned her so that her back pressed against him and his arms pinned hers against her sides. He clamped his legs around hers. She tried to kick, but he held her tight.

"Don't worry," he said. "I won't taint myself with your disgusting body."

Elysen clenched her teeth and lay there, as rigid as the lodge pole pine of the western mountains. Grayson's shivering body shook hers. The soot-colored day turned to darkest night. Elysen slept fitfully. She woke many times and tried to break away, but each time Grayson pulled her back. Finally, in the gray light of early dawn, he let her go. They stood, facing each other, naked, her feet on the ice, his on the pile of furs and wool that had made their bed. He threw her clothes to her and put on his own. He picked her pouch off the ice and looked inside.

"What is this stuff?" he asked.

"Keepsakes," she said. She wrapped her clothes around her body and held out her hand. Grayson stuck the pouch under his belt.

"Now," he said. "We'll finish this."

He pushed her forward. She moved slowly, looking back once at the two frozen bodies that lay sprawled on the endless expanse of ice. Even from a few paces away, they were nothing but tiny specks against the immensity of the glacier.

"You'll die here, too," Elysen said as she walked. Grayson sulked a few paced behind her. "Everyone that touches me dies."

"Everyone dies," Grayson said. "The point is to die well."

The familiar words startled Elysen.

"You would do well to just die," she said quietly. He pushed her in the back. She stumbled once before she regained her stride.

"You would do well to walk in silence," he said.

They traveled for three more days and nights. Each night Grayson disrobed her roughly and warmed his body against hers. She broke the silence only on the morning of the fourth day.

"I'm losing my body heat," she said as she pieced together her tattered clothes. "I need food."

"Suffer," Grayson said.

"You fool," she said. "If I die, so do you. Who will keep your filthy body warm at night if I die?"

He tossed her a piece of smoked beef and a frozen turnip. "This is all I have left," he said.

"According to Sethe, we should have come to the headwaters of the Mortain by now," Elysen reminded him.

"Just keep walking," Grayson said. His teeth were chattering again.

A damp mist hung around them. Between the gray of the ice and the gray of the sky and the stagnant vapor, the whole world became a thin cloud.

"We can't go any farther," Elysen said. "I can't see a thing."

"We're close," Grayson said quietly. A touch of awe and fear came through in his voice.

"How can you tell? This fog obscures everything."

"Can't you feel the temperature rising?" Grayson asked.

She nodded and opened her coat. "It is warmer," she said. "Maybe I won't have to sleep with you tonight."

He grunted. "Just keep moving forward."

"I don't know which way is forward," she said.

Her foot slipped and she fell. The ground turned wet and slippery, covered with a layer of slush.

"Follow the slope," he said.

As she peered more closely at the dingy ice, she could see tiny rivulets of water, streaming in the direction of her feet that now jutted out in front of her as she sat on the melting ice. She watched as the water pooled around the heels of her hands, felt it soaking into her clothes along her legs and lower back. She looked at her palms, now dripping with gritty water.

"The headwaters," she said.

"We are close," Grayson said.

"No, look." She showed him her palms. "We are here. These tiny streams of water. These are the headwaters. Trickling along here, pooling up somewhere ahead of us, one adding to another."

"Enough," Grayson said. "Get up and get moving again." She stared at her hands for a moment longer before Grayson yanked her to her feet by pulling on the back of her coat.

As they followed the flow of water, the ice began to slope downward at a more severe angle, forcing them to walk northward again, across the slope. Several times they had to leap over small rifts and cracks in the ice mass. The surface of the glacier became even more slippery. They slid and fell over and over again, until Elysen begged for rest.

"We have to keep moving," Grayson said. His eyes were wild with excitement.

"We'll kill ourselves," Elysen said. "We can't see where we are going, and the ice is unstable. We have no idea what's in front of us." She sat on the ground again in a puddle of water.

Grayson pulled her up once more. She stripped off her coat and carried it over her arm. She walked a few paces and fell again on the wet ice, skidding along quickly before the heels of her boots dug in. Grayson rushed to catch up with her, slipped himself, and skidded past. Elysen reached out and grabbed the hood of his cloak, but instead of stopping his forward slide, he pulled her along with him. She let go, but her momentum now carried her along an ever-increasing slope. Grayson slid on his back, his feet and hands moving in a kind of backwards crawl as a look of surprise and fear twisted his face. Elysen twisted onto her stomach and lost her coat.

The gray fog hung so still and thick that they could hardly tell they were moving. Only the scrape of ice under their hands and the spray of water from the heels of their boots assured them that they were sliding rapidly. Neither one uttered a sound as they scrambled for purchase on the ice. Elysen managed to roll onto her back, using her elbows to rotate so that her feet faced into the mounting wind as she picked up speed. Grayson slid faster and faster, and finally passed out of sight completely. The pitch of the slope became fearsome. Elysen's breath caught high in her throat as she moved faster than she had ever moved before, faster even than Temper's frothing gallop. The ground began to curve, her speed increased. Now skidding, now sliding, now falling, weightless, with the ice under her as if it were a vertical surface, her body barely touching it. The wind whistled around her, and then, suddenly, the grayness parted. She fell through the air riding a sheet of water, her feet pointing downward toward an icy lake of green water. It rushed toward her and swallowed her.

The whole world stopped suddenly. Hitting the water felt like falling onto a stone slab. The impact and the coldness paralyzed her lungs and pricked her skin with tiny needles. Tiny bubbles surrounded her, and her clothes twisted about her in a slow and savage parody of the winds that blew on the surface. She twisted and struggled, no air in her lungs, her head and eyes pounding. She kicked off her heavy boots and her feet hit something hard. She glanced downward. Grayson hung, suspended in the water as if he were a ghost, his gray-blue eyes imploring her. His fur coat billowed out around him. She reached down, grabbed the collar of his tunic with one hand and kicked his shoulder with her foot. She managed to peel his coat from his arms. The coat fell away from him, and she returned her gaze to the surface. Her body screamed for air.

She pulled hard on Grayson, but his weight just drew her downward. She let go of him and shed what remained of her makeshift garments. The irony of being naked again crossed her mind. She lost the last bit of air in her lungs as she giggled involuntarily and the cold clutched at her body. She looked down again and saw Grayson, still hanging there with his arms outstretched. Her sudden rush of inappropriate humor dissipated. She reached down and grabbed him and kicked and flailed for the surface. Her head broke into cold air. She sucked in as much as she could before Grayson pulled her under again. She let go of him and her body cramped from the cold. Darkness enveloped her once more.

Twenty-one

Elysen opened her eyes. Someone rocked her, awkwardly, in a wooden cradle. In the mist, she saw someone smiling at her. The face looked young and smooth, the hair light like wheat dried under the heat of the Soel. Elysen tried to call out, but no sound came from her lips. She tried to breathe, could not, tried again, but her chest filled with ice. She gagged, coughing and vomiting at the same time. The muscles in her chest and stomach all contracted at the same time, cramping her into a huddled ball. Someone picked her up as if she were a child and she hung for a moment, bent over in the middle, with a hard knot of something punching her in the stomach. She felt her body convulse violently again, but this time water gushed from her open mouth. She coughed and gagged at the same time, the cough tearing at her throat. More water. Then a moment's reprieve. She gasped, sucked in some air. Coughed again, this time a hoarse, racking sound followed by a mouthful of water that came bubbling up her throat.

"Just let me die," Elysen moaned.

She coughed again, spewing water and gagging on it as she tried to catch another breath. Someone rolled her onto her side. She retched again, coughing. More water.

"Not today, young lady," came a soothing voice.

Elysen opened her eyes. She looked into a puddle of mucous and water that slid back and forth across a wooden floor made of small strips of a dark brown wood. The smell of damp cedar stung her nose. Above her, the gray sky hung like fabric between the cliffs on either side of the small valley. Overhanging lips of dripping ice topped the steep cliffs. A sheet of water cascaded from a cleft in the ice above. Several boats bobbed in the water around the base of the waterfall, people prodding the water with their oars amidst the roaring spray.

A young man's voice drifted into her thoughts.

"She's awake."

Elysen turned her head slightly. The boy's ruddy blonde hair and pale skin accentuated his cheeks, reddened by the harsh cold. His blue eyes matched the sky above the distant Vyr. Something about him made her long for home.

Another man, older, but with merrier eyes, spoke as he rowed.

"We'll get her back to shore and then join the others." He leaned forward and peered at Elysen. She turned her head away and coughed out another mouthful of water against a pair of brown boots. She wiped her face on the rough blanket.

"Where am I?" she asked.

"You have fallen into the Cevante," the young man said. He seemed both excited and happy at her misfortune. "This is a most unusual occurrence. We have never heard of such a thing happening, not with a human anyway. My grandfather once told me of a great white bear that fell from these cliffs among the fleet, and that they tried to haul it aboard one of the boats but it flailed and slashed them so much with its great claws that they had to pull away, and that it swam all they way to shore and maybe lives there still in the forest of Ardien."

"Enough, enough," the old man said with a smile and a twinkle in his blue eyes. "Our young adventurer here is not ready for your stories."

The younger man smiled and spoke slowly.

"I'm Tobias," he said. "And this is my father Kendar. We were fishing. Imagine our surprise when you fell from the sky, almost directly into our nets."

Elysen suffered through another hoarse, rattling cough from deep within her chest.

His face became serious again. "Are you all right?"

"Of course she's not all right," Kendar said, frowning at his son. "She just fell from the cliffs and practically drowned in freezing water. She's lucky to be alive." He turned his attention toward Elysen and his voice softened.

"You chose a strange method of travel," he said. "That was a very dangerous fall. And the water is severely cold."

She nodded. "We got lost in the fog."

Tobias looked up at the cascading sheets of water. "We don't travel up to the ice very often. I have never ascended to the world above. But father has," he said with a moment of excitement in his voice.

"Leave her be now, Tobias," Kendar said. "She needs time to recover. She's in shock."

Tobias crossed his arms and watched Elysen. She turned her face away from his gaze and looked out across the water. The lake occupied most of the valley. Broad-leafed trees and thick bushes surrounded the shore. Kendar rowed with his back to the bow of the small boat. Tobias sat on a plank between Kendar and Elysen, facing her. Elysen faced forward, watching the shore draw nearer. They approached a grassy meadow that sloped into the green water, where short, tough rushes sprung up along the shoreline. Wooden piers supported a dock made of planks of wet, black wood that looked half-rotted. A group of people gathered around the edge of the water, watching as the boat approached.

Kendar guided his boat against the dock with barely a glance, as if he had done this same small task as often as Elysen had stepped into a stirrup. The people that stood along the shore stared at the strange figure huddled under the coarse blanket. Tobias followed Elysen's gaze.

"Word travels fast in our village," he said.

Kendar smiled and stepped out of the boat and onto the dock. He held his hand out for Elysen. She took it and stood up. Her slender leg slipped from under the blanket as she stepped onto the dock, at the same moment that the brown woolen fabric fell around her shoulders, exposing the stark black and white features of her neck and upper back, as well as her head and face. She collapsed into Kendar's arms and he lifted her up. A murmur of voices ran along the shoreline, following the rippling wake left by the boat. Elysen felt her heart pounding.

Tobias noticed Elysen's distress.

"Please forgive them," he said. "We've never seen a Vyrlander before."

"I'm not like most," Elysen said.

Tobias looped the bow rope around the top of the nearest piling. Elysen held the blanket closed with one hand, and used the other to pull it back over her head so that only her lower legs and feet showed.

"Let me walk," she said.

Kendar set her down and took her gently by the arm. She stumbled and he caught her.

"You're too weak to walk on your own," he said.

He swept her up into his arms again and carried her like a child, Tobias following a few step behind. The people stepped back and held their hands in the air, palms facing toward them.

"What are they doing?" she asked.

"They are asking for blessing to be bestowed upon you," Kendar said. "It is their way of greeting you."

"They don't seem very surprised to see me," Elysen said.

"Some of them have been waiting for you," Kendar said. "Look," he said. "Your presence has even brought out the doubters and those of little faith." He smiled and waved at a man who did not wave back, but instead carried a worried look on his face.

Some of the people placed their palms together and bowed their heads, murmuring with lips that moved but made little sound. Some showed curiosity in their eyes. But most were unwilling to even make eye contact with her. A bead of sweat trickled down her temple and she let the blanket slide off her head again as she opened the front just a bit to let more air in. An old man studied her intently, staring at the runes and spells that covered her scalp and face, but not looking into her eyes. A child tugged on the flared waist of his mother's tunic and looked up with imploring eyes. The mother ignored the child and kept her eyes fixed on Elysen as Kendar walked slowly by.

"What is this place?" Elysen asked.

"This is the beginning of the Rift," Tobias said as they walked up the grassy slope.

The small gathering of people began to follow them, at a distance. They chatted and mingled as they walked, but Elysen sensed an underlying current of concern. She glanced over her shoulder at the wary villagers. Tobias smiled at Elysen and continued to explain.

"The heart of the world pours forth heat, just as our hearts heat our bodies. Except the heart of the world is mighty, and the heat it creates melts the ice. The water runs toward the far sea as the river Mortain. The Cevante is the beginning of the Mortain, the blood of the Vyr." He glanced at her face. "You have the eyes of the Mortain. The same bright green."

"They are my mother's eyes," Elysen said.

"Yes," Kendar said. "They are."

"Did you know my mother?" Elysen asked. Her eyes opened wide.

"She was a great servant of the people," Kendar said. "She was a teacher and a scribe. Everyone knew her."

Elysen looked disappointed.

"What's the matter?" Tobias asked.

"I thought that my mother was a leader of some kind, not a servant."

Tobias laughed. Kendar smiled. They crested a small rise and now stood looking at a sloping meadow dotted with cabins. Kendar took her to one of the larger cabins and pushed the door open with his foot. Tobias brought in wood and made a fire.

"Where is my traveling companion," Elysen asked.

"One of the other boats recovered him," Kendar said. "I'll send Tobias to check on him later. Right now you should just worry about yourself."

While Elysen huddled in the corner, wrapped tightly in her blanket, Kendar boiled fish in an amber colored bowl. The outside had been blackened by many fires, but she caught glimpses of the inside surface of the bowl gleaming in the firelight. She tilted her head slightly, a puzzled look on her face. She pointed at the strange pot.

"What is that?" Elysen asked.

"A pot?" Tobias suggested.

"She's never seen bronze before," Kendar said.

Tobias's face registered a look of understanding. He walked over and tapped the metal bowl with a ladle of the same cedar-colored metal. The ringing sound made Elysen's skin crawl and she pushed against the wooden floor with her bare heels, pressing her back into the corner and baring her teeth.

"Easy there," Kendar said, holding out one palm toward Tobias, who stood in stunned silence, and the other palm toward Elysen.

"You are in alliance with the Uemn," she said. "I have seen this hard metal before. They have weapons like this." Her eyes were wide, frozen on the small round pot that dangled and swayed over the hot coals.

Kendar spoke, keeping his voice low and calm.

"We don't use our metal for weapons. We have no enemies, and the Uemn don't venture this far north."

Elysen remained stiffly planted against the corner wall.

"We have never knowingly disclosed the secrets of bronze to the Uemn," he said. "They would use such knowledge for violence. We are peaceful artisans and craftsmen. We don't make weapons." He held his arms wide. "Have you seen any weapons here?" He watched Elysen's face for a moment and then continued. "Only tools. We use our metal only for tools."

"That is not a tool," she said, pointing at the pot.

"And for cooking," Kendar chuckled. "This is hardly a weapon."

She took a deep breath, the first in several moments, and then coughed again, doubling over. She dropped to one knee, tried to stand up again, and then fainted.

She came awake wrapped in a softer blanket, lying on a lumpy pad covered with smooth fabric. She struggled into a sitting position, and then dropped back. She stared at the rafters above her, at the underside of the thatched roof. Tobias came over. He sat next to her and helped her to sit halfway up. He let her take a sip of the fish stew from a cup made of baked clay painted with a smooth, white covering. The soup steamed in the cool air of the cabin. The fire still glowed warmly on the far side of the room. Elysen swallowed, and then collapsed again.

"There is no need to be frightened of us," Tobias said. "You fell into friendly hands."

"I'm not frightened," Elysen said.

She tried to keep her eyes on him, but something drew her into the darkness. She yawned and her eyes closed. She woke to the quiet sounds of people moving about. She stared at the ceiling. A natural light filled the room, not firelight. Dim. Cold. Early morning. Low voices murmured around her.

"Are you hungry? Thirsty?" Tobias asked quietly.

Elysen held very still and listened for a moment to the voices.

"What is that sound?" she asked.

Tobias helped her to sit, propping her up with his arm. His warm hand touched her bare skin, and she shivered. He jumped and moved his hand around so that it touched only blanket. His cheeks turned red.

"Some of the villagers have gathered outside," he said.

"Let me see," Elysen said.

She struggled to her feet. She pulled the blanket around her back, rolling it around her body and tucking it under at the center of her chest, wearing it like a royal gown, her black and white shoulders and arms gleaming in the soft light. Tobias helped her to the window. She touched the window, and her fingers met with an almost invisible layer of hard material.

"Glazing," Tobias said.

"You have many strange things here," she said.

Tobias' eyes kept drifting toward the dark runes carved into her skin. Elysen stared out the window, ignoring his glances. She saw her own reflection in the smooth surface that covered the opening like a skin of water. She touched her damaged jaw and made a sour face.

Outside, people sat all around the cabin, paying no attention to the cold mist of gray dawn. One man rocked back and forth, chanting. Several of the women sat cross-legged, each one with several candles burning in front of them.

"What are they doing?" Elysen asked.

"They are praying," Kendar said.

"Why?"

He shrugged. "Why do any of us pray? For guidance. To calm our fears. To express our gratitude."

"To whom do they pray? The ice lord?"

Kendar shook his head. "The ice lord is but a name. We believe in the one power. Creator of the universe."

"What is the universe?" Elysen asked.

"The universe is everything," Kendar said.

"Thorsen created everything," Elysen said. She watched Kendar's face carefully.

Kendar smiled. "It is hard for a Vyr mind to grasp the greatness of the realms beyond our limited vision."

"Maybe I know more about other realms that you think I do," Elysen said. She turned and gazed out the window again. "Can you send those people away?"

Kendar shook his head.

"They have a right to stay there as long as they like," he said. He paused and studied Elysen's face for a moment as she gazed out the window. He clasped his hands together and spoke quietly.

"As soon as you are able to travel, we will walk to Hashanah, our ancient city. We will seek counsel from your…from the Madeire, who resides there. She is our most revered spiritual leader. Tobias and I are but humble boat builders and fishermen. The Madeire will be able to answer your questions far better than we can."

Elysen reached up and touched the stubble that used to be her hair. "I have to do something with this," she said. "I want to scrape it off."

"All of it?" Tobias asked.

She nodded. "I just need a sharp blade."

Tobias touched her shoulder. "Let me," he said.

He led her to the table and she sat down. Tobias brought a bowl of hot water and a bronze blade. Elysen reared back when she saw the flat knife.

"Don't be afraid," he said.

"I thought you said that you only make tools out of metal," she said.

Tobias rotated the blade so that she could see it better. "This is a tool," he said. "We use it to shave with. It's much better than a stone blade."

He dipped his hands in the steaming water and rubbed a lathering lotion onto her scalp. Elysen tried to relax.

"You build boats?" she asked.

Tobias began to scrape the top of her head lightly.

"Yes," Tobias said. "Boat building has been the art of our family for generations."

He continued to shave her as they talked, his fingers dancing across her scalp. She felt her shoulders relax. The sky brightened and Elysen stared out the window. A small group of crafts moving slowly into the lake, white sails tilting in the wind.

"Why do they tip like that?" she asked. "Can't you build a boat that stands up straight?"

Tobias laughed. "They are tacking. See?" He pointed out the window. "They set their sails against the wind. It pushes them sideways. Underneath each boat we have secured a keel, a long blade of wood that slices through the water like a knife." He tried to show her with his hand, fingers pointing downward, hand moving forward. "See? The sideways pressure pushes the keel forward."

"They look like they're going to fall over."

"Never," Tobias said. "We craft our ships to tack like that. It is their way. They use the power of the wind to steer their course, even if it is directly into the wind. See them come about?"

The fleet turned, one by one. The sails flapped loosely in the wind for a moment, then filled again, and the ships began to move forward again, at an angle opposite to their original course.

Tobias continued. "Rather than fight against the wind, like an oarsman, they use the power of the wind, bending with it rather than fighting against it."

"They are quite beautiful," Elysen conceded. "I would like to sail in one someday."

"You did, yesterday."

"But your father was rowing."

"We furled the sail to keep the boom from swinging around," he said. "The last thing we needed was to knock you out of the boat. But, I have had an idea, for running with the wind, as we were last night. A large sail, deployed off the bow, to catch the wind and pull us forward."

Kendar smiled. "Our attempts so far have failed," he said. "Our sailcloth is too heavy. It will not fill with wind. It just drags in the water."

"I know it can work," Tobias insisted.

Kendar patted Tobias on the back and smiled.

"This one is a dreamer," he said.

"You need silk," Elysen said.

"What is silk?" Tobias asked. His eyes showed his excitement.

"It is the yarn of the silkworm. It spins a cocoon of silk. We harvest the cocoons and unravel them. The thread is as fine as my hair, when I have hair." She touched her naked scalp. "But silk thread is far stronger than these woolen twines you use to weave this blanket."

Tobias looked doubtful. He rubbed her head with a towel and then he was done. The absence of his touch left her feeling empty.

"Well," Kendar said. "Even if a worm could make thread light enough and strong enough to make a sail, there are no such creatures here. Do you feel well enough to travel?"

Elysen nodded.

"You'll need some clothes," he said. "You may take a shirt and boots. We have little else to offer."

Tobias gave Elysen an extra pair of his boots, made of soft brown leather and designed to cover his legs up to his knees. They hung loose below her knees, gathering a bit around her calves and ankles. He handed her a heavy, cream-colored woolen shirt that had been quilt-stitched and padded and lined with a softer fabric.

"I'll give you my pants, if you need them," he said.

The shirt hung long enough to cover her hips and upper thighs.

"This will do," she said. "I don't want to see you go without pants." Tobias smiled at her and gave her a leather belt to tie around her waist.

"Your friend left this," Kendar said.

He handed her a pouch. She stared at it for a moment and rubbed the soft leather between her fingers before she tied it to her belt.

"And here," Kendar said. He handed her a knife in a leather sheath. "He left this behind too."

Elysen slipped the knife free. The red obsidian blade and leather handle were unmistakable. Holding it sent a shiver up her spine. She closed her eyes and tried to remember Raes, but all that came to her was the feel of Tobias shaving her head.

"And where is friend Grayson?" she asked.

"He seems to have slipped away," Kendar replied.

"Well, I'll be sure to thank him when I next see him," Elysen said as she pushed the knife back into the sheath and tucked it under her belt. Again, instead of imagining the red blade sliding across Grayson's throat, all she could think of was the feel of Tobias' finger on her bare scalp.

Kendar made fish rolls with sticky boiled grain and wrapped them in cornhusks. He stuffed them into a small pack and they stepped out, into the circle of peasants that surrounded the small cabin.

"They have come from very far away," Kendar said. "I don't even recognize many of these people. They must have traveled all night." He scratched his beard. "Many of them knew your mother. They honor her memory."

"You said she was a servant," Elysen reminded him.

"In our culture," Kendar said. "There is no greater station, no greater honor, than to serve. Your mother was an example to us all. These people remember her with reverence."

They walked away from the cabin. The people that had been kneeling and sitting now stood, some staring, some with eyes closed and hands clasped.

"Why did she leave?" Elysen asked Kendar.

"She left as an emissary to your people," Kendar said. "In order to serve the

Vyr. It was a dream she had always had, to be able to share our culture, our ways, our beliefs with the people of the high plains and the deserts. Even as a young girl, she wanted to unite all the people of the world in peace."

"She did not succeed," Elysen said.

"Maybe she isn't done yet," Kendar replied.

"She's dead," Elysen reminded him.

"We have heard that her body is dead. Yet her spirit lives on."

Elysen pondered as they walked through the silent forest. After a while, they stopped and Kendar handed out the fish rolls. Elysen made a face as she tasted hers. Kendar looked concerned for a moment, and then smiled.

"Maybe my fish rolls take some getting used to," he said.

"The fish tastes raw," Elysen said.

"It is," Kendar replied.

Tobias smiled and stuffed his roll into his mouth. Elysen ate slowly. Pieces of sticky, brown grain stuck to her fingers, and Tobias brushed one from the corner of her mouth.

"That was really awful," she said. "But thank you."

Kendar took it good-naturedly.

"See? If your mother had lived, you would have gotten to taste fish rolls a long time ago."

They stood and walked again in silence. The woods became dark but they finally emerged from the forest and stepped onto a vast plain. Hashana sprawled in front of them. Rows and rows of small buildings, some with large stone fireplaces and foundations, stretched out along pleasant winding avenues that were paved with small, square flagstones.

Near the center of the town, on a small rise that stood above a group of tall, stone buildings, an immense structure towered above the surrounding homes like a mountain above foothills. From the distance, it appeared to be as long as twenty of the smaller buildings around it. The stone roof peaked into a single tall spire and remarkable arched supports jutted out along the roofline, giving it an almost skeletal appearance. Elysen sensed that the building made the shape of a short sword, with the entrance at the base of the hilt. Two tall, pointed towers guarded the main doors.

"There will be a great feast tonight to celebrate your safe arrival," Kendar told her.

He took her arm and she forced her eyes away from the giant stone palace.

They walked into town down a narrow, winding street. The constant mist of the valley diffused the evening light, making everything a dull gray color.

"Where will I stay?" she asked.

"We will take you to the home of our Madeire," Kendar said. "She is our spiritual leader. She'll take good care of you."

They stopped at the intersection of two avenues. Elysen glanced upward, toward the cliffs that loomed over the valley like silent leviathans; their white mantles perched precariously, as if they were only moments from sliding into the valley, crushing it under mountains of frozen rock and ice.

"I have to leave you here," Tobias said. "There are duties that I have to attend to."

Tobias turned and walked away. He glanced back over his shoulder and smiled as he left.

"Not everyone appears to be as happy to see me as you two are," Elysen said, remembering the faces of the people on the shore of the Cevante, and the expressions of the villagers that waited around Kendar's hut.

Kendar shrugged and motioned for her to proceed.

"Some refuse to believe the obvious," he said. "Your coming has been foretold. The signs are abundant. Our valley grows hotter every year. The Soel used to peek through the upper mists every now and then during your summer months, but it has been years since we have seen it. I don't think that Tobias has ever seen it."

"How old is he?"

Kendar smiled. "We don't measure time as you do. We have only two seasons. This is the season of darkness, where our days become shorter and shorter until we have but dawn and dusk, and nothing between, and then, gradually, the days lengthen until we have no night at all. We are in the season of darkness now. This day is almost done, and it seems as if it had only begun."

"I feel that so much has happened to me in such a short day," Elysen said. "At times in my life, the seasons have come and gone with nothing but boredom between. These last days, since the season began to turn, have been…" Her voice trailed off. She stood, staring at nothing.

"You have much on your mind," Kendar said. "Come along, I will introduce you to our Madeire."

They began to walk again.

"You did not answer my question," Elysen said.

"What question was that?"

"About your son. How old is he?"

"We measure age in turns of the world. He has seen twenty turns."

"What do you mean by 'turns of the world'?" Elysen asked.

Kendar scratched his forehead just above a bushy eyebrow.

"The Soel is fixed in the heavens," he said. "And the world turns, rotating on an axis like this."

With his hands, he tried to show Elysen a ball, turning in the air. She said nothing, but her blank stare caused him to clasp his hands together.

"Maybe you should ask Tobias to explain it," he said. "He can take you to the observatory and show you."

They stopped in front of a large home. Just east of them, the towering citadel rose above the town like a crouching animal.

"What is that place?" Elysen asked, pointing.

"That is our cathedral," Kendar answered. "The observatory is in the east wing. Tobias can show it to you tomorrow."

"It is magnificent," she said.

Kendar looked at it for a moment and then nodded.

The light began to fade around them, plunging the world into dusk, and the cathedral turned into a cold stone shadow that watched over the town. Kendar knocked on the wooden door in front of them. A cool wind whipped down the street and slipped down the back of Elysen's shirt, brushing icy fingers against her body.

The door swung open. Inside, an elderly woman beamed. Her face wrinkled in a hundred ways as she smiled. She carried a small storm lantern in her hand, dangling from a short wicker handle, and the light danced in her eyes.

"Lady Elysen," she said. "We meet at last. There has been much excitement in our village since your strange arrival." She took Elysen's arm with a gentle hand and led her inside. "Come in as well, Kendar," she said.

He smiled. "Please pardon me, honorable Madeire, but I have things to attend to before the feast."

He left. Elysen looked puzzled. "Why do you throw a feast for me?"

The Madeire laughed, sounding like the soft clatter of golden bells.

"You landed here during the time of the Feast of Jihn, one of our patrons. We feast each turn on this same day, to honor him. He believed in man's goodness and the Lord's abundance. He was a great teacher."

"He's dead?" Elysen asked.

"Oh my, yes. He's been dead for a thousand turnings. His spirit lives on, as do his teachings. Through prayer and mediation, he became aware of many truths. He started his life as a warrior, ended it as a monk, hiding in this valley."

"What caused him to lay down his arms?"

"He came to conquer us, but we welcomed him with open arms and he became curious about our culture, and began to study it. One day, he found that he had forgotten about his quest. His men abandoned him, although it is said that none of them ever returned to their homes. Their ignorance doomed them. Jihn's spirit lives on within us, reminding us to place study and worship above any worldly desires. You must be looking forward to the feast. You look as if you have not eaten in weeks."

"I had fish rolls for lunch," she said. She wrinkled up her nose and the Madeire smiled.

"Well," the Madeire said, "we need to get you well fed and rested. All this coldness and travel and hunger can't be good for the baby. And we need to get you some clothes as well. Let me see what they did to you."

Elysen stood with a strange look in her eyes. "How did you know about the baby?" she asked.

The Madeire smiled and gently led her into a large room kept comfortable with a cozy fire. The warm orange light filled the room, but left darkness around the corners and in the nooks and crannies of the shelves and sparse furnishings. The two women stood facing each other in the center of the room, next to the only two chairs.

"Now," said the Madeire. "Let me see what they have done to you."

Elysen slowly opened the blanket and let it fall to the floor. The Madeire nodded and then shook her head, clicking her tongue.

"Was it painful?" she asked.

"Yes."

"May I take a closer look?"

"I'd rather you didn't."

"I have some robes that I can give you. Do you have a preference for color? I have a wonderful blue-green that would match your eyes."

"I prefer black."

The Madeire smiled and said nothing more. She stepped away for a moment, into the next room, and came back with a pile of clothes. Elysen sorted through the pile and chose a thick, long-sleeved wool shirt and pants made of smooth but tough fabric. Though the clothes fit snugly, they gave and stretched as she moved, without a hint of stress on the almost invisible seams. She slipped on a pair of dark socks and black leather boots that were slightly large on her narrow feet. She pulled a sleeveless, black leather tunic over her head. It covered her chest and shoulders and laced closed along a wedge shaped opening in the front that came to a point at the waist, just above her hips. A short, skirt like flare covered her upper thighs.

"You have chosen well," the Madeire said. She looked at Elysen's feet. "We will have a better pair of boots made for you," she said. "And I have a cloak and gloves that will serve you during the cold of night." The Madeire tapped her finger against her upper lip in thought, and then scratched her chin. "I have," she said, "a hat that I wove myself, that I think you might like to wear, at least until your hair grows back completely."

The Madeire brought out a black woolen cap and handed it to Elysen. The simple cap stretched over her scalp like a stocking.

"Thank you," Elysen said. She took the cap off again and held it in her hands.

The Madeire dismissed her gratitude with a wave and a smile.

"It is the very least that I can do for you, my dear. Now, let us sit for a while before we have to go out again and join in the feast."

"Do you think we might be able to sit on the floor?" Elysen asked.

The Madeire looked puzzled.

"Of course," she said.

They pulled the cushions off the hard wooden chairs and placed them on the floor. Elysen sat cross-legged, and the Madeire tried to imitate her.

"I'm afraid my old bones won't let me sit like this," she said as she struggled to get comfortable.

She grabbed another cushion from the floor behind her and stuffed it up against the base of the chair so that she could sit with her back propped up.

"Are you warm enough?" the Madeire asked.

"Too warm," Elysen said.

"Well, no wonder. You have completely dressed yourself for outdoor weather."

"It seems like forever since I slept in a house, in a bed."

"There are times in our lives like that," the Madeire said. "I too once went on a journey far from home, far from the comforts of this place."

"Why?"

The Madeire shrugged. "Why do you journey?"

"I am forced to. Were you also forced to flee?"

"No," she said, pondering for a moment. She sighed and closed her eyes, and then smiled as she recalled something fond to her. "It is our custom to leave our village. We wander into the wilderness to follow our hearts, with nothing but the clothes upon our backs. No weapons, no provisions. We travel until we receive our calling." She paused for a moment. "My calling was to return here. Your mother's calling was to travel southward, to the plains."

Elysen sat quietly.

The Madeire pointed at Elysen. "The clothes that you now wear were clothes that I wore on my sojourn. I have kept them all these years, tucked safely away in a box made of yellow cedar to keep the moths and bugs away, for what reason I did not know until now." She paused again. "You see? You are well provided for along your way."

"I have been starved, beaten, tortured, stripped, lied to, and abused in all manner of ways. Not well provided for at all."

"Ah, but here you are, and you are alive and well. You have everything you need. Nothing more, nothing less."

Elysen yawned. "Pardon me," she said.

"You are exhausted," the Madeire said.

"No. Not at all."

With the warm, soft glow of the fire against her cheeks, Elysen yawned again.

"Rest for a few moments," the Madeire said.

"There will be plenty of time to rest when I am dead," she said. She yawned again.

"Take off your boots, and your tunic, and lie down for a short while here in front of the fire," the Madeire said.

Elysen shook her head, but her eyes were drifting toward the floor. The Madeire went on.

"Settle down here for a moment," she said. "And I will tell you about your mother."

Elysen took off her boots and placed them within reach, and then unlaced the tunic and placed it on a chair behind her. The Madeire reached out and gently guided Elysen's head toward her lap. Elysen rested her head on the Madeire like a child finding comfort with her mother, a comfort that Elysen had never known. They both stared into the fire.

"Everyone I care for meets with a terrible fate," Elysen said. The Madeire's hands settled onto Elysen's scalp like cool, dry leaves.

"You are seeing only the circumstances around you," the Madeire replied. "You are not the cause of pain and suffering in this world. If anything, you give us hope."

"How could that be? Hope for death?"

The Madeire stroked Elysen's shining head and studied the glyphs and runes carved there.

"Hope for peace, and harmony," the Madeire said.

"Peace is what my mother dreamed of," Elysen said.

The Madeire nodded and stared into the fire.

"Your mother was a spirit-singer," the Madeire said. "She could hear the songs of people's hearts. It was her gift. And yet, she could not hear her own song. She drowned it in sorrow, blocked by a darkness that she could not avoid. She yearned so much for peace for herself. I think that she believed that she was destined to suffer."

"Maybe she was right," Elysen said. She struggled to stay awake. "Tell me what she looked like," she asked. "Was she like me?"

"No," the Madeire said. "She had freckles. And dark, silky hair that glowed red in the light of the Soel. She was so beautiful. So beautiful. Graceful, strong, and she could capture you with her eyes."

The Madeire paused, lost in thoughts and memories.

Tears filled Elysen's eyes. "I wish I could have known her. Maybe everything would have been different if she had lived."

"But she did not," the Madeire said quietly.

The Madeire stroked Elysen's head with a gentle hand. The pain and sorrow welled up inside Elysen and spilled out in salty tears.

A warrior feels no pain. A warrior feels no pain.

The Madeire closed her eyes and whispered softly, almost singing, but the tune sounded more like breathing, and the words were simple.

"Father, who watches over us, father, who created all, hear our prayer for your daughter here on earth, and her child, your child. Guide her and protect her, lead her and comfort her. Let her find joy, even in sorrow. For her life will be hard, and she will feel much of the world."

Elysen felt her chest relax, and her sobs floated away into the cool, damp air.

"Who were you talking to?" she whispered.

"I speak to the trees and the sky and the fish of the sea," the Madeire replied.

Elysen dozed, and awoke to the sound of quiet voices. She found herself curled in a comfortable kitten-like ball in a pile of pillows. Light filled the room. The boots and gloves and hat and tunic that the Madeire had given her sat neatly piled, still within easy reach of Elysen's hands. Elysen pushed herself into a sitting position, and then rocked back and forth for a moment before she fainted.

She awoke again, and this time the Madeire held her head and gave her a sip of warm broth.

"You will need to drink all of this before you try to sit up again," she said.

Across the room, Corde sat in one of the large, wooden chairs, waiting patiently. Elysen stared at him in disbelief.

"I thought I'd pop in and check on you," he said. "After you didn't show up at the feast. We were worried."

Tears filled Elysen's eyes and her chest heaved. "Oh Corde," she said. "It is so good to see you again."

Seeing tears in Elysen's eyes brought tears to his own.

"I came by earlier," Corde said. "But you were still sleeping."

"Slept through both day and night," the Madeire said. She turned toward Elysen. "Corde has been by seven times now."

Elysen pushed herself up to a sitting position. She wiped her eyes with her fingers.

"Are you ill?" Corde asked.

"I feel as if there are worms crawling in my belly," she said.

"Your body is adjusting to the baby," the Madeire said. She smiled as widely as a new father.

Elysen touched her stomach. "I fear for his safety," she said. She glanced at the Madeire and tears began to fill her eyes again.

"Now, now," the Madeire said. She stroked Elysen's head and wiped away the tears with the back of her old, wrinkled fingers. "Your baby is just fine. You would be surprised how your body protects the new life within it."

"But we were so cold, so hungry, so tired."

"All that is behind you now," the Madeire said. "Corde, please fetch another cup of this broth."

Corde hurried into the next room and reappeared with another cup. Elysen took it from his hands. She paused for a moment and shut her eyes as her fingers touched his. Then she took the cup and began to gulp down the steaming greenish-brown liquid.

"Slowly," the Madeire cautioned. "You need to keep this broth down. If you drink too fast, you will likely waste it on my floorboards."

Someone knocked softly at the door. Corde answered and admitted Tobias into the room. He sat on the floor and watched Elysen sip broth.

"Why are you staring?" she asked.

He blushed and turned his attention toward his fingers.

"He must have told the story of your landing a hundred times or more during the last few days," Corde said, smiling. "He has talked of nothing else but you."

"Enough," Tobias said. He rolled his eyes and his cheeks grew a shade redder.

Elysen smiled, but the moment passed as she noticed Corde and Tobias, both staring at her as if she floated in the air. A look of concern replaced her smile.

"What's the matter?" she asked.

Corde laughed. Tobias suddenly took interest in his fingers again. The Madeire took Elysen's hands and clasped them between her own.

"Your smile," she said. "It lights up your whole face. Your eyes come alive, and our hearts share your joy. You should smile more often." The Madeire smiled, but as she saw Elysen's horrified reaction, her smile faded.

"I have nothing to smile about," she said. She turned her head away from them and stared at the gray sky.

"There is much to be happy about," the Madeire said.

"You're alive," Tobias said, "You're with friends now. You're with child." His voice trailed off.

Elysen shook her head. Her eyes gleamed but she held back her tears.

No more crying, she told herself.

"You're all in great danger," she said. "They will come looking for me."

"You're safe here for now," the Madeire said. "Enjoy this moment."

"It won't last," Elysen said.

"Nothing lasts," the Madeire said. "We are but shadows. One moment here, the next gone." She paused and closed her eyes before she continued. "One learns to appreciate the moments of happiness."

"I can't," Elysen said. "I won't let myself care again. I couldn't stand to see any more of my friends hurt."

They all sat in silence, pondering their own thoughts. Elysen broke the silence.

"Before I go, I'd like to see your temple," Elysen said.

Tobias jumped up.

"I can take you there," he said.

Corde put his hand on the boy's arm to calm him down. The Madeire smiled and winked at Corde. He removed his hand from Tobias' arm. Tobias helped Elysen to her feet and Corde helped her get dressed.

"I'm like a baby," she said as Corde pulled her leather tunic over her head and laced it for her. The Madeire placed a dark cloak over Elysen's shoulder and shooed her and Tobias out the door. Corde watched them walk away.

Tobias led Elysen up the hill.

"Slow down," she said. "My legs don't seem to be fully awake yet."

"Sorry," he said with an edge of excitement in his voice. He almost danced as he walked. "It isn't a temple," he said. "We call it the Citadel d'Vie, the place of life. Built long ago by our ancestors. Much of the knowledge that they tried to retain has been lost over time. But some of us persist. We try to keep the flame of knowledge alive."

They were walking uphill, and as they came around a corner Elysen stopped to catch her breath. The Citadel rose before her, stark and gray and imposing against the misty sky. She felt a tremor of fear and awe as she thought of the power that created such a thing.

"It's beautiful," she said.

"Come on," Tobias insisted. "There is something I want to show you."

He took her hand and they climbed a long flight of stone steps that led up to the citadel. They stopped in front of a set of doors hewn from giant planks. The wood showed a darkness that came only with age. Elysen craned her neck back and looked up toward the peaks of the twin towers that guarded the doors.

"Is it as big as Sunder Keep?" Tobias asked.

Elysen smiled. "Oh, no. Sunder Keep is much larger. But this is far more intricate. Sunder Keep is like a block of stone compared to this."

Tobias pushed open a smaller door cut into the bottom of one of the huge arched ones.

"Are there no guards?" Elysen asked.

"Why would there be guards?" Tobias responded.

Elysen glanced at him. He pulled her inside, into a dark, empty cavern. Even through their gloves, the feel of his hand, clutching hers, gave her a chill of excitement. The high ceilings arched above them, and the sounds of their boots echoed off the walls. Elysen turned as she walked, trying to see everything. The dim light filtered in through cross-shaped openings in the walls, throwing white streams across the emptiness. Tobias pulled on her arm and she hurried along with him.

If only all of life could be like this moment, she thought. It suddenly came to her that they were completely alone.

"Why is it so empty?" she asked.

"Not many people come here any more," he said. "My father says that the Norgarden are losing their faith." He looked around at the empty Citadel and shrugged. "Anyway, here is what I wanted to show you."

He led her around a corner and into one of the large side wings. Elysen stopped and stared. A tiny flame hung in the center of the room, high above the floor, suspended from the end of a long, curved pole. It burned hot and bright. Large loops circling at odd angles filled the rest of the room. Each loop had a ball; each ball sized and shaped differently than all the others. A brown and blue ball hung affixed to one loop, halfway across the chamber. An old man sat on a stool, watching that ball, as if he expected it to do something.

"What is this place?" Elysen asked.

"This is our observatory," Tobias whispered.

Elysen raised her eyebrows and tipped her head. "What is he doing?" she asked. She pointed at the old man.

"That is Veger," Tobias said quietly. "He is the keeper of the history of the universe. Come on."

As Tobias led her to Veger, they stepped over a thin slot in the floor. A pointed post protruded from the slot, just touching the blue-ball hoop. As they approached the old man, he glanced at Elysen and nodded, and then returned his gaze to the ball.

"What is he doing?" Elysen whispered to Tobias.

Veger glared at her. "I am observing," he said.

Elysen glanced toward Tobias. Veger peered at Elysen and then slid off his stool and came close to her.

"You are Elysen," he said. "Daughter of Aephia."

She nodded.

"The Madeire must be very happy to see you," Veger said.

Elysen looked confused. "She was very gracious," she said.

Veger nodded.

"Kendar was trying to explain the universe to Lady Elysen," Tobias told Veger. "He thought you might be able to show her."

Elysen reached out and lightly touched the cold black curve of the loop. Veger swatted at her hand and she pulled it back.

"What is that?" she asked.

"What does it feel like?" Veger asked her.

"It feels like metal," she said.

He nodded. "You have seen metal before."

"We had some at the Keep," she said. She remembered the look and feel of her simple crown made of silver, and then she felt the long blade of hard metal in her hands again, heard it scrape against the stone floor. She shivered.

"You have quite a bit of metal here," she said. "I've seen pots and pans and plates and even cups. And a representation of a bird. And now this."

Veger nodded. "We mix two ores together to make our bronze. But this is something much more ancient and advanced. We do not even know what it is."

He tapped the loop with his fingernail and the chamber filled with a sweet ringing sound. Elysen suppressed another shiver.

"Show her the observation," Tobias said. His voice quavered with excitement.

Veger chuckled. "There are not many Norgarden who have any respect for my science," he said. "There are a few who tolerate me. And then there is little Tobias."

He reached out and ruffled Tobias's hair. Tobias smiled but pulled his head out of the old man's reach.

"What is this?" Elysen asked.

"We study the universe here," he said. Veger pointed at the flame that hissed above them. "That is the Soel." He touched the blue ball. "And this is our world," he said.

He took Elysen's arm and pulled her closer. A smaller, gray ball hung on a loop around the blue and green one.

"That is what you call Turoc," he said. "As you can see, it is just a small ball of rock that circles our world in endless procession."

As Elysen struggled with her confusion, Veger walked over to the post and began to turn a small handle. As he did, the post moved in the slot, sliding very slowly backwards. At the same time, all of the hoops moved, spinning slowly around each other. Elysen jumped back as the blue ball spun inside its tiny loop. The room filled with the sounds of creaking saddles and swarms of bees.

Veger stopped and the array came to a rest as suddenly as it had come to life. Elysen leaned closer to the brown ball and watched carefully as the tiny orb Veger had called Turoc came to a stop.

Veger returned and leaned forward as well.

"This is our world," Veger said, pointing at the larger of the two balls. "And with this array we can predict the positions of Turoc and the Soel at any point in time."

Elysen frowned. "I thought that the Vyr was flat, and green."

"It depends on what you call the Vyr," he said.

He pulled a thin, straight stick from his pocket and used it to point to a spot on the ball. Elysen placed her hands on her knees and leaned even closer to the ball.

"See this spot of green?" Veger asked.

She nodded and squinted.

"That is the plains of the Vyr. And here is the Rift, and this blue down here is the Sud de Mer."

Elysen pointed at the sparkling white cap on the top of the ball.

"Then these are the icelands," she said.

Veger nodded. Elysen frowned.

"Most of this world is covered with ice and water and desert," she said. Veger nodded again and crossed his arms. "It looks almost dead," she noted.

"It is," Veger said. "Mostly dead. Killed in the days of Thorsen and Kaan."

Elysen leaned ever closer, examining the tiny patch of green.

"Turoc's Cauldron," she whispered. Elysen used her finger to point and Veger pushed it away with his stick. "Careful," he said. "This is very delicate."

Elysen could not contain her excitement. "And there are the Mountains of Oken." Her eyes glistened.

"Yes, yes," Veger said. Elysen came upright suddenly. She looked up at the burning flame, and then returned her gaze to the orb of the Vyr.

"There is a shadow on the Cauldron," she said.

Veger nodded. "I have returned the array to the time of your birth. A shadow passed over the Soel that day." He used his stick to point at Turoc. "See? Turoc, in its rotation, passed in front of the Soel." He stood up and put a hand on his lower back. He winced and then continued. "This happens every once in a while. It is nothing to fear. Nothing to be alarmed about."

Elysen walked over and pushed on the post. Veger's eyes popped open and his mouth opened, but it was too late. The array hummed and the pieces moved again. They came to rest slowly and Elysen looked closely.

"The shadow again," she said.

Veger pushed her away and then leaned over so that he could see. The array seemed to have returned to almost exactly the same position.

"Interesting," he said. He glanced up at the complex web of loops with a puzzled look on his face. He did some calculations in his head, humming and chewing on his lip as Elysen and Tobias waited. He finally spoke.

"If you are in the hills of the Vyr, just south of Sunder Keep, during the hot months two summers from now. You will see this shadow again."

Elysen took a deep breath and put her hands on her hips.

"Why did it move to that position?" she asked.

Veger tipped his head.

"This is an extremely unlikely result," he said. "Very odd. There is a power here that speaks to you."

Elysen blew a bit of air out of her nose.

"And what exactly is it saying?" she asked.

"You will not know until your mind is open," he said. In the meantime, I have a gift for you."

He tottered out of the room, leaving Elysen and Tobias alone for a moment. Tobias grinned at her. Elysen felt her happiness slipping away. She stared at the tiny shadow on the speck that was the Vyr. Her eyes strayed upward, to Turoc, and then on to the Soel.

How could the Vyr be so small?

Veger rescued her from her thoughts. He handed Elysen a tapered tube made of bronze.

"Look in this end," he said. She put the small end up to her eye.

"I can't see anything," she said.

"Point it over there," Veger said, motioning toward the door.

Elysen glanced at him, swiveled in the direction he pointed, and looked again. Her mouth dropped open and she pulled the tube away from her eye quickly. She put it back up slowly and looked again.

"What kind of myst is this?" she asked.

"Not myst," Veger said. "Science."

"Explain," Elysen said.

Veger shook his head, but Elysen did not notice. She stared through the tube with one eye. Her other eye was squeezed shut.

"We do not know the science," Veger said. "It is lost to us. I have had this viewing scope in my possession since my father gave it to me. His father gave it to him. It has been handed down for generations."

Elysen pulled her head back and then examined the scope, rotating it back and forth in her hands.

"It's very beautiful," she said. She offered it to Veger, but he refused it.

"It is my gift to you," he said.

She shook her head. "I can't take it. It will come to some harm if it follows me."

Veger smiled. "That may be," he said. "But it does no good here. I used to use it to examine the stars and Turoc before this eternal mist settled over our valley. The world has changed. It is time that this gift left the icelands and went on a journey. I can think of no one better to have it than you."

He took it from her and slid it into a leather case with a long strap. He slung the case over her shoulder.

"Use it well," Veger said. "And may you bring knowledge and power and beauty back to the world."

Tobias took her arm. "Thank you, Veger," he said. "We have to go now."

He tugged on Elysen's arm and she took a few steps backwards. Veger turned his gaze back to the fire in his imaginary sky.

"Veger," Elysen said.

He grunted.

"Are you sure the rest of the world is dead?"

He shook his head. "I don't know. I have never been beyond this valley. Perhaps that is a question that you will have to answer." His eyes narrowed and his face broke into a smile. "Or maybe that is a journey for you, young Tobias."

Tobias chuckled and shook his head. Veger spun the array a bit and then crawled back onto his stool.

Tobias led Elysen back to the Madeire's cabin.

"What are you thinking about?" Tobias asked her as they walked.

Elysen stopped and held his arms. "If you wish to help me, please provide me with a pack and some rations and a blanket to sleep on. I will leave in the morning."

"Where will you go?" Tobias asked.

"South," she said. "To the desert."

"But why?" Tobias asked. "You're safe here. You can stay as long as you wish."

Elysen shook her head. "I feel safe here," she said. "But we are not. The Kaanites will come looking for me, or, worse yet, the Uemn. I won't have any more blood on my hands. I'll go to them. There's no other choice."

"There are many choices," Tobias said. "You could stay here. You could hide in the mountains." His voice trailed off to nothing.

"No," Elysen said. "In the quiet times, when all else is still in my mind, I see that the way for me is south, toward the Uemn. I see the desert in my dreams."

And a dark shadow.

"But the Uemn are beasts," Tobias insisted. "You have no idea what they will do to you."

Elysen sighed and closed her eyes.

"There is little more that can be done to me that has not already been done. And death would be a welcome friend. So I have little to fear. I will go on. I will finish the path that has been set for me. I will find the Uemn hordes and surrender myself to them."

"That sounds like a crazy idea," he said.

They finished their walk. Corde had a stew waiting for them. They sat with

Corde and the Madeire at a wooden table and ate from bowls of bronze.

Corde's eyes went from one woman to the other as they spoke.

"The Kaanites and the Uemn will come for me," Elysen said. "I have decided to leave."

"We don't fear the Kaanites or the Uemn," the Madeire said. She kept her face calm but there was concern in her eyes. "Even so, you should be wary. You will be safer here."

"According to the Kaanites," Elysen said, "the Uemn believe that I will lead them to victory over the people of the Vyr. As long as they believe that, I will be safe with them."

Corde spoke. "They may also believe that if your son lives, their victory will be short, and their reign will end during his lifetime. They will not want to let that happen."

"I will not lead them to victory if they harm my son in any way," Elysen said. "Once they have conquered the armies of the Vyr Lord, I will escape with my son."

"Where will you go after that?" Tobias asked.

Elysen shrugged. "Across the mountains, to the empty world beyond."

"You have seen the world beyond the Mountains of Oken?" Tobias asked.

Elysen nodded. "Rolling hills, as far as the eye can see. And the winds of life do not blow there. The part that I saw is as Veger described it. Barren and dead. The Uemn will not follow me there."

"Don't be so sure," the Madeire said. "The Uemn don't fear the old superstitions about angry spirits at the edge of the world. They have been beyond the edge of their own world, into the great ruins of the ancients, and have met the spirits there. They will have no problem following you into the unknown world beyond the mountains."

"You seem to know much about the Uemn," Elysen said.

"We have had our dealings with them," she said.

"You met them on your journey," Elysen said.

The Madeire nodded. "Your mother went west. I went east."

Elysen frowned. "You returned and she did not."

"You are surprised?"

"It just seems ironic, that she went to the west, toward civilization, and that you went east, toward chaos, and yet she was killed and you returned."

"Perhaps your civilization is not as civil as you have always believed," the

Madeire said.

"Everything I was ever told to believe in was a lie," Elysen said. "It would not surprise me one bit if the people of the plains were the monsters and the Uemn were righteous."

"I don't think that is the case," the Madeire said. She reached out and stroked Elysen's bare head. "The voices you hear in the quiet times, there is guidance there. Try to forget the pain of your past. Dwell not on vengeance and retribution. Your destiny is not in the way of violence."

Elysen pulled her head away from the Madeire's touch. "You can not know of my destiny," she said. "Vengeance is all I live for."

They sat in silence again for a while before Tobias spoke up.

"I will go with you," he said. "To the desert."

"Absolutely not," Elysen said. "This is my trial, not yours. I will have no one else die because of me."

The Madeire touched her knee. "The circumstances around you are not within your control. People will die, people will live. You must not come to believe that you are the cause of every effect."

Elysen turned and looked out the window at the gathering dusk.

"Nevertheless," she said. "Tomorrow I leave for the desert. I will face whatever awaits me there. Alone."

"You will not be alone," the Madeire said. "You have never been alone."

The next morning, the Madeire made Elysen a hot breakfast of eggs and fish. They ate in silence. When Elysen finished, the Madeire took her by the hand. She slipped her arms around Elysen and hugged her. Elysen slowly reached up and gently touched the Madeire's back.

"May peace and love be with you," the Madeire said. She smiled as Elysen stepped out the door and almost ran into Tobias and Corde who stood waiting with packs on their backs. Tobias held up his hand.

"Before you object," he said. "I am walking with you to the edge of the forest. I'll point you in the right direction from there."

Elysen nodded.

"Thank you, Tobias," she said. She turned to Corde. "And what about you, old man? What is your intention?"

"M'lady," he said. "I'll stay with you from now on. It's entirely clear that you can't get along without me. I've never forgiven myself for leaving you, and I will not let you slip away from me again. Look at you. You don't eat right, you consort with all kinds of ruffians and riff-raff, and you even get…"

His lips opened, but no sound came out. He made a rolling motion with his hand as he searched for the right word.

"Poked," Elysen said.

Corde smacked his forehead with the palm of his hand.

"I hope that you mean poked by arrows, m'lady."

Elysen smiled. "Poked by arrows and knives and all kinds of things that men poke with."

Tobias' mouth dropped open. The Madeire smiled and shook her head. Corde closed his eyes and shook his head sadly

"I have left you without good teaching for far too long," he said. He rubbed his forehead. The Madeire slipped inside and the came back out with a light pack and Veger's scope. Elysen slung them both over her shoulder and then shifted the pack so that it rode high up on the center of her back.

"There is food in there," the Madeire said, pointing at Elysen's pack. "Enough for a week if you are frugal. You should be able to provide for yourself along the way too. And water will be plentiful until you hit the edge of the forest, so keep your goatskin bag full. And there are some simple clothes and a light cloak that you can wear during the day in the desert. The white fabric will reflect the heat. And there is a visor, made of bone. Wear it when the fire is bright. It will save your eyes, and will make it easier for you to see." She shook her finger at Elysen. "Listen to me on this. Don't wear black during the daylight hours in the high desert unless you want to kill yourself."

"Thank you," Elysen said. "You've been kind and generous, all of you. I may never be able to repay you for all you have done."

"All that we have, all that we are, all that we circulate, comes back to us in its own time, its own way," the Madeire said.

Elysen parted from her with a simple hug. No more words passed between them. The three travelers walked away, down the narrow, winding street. Only Tobias looked back.

Twenty-two

They traveled during the short period of light, walking along a wide and well-worn path, making it to the next village by the fall of darkness. They stopped at a small house that took in short term borders. Elysen kept her hood over her face and her gloves on her hands and ate with Tobias in a far, dark corner of the tiny dining hall. The other guests kept to themselves, but glanced at the two travelers often, and whispered between themselves. Corde came back and led them upstairs to a large room with a dozen beds nestled close together like a barracks. Only a few of the other beds had occupants. Elysen slipped out of her cloak and under her blanket before she removed her gloves and boots. She curled up in a ball and tried to keep her eyes open, but they fluttered shut of their own accord. Tobias woke her in the morning. She came alive slowly, sat up and rubbed her eyes.

"My sleeping habits alarm me," she said softly. The cold, damp air of morning filled the room. Everyone else still slept.

"You rest according to your needs," Tobias said. He waited while she donned her boots and gloves, and then helped her into her cloak. She hesitated, and then relented, letting him drape the black cape over her shoulders.

"I never used to sleep this soundly," she whispered.

"Your baby is making demands on your body," Tobias reminded her. They slipped outside, into the cool morning air.

Corde came up to them, carrying all three packs, breathing hard. He dropped the packs on the ground at their feet and stretched his back. Elysen smiled at the plume of vapor that came from his open mouth.

"You spew like a pot of boiling water," she said.

"As well I should," he said. He put his hands on his hips. "While you two are dawdling around here in front of the inn, I was out gathering supplies."

"You should have been the one sleeping in, old man," Elysen said.

"Well, if I was with child, perhaps I would be inclined to sleep in. But I am not. And you are. And you, young Tobias, are you with child as well?"

Tobias frowned. "Your stomping and fuming woke me up this morning. I stayed to watch over Lady Elysen."

"Ah, I see." He began to shake his finger at Tobias, but Elysen bumped against Corde as she lifted her pack. He stumbled forward and she teased him with a smile.

Corde stooped over and put one hand on his lower back. "Can't you see that I am an old man?" he said. "Why do you abuse me so?"

Elysen rolled her eyes. "You are younger at heart than either one of us," she said. Her smile faded a bit. "Just put up with me this morning," she said. "I am in a bit of a light mood for some reason."

Corde smiled, and then winked at her. She smiled back.

Tobias shouldered his pack and then helped Corde get the smallest of the three packs into place on his back. The three travelers stood facing each other in a small circle. Corde took Tobias' hand and held his other out for Elysen. Elysen completed the circle and the two men closed their eyes. Tobias led a short prayer.

"We set out on this path, knowing that we have everything we need. Thank you."

They each let go of a deep breath and opened their eyes again.

"Why did we do that?" Elysen asked.

"It is tradition with our people," Tobias said. "Before we depart on a long journey."

They began to walk, with Tobias in the lead. He kept his eyes on the path ahead of them. They passed the last small house on the outskirts of the town and traveled through forest again. Tall fir trees lined either side of the path. Under the canopy of trees, the forest stood dark and still.

Corde walked just behind Elysen.

"Your grandmother walked along this same road when she was your age," he said.

Elysen allowed herself to be lost in thought for a moment. "The Madeire," she said. "She is my grandmother, isn't she?"

Corde smiled and nodded.

"Why wouldn't she tell me that?"

Corde shrugged. "She is a spiritual leader. She has her own reasons."

Elysen shook her head. "Do you know what I just realized?" She did not wait for an answer. "All my life, I have been raised to be a warrior. I know how to fight, and how to kill, and how to be merciless and strong and mean. But I don't know anything about raising a baby."

"A mother's instincts are strong," Corde said. "Her love for her child is the most natural love in the world." He paused. "Somehow, I think that you will know what to do when the time comes."

Love, she thought. *The spirit connection.* She realized that she had never heard Corde use that word before.

She stopped and closed her eyes, and the two men stood still, waiting patiently as Elysen listened. Curiosity finally overcame Tobias.

"What are you listening to?" he whispered.

She shook her head and frowned at him. "I'm trying to hear my baby. I'm trying to hear his song."

She stomped her foot and grunted. "What's wrong with me?" she asked as she opened her eyes. "I can't hear a thing." Her eyes suddenly went wide. "Maybe there is something wrong with him."

Corde touched her on the back and peered into her eyes.

"Your gift is different than your mother's gift. Don't try to be something that you are not."

She glared at him and shook her head. "My baby is dying and you are giving me philosophy lessons again," she said.

Corde leaned back a bit, his face full of surprise. He relaxed a bit and closed his mouth.

"Fear consumes you," he said. "What happened to your light mood? Would you like to hit me again?"

His humor fell on deaf ears. Elysen's shoulders fell forward. Corde and Tobias both reached out at the same time, as if to catch her. She fell into Corde's arms and cried. Tobias stood steadfast while Corde held her and rocked her back and forth like a child. Her tears turned to racking sobs that shook her body, and finally to great gulps that were like the gasps of a drowning person finding moments of sweet air. Finally, Elysen relaxed and let go.

"It looks as if it has been a long time since you let yourself have a good cry," Tobias said.

"It's a sign of weakness," she said. "I'm falling apart."

"It is a sign of strength, a way of healing," Corde said. "Those who don't let themselves grieve and cry and feel emotions are like ships without wind in their sails. They try to power through the water with just their oars. The wise one unfurls the sails, fills them with the winds of the universe, and steers a course accordingly."

Elysen's smile returned, but it held only a shadow of the earlier one.

"Ahh," Corde remarked. "To see that smile is one of the greatest treasures of the Vyr."

The smile faded.

"What's wrong now?" Tobias asked. His brow furrowed with concern.

"I just keep thinking about what lies ahead. There's nothing to smile about out there."

She tipped her head forward and hitched her thumbs under the straps of her pack.

"And look at me. I'm a wreck. I hurt all over. I'm sick, and I can't control my emotions."

She stopped again and turned toward Tobias with a glazed look in her eyes. "What kind of warrior am I?" she asked. "How am I going to get through this?"

"Try not to focus on tomorrow," Tobias said. "Enjoy the day. Concentrate on the peacefulness of these woods. The coolness of this air. Live in today, m'lady. Tomorrow will come soon enough."

Elysen took a deep breath. Tobias headed down the path. Elysen took a few long strides to catch up with him. Corde lagged behind.

"So," Elysen said to Tobias. "Are you a philosopher as well? Like the Madeire? And Corde?"

She glanced back at the old man and he gave her a quick, courtesy smile.

Tobias laughed. "No. I'm just a simple fisherman. Like my father. And his father before him."

"And a builder of boats."

"Yes, that too."

"And a dreamer."

"Much to my father's dismay."

"And a scientist?'

He nodded.

"Tell me about your dreams," she said. "What else do you dream of besides boats and stars?"

His eyes glowed. "I dream of a sailing ship so large that it would hold a hundred men, and that could chase down a fish the size of a small mountain."

"More boats," Elysen said.

He shrugged. "Boats are my passion."

"Are there fish the size of small mountains in the Cevante?"

Tobias laughed. "No. Of course not."

"Then why would you dream of building a boat that large?"

He shrugged. "It is just a dream. But what good is life if we don't dream of things that appear to be impossible? Our ancestors must have dreamed once. Magnificent dreams that became real, like your Sunder Keep, and our Citadel d'Vie."

"Young Tobias, you seem to speak with wisdom beyond your years." Elysen mused.

"Do I speak like a fool then?"

"Oh no," Elysen said. "I like what you have to say."

"But?"

She shook her head. "I just have trouble…trusting."

"You mean you think I am insincere?"

"Oh no, not at all. I'm worried about tomorrow, and the next day. These brief moments of comfort and serenity, of idle chatter about dreams and fish and boats, it will all end again. I'll be back to fighting and I'll feel as if I'm dying again, instead of living."

"But you are enjoying the moment?"

"Yes," she said. "I feel alive. For the moment." She paused. "I really am glad you came with me."

"Then I do speak some truth," he said. "We are here, in the woods, fellow travelers, and although there are weighty matters ahead of us, right now, nothing troubles us. So, we enjoy this moment. Expect the best right now. The early morning light. A bird singing, a doe, jumping out of the woods ahead of us, bounding into the darkness of the deeper woods. A light rain. You can find comfort in these things."

"I do," she said. "And I find comfort in your presence too."

"Then go forth with confidence." He pointed his finger at her and glared in mock anger. "And don't worry about me. I can take care of myself."

Elysen sighed. Her next step angled toward Tobias, and their shoulders bumped together. She held her position there as they walked, their arms touching lightly. She stared at the ground and watched as their feet brushed against the grass that grew in patches, kicked pebbles, splashed in small puddles. A rabbit appeared from nowhere, shot across the path, and then cowered in the low grass beside them. Elysen suppressed an urge to kill it, and then Arador's face appeared to her, and she remembered the look in his eyes as his spirit left his body. She glanced at Tobias, and then held her gaze there, staring at his boyish face.

A voice called out from behind them. "Please don't forget old Corde, back here, walking all alone."

Elysen looked back at him and smiled, and they all stopped and sat side by side on a log just off the path to share a piece of hard yellow cheese and a large, flat piece of dry bread. Elysen stopped chewing for a moment. Tobias and Corde noticed her stillness and stopped chewing as well.

She stood up, her back straight and her eyes narrow. She chewed again slowly. Stopped again. Tobias frowned. They sat very still, as if frozen. Elysen slowly leaned forward and spit out a half-chewed piece of bread. Tobias glanced at her, swallowed his own piece of bread, and then watched her intently. She tilted her head to one side, just slightly, as if listening to something distant.

"What is it?" Tobias whispered.

Elysen shook her head. "Something's not right," she said.

"I can't hear anything," he said.

She shook her head again. "It is a feeling."

Her frown deepened. Her breathing came quick and shallow. She turned toward Tobias, stood up and took his hands in hers. He stood and faced her.

"Tobias, Corde, listen to me. I want you to run. Run back. All the way back. Don't stop. Don't sleep. Eat as you run. Just run."

"What is it? What do you hear?" Tobias asked.

"Horses," she said. "Lots of them. I can feel them in the ground. Smell them in the wind."

Tobias glanced around. "I don't feel anything."

Corde touched his arm. "You can trust what she says."

"They're coming from the south," she said.

She leaned forward and kissed Tobias on the cheek.

"Go now," she said. "Warn the villagers as you go. Hide in the forests when you get home. Warn everyone. They want me. But my fear tells me that they will not stop once they get me. Please promise me you will run and hide."

Tobias shook his head.

"I can't leave you," he said.

"You have to." She touched his face and smiled. "They won't hurt me. And I won't give them the satisfaction of seeing my fear. I will live in each moment, expecting better things to come, and they will learn to fear me, because they will see that I don't fear them and I don't fear death. Now go, before I have to beat you. And you too, Corde."

Tobias took a deep breath, grabbed her and kissed her hard, and then stepped away. He started at a trot, turned around once, and then began running, disappearing out of sight in a moment. Elysen turned to Corde and put her hands on her hips.

"Don't stay with me," she said.

Corde bunched up his shoulders and tipped his head slightly. "I can't leave you again," he said.

"You are a fool then," Elysen said.

"Oh, yes. I am that. It is my lot in life, I am afraid. The last time I left you, I became suddenly sensible, and I have not been able to live with myself since."

"Do as you will then," she said.

She turned her back to him and walked to the center of the wide pathway. She stood alone, her arms hanging relaxed at her sides, her head and eyes held high. Before her, the path dwindled into the dark forest. Above her, the gray sky whispered in the tops of the trees. Under her feet, the ground trembled. She glanced back toward Corde. He stood gazing at her and her shoulders sagged a bit.

"You really are a fool, aren't you?" she said.

He nodded.

"Well, come here then," she said.

He came to her and she held his hand. He gazed at her for a moment and then they both stared down the road toward the oncoming storm.

"I love you, m'lady," Corde said.

Elysen closed her eyes and let a lonely tear slide down her cheek.

Twenty-three

The Uemn troops emerged from the gloom; riding two by two on horses with hooves the size of stone battle hammers. The first two riders pulled up twenty paces from Elysen. She let go of Corde's hand and pulled her hood off her head. The two riders glanced at each other, and then one of the soldiers peeled off and galloped back along the path. Elysen waited.

The Uemn column stretched off into the gloomy distance as far as Elysen could see. Their appearance tied her stomach in a knot. Where Elysen and her people wore plates of hard wood to protect the most vulnerable and easily attacked portions of their bodies, the Uemn wore broad plates of oily black metal, hammered and shaped to fit their chests. Similar plates protected their arms and legs. Even their boots and gloves glistened of metal. Sheets of small, linked circles of the same dark metal showed from under their armor.

The metal Uemn helmets flared out at the back of the neck and each Uemn hid behind a faceplate of metal and bone. The Uemn guard who now waited for his companion to return had used thin strips of gold to fashion thin eyebrows above two large holes, behind which the eyes of the Uemn lurked. The faceplate came to a point along a beak-like nose guard made of a piece of exotic brown horn, and below that gaped a mouth, fixed into a warlike scream, adorned with sharp yellow canines. Behind him, the riders were similar in mount and armor, but not one faceplate resembled any other. Some helmets were adorned with horns, some were conical, some round, some even flat on top.

Each warrior wore a long blade on his left, and a shorter one on his right, and had a round wooden shield affixed to his saddle. Metal straps ran across the boards of each shield. Every piece of armor showed the chips, dents and scratches that came from ceaseless fighting. Even the horses wore faceplates of metal and blankets of the woven chain over their flanks and necks.

The horses shuffled impatiently as the riders stared at the apparition before them. The first rider came back at a quick trot and took his place next to his comrade as three mounted Uemn made their way alongside the column. Two stopped a short distance away, but the third approached Elysen, carefully, cautiously. He dismounted and stepped forward, his face shield still in place.

Elysen stood with her feet planted squarely in the path, staring at the stranger. His garb was more ornate than the others, with gold and silver inlay. His faceplate turned Elysen's stomach, with decayed human teeth bared in a snarl and the same dark, deep recessed eyes that were common to all of the Uemn masks. Elysen frowned at the shadow that she imagined around him – the same shadow she had seen in her visions in the Kaanite camp. Corde stood slightly behind Elysen with his hands clasped tightly together.

"Then it's true," the Uemn said. He walked around her slowly. The shadow seemed to reach for her.

"The Kaanites are certainly an odd bunch," he said. His nightmarish facemask muffled the sound of his voice. He reached out to touch her, but she pulled her shoulder away from his finger. "Did this hurt?"

"Who is asking?" she replied.

He reached up and pointed to a series of strange markings on the metal plates that covered his shoulder. His other hand touched the hilt of his sword.

"I am Ser Kreid, General of the Uemn Front Guard."

"I am Elysen, daughter of Lord Vollen."

He nodded. "I know who you are, cousin. You are just a strange sight to see." He walked around her again.

"As are you," she said, frowning even deeper as she tried to ignore the dark cloud that hung behind him.

Ser Kreid removed his helmet, revealing skin darkly tanned and deeply creased, especially around the corners of his eyes. His fine, blond hair, bleached by years in the hot Soel, fell around his shoulders. But a look of weariness marred his handsome face. His blue eyes were tired, slightly sunken, the skin under them lighter than the bronze of his cheeks and forehead, and his skin clung to the bones of his face.

"What do these marks mean?" he asked, pointing at Elysen's cheek.

"Nothing to you," she said.

His eyes became livid, as if he was about to strike her down, then he calmed again.

"What is that?" she asked. She waved her hand in the air beside him. Suddenly she gasped and stepped back.

"There is something crawling on you," she said quietly.

He smiled and nodded. "That is the Addiss," he said. "The emissary of the dark lord. I have been chosen by him, as his host in this realm."

The Addiss wound around Ser Kreid's body like black smoke with tentacles snaking in and out of his armor. Suddenly, a wet, glistening face appeared above Ser Kreid's shoulder, a gaping visage with a mouth open in a silent, angry scream, eyes wide and empty. Elysen took a step backwards.

"I don't understand," she said. "What is that thing?"

"The Addiss is my protector, my Lord."

As they spoke, it emerged from within Ser Kreid's armor, through it, as though it were shedding a blanket, waking from sleep, or coming out of hiding. As it reared upwards, its horrible face poised above and behind Ser Kreid's head and its black shape became more distinct, darker, defined. Its tentacles caressed Ser Kreid's body like the arms of a lover. Elysen moved another step away.

"It is horrible," she said.

Ser Kreid turned away from her. He grabbed the horn of his saddle and mounted his horse. The creaking leather awoke Elysen from her trance.

"Is it alive?" Elysen asked. She could not take her eyes off the sneering apparition that clung to Ser Kreid like a jealous lover.

"Everything will be explained," he said.

She snorted softly through her nose. "People always tell me that," she said. "And yet nothing is ever explained."

"Come with me," he said. He held out his hand. She stared at the thing on his back, stared at his hand, and then shook her head.

"I prefer to walk. I'll not ride with you as long as that thing is there."

"Walk then," he said.

He turned his horse and motioned to the column.

"Break ranks," he shouted. "We will camp here tonight." He placed his helmet back on his head and sat, tall and proud in his saddle.

The soldiers dismounted and dispersed themselves into the woods, leading their horses. Ser Kreid rode slowly down the ranks as they pitched their tents in the woods. The tents were made of mottled fabric that blended with the soft, dappled light sifting through the trees from the gray sky above, making them almost invisible in the gloomy forest. Elysen followed Ser Kreid as he inspected the activity, and in turn, two mounted guards followed her, their hands resting on the hilts of their swords. The procession stopped at a small meadow where a group of pack animals stood waiting, surrounded by more troops. In addition to nearly forty armed guards, the mules were guarded by black dogs the size of small bears, fangs dripping white foamy saliva. Their black eyes peered at Elysen and they snarled softly, as if warning her to stay away. A dozen men, dressed in simple cotton clothes with no weapons and no armor, tended to the mules and dogs. As she passed, she could smell the musky odor of sweaty animals and men, mixed together, and her heart longed for Temper and a longbow.

Ser Kreid stopped in the middle of the clearing and waited, his arms resting on the pommel of his saddle. The slaves and guardsmen all pitched in together to unload the animals. They unrolled a large canvas and hoisted it with poles into a large wall tent. One of the slaves, dressed in a white sleeveless surcoat, took the reins of Ser Kreid's impatient horse, and he dismounted. Elysen followed him, but hesitated when he entered the tent. The two guards still hovered behind her. She glanced at them, and then ducked through the opening and stood in the gloom within.

The servants brought in canvas chairs and a cot. Ser Kreid sat on the cot and motioned for Elysen to take a chair. She refused, choosing instead to stand. The two guards stood just inside the door with their arms crossed. Ser Kreid began to release the armor from his arms and legs as he spoke.

"The Addiss saved us from starvation, taught us how to forge metal into tools and weapons. They know the secrets of the universe, and are our benevolent guardians and lords."

"They speak to you?"

"Only in our thoughts, our ideas. Most of what they know we cannot yet understand, and only the quiet of mind can even hear them. That is why only certain Uemn are chosen to merge with the Addiss. We have to be completely ready to accept our lord and master, in order to hear their wisdom."

He glanced up at the guards as if he had only just noticed them.

"You may go," he said. They dropped their arms to their sides, bowed their heads, turned sharply and stepped outside.

"Aren't you afraid that I will escape?" Elysen asked.

Ser Kreid laughed, and his face filled with an energy that had been absent a few moments before.

"You came here of your own free will," he reminded her. "Besides, you have nowhere to go. This is your home now."

He finished unbuckling the armor plates on his legs and unstrapped his chest plate. A lean man with thinning gray hair and cracked skin stepped in as if silently bidden. He gathered the various pieces of armor and hung them from wooden pegs hammered into one of the crossbeams.

"May I be of any other service to your lordship?" the man asked in a quiet voice. He glanced quickly at Elysen. Ser Kreid waved him away. The servant shuffled out with his head down.

"A Vyrlander?" Elysen asked.

Ser Kreid nodded. He stretched out his legs and braced his arms against the cot. Behind him and around him, the snake-like Addiss coiled and uncoiled itself, bobbing up and down as if eternally restless. She could see its gaping eyes, surveying the room, glaring at her, rolling back in disgust.

"We sometimes take the Vyr Lord's people for slaves," he said. "But we find most are unsuited to our harsh climate, and for the most part they are just plain lazy. Not good workers."

He leaned forward suddenly and rested his forearms on his knees.

"But you, dear cousin, tell us about you. Tell us everything. We are especially eager to hear about those strange markings. What do they mean? We can't read them. The language is too ancient. And I'd like to see more, see all of it."

"Why do you call me cousin?" she asked.

Ser Kreid looked as if her were appalled.

"Is your mother not Aephia, of the Norgarden?"

She nodded.

He clasped his hands to his chest and smiled broadly, as if he had just won a prize.

"My uncle," he said, "was Aephia's father."

Elysen frowned. Ser Kreid continued.

"My uncle, Stratus, ruled the lands of the desert when my father was just a boy. As a young girl, your grandmother journeyed to our lands on her vision quest. Stratus took her as a concubine, but she escaped back to the icelands and raised your mother there." He tapped his chest proudly. "I was born in the desert. I am pure-blooded Uemn."

Elysen pondered for a moment. "The Madeire," she said to herself. "Then your uncle is my grandfather?" she asked.

He nodded. "That makes you a cousin. Granddaughter of Lord Stratus of the Uemn. We've been waiting for your arrival for a long time." He clasped his hands together and waited.

Elysen let the silence hang heavy in the air. She bided her time by watching the ceaseless, slow, agitated movements of the beast that infected Kreid like the morgred fungus infested the alder trees in the valley of the Ryn Gladde. She studied Ser Kreid's tired face for a while as he sat locked in a trance.

"Why?" she asked. "Why are you waiting for me?"

He smiled.

"You will lead us to victory over the people of the Vyr. You will lead us to Sunder Keep, and we will take our rightful place again as rulers of this world. And," he leaned forward a bit, "we will unlock the secrets of the Keep. All of the knowledge and power that Thorsen stole from the world."

Ser Kreid smiled, but under the smile was a look of pain. It showed in his eyes and along the corners of his mouth.

"We have expected you for some time now. Our spies in the Vyr told us that you were on the run. We headed north and our man Grayson returned to us last night. He told us that you were here. Besides, this is all as it should be. The ancient prophecy fulfils itself. The white storm, from the north, that will destroy the people of the Vyr and will bring the people of the fire out of the desert and into their rightful place as rulers of the world. And our son shall rule the world."

"That is your prophecy," she said. "Not mine."

He shrugged. "We shall see."

She sat with her arms crossed. "I will not cooperate with you. I will not let you attack and butcher my people."

"You have no people," he snarled. A servant ducked his head in the door.

"And perhaps it will be Yergen's son that will rule the world," Elysen said.

"What do you mean by that?" Ser Kreid asked sharply.

"I am with child already. Yergen's child."

Ser Kreid bolted out of his chair and stood with his fists clenched and his legs braced wide. He glared at Elysen.

The servant interrupted, trying to get the general's attention. "Your dinner is ready, my lord," he said.

"Get out," Ser Kreid snarled back at him.

The man disappeared in an instant. Ser Kreid turned back toward Elysen and bared his teeth, suddenly possessed by a burst of anger. A hot glare formed in his eyes and Elysen found herself pushing against the ground, pushing her body away from him. He spit words like coals from a cedar fire.

"Let me give you the real story," he said. "You are the bastard grandchild of an icelander whore who trespassed onto our land bringing word of a false prophet and causing unrest amongst the people of fire. She blasphemed against the Addiss, our true lords. As punishment, my uncle raped her and beat her and imprisoned her. In our eyes, she was lowlier than the pig slop we fed her. When my uncle found out she was pregnant he beat her again and sent her naked into the desert. She survived and made her way back to the icelands. But her daughter, Aephia, was never one of us. And you, then, are the bastard daughter of a dead Vyr Lord and a despised Uemn half-breed. You are not of the Vyr. You are not of the ice. And you are certainly not of the fire. You are no one. And this baby that you carry, if in fact you carry one, is even worse. You should let me cut it from your body right now."

He sat back and took a breath.

"If all that is true, then why don't you just kill me now?" Elysen asked quietly.

"Get out," he said.

"Gladly," she replied.

She stood up and walked outside. Her legs shook. Dusk settled on the encampment, and there were fires burning in a rough circle around Ser Kreid's tent. As Elysen stood there, studying the layout of the camp, she heard Ser Kreid yell something incoherent from within the tent, and a servant bustled by her carrying a small box. He had a worried look on his face as he ducked inside. Elysen stood for a moment, gazing at the door. She moved toward it but the armored guards stopped her.

"Is there food here?" she asked. She tried to peer into the darkness behind their fearsome masks. "Can you speak? I'm hungry." They stood like statues as she spoke to them, but followed her as she wandered toward a large fire where the slaves had gathered. As she came near, they dropped to their knees, cowering in fear, their faces in the trampled grass.

Elysen sighed and sat down on a small log near the fire. She could smell roasted meat, and her stomach growled.

"Can I get something to eat?" she asked.

"Lady Elysen." Ser Kreid's voice came out calmer now.

She turned. He stood behind her, framed by two guards.

"You consort with the slaves. Are you hungry?"

"Yes," she said.

He had suddenly changed into a more personable demeanor. She stood and he led her toward one of the smaller fires. A soldier stood up sharply as they approached. Ser Kreid smiled.

"At ease, Veldon," he said.

Veldon appeared to be quite a bit younger than Ser Kreid, bright eyed, with a quick, darting tongue that touched his lips almost continuously as he ate pieces off a large bird roasted on a stick. Ser Kreid presented Elysen as if she were royalty.

"The Lady Elysen," he said.

A servant appeared and placed three wooden stools on the ground. Elysen nodded at Veldon and then sat down. Veldon tore off a small chunk of the steaming meat with his fingers and offered it to Elysen. She took it and ate, watching Ser Kreid and Veldon carefully. She picked up her chair and moved it so that she sat on the other side of the fire from the two men.

"Veldon is my captain," he said. "Very able. An accomplished tactician for his age." Ser Kreid slapped him on the back and Veldon smiled.

"I have applied to host an Addiss," he said proudly.

"And been accepted," Ser Kreid added. "It is a great honor to become an Addicere; keeper of the Addiss."

Elysen watched them carefully as she ate. The two guards stood at attention behind her, hovering over her. She squirmed a bit, trying to get more comfortable on the strange chair.

"This is a great day for our people," Ser Kreid said. Veldon nodded. Ser Kreid leaned forward, addressing his next comment toward Elysen.

"Tomorrow," he said, "we will march northward, into the land of the ice people, and we will wipe them from the face of this world." He sat back. "Then we will go on into the lands of the Vyr Lord, and cleanse the world of them as well, once and for all." He crossed his arms and grinned.

"What say you to that, m'lady?" he asked.

Elysen stopped eating.

"The northern people are peaceful, they don't even have any weapons," she said. Ser Kreid confused her.

"They are a scourge, an insult against the natural order of the world," Ser Kreid countered. Veldon nodded.

"Leave them in peace," Elysen said. "You have me now."

A guard interrupted them. The metal of his armor gleamed in the firelight.

"We sent out an advance scout, sire. They have returned with a prisoner. A boy."

"Why didn't they kill him?" Ser Kreid asked.

"In order that you may torture him for information, sire. He was running from them. They felt that he was attempting to warn the villages of our coming."

"I know this boy," Elysen said. "He is no threat to you. And he knows nothing."

"Then we shall simply kill him outright," Ser Kreid said.

"Please don't," Elysen pleaded.

"They will all die anyway," Ser Kreid said. He smiled at Veldon. "We will march through and butcher them like cattle."

"Please leave them alone," Elysen begged. She felt panic rising in her chest.

Ser Kreid leaned forward. "I have no reason to leave them alone, and every reason to kill them."

Elysen shook her head and gazed at him with sadness in her eyes.

"How can you say that? What reason could you have to kill them? They've done nothing to you."

Veldon spoke up. "They send their ambassadors to our lands, to pervert the minds of the people, to turn them against us. They spread the words of a false prophet, and our people gather hope and courage, falsely, and then become dissatisfied with their lives. They disrupt our society, like a pox, a subtle, silent plague against us. And like a plague-ridden village, they have to be burned to the ground, so that they don't spread."

Ser Kreid nodded as Veldon spoke. Elysen stared at them.

"Leave them be," she said. "Promise me that you will leave them be, and I will cooperate with you."

Ser Kreid waved his hand at her.

"We don't need your cooperation," he said. "You are as impotent as your father was."

"If you take your army over the ice, they will die," she said. "And you have tried to take them up the walls of the Great Rift with disastrous results."

Ser Kreid revealed nothing with his expression, but sat listening in silence. Elysen continued.

"And your victories in the swamps leave your troops spread out and spent. Our crossbows pierce your armor, and our people continue to resist you. You have never made it north of the lower plains, have you?"

Ser Kreid crossed his arms. Veldon glanced at him.

Elysen took a bite of her meat and chewed thoughtfully as she realized that the Uemn did not know how badly the armies of the Vyr suffered.

"There is a way to get to Sunder Keep without going over the ice or through the swamps of the Rift," she said. "A fourth option."

Ser Kreid grinned. "Tell me."

"I will tell you when the time is right," she said.

"Tell me now."

She frowned, peering at the Addiss as it slid its tentacle around Ser Kreid's body, under his arms, around his waist, as if it were unashamedly caressing his body for its own pleasure. She let her disgust show.

"If the Addiss are so wise, why have they not told you of the fourth option?"

Ser Kreid's face grew serious.

"They have tried," he said. "But we can't understand what they are trying to tell us. Our minds are not yet open enough. We are not yet worthy. But they will guide us when our time comes to take the Keep. Of that you can be sure."

"Fine," she said. "Let them lead you to Sunder Keep."

Ser Kreid licked his lips.

"Tell me about the fourth option," he said.

"I will," she said. "But I have conditions."

"No conditions," Ser Kreid said.

"How badly do you want this?"

He frowned and waited. "Go on."

"Leave the northern people alone. Let them be. They are of no consequence to us. And I need the prisoner, the boy Tobias. He has knowledge and skills that we need. He will not be a problem if you release him to me."

Ser Kreid glanced at Veldon. Veldon shrugged.

"If he gets out of line, I will kill him," Veldon said. Ser Kreid nodded at Elysen. She continued.

"And my servant, Corde. You will not harm him either. These two men will stay with me."

Veldon crossed his arms. Ser Kreid looked amused.

Elysen continued. "We will march into Sunder Keep as peacefully as possible. We will not attack anyone along the way unless we are attacked first."

Ser Kreid shook his head. "That is an insane request."

Elysen put up her hand. "If you believe in your prophecy, then you believe that I am the one to lead you to Sunder Keep. If I lead you, the people will let you through. They hate Yergen, and they will welcome me back. They will cooperate."

"If they don't, we will cut them in half," Ser Kreid said.

Elysen nodded. "Just three more things then."

"Three more?" Ser Kreid looked as if he were at the end of his patience again.

"My cousin, Yergen. If he is not killed in battle, if he is captured, he will be brought to me."

Ser Kreid pursed his lips, but nodded reluctantly.

"The same with his Master Dage, Raes."

Ser Kreid nodded again.

"I will give you a description of both men. They are not to be harmed if captured. Not to be killed unless absolutely necessary. Do you understand?"

"I understand perfectly," Ser Kreid said. "And the third concession?"

"My baby is not to be harmed in any way. If you try to harm him, I will turn the people against you, and no amount of hard metal armor or weapons will protect you from my fury."

He shook his head. "I can't promise you that. I can't stop my people from trying to do harm to you or your child, if it is true that you are with child."

"But you can promise me your protection, and the protection of the men who are loyal to you."

He pressed his lips together as he considered her request.

"I will promise you this," he said. "I will protect you, to the best of my ability, until such time as we take the Keep. After that, I promise nothing. Your child is a threat to us all. My people will not abide his life. There will be many who will demand his death."

Elysen sat staring at Ser Kreid across the flickering flames. The roasting bird dripped grease into the fire, making sizzling, popping sounds and spewing forth black smoke. Ser Kreid broke the long silence.

"The lives of the northerners, the lives of the plainsmen, the lives of your men, and your child's life until we have taken the Keep. That is the best I can do." He glared at her and leaned even farther forward. "For every life I spare, I may lose the life of ten score of my men. Don't forget that, m'lady. You have made your deal, now say no more, except for the word 'yes'."

Elysen glared at him for a long time. Veldon watched both of them, his tongue flicking across his lips. Behind Ser Kreid, the Addiss reeled and stretched as if it had been sated, satisfied somehow.

Elysen swallowed the piece of meat and threw the bone in the fire. She watched it sizzle amid the ashes and glowing embers and then she looked back at Ser Kreid and spat into the fire before she spoke.

"Yes."

Twenty-four

The army packed up the next morning. Ser Kreid freed Tobias and gave Elysen a horse to ride. She pulled the boy up and let him ride behind her. He turned his head in an attempt to hide the bruises on his face.

"Where is Corde?" Elysen asked.

"He's with the other servants," Tobias said. "They have wagons and mules. I think that he'll be fine."

"I'm sure he will," Elysen said.

Tobias grimaced with every lurching step. They stopped at the brink of the wooded plateau facing the pale low Soel as it traversed the southern horizon. A barren hill sloped away from them to the west, disappearing into the great rift. To the south and east lay an endless flat tundra, blanketed by a cold wind. The tundra looked smooth and flat at first, but as Elysen's eyes adjusted to the expansive openness, she could see broken ground, jumbled with boulders.

"It looks like our northern lands," she said.

Ser Kreid smiled. "You'll find it quite different, I think."

They rode south, across the rocky ground, making the most of the short days by riding until dark and pitching their camp in the twilight. The clouds cleared and the nights became cold. Elysen welcomed the sparkling lights of her ancestors. She stared upward, wondering which one might be Aephia. She made a diamond shape with her hands and held them above her head as she lay on her back. Tobias turned toward her.

"What are you doing?" he asked.

"Do what I do," she said quietly. "I will show you an old trick that my father showed me."

Tobias copied her, placing thumb to thumb and pointer to pointer. He lifted his arms above his head and peered into the heavens.

"Look straight up," she said. "Now find the Arm of Thorsen."

"What is that?"

"Five stars, in the shape of a forearm with fingers cupped."

"I don't see it."

"It looks like a ladle," she said. "Off to your right."

"Maybe I see it," he said.

"Follow the fingers to the bright star."

"Yes."

"That star is Graden."

They found it in the sky above their feet.

"Yes, I know that one," Tobias said. "We call it the Watcher.

"It always lies directly north," Elysen said. She turned to look at Tobias. "I'm surprised you don't know how to orient yourself by the stars."

"I have never had a need to learn. Our world is very small."

She let her arms fall and turned her face back to the sky. "If you ever get the chance to go home, that is what you will follow. It will lead you to the lands of ice."

"Why did they spare me?" Tobias asked.

"I asked them to."

"But why did they agree?"

"I told them you would be useful. They agreed to spare your people if you would agree to help me."

"But help you do what?"

"You will see. Soon enough. Get some sleep now."

Elysen rolled over and stared into the darkness of the desert. She placed her hands on her belly, following her hard pelvic bones toward the soft skin in between and then upward toward the slightly swollen roundness of her baby. She closed her eyes and listened. In the desert, an insect rubbed its legs together. Something flitted through the air above their resting place. Far off in the distance, an owl called out. Elysen heard nothing from within.

Night came and went. Morning turned to day and day to night again, and the army marched onward. As they traveled south, the landscape changed. The days grew hotter, but the nights remained bitter cold. The terrain became gritty, covered with a dusty soil that sustained nothing. Ser Kreid and Veldon ignored Elysen and Tobias for the most part, satisfied to keep them under light guard as they traveled.

Occasionally, a group of soldiers would kill a deer and the camp would roast and share the tough meat that tasted strongly of the sage that it ate every day. The army scrounged rabbits and other small rodents for food. Tobias and Elysen ate last, or not at all. Water came in short supply, and Elysen made sure to fill her goatskin bag at every opportunity. Ser Kreid allowed her to keep her pack and her scope and her knife, and Tobias would sneak off in the night and kill a rabbit or a mouse so that he could roast it long after the others had drifted off to sleep. If the guards noticed, they said nothing, if they said something, Ser Kreid ignored it. Elysen took comfort in Tobias' gentle touch, so she asked him to shave her head every night. It became a silent ritual between them.

During this time, Elysen became ill, and by the time Turoc cycled from a thin sliver to a fingernail to full again, she could barely ride. Tobias gave her extra water when he could. At twilight, when they stopped to camp, Tobias would boil table scraps for broth. Elysen could keep nothing else down.

"She is wasting precious water," Ser Kreid said as he made his round one night. Even as he spoke, Elysen threw up, perched on her hands and knees. A stream of drool hung from her mouth as she glared up at him.

"How much longer must we travel in this deserted land?" Tobias asked.

Ser Kreid looked out across the pale blue sky. The Soel settled below the edge of the world, leaving a strange, orange tinted dusk.

"We still have many more days ahead of us."

Ser Kreid rode off, leaving Tobias holding Elysen. He placed her head in his lap and she slept.

The days grew longer as they traveled farther and farther south. The ground grew more barren, finally becoming nothing more than dust. They finally came to a cart path that ran across their line of travel. The army stopped and Ser Kreid rode to the front. They turned west and began to follow the path to the edge of a small valley filled with sparkling blue water. The wall on the other side of the canyon was lower than the one upon which they stood, and beyond that, the land dropped away.

Between the sloping piles of rock at the base of the cliff and the flat expanse of glimmering water sat a narrow strip of land, alive with trees and bushes.

Tobias pulled Elysen's horse up next to Ser Kreid's and stopped. Elysen hung on to Tobias' waist with her head resting on his bony shoulder.

"We are nearly there," Ser Kreid said quietly. He called Veldon forward.

"Take the men down and cordon off the town. No one leaves without my permission. I want marshal law until we are ready to march to Kardesh. Do you understand?"

Veldon nodded. "Yes sir."

"I will bring Elysen down last. Your men will clear the streets so that we can bring her in secret. No one talks about her until we have had time to clean her up. I want utmost secrecy maintained."

"How do we explain our taking of the town?" Veldon asked. "Won't your father be suspicious?"

"He will," Ser Kreid answered. "And we will let him be suspicious. He grows old and foolish, and the army follows me now. He will sit in his fortress, brooding, wondering, while we prepare."

"Your will be done," Veldon said.

"Go now," Ser Kreid said.

On Veldon's command, the army dismounted and began the shuffling, treacherous journey downward, into the valley. Ser Kreid let the main force go first. He watched them from his mount as they passed before him, weary but excited. Elysen and Tobias went last, followed by their appointed guards for the day.

"Are we descending into the Great Rift?" Tobias asked as they passed by the Addicere General.

"Hardly," he said. "This is Asaka. We are still high above the floor of the Rift." He pointed toward the shimmering expanse to the west. It stretched out like a different world, vast, unclaimed and unforgiving. "That is the Rift, out there beyond Asaka."

"Where does the water come from," Tobias asked as he admired the blue lake.

"We don't know. It comes from the world below." He turned his horse and dismounted. "We don't question it. We just accept. You will have to walk your horse from here. We don't ride down this path."

Tobias helped Elysen off her horse. Her white robe slipped open, revealing her bulging stomach. Tobias placed her arm across his shoulders and helped her walk.

"Stay with them," Ser Kreid ordered. The guards nodded. Even in the heat, the guards maintained their full armor. They walked slowly behind the struggling outsiders. From the valley below, the sounds of metal striking metal resounded and echoed off the rock walls, interspersed with spurts of laughter and loud voices that pierced the afternoon stillness.

"Where are we?" Elysen asked. She felt groggy and tired, but lucid.

"Some Uemn town. On the eastern rim of the rift. There is water here. Perhaps we'll be able to rest for a while."

"Where is Corde?"

"He has been relegated to the cooking wagon, where he entertains the slaves while preparing fat meals for the Uemn."

"I hope that he spits in their bowls every night," Elysen said.

Tobias smiled. "I'm sure he does."

"How long since we left the forest?" Elysen asked.

"It has been nearly three cycles of Turoc."

Elysen groaned. "It has been a living nightmare for me, I barely remember it."

"You have been ill. It is the changing. Your body is adjusting to the baby."

"Something is terribly wrong."

"It is not abnormal. It will pass."

"It had better. I can't go on like this. I think I may be dying."

Tobias looked worried.

"They're not treating you well," he said.

"They don't want this boy child to survive."

"What if it turns out to be a girl?" he asked.

Elysen managed a weak smile. "I have never even thought about that. I guess I had always assumed that Joryn was right, that it was a boy."

"I haven't seen you smile for quite a while," Tobias said.

"There has not been much to smile about." Her smile faded. "I'm worried about the baby."

"Your worry does you no good. It's bad for your body."

"I can't help it."

"I know," he said. "Perhaps we could pray together tonight."

"Will that help?"

He looked at her face. Her eyes held anguish and desperation.

"Won't hurt to try."

She lifted her head and pushed her hand across her scalp, feeling the hot sweat with her fingers.

"It's too warm here," she said.

"We are in the southern desert now," Tobias said. "And this is still the season of the Proste. In two more cycles, the heat will be unbearable."

"My son will be born in a terrible heat," she said.

Tobias nodded. Elysen's eyes pleaded with him.

"How will we ever get through this?"

He shook his head. "I don't know."

They walked in silence for a while, ignoring the guardsmen behind them. The trail wound in and out of the rocks, spiraling downward toward the lake below. The sounds of the forges and metal smiths faded in and out as they moved through the rocky draws and ravines that led them to the lower plateau.

"Your father must be very worried," Elysen said.

Tobias nodded. "He'll be worried. But he knows that I'm doing what I have to do. We prepare for our journey from birth. It's our way. Our rite of passage. Your mother did it. So did mine, and my father. And now me. We all leave our tribe in order to find our purpose, our giftedness. When I return, the village will gather together and sing my song of remembrance, and I will be welcomed back into the tribe. It will be a great day. There will be a feast, with music and song and dance."

"What if you never return?"

"Then they will sing my song to remember me, and they will laugh and sing and dance anyway, as a celebration of my life."

They walked for a while in silence.

Elysen kept her voice low and quiet. "I don't want you to waste your life in the desert with me," she said. "The first chance you get, run away. Go north. Go home."

"My life will never be wasted, wherever I go," he said.

"I wish I could feel the same way," Elysen said.

Ser Kreid led Elysen and Tobias around the edge of the wooded area to a clearing by the water, where Tobias helped her clean up and cool down. She sat naked in the cool water, exhausted, until Tobias waded out and pulled her away. He dried her and helped her to dress in the soft, white desert gear that the Madeire had given her. Elysen kept her knife with her.

"The baby is really showing," Tobias said.

"Nonsense," Corde countered. "This girl is as skinny as a willow branch. We need to get her some food."

Elysen turned at his voice. It took her only three quick steps to reach him. She threw her arms around his neck and hugged him.

"Food would be good," she said.

"Feeling better are we?" Ser Kreid stood at the edge of the clearing.

"How long have you been standing there?" Elysen asked.

"Does it matter?"

"No." She turned away from him and pulled her hood over her head, securing it with her bone visor. She pulled a flap of fabric over her mouth. The white garb completely concealed her skin.

"Are you ready to be presented?" Ser Kreid said.

"I am ready to see your village, but it is no thanks to you," she said. She tipped her head to Tobias and Corde. "Thank you, gentlemen."

"Our pleasure," Tobias said.

Corde watched Ser Kreid suspiciously. The prince presented his arm to Elysen and she placed her hand on it lightly, following him from the shady glade onto a well-worn dirt path that led toward the noise and activity of the village.

"You will stay in my villa," he said.

He pointed toward a large stone building on a small ridge that overlooked the commune. It looked as if it could be home to a dozen families.

"Where will Tobias be staying?" she asked.

"He will stay with the slaves at the bottom of the hill there."

"I will stay with them," she said.

"That is not appropriate," Ser Kreid said.

"Nevertheless, I will stay with them."

Ser Kreid stopped and glared at her. "It is inappropriate for a lady to stay with peasants, much less slaves. I forbid it."

"I prefer their company to yours," she said, keeping her voice calm and her expression hidden behind her white mask.

Ser Kreid clenched his teeth.

"If you allow me to stay with my friends, I'll cooperate quietly. I'll stay out of sight. I'll be no trouble."

"And if I refuse."

"Then I will be noisy and horrible."

He smiled suddenly, but it was a blank smile that did not extend into his eyes. The Addiss on his back remained calm, almost distracted.

"I don't really care where you stay," he said.

"Fine," she said. They continued walking in silence.

On approach, Asaka did not look like the villages of the plains at all. Rather than a gathering place where many things were traded and where people met for community, it was a working commune of metallurgists and artisans. There were no stores, no meeting places, no hostels. Just an unorganized array of sheds and huts, mostly dug into the ground itself in order to take advantage of what little coolness the desert retained during the day.

In the center of the gathering of squat, adobe buildings, under a large, shaky tent, a group of young men pumped up and down on huge articulated bladders, blowing gusts of air across a bed of coals so hot that Elysen could barely look at it. The ceaseless Soel tanned their backs and shoulders almost black, and their faces were red from the heat of the fires. Within the fires sat great crucibles of bubbling iron, suspended from heavy chains that glowed red over the fire, then yellow, then orange, and then a dull auburn, finally returning to their true black color as they extended outward, where they looped around large iron pulleys that were looped around giant posts.

A bald, leathery man hauled a crucible out of the fire by turning a large wooden-handled crank. His muscles bulged and his veins strained against his skin as if he could explode. Beads of sweat dripped from his nose and chin as he grabbed a long metal prod and tipped molten iron into a clay mold that shouted and cracked like a living thing, seared and scalded under the heat of the liquid metal.

"Asaka is the birthplace of our finest weapons," Ser Kreid said as they stopped just outside the large tent, less than a dozen paces from the blazing inferno. "This is the foundry," he said. He placed his hands on his hips. Elysen let her arm drift to her side as she gazed at the activity around her. Men stood at long benches made of thick wooden planks that looked and smelled like charred oak.

A reddish-skinned man took a long rod of iron out of the forge with a huge pair of black tongs. It smoked, cherry-red, in the hot air. He carried the hot iron over to an anvil and began to hammer on it, working his way down the length of the rod with quick, deft strokes, sending a shower of sparks with every blow. The sound rang in Elysen's ears and echoed off the cliffs.

Ser Kreid shouted over the chaos of noisy hammering and shouted commands that passed from one worker to the next.

"These are the forges," he said. "Where the iron bars are heated so that they can be drawn out." He pointed at the man she had been watching. "That is Rodan, our best blade smith." He leaned close to her and whispered in her ear. "His coupling with the Addiss is unique. It muddled his mind and nearly destroyed his Addiss. Yet he still produces excellent work." The violent noise and layers of shouting voices faded away as more and more of the men stopped to gawk at the visitors. Ser Kreid took advantage of the lull in the activity to approach Rodan, who continued to work as if nothing odd were going on.

"The Lady Elysen," Ser Kreid announced as they came close to him.

Rodan tipped his head up slightly so that he could peer at her, but he kept hammering as if he needed only the corner of one eye to place the blows that fell in expert measure, one overlapping the next. The other hammers fell silent, leaving only Rodan's, playing a lonely, monotonous melody that filled the entire canyon. He finished his chore. The iron faded to dull amber. He placed his hammer on the workbench and bowed his head.

"M'lord," he said. "M'lady."

"It is good to see you, old man," Ser Kreid said, clasping his shoulders.

Rodan smiled, showing only a few remaining teeth. As he turned, Elysen could see an Addiss, wrapped tightly around his body, hugging his back like a child afraid of slipping off. It hung there, clutching, not agitated, and yet not satisfied.

"How was your campaign in the north?" Rodan asked. He glanced at Ser Kreid's sheathed sword and frowned. "That blade looks as fresh as the day I made it. No blood? Not even a fight to test the metal of that blade?"

"We found what we were looking for," he said.

Rodan turned his gray eyes to Elysen, looked her up and down, and squinted at her face as if his eyes could pierce her shroud.

"So," he said. "The lady Elysen. They say you killed your uncle with Griever, one of my finest blades, made for Ser Kreid's brother Zegra, wrested from his dying grip by the coward Yergen, after the people of the Vyr punctured Zegra's body with forty bolts." Rodan's eyes were gleaming as he recounted the tale in his gravely voice, his tongue running afoul of his toothless gums as he spoke.

Elysen noticed that Ser Kreid seemed agitated, so she changed the subject. "Do you name all your swords?" she asked.

"Ah, yes, m'lady. This one that Lord Ser Kreid wears is the brother of Griever, named Mourning, and not the morning of the Soel, but the mourning of women and children as they weep over the bodies of their husbands and fathers, cleft of head, cleft of arms, cleft of legs, and cleaved down the middle, or with their guts spilling out, steaming on the fair, dewy grass of the plains."

Ser Kreid turned away and gazed out at the lake. A wind blew across the water, bringing a refreshing breath of coolness with it. Rodan smiled and winked at Elysen. His action startled her. She paused for a moment and then tipped her head to the side slightly as she eyed the old man with curiosity. Just then, Ser Kreid returned his attention to the blade smith, and Rodan turned back to his workbench.

"And what is the name of this blade that you craft now?" Elysen asked.

"We won't know that until we are finished. When my sweat and my life drip into the fires that forge these blades, I give them life, birthing them like little children, and I name them accordingly, when they come out all shiny and slick and oily. Then I see them and I hear them and in my heart I know their names, and I know what they can do, and I see all the places they will go."

Ser Kreid smiled, but his eyes looked tired.

"I can tell that you love your work," Elysen said.

"This piece that I have here," Rodan said. "The others spurned it. They said it was too narrow, too thin, that it would not make a good blade, but I saw something in it. In the color of the metal, I see something tough and special, so when the others sought to throw it back, I took it and said 'give it to me.' I will show you how the craftsman sees no mistakes, only uniqueness and beauty."

He paused, staring at Elysen. "I see now that I make this blade for you," he said. "It will not be as heavy as Griever and Mourning, but where it is smaller, it will slip between your enemy's armor plates, and where it is lighter, it will be quicker, like the strike of a snake, and where it is thinner, it will sing all the more beautifully as it swings in a graceful arc before slicing through leather and skin and bone. I will make it sharper and keener than any blade we have ever made. When it is done, I will come find you and give it to you." He put up a stubby, hard finger. "I will tell you its name on that day, and I will sing to you a song about its glory."

Ser Kreid laughed. "You are a treasure, old man," he said. "If you were not such a great blade smith, we would have used you in the Lord's court to entertain us with your wit and colorful language."

Ser Kreid took Elysen by the arm and led her away. Rodan watched them for a moment, and then thrust the bar of iron back into the forge, deep into the smoking coals. He nodded his head with some secret song as he worked the bellows with his foot, fanning the coals into a frenzy of swirling sparks and white heat.

"You see Rodan's affection," Ser Kreid said. "His Addiss became ill, malnourished, unable to thrive. It has driven the poor man mad, but he continues to be a great blade smith." Ser Kreid shook his head sadly. "His case is rare indeed. Even the Addiss feel badly for him."

"And what will happen to him?"

Ser Kreid shrugged. "As long as he continues to forge great weapons, he will stay in our service. Yet, we watch him closely."

"Why?" Elysen asked.

"Because, like you, he is not Uemn."

Elysen glanced back at Rodan, hammering away again, and at the clutching black monster that watched her as if it longed for something it could not have.

Twenty-five

Ser Kreid rode for the capital city of Kardesh the next day, leaving Veldon in charge of Asaka. Elysen stayed close to the water's edge during the day, hiding under her white robe, protected from prying eyes and biting bugs. In the evenings, as the sky turned from blue to purple, she changed into black and hid in the shadows, watching Rodan work. He never rested. He pounded the mysterious metal over and over, tirelessly. Sometimes, other men stopped to watch him briefly before returning to their own work. But Elysen never tired of the rhythmic pounding of the heavy hammer against the impossibly hard iron. Day by day, the iron bar grew longer, thinner, flatter, as Rodan folded it, red hot, against itself, and then pounded it thin again.

One night, Rodan stopped for a long drink of water from the well near where Elysen crouched in the darkness. The other workers had stopped for dinner. The compound rested quietly.

"Come out of there, little one," Rodan said to her. He took another long drink, wiped his chin with his bare arm, and then motioned to her. "Come out. I see you there, hiding, watching me every night. Come out here, and I will show you something."

She stood and took a step forward then stopped.

"You have nothing to be afraid of from me," he said. "Come over here, into the light. I will show you the blade that I have been working on."

Elysen stepped forward, into the light from a dozen bright lanterns that burned under the canvas canopy.

"Don't you ever worry about this place burning down?" she asked.

Rodan laughed. "My dear," he said. "That would be the greatest blessing in my life."

She let her hood fall back, exposing her head and face. The dark runes were like flickering shadows against her white skin.

"So," he said. "It is true." He took a step toward her and she took a step back. "Now, now," he said. "I am not going to hurt you. I just wanted to take a closer look at those runes."

The sour smell of burnt oil and sweat hung on his body. He peered at her, and then shook his head. "I have seen writing like that before. Very old. Very strange." Elysen's body broke out in tiny bumps as he examined her. She tried to swallow, but could find no moisture in her mouth or throat.

"Can you interpret their meaning?" she asked, her voice barely more than a whisper.

He shook his head.

"Kreid said the language is too ancient for even the Addiss."

"Ha," Rodan laughed. "The Addiss know nothing."

Elysen blinked. "Kreid says they know everything. That they taught you how to forge metal, how to survive in the desert."

"Nonsense," he said. He spat on the ground. "The Addiss take credit for our own accomplishments. They are leeches. Without them, we would flourish. With them, we are sliding into a cesspool of degeneration. Everything they say is a lie. Remember that, little one."

He picked up the weapon and examined it, turning it under the hot lights that drew swarms of tiny insects.

"The Addiss are demons," he said. "Spawned from some unholy venture with a dark power from long ago. The Uemn should never have dragged them up from the depths where they were imprisoned."

"You speak of the Addiss as if you were not one of them. Yet you carry the shadow of the Addiss on your back."

"I don't let the Addiss control me. They leave me alone because they think I am sick. Maybe I am sick. I do think that I have lost some of my mind working in this heat and noise for so long. I have spent most of my life here, with only the fire and the metal for company." He ran his fingers along the metal as if he were admiring a lover.

"What did you do before this?" she asked.

"I am a Norgarden, like you," he said. "Captured and enslaved here for this eternal summer. I was but a young lad, no older than you are, when I came to this place."

"Why did you leave the ice lands?"

"It was my rite of passage. I chose to leave, to find my spirit and purpose here in the world."

"And you ended up here, making weapons of death."

He nodded and held up the partially completed blade. "I think this is the last weapon I will make," he said.

"I don't need a weapon," Elysen said. "I appreciate the task you have undertaken for me, but I can't deal in death any more. I'm weary of it."

He gazed at her. "I come across as crazy when you first meet me," he said. "I have been making these weapons for so long. And yet, I have been hammering out this metal, for this blade, for you, and the days have gone by like minutes. You are a warrior, and I see great things in this blade. You've already shown that you know how to use one."

"I have a confession to make," Elysen said.

"Oh?"

"I did not kill my uncle. Not with your blade, nor any blade."

"I know."

"How could you know that?"

"Because when I look at you now, when I look into your eyes, I don't see the eyes of one who kills for power."

"Yet I have killed."

Rodan nodded. "And I have made many weapons that have dealt death to many men and women and children. May the universe forgive me."

"Why do you keep doing it?" Elysen asked.

"I slave away here, toiling in the heat, making weapons for the Uemn, watching the Addiss take over people's lives and bodies and ruin them, and yet, I find a strange comfort in knowing that all of these things are but temporary, and that there is a large and unexplained wholeness to the universe. I believe that there is a power greater than the Addiss, greater than the Vyr Lords, greater then everything."

Elysen smiled. "You are much different than I first thought."

"My bravado is just a mask I wear to hide myself from the world."

Elysen sat on a wooden stool and watched as Rodan hefted the roughly hewn blade, rotated it in his hand, and then flipped it over and over.

"What would you have been if you had returned to the ice lands?" Elysen asked.

"I would have been a metal worker," he said. "In bronze, though. Not this horrid iron. I would have made tools, and works of art."

"I saw a beautiful statue of a swan, outside the citadel," Elysen said.

Rodan's eyes brightened. "I know that one," he said. "Can it be that it is still there after all these years?"

She nodded. "Its wings were outstretched, and it looked as if it were poised for flight, caught in that instant when its body is weightless upon the Vyr, yet the tips of its long toes still feel the ground beneath."

"I can see it, just as you describe it," he said. He closed his eyes. "The swan is the spirit, reaching for the great creator, striving for perfection, and the feet are the soul, touching the Vyr but for a short while, feeling the gritty, solid world, experiencing the pain and the joy of life."

"So, you are a philosopher too?"

"I am an artist. Art is creation. Creation is an act of the spirit. The spirit reaches for the universe. Contemplation of the universe is philosophy, therefore, as an artist, I must be a philosopher."

"Any other secret talents?"

"Ah yes, too many to tell."

"I have to go," Elysen said. "Some of the men are returning from their dinners."

"Take this," he said, handing her two wooden sticks fashioned to look like long blades. "During the long hot days and sleepless nights, practice with your friend the art of wielding a sword. I will finish this blade of yours, and you will wear it, for what purpose we don't know. Just know that I feel in my heart that this blade is the end of my toils. I have prayed to the swan, and she has answered. She sent you here, to me. All these years of labor, of practicing this craft, which was not the craft of my choosing, all these years of perfecting my art, the art of making weapons, which was also not of my choosing, have all led to this moment. I feel that my trials are almost over. I will return home after this, or, I shall die on the journey, and my spirit, the spirit of the swan, will finally fly away from this human journey." He shook his finger at her. "But, if you carry the blade, you have to learn to defend yourself with it. That is the rule of weaponry."

"I know," she said.

He forced the wooden swords into her hands and she took them reluctantly.

"Tomorrow, when you come back, I will begin to teach you the fundamentals of sword fighting. You will see that I have much to teach you. In the meantime, you practice with these. Just hit each other for a while. It can be rejuvenating."

She stepped back into the darkness and covered her face again.

"Rodan," she said quietly.

"Yes?"

"The Addiss with you…"

He smiled. "I have come to an agreement with my Addiss," he said.

"What kind of an agreement?"

The other workers were taking their places at the workbenches and forges, and were glancing suspiciously at Elysen and Rodan.

He smiled again. "It is not actually an agreement," he said. "I think that my Addiss is actually not happy with our arrangement."

"It does not act like the others."

"It does not control me."

"You have overcome the Addiss?"

He shook his head.

"No, but I have regained control of my own life. I no longer worship it."

One of the other men came over to Rodan and stood, waiting to ask a question. Elysen took another step backward, and Rodan turned away from her. She stood for a moment, waiting, but after Rodan had answered the question he went back to his bench and began his endless hammering again. Elysen slipped away into the night.

Early the next morning she handed one of the wooden blades to Tobias.

"Try to strike me," she said.

Tobias stared at the blunt weapon and frowned.

"I would rather not."

"Come on, winney," she said.

"What is a winney?" he asked. He hefted the stick, holding it out in front of his body as if it were a torch.

Corde came out of the stable-house, wiping his hands on a piece of cloth. "You had better not let Veldon catch you playing with those," he said. "It is a capital offense for slaves to practice weaponry."

"Of course it is," Elysen said.

She stripped off her clothes and tied a long strip of white cloth around her chest, leaving her bulging stomach and sculpted shoulders bare. She tied a wider strip of the same lightweight fabric around her hips in a makeshift skirt. The blackness of the runes and spells showed through the thin fabric.

"Come on," she said. She swung her own stick in a circle, holding it with both hands as she had seen the soldiers do in practice.

"What is a winney?" Tobias asked again.

"A winney," she said, "is someone who is afraid to try something new."

"I don't want to learn to fight," Tobias said.

"Then learn to defend yourself," Elysen countered.

She lunged at him, purposefully swinging for his sword instead of his body. Tobias ducked his head as the wooden sticks knocked together.

"Why are you smiling," he said.

"Because, you ducked," she said. "I wasn't even swinging at your head. You closed your eyes and ducked. That was not a very good defensive move."

Tobias looked at his wooden weapon. Pursed his lips, and then swung it gently towards her. She easily deflected the blow.

"Winney, winney," she said. Her smile broadened, and Tobias smiled back. He swung again, harder this time. The sound of the sticks striking each other echoed in the cool morning air, and Corde cringed.

"Don't worry so, Corde," Elysen said. "They have to put up with me for now."

She swung again at Tobias and almost knocked the sword from his hands. He lunged, she parried, he lunged again, she stepped backwards. They began to lunge and parry more seriously, moving around the small glade until Elysen's feet slipped into the edge of the lake and she turned to look down. Tobias's thrust nearly caught her off guard. She deflected the blow but stumbled backwards and tripped, falling into the water and landing with a splash. Her eyes opened wide and Tobias looked appalled until Elysen began to laugh, quietly at first, and then with more gusto, until Tobias laughed as well and even the somber, worrisome Corde began to chuckle. Elysen's laugh peeled through the valley like music. A harsh voice interrupted their mirth.

"Where did you get those weapons?"

Veldon stood on the shoreline with his hands on his hips, frowning.

"We borrowed them from the foundry," Elysen said, a trace of her laugh still musing about the corners of her mouth and eyes. She stood up and trudged out of the water, dragging her skirt along with the help of her free hand.

"It is forbidden for you to have those," he said.

Elysen walked up to him and stopped in front of him.

"I am no slave," she said. "Remember that, child soldier. I will lead your army to Sunder Keep, and I will do it with my blade on my hip, not with flowers in my hair."

They glared at each other. Elysen held firm, but Veldon's mouth curled up in fierce indignation and rage.

"We shall see about that," he said.

"Yes, we shall," Elysen said. Veldon turned to go. Elysen called after him.

"Please announce yourself next time you decide to visit here," she said.

He stomped away without turning back.

"Winney," she said to his back.

Tobias smiled. "Um, m'lady?"

"Yes?"

"You don't have any hair," Tobias reminded her. He pointed at her head.

"What?"

"You can't wear flowers in your hair," he reminded her.

Elysen laughed, but her mirth faded quickly.

"We will practice again tonight," she said. "When the canyon has cooled down."

She walked toward the house with her sword in her hand. She stopped and turned toward Tobias.

"By the time we leave for the land of my people, I will be as good with a sword as any desert man."

The night came on as cold as any winter night in the high plains, but Elysen made Tobias practice until he dropped from exhaustion. In the morning, she made Tobias fight again before breakfast. Corde finally came out and pulled Elysen into the cabin. She sat down as he finished making her morning meal.

"This is their best season," Corde said.

He gazed out at the Soel as it peeked above the rim of the canyon. He served her wheat cakes and salted meat with a bowl full of red, sour winterberries. Corde ate standing up, staring out the window. When he finished, he wiped his hands on a towel, as he always did. He handed it to Elysen.

"Your new friends teach you much about this land and its customs," Elysen remarked.

"There is a network of communication among the slaves and servants that is unequalled in all the lands," he said.

Elysen frowned and stood next to him. "How hot will it get in the summer?"

He shook his head slowly. "I fear that we have nothing to compare it to."

"Even now the days grow longer," she said.

Tobias came running up. He jumped up on the porch.

"Ser Kreid is back," he panted. "He has summoned you to his villa for a meeting."

Elysen pursed her lips. "I want you to come with me," she said to Tobias.

She changed into the white desert gear that Corde kept so perfectly clean. She donned her visor and covered her face, and Tobias followed her up the hill. A guard met them at the door to the villa and put out his hand to stop Tobias, but Elysen grabbed the man's arm.

"If you don't let him pass, then we both leave and you will have to explain to the Ser Kreid how you sent me away."

The guard relented, and Elysen and Tobias passed into a great room. An open door at the far end of the room led to a smaller room. Ser Kreid sat at a large wooden table with Veldon. Another man, older, also an Addicere, sat between them, commanding the center of the table. The men all stood up as Elysen entered. She removed her visor and her cowl and stood at the end of the table with her arms hanging at her sides. There were bowls and cups on the table and a partial loaf of bread and scraps of meat on a tray. The pungent smell of wine drifted through the room.

"Good morning," Ser Kreid said. "I see you have brought a guest."

"Tobias is the captain of my personal guard," she said. "Where I go, he goes."

Ser Kreid smiled and nodded.

"May I introduce my father," he said. "The Consilium Addicere Jenus." He motioned toward the older man.

The Consilium bowed his head. "I am honored." He tried to clear his throat but instead launched into a weak, wet cough. The skin of his face looked like old leather that had been stretched too tightly over his bones. He wore a gaunt, starved look, and although years of desert heat had tanned his skin, there was an underlying grayness to his complexion like rotten meat, that spoke of impending death. He fidgeted a bit. The Addiss was flicking its tentacles as if it were cleaning crumbs from the Consilium's shirt.

Elysen bowed her head slightly. Tobias followed suit, but bowed more deeply and held it longer.

"Why do you summon me on such short notice?" she asked. The Consilium glanced at his son with a questioning look, and then turned back to Elysen. He took a breath and nodded toward her.

"We sense your confusion," he said. "Our people have been at war since the time of Thorsen." He leaned forward in his chair. "But you and I will change all that," he said. "With you, the bloodlines are complete again. Just as Kaan foretold. The legend of your coming comes down from generation to generation. We have waited for countless thousands of cycles for you."

The Consilium leaned back again and coughed quietly. Ser Kreid gestured for Elysen to take a seat. There were several empty chairs in front of her. She chose to remain standing.

"Your brother was my grandfather," Elysen said.

The Consilium nodded.

"Will I meet him?"

"Consilium Stratus is dead. My son Kreid now hosts his Addiss."

Elysen turned his words over in her mind, trying to concentrate without showing it.

"Stratus was your elder, then?" she asked.

The Consilium nodded. "He was a great leader. We all miss him."

Elysen bowed her head. "I'm sorry that I never got to meet him."

"Ser Kreid tells me you are with child," the Consilium said. "Yergen's child," he added.

Elysen responded with a small, curt nod.

"That is unfortunate," he said. "But, we shall see when the time comes."

He put his elbow on the armrest and touched the side of his face with his fingers. His other hand gripped the other armrest, and he settled deeper into his chair.

"We are prepared now to listen to your plan for taking Sunder Keep," he said.

Elysen stared at him, transfixed by the squirming, restless beast on his back.

"You do have a plan, don't you?" the Consilium asked.

Elysen nodded. Veldon slumped in his chair, gritting his teeth.

"I will tell you my plan," she said. "But don't interrupt me. You can ask questions when I am done."

"Impertinent, isn't she?" the Consilium said to Ser Kreid.

Elysen approached the table and pulled Raes' knife from its sheath behind her back. Veldon stood suddenly and drew his blade halfway out of its scabbard. The Consilium put his hand on Veldon's arm and pushed him back into his seat. Elysen plunged the stone blade into the center of the wooden table and left it there. She grabbed a cup, keeping her eye on Veldon. Elysen turned the cup over, spilling the contents into a large bowl. She slammed the cup down inside the bowl.

"Sunder Keep," she said. "Floating along the western edge of Turoc's Cauldron."

She dislodged the red-bladed knife from where it stood in the middle of the table and slowly, purposefully scratched a long line to the far end of the table where Tobias stood silently. She reached across the table and scratched another slow, grating line parallel to the first.

"The Great Rift," she said. She kept her eye on the Consilium and his men as she marred the table. They in turn watched her eyes, not her hand.

"Tobias stands in the Sud de Mer, the endless sea. You sit at the crown of the world, even north of the ice lands."

The Consilium leaned forward a bit, as if some life had seeped back into his body.

"How many times have you tried to cross the ice, and failed? Your men's lips turning blue, then black, as they fell one after the other to the numbing cold. They became tired, slept, never to rise again, their bodies stiff as the swords they carried, lost in the great expanse of ice." Her words came out as a statement rather than a question.

"Go on," the Consilium said.

"And for how many centuries have your warriors battled against the armies of the Vyr Lord in the southern swamps? By the time your men broke into the southern lands, they were scattered, weakened. Even with their armor and weapons of hard metal, our crossbows eventually defeated them and drove them back, and the swamps swallowed them in their heavy garb. Your men were fearsome and frightening and vicious, and yet you still suffer defeat after defeat after defeat at the hands of the plainsmen."

She tapped her blade against the end of the table as she considered the imaginary swamps that spread out in front of Tobias.

"The western walls of the Rift are too steep, and are too easily patrolled. You have tried to scale them with horrible results. We waited for you near the top, and pummeled you with rocks and arrows. Your men died horribly."

"You were there?" the Consilium asked.

"I sent my share of your Uemn dogs to hell," Elysen said.

The Consilium smiled and nodded.

"Your people believe that I will lead them to victory," Elysen said.

He nodded again.

"What about you?" she asked.

"What do you mean?"

"What do you believe?"

"I believe that what our people believe is a great asset to us."

"My plan is dangerous, and will involve much trust on the part of your soldiers."

The Consilium pursed his lips. "What reason do you have to help us to victory? Why would you not lead us into a trap?"

"I did not kill Lord Owen," she said. "The beast Yergen did. I attempted to protect my lord. I failed. I am not Norgarden, nor Vyr, nor Uemn. I have no loyalty to anyone. I will lead you to Sunder Keep. I have no love for that place, or for the people it purports to serve and protect. You will deliver Yergen to me, alive. And Raes. I will have my revenge, and the reign of the Vyr Lords will end."

The Consilium pondered her statement for a moment.

"So, what is your proposal?"

Elysen grabbed a tray of meat and stood at the end of the table, next to Tobias.

"This man," she said, nodding toward Tobias, "will help us build a dozen or more great sailing ships, of the kind they use in the northern lakes for fishing, but much, much larger. You will deploy an army to attack the southern villages through the swamps, thus occupying Lord Yergen's army in the south, drawing them away from the Keep. We will sail our vessels south, into the Sud de Mer, then west, and finally north again, where we will disembark on the far side of the Mountains of Oken."

Ser Kreid stood up, glaring.

"Impossible," he said. "We will drop off the end of the world."

"If your Addiss are as wise and all knowing as you say they are, then they know that the world does not end at the far mountains."

"Enough," the Consilium said. He shook his finger at Elysen. "There will be no more remarks about the Addiss. They are all-knowing, all-powerful. It is only our ignorance that clouds our ability to understand them." He closed his eyes. "They reveal the truth to me now. Just as we once believed that our world ended somewhere beyond the desert, we must now accept that possibility that there is world beyond the western mountains."

"There is," Elysen said. "I have seen it."

"Impossible," Veldon said. "Even if there were something beyond the mountains, no one could survive the journey."

"That is all ignorance. You are limited only by what you believe. If you choose to believe that the world ends at the mountains, then for you it does, and I am of no use to you. If you choose to believe that the world goes on, then I can lead you there, and I can lead you back across the mountains, into the very back door of Sunder Keep. We will meet with little resistance. I will lead the advance guard. I will rally the people against the Vyr Lord, and you can walk into Sunder Keep. If you keep your word, and if you don't harm my child, I will abdicate the Vyr and you can have it."

She leaned against the table.

"Then I will be gone. Forever. But, if you betray me, if you harm my child, I will turn the army of the Vyr against you, and I will bring death and destruction down upon you, just as the ancient prophecies have foretold."

The men sat silently, considering her words.

Finally, the Consilium broke the silence, but he spoke quietly.

"I will not lie to you, Lady Elysen. We will not let the boy child live. You know this as well as we do."

"You don't even know if it is a boy yet. At least let me have the child."

He nodded. "The prophecy is vague about the boy," he conceded.

Elysen stood firm, her lips pressed tightly together, her face grim. She realized that she held her belly with both hands, and she let go.

The Consilium considered her plan for a moment, and then pounded on the table with his fist.

"What stories our grandchildren will tell of us," he said. "You will build your boats. We will plan to arrive at the far side of the mountains in the middle of the next summer, so that the crossing will not be in the deadly cold."

"Then we will have to embark across the sea in the late winter," Ser Kreid said. "That will give us time to make our way northward during the time of planting."

"We will have to begin building the ships immediately," Veldon said.

The Consilium put his hand in the air. "We will see one of these ships before we commit to the plan. Boy, you will teach my craftsmen how to build a giant sailing vessel here, in Asaka. We will test it in the lake."

Tobias turned pale. He said nothing.

"We will let two cycles of Turoc pass before we return to this place," the Consilium said. "In the meantime, we will travel across the great desert to the ancient burial grounds of the Addiss, where Sire Veldon and the other warriors of good merit and clear hearts will couple with their Addiss. Lady Elysen will accompany us. But the young boat builder will stay here." He looked toward Tobias. "Have that sailing ship done by the time we return," he said. "This summer shall pass as we prepare for war." He turned slightly in his chair and addressed his son. "Ser Kreid, gather an army. Recruit two thousand men to attack in the south as we pick our way northward along the western side of the mountains. How many can we take on these sailing ships of yours?"

Elysen shook her head. "We will build one, then we will know how long it will take your men to build more, and how many we can carry."

"We shall take the Addiss with us on each ship to lead the way," the Consilium said. "We shall finally occupy Sunder Keep, and we shall have all of its secrets." He smiled joyfully. "This is a great day in our history. Make preparations now. We set off tomorrow for Kardesh and the Temple of the Addiss."

Ser Kreid and Veldon stood as the Consilium stood. They bowed their heads as the Consilium walked out. Veldon glared at Elysen. Ser Kreid walked by without even a glance. Veldon leaned close to Elysen as he passed her and whispered.

"After we have taken the Keep, I will take pleasure in hunting you down and killing you."

She picked up her knife and tucked it into the sheath behind her back.

"You and everyone else," she said.

They stepped out into the heat, following the three men, who mounted horses. A dozen more Addiss warriors joined them plus a few uncoupled riders like Veldon, who fell to the back of the procession.

"I can't build such a thing as you have promised," Tobias hissed. His eyes were wide and there were tiny drops of sweat on his upper lip. Elysen touched them with her finger and Tobias nearly jumped out of his boots.

"You can build the ships," she said to Tobias. "It is your chance to live out your dream."

"My dream did not include hauling an invading army of demons into your homeland."

They walked slowly back to the hut at the shore of the lake. Corde waited outside the door, his ever-present towel swinging from one hand to the other. He looked worried.

Elysen touched Tobias' shoulder. "You will build your ship. I know that you will. And I know that it will be done by the time I get back."

"Back from where?" Corde asked.

"We go to the capital city of Kardesh, the ancient burial place of the Addiss, where Veldon and the others will be coupled."

Corde's worried look deepened.

"They mean to couple you as well, m'lady," he said. "In order to gain more control over you."

Elysen and Tobias stood in shocked silence.

"How do you know this?" Elysen asked.

"The slaves have their own communication routes, m'lady. I had heard this before, but I discounted it until now."

"I will not have it," she said.

"They will force you."

"I thought that one had to have an open mind and a clear heart, to be ready for the Addiss before coupling could take place."

Corde shook his head. "There have been those that have been coupled against their will before. Most of them go mad."

Elysen stood, transfixed.

"If I resist I will go mad?"

Corde nodded.

She looked around at the glade, the simple hut, the water lapping at the shoreline. "What about the baby?" she asked. Corde shook his head sadly.

"I know nothing of that. The slaves have seen Addiss coupled with women before, but I don't know what affect they might have on unborn children." He paused.

"What is it?" Elysen asked.

"Have you seen any women possessed by Addiss?" Corde asked.

Elysen thought about it for a moment. "No," she said.

Corde set his jaw and took a deep breath. "No woman has ever survived the coupling," he said.

Elysen just stared at him and shook her head.

"There is something even worse that I have not yet told you," he said.

Elysen frowned. "What could be worse?" she asked. "Go on, tell me."

"The Addiss are nourished by a poison that is fed into the bodies of their hosts. They crave this poison to the exclusion of all else. It drives them, feeds them, sates them for a time, then they need more, and more, and more, until the host body can take no more. The Addiss kill their hosts, just as surely as they themselves cannot be killed."

Elysen's eyes were glaring, intense. "If the Addiss don't die, what happens to them when the host dies?"

"They are transferred. There is a ceremony."

"This poison. How will it affect the baby?"

Corde shook his head. "The slaves have never seen a woman with child coupled with an Addiss, much less ingest the potion."

"They can't do this," Elysen said.

She sat down and her shoulders slumped. She wrapped her fingers together. Tobias stared out the window. Corde took a deep breath and exhaled through his nose.

"How will we stop them?" he asked.

"I'll offer to help them," Elysen said. "If they will forego the coupling."

"You have helped them already," Corde reminded her.

"We can run," Tobias said. "We have to run away. It is the only choice."

"Run where?" Elysen asked. "Through the desert? Back to the northlands, so that they can follow us and butcher your people?" She shook her head. "We're committed to this course of action. My only choice is to go with them.

I'll show them that we are with them, that we are cooperating. They won't chance a coupling if it means losing my support."

Corde's lips were tight. "Or your life," he said.

"I have to go with you," Tobias said.

Elysen took his hands. "Brave Tobias, you have to stay here and build that ship. I can take care of myself. Besides, maybe Corde is wrong about the coupling."

Tobias shook his head. "He's not. I can see it in their eyes when they look at you."

"You imagine the worst," she said.

He hung his head and nodded.

"Don't worry so much about what might come to pass. Remember what you told me, a long time ago, in the woods of the northern lands? Enjoy the day today. It may be all we have. Take solace in our time together, right here, right now."

"What will I do if you come back…different?"

"Do you still believe in a greater power?" Elysen asked.

Tobias nodded.

"Then pray to it."

"What about you?"

"I will do whatever I have to do to protect my baby. His life is all that matters to me now."

"We will both pray for you," Corde said. "I wish we could do more."

Elysen's eyes grew bright, intensely green in the bright light of the hot Soel.

"Others have tried in their own way to hurt me, to stop me from becoming what I am. They failed, despite their best attempts. Let the Uemn do their best against me. They will only make me stronger."

"The Addiss will take you from us," Tobias said.

"It's true," Corde said. "When you return, you won't care about the baby anymore, or about us. You'll care about nothing but yourself and the Addiss and their poisonous hydria. That is their way."

"We'll see about that," she said.

Twenty-six

The heat drove Elysen into the cool water of the lake, where she spent the rest of the day practicing swordplay with Tobias. But the play turned more serious. Elysen made her strikes more directed, and the force behind them increased. It was all Tobias could do to defend himself.

"You're not trying," Elysen said.

She stood waist deep in the water, her feet mired in the mud. Her wet tunic clung to her heavy breasts and swollen stomach. The morning Soel reflected off the surface of the lake and warmed Elysen's back.

"I am trying," Tobias protested. "You're too aggressive. I can't fend off your blows any more. My arms are tired, my legs quiver with exhaustion, and yet you keep pummeling me. When can we stop?"

"We'll stop when you start trying," she said.

"The Soel is getting high. Your skin will burn."

"Then I'll get a heavier shirt," she said.

Tobias put his hands on his knees and leaned over, waiting for his breathing to return to normal. He shook his head.

"You have long ago become too good for me. I am not a fighter. I just build boats and catch fish. I'm afraid my heart is not in this play."

"This is not play any longer," Elysen said. She placed her hand on Tobias's shoulder. "Come on. Let's go in and have some dinner. I can smell Corde's awful cooking, and it is making me hungry."

Tobias stood and smiled. "You are always hungry these days," he said.

She smiled and patted her stomach, and then her smile faded.

Tobias' smiled faded as well.

"Are you scared?" he asked.

"About the trip?"

He nodded.

"Yes," she said.

They slogged through the muddy water towards the cabin.

"Tonight I'll go see Rodan for the last time," Elysen said.

Tobias nodded again. "He's been a good teacher for you."

"And a friend."

The day passed, long and hot. Elysen cooled her body in the water at the edge of the lake under the shade of a willow tree. As night fell, she wandered toward the workshops. Rodan waited for her. She sat on his stool as he toyed with the mechanism on a small crossbow.

"I have lost my taste for this work," he said.

She nodded.

"I've spent my whole life making weapons of war," he continued. He held up the small crossbow, finely crafted of steel. The haft attached to an armband, etched with a delicate design inspired by the runes that Elysen now took for granted, as if they had always been a part of her. The steel had been blued by bathing it in a bath of caustic acid, polished, bathed again, the process repeated until the smooth metal took on a blackness like the deep evening sky. Rodan slipped it on Elysen's arm. The gauntlet fit perfectly and she hid it easily under the black fabric of her tunic. She examined the weapon carefully.

"Where is the release?" she asked.

He smiled. "Let me show you," he said. "Relax your arm, let it go limp."

He wrapped his arm around hers and used both hands to cock the weapon, using a lever to pull the small spring steel bow into a high tension. From the bottom of the gauntlet, he removed an iron bolt with a hardened tip and fitted it through a hole in the front of the bow. It snapped into place, the nock of the bolt against the woven steel thread that hummed between the ends of the straining bow. He walked over to the other side of the open tent and placed an iron breastplate against one of the poles. He stepped back.

"Point your arm at the breastplate," he said. "Now, tense the muscles in your forearm, make a fist, but keep your wrist bent downward."

The moment she did, the bolt released and a hole appeared in the armor plating. It was a clean puncture, almost square, with the edges bent inward. As she stared at the effect of the weapon, she noticed that the tent pole buckled slightly from the damage. Rodan grabbed the broken pole in an attempt to keep the tent from collapsing. Elysen stood wide-eyed, but Rodan laughed. He grabbed an iron rod and jammed it against the grommet at the top of the tent in a makeshift replacement for the damaged support.

"That was murderous," Elysen whispered.

Rodan winked at her and put his finger against his nose. He beckoned to her, glancing to his left and right, and she came to him. He took her hand and led her to a wooden box. Before he opened it, he stared into her eyes.

"Never tell anyone what I am about to show you," he said. "Even if they do think that you are the savior of the world, they would kill both of us if they knew that we had seen their secret weapon."

Rodan slowly unclasped a metal hasp and lifted the lid to the box. Elysen peered over his shoulder, straining to see inside. Rodan dipped his hand into the box and drew forth a handful of black powder that trickled between his fingers like dried blood.

"Coal dust?" Elysen asked. "That is your secret weapon?"

Rodan shook his head and smiled like a boy playing a prank.

"They call this golgrit," he said. "They have added compounds from the high desert, a stinky yellow substance that smells like rotten eggs, and an ashen-gray powder from the rift. Watch this."

He took a small amount and tossed it into the flame of a nearby torch. The golgrit became a cloud of hot flames as it exploded with a soft grunt like the sound of a man hit in the stomach. Elysen jumped back, her eyes wide, and then she frowned and shook her head.

"Very impressive," she said. "But hardly a weapon."

"Don't be misled," Rodan warned her. He picked up a small metal canister from a table and handed it to her. She nearly dropped it.

"It's heavy," she said. She hefted it several times before she handed it back to Rodan.

"The golgrit is compressed in these canisters made of thick iron that is designed to fracture along several points."

He pointed to a small hole in one side of the canister.

"This is where we insert a short length of cord that has been wrapped with the golgrit as well. We light the cord, and when the flame reaches the golgrit inside, the golgrit turns to flame, expanding a thousand times in one instant. It blows the iron canister apart with a sound like thunder, and it destroys anything within sight."

Elysen reached out and Rodan handed it back to her.

"What do you call this thing?" she asked. She tried to peer into the tiny hole.

"We call them armenders, because of all the men who have lost their arms to these things."

"In battle?" Elysen asked.

"No. We have never used them in battle. Our men lose their arms making them. They tend to blow up without warning sometimes."

Elysen shoved the armender back into Rodan's hand and he laughed. He put it back on the table and motioned for her to follow him again. She glanced back at the armender and realized that it was only one of several dozen that sat on the table, looking like simple metal ingots.

Rodan walked over to the workbench and picked up two leather scabbards, each with a long sling. One scabbard fit a short knife, the other a long blade. He slid them over Elysen's shoulders so that the hilt of the long blade would project above her left shoulder, and the hilt of the short blade would project above her right shoulder.

"The fiercest Uemn warriors carry two blades," he said.

He walked back to the bench and unrolled a leather package, revealing the blade he had been working on for so long. He presented it to her, holding it across his upraised palms. The thin blade had been polished to a high gleam that made it appear almost clear, sharpened on both edges, with a wide, shallow groove down the middle of each flat side. The pointed tip glistened. A thin, bronze cable, blackened like the crossbow, wound around and around the hilt, building it up to a size perfect for Elysen's small hands. Rodan had cast the crosspiece at the top of the handle into a likeness of a skull headed beast that reached outward with muscular arms ending in three-fingered claws. He had repeated the claw shape at the pommel. Each claw held a ball of round, black obsidian. Rodan handed the blade to Elysen.

"Her name is Soul-Reaver," he said sadly. "And here is her little sister, Soul-Stealer." He handed her the dagger. He looked at them sadly as Elysen held one in each arm. The muscles of her arms rippled as she moved each weapon in a slow arc, watching the light reflect from the silver surfaces.

"They're beautiful," she said. "If only I would never have to use them."

He sighed. "That is up to you."

They sat in silence for a moment.

"I felt the baby move today," she said.

Rodan smiled and nodded, and a cloak of silence descended upon them again.

"How did you defeat the Addiss?" she asked suddenly.

He tilted his head a bit. Elysen flipped the blades over her shoulder and fumbled a bit as she tried to slip them into their scabbards. Rodan helped her slide them home. She sat again, and he began to sweep small bits of debris off the workbench onto the ground.

"I never did defeat my Addiss," he said. "It still taunts me, still whispers to me in the night. I pretend to be mad. I make my weapons by day, and I survive as best I can. But I did not defeat the Addiss. If anything, it defeated me. I simply gave up. I hit my knees one day and prayed to whatever power created them, and I realized that they were just part of this existence, like me. They did not create everything, they don't have power over everything. If they did, they would not be stuck here with me, begging for more hydria. I laughed, I cried, I begged for help from whatever power might be out there listening. I hoped. That was it. I hoped. My hope gave me faith to try harder."

"How long has it been since your Addiss was nourished?"

He shook his head. "I'm not sure. A long time. The other Addiss think it is sick."

"Then there is hope. Hope for me."

"I have hope for you. But it will not be easy."

"I have to be strong, for my baby."

Rodan nodded. "I fear for the baby. The evil of the Addiss will follow him all of his days. I fear he will be drawn to them."

Elysen stared at him, her nostrils flared, her eyes bright, intense and deep as the green water of the Cevante in the far north. Rodan sighed, and handed her a cloak, white on one side, black on the other.

"I had this made for you as well," he said. She almost dropped it.

"It is heavy," she said, gathering it up in her arms.

"There are metal plates riveted into the padding," he said, pointing out the rows and rows of metal buttons that ran lengthwise down the long cape. It split at the back up to her waist, for riding.

"You won't be able to wear armor until after the baby is born, so I had this cloak made special. It will protect you from the Soel during the day, the white surface will reflect the heat, and at night you can turn the dark side out, to help you hide in the shadows. The metal plates woven inside will protect you from most arrows and blades."

He draped it over her shoulders and showed her how to separate the hood from the rest of the cloak so that she could wear her scabbards underneath and yet still have the hilts of her swords protrude above her shoulders.

"Thank you, Rodan," she said. They held an awkward silence between them. "You won't go north, will you?" she said.

He shook his head. "The Uemn will follow me there if I do. Besides, I don't belong there any more. I'm more Uemn than Norgarden now."

"Where then?"

He smiled. "Remember, you will be one of them when you return."

"I will never be one of them. I will overcome the Addiss as you did."

"It's not that easy."

"Why not? You did it. So can I."

"It took me many years."

"What made the difference? Tell me now, so that I don't have to suffer as a slave for those many years. I will take your secret and spread it among the others. I will free them all."

Rodan laughed. "They don't want to be free," he said. "That is the secret. You only have to want it bad enough."

"But how can they stand to be slaves to those creatures? Surely they want to be free, just as you did?"

He shook his head. "The Addiss give them a sense of power, of purpose, of invincibility. It is all false, but it is there nonetheless. It is like a need that cannot be quenched. They don't want to be free of the Addiss."

"Are they happy?"

He shook his head again. "They are miserable. They are dying. But the Addiss are persuasive, cunning, powerful. And the hydria numbs the true self."

"Is that why there are so few Addiss?"

Rodan nodded. "They kill the host, eventually. At first, most of the Uemn only lasted a few weeks with an Addiss. Many simply killed themselves, or drowned in the hydria. The Addiss have become selective, choosing only the strong."

"I still don't understand how you broke free, and how you have survived."

"I simply wanted it badly enough. Badly enough to turn away from the momentary pleasure and sense of power that the Addiss gave me. But it still nags at me, clutching there like a bad dream. Sometimes I feel that I will succumb at any moment. Unable to resist that first suggestion, that first hint of need."

He stared into the darkness for a moment.

"I will strike out across the Rift," he said. "If the Uemn wish to follow me there, let them. I will wander in the desert until I am cleansed of my guilt and shame. I will beg for forgiveness from whatever power for goodness and mercy delivered me from the binding of the Addiss. And when I have found peace in my heart, and when I have forgiven myself for so much death and wrongdoing, then I will lay down in the heat and die, and I will let my body return to the ground as food for the carrion eaters and dust for the desert winds."

"You are a hopeless romantic," she said softly. "Maybe I will meet you there in the desert someday, and we can let the Soel bleach our bones together."

"Perhaps," he said. He sighed and stood up, pushing Elysen away gently, as a father would a child. "For now, m'lady, our paths head in different directions."

"I shall not forget you," she said.

"No, I expect you will not."

"I will not come after you either."

He smiled again. "Oh, yes you will." He gazed at her for a moment. "But, if I die by the hand of a warrior, I would that it be yours, wielding Soul-Reaver with one arm and Soul-Stealer with the other. I made these two blades sharp. The sharpest blades ever made by the hand of man, at least by the hands of this man. I folded the steel a hundred times, hammered thinner than the thickness of a hair, folded over and over upon itself and hammered thin again, until it holds an edge fine enough to shave your delicate scalp."

"You talk madness again, old man," she said. "Stop rattling on so, and get on with your work. I will not kill you."

He nodded. “My work is done here.” He picked up his hammer, looked at it lovingly, and then set it down again. “M’lady,” he began to speak, and then stopped.

“Yes?”

“I never meant to make blades to kill,” he said.

“And yet they do.”

“I shall forever be sorrowful for that. Good bye, m’lady.”

He stepped out of the cover of the tent and into the darkness. Elysen took a step backwards. The other workers stared at her now, with wondering looks on their faces. Some glanced around, as if looking for Rodan, frowned, went back to work, stopped again. Elysen turned and walked away.

“I shall not let the Addiss take my will,” she said as she walked. “I will find a way.”

Twenty-seven

Ser Kreid waited outside the cabin the next morning, mounted on his horse. Veldon and two of the Regular Guard accompanied him. Veldon led a spare horse, small and dark with a narrow face and a calm demeanor. Corde followed Elysen outside, carrying her armored cloak and her weapons in his arms, staggering under the weight of them.

"I see that Rodan has equipped you well," Ser Kreid said.

"He is a fine bladesmith, as you said."

"He has gone missing this morning. No one can find him anywhere."

Elysen's eyes revealed nothing.

"You saw him last night," Ser Kreid said. "He gave you these things."

She nodded.

"He said nothing of his plans for today?"

"He spoke of a journey that he longed to take, and of resting from the heat of the forges."

"Nothing else?"

"Nothing that I remember."

"You should not let her keep those weapons," Veldon protested.

"You should not try to take them from me."

Ser Kreid smiled. "No matter. You will need them against the armies of the Vyr Lord soon enough." He turned toward Corde and spoke to him. "You."

Corde snapped to attention. "Yes, sire."

"You will accompany us as well. I seem to remember that your cooking on the trail is very good. Gather your things and then join the other servants with the pack animals."

"Yes, sire. Thank you, sire. An honor, to be sure."

Elysen bit the inside of her cheek to keep from laughing. Corde strapped Elysen's gear to the back of the spare horse. The sleek mare snorted and shook her head as Elysen mounted. Elysen struggled to get comfortable, her large belly rubbing against the pommel of the saddle no matter how she sat.

"You will ride with me, at the front of the regiment," Ser Kreid said.

Veldon glared. "Look at her," he said. She dresses like a dancer and looks like a white cow."

Ser Kreid bared his teeth and almost growled. "Remember your place, Veldon. You are not an Addicere yet." Veldon lowered his eyes, but his face clearly showed his anger.

"He's right," Elysen said. "I can't ride like this. Let me ride in a wagon until we reach the outskirts of Kardesh. Then I'll ride with you."

Ser Kreid and Veldon continued to stare at each other for a moment, and then they broke away and turned their horses toward the long path upward, out of the canyon.

Ser Kreid led the procession across the high desert, followed by a dozen armored and highly adorned Addicere, each carrying a distinct banner from each of the honored households that followed. Veldon rode with members of the tribe of Grevendal, a large village in the south represented by a white lion. There were a nearly a dozen more men riding in his group, and just as many in the others. Behind the honored initiates rode another brigade of Addicere, in full armor, riding proudly. Lagging far behind by the end of the day came the servants accompanied by a regiment of Regulars and the support wagons drawn by humped-backed oxen.

Elysen rode in a small supply wagon near the back of the expedition. For most of the first day, she stared upward at the white fabric that domed over the cart like a tent. A drip of sweat slid across her eyebrow and down her temple. It dried in the heat as it tried to trickle down her scalp towards the bags of rice and wheat that she used for pillows. Bits of skin flaked off her lips, and she felt as if every fiber of her body had become dry and hot. She raised her head, touching her chin to her chest. Her body was a strange white bubble, covered with the black runes, now stretched into contortions of their former shapes.

Elysen rolled right and left, unable to get comfortable. She finally grabbed a handful of the thick, rough fabric under her and peeled it back. Her heart jumped and her eyes froze in their sockets. Underneath her, covering the bottom of the wagon, were rows and rows of armenders. She threw back more of the blanket and sat up. She tried to count, but there were too many. Tens and tens. She picked one up, and found another underneath. She peeked from under the canvas cover, and counted tens and tens more of the slow, cumbersome supply wagons. Each one rode hard and heavy on the ground. She closed her eyes and let her breath out just as Corde stuck his head into the back of the wagon. Elysen noticed his concerned look. She let her head fall back against a hard, burlap sack.

"I'm not going to make it," she said. She decided that he did not need to know the contents of the wagon. "I'm dying. I can't live in this heat."

"You will make it, m'lady," he said. "Somehow, you will make it."

"Maybe it's better that I die now. Better to be bones in the desert than to be taken by the Addiss, my baby poisoned by their hydria."

"Keep hope, m'lady."

Later that day, the desert gave way to sparse pines that stretched out forever in rolling hills and swells. The army made their way down a dusty slope and began a silent journey through the pine forest. Finally, they stopped, and Elysen groaned from the aching in her tired body.

"M'lady," Corde said. He roused her and helped her out of the wagon.

She groaned. "I was made for cold," she said. "Not heat."

Corde helped her sit so that she could drink tepid water from her flask. She touched her stomach. The skin seemed stretched to the bursting point.

"Ser Kreid summons you," Corde said. "We are at the outskirts of Kardesh. You have to ride now."

"I can't," she said, shaking her head.

"You promised him," Corde reminded her. "And he is in a bad mood today. The Addiss have run out of their hydria and are anxious to enter the city."

"I can't remember why I am even doing this," she said.

"Sometimes it feels as if we are just being pushed by the wind," Corde said.

Elysen shook her head. "I feel like I've lost my way again." She looked up at Corde. "There are nights when I don't sleep at all, and Yergen's face is all I can see. My heart burns all night long, and I imagine every way of killing him. But then the Soel comes up and I lose my resolve. I feel like one of Rodan's forgers, trudging back and forth from the fire to the anvil. Moving almost without thinking." She collapsed back onto the hard sacks. "Today is like that," she said. "My body is awake, but my mind and my heart are not."

Corde helped her stand up. She took the rest of his water and poured it over her chest. The soft fabric soaked up the moisture and clung to her like a skin. She left her weapons and the heavy armored cloak in the wagon, but took the lightweight white cloak she had brought with her from the north. She pulled the hood over her face and affixed the Madeire's bone visor over her eyes.

A servant arrived leading a tired-looking mare. Elysen took one look at the saddle and then unstrapped it and let it fall in the dust. Corde helped her mount. As she perched on top of the little horse, with her stomach bulging out from under her cloak, she laughed.

"The destroyer of the world is here," she announced. The servants watched her nervously. Even Corde looked worried.

"My dear Corde," she said. "You have lost all your mirth. I fear that this journey has taken your spirit."

He smiled. "These are trying times," he said. "And yet, I would not have you here without me."

She leaned over as best she could and touched his cheek for a moment before she tapped the little mare's sides with her bare feet. The horse plodded forward lethargically, through the waiting hordes of Uemn. They watched her carefully, as if they expected some trouble. She pulled the mare to a stop next to Ser Kreid and gazed out at Kardesh.

The city of the Addiss filled the bottom of a great round pit, far larger than Turoc's Cauldron. At the bottom of the crater, precious water had pooled in the lowest spots, creating a myriad of brownish-green ponds and lakes. Scattered pine trees stood between stocky, white buildings. At the far side of the canyon, the cliffs hung above a series of carved terraces. The giant steps receded into darkness, undercutting the towering columns of red rock.

"Marvelous, isn't it?" Ser Kreid asked.

Elysen kept her face hidden under her visor and hood.

"This is Kardesh?" she asked, letting disappointment show in her voice. In her mind, she could still see the beauty of Hashana and the Citadel d'Vie, and the smooth, red walls of Sunder Keep.

"There is more to Kardesh than just buildings," he said. "You will see."

She sighed. "Let's get on with it then," she said.

The army rode down a winding path and across the bottom of the canyon with Ser Kreid and Elysen leading. The brightness of the Soel reflected off the white fabric of her cloak as if she were a source of light herself. The army plodded across the sweltering hot desert floor, stopping for just a moment to push the supply wagons into a series of lean-to sheds, stacking them ten deep in rows and rows. Elysen sat and waited, feeling poisoned by the Soel and the dust and dry wind that sucked the water from her body. Finally, the army moved again, toward the far side of the valley.

As they moved closer to the cliffs, Uemn men and women gathered along the main road, watching the procession with blank stares. At the base of the cliffs, the army stopped in a wide plaza and waited while Ser Kreid dismounted. He helped Elysen down and led her up a wide flight of carved stairs to a series of arches cut into the giant stone terraces. The largest arch was framed with stone blocks, intricately grooved and carved into graceful curves. They stepped through the arch and into a vast hall. Elysen closed her eyes and smiled as her feet touched cool white tiles. Compared to the hot desert sand, the polished surface felt like snow. Elysen took a deep breath of air that smelled like dry soil, and then yawned as she pulled her hood back off her head. Ser Kreid stopped, and she almost ran into him.

"Are you bored?" he snapped.

"No," she said. "Please pardon me. I am fatigued."

"There is no time for fatigue," he said. "You are our honored guest tonight. The Consilium Addicere Jenus is dying, and his Addiss wants to take you for its host. It is a great honor, and not one to be taken lightly. There are many here who think you should be destroyed, and that we should carry your head to Sunder Keep on a pike."

Elysen stopped walking. She stared at Ser Kreid's back.

"This is it?" she asked.

He turned and frowned at her. "What do you mean?" he asked.

"We are going straight to the coupling?" Isn't there some kind of ceremony first? Some time to get settled in?"

She felt fear clutching at her throat. Her heart labored in her chest, and the dry air didn't satisfy her need to breathe. Fear wrapped around her chest and crushed her.

"I've already told you," she said. "I won't take an Addiss."

He turned around and grabbed her arm.

"You will not argue with me," he said.

She pulled hard against his grip, but his hand tightened.

"I won't be a servant to anyone or anything," she snarled.

She took a deep breath and compressed her body into a tight crouch. She sprung up and brought her leg around, hitting him in low in the chest with her knee. He lost his grip on her arm as she spun around. She used the momentum of her turn to add force to her forearm as she whipped it against the side of his head. He staggered and fell against the wall, shaking his head. Elysen stepped forward and tried to stab the heel of her hand at his exposed chin, but she moved too slowly. Ser Kreid ducked sideways and hit her in the back of the head with his fist, propelling her body against the wall. Her head bounced against the stone and she slid to the floor, curled around her bulging belly. Ser Kreid grabbed her by the back of her cloak and dragged her to her feet.

His fingers cut into her arm as he pulled her along the hallway and into a giant chamber filled with rows and rows of benches, carved from the same smooth stone as the rest of the temple. They radiated outward from a raised platform in the middle of the room. Other Uemn were already filling the chamber and taking seats.

Elysen pulled away again but a burly Regular grabbed her from behind and picked her up, kicking and pounding with her fists. The sounds of the crowd filled her ears like the chattering of a flock of blackbirds. She recognized words, but heard only the thrumming sounds of countless voices. The guard carried her to the platform, where Consilium Addicere Jenus lay on one of two stone slabs, his tired eyes vacant, his mouth open. He glanced at Elysen, but his eyes held no sense of recognition. He turned his head again so that he stared upward, into the dim upper reaches, watching nothing but the flickering of the light against the far away stone. His Addiss struggled, lashing out, desperately feeling the air around it. Ser Kreid forced her down onto the second slab and two burly guards strapped her down. The murmuring crowd grew silent. Elysen struggled against the guards' grip, and then against the thick leather straps that held her wrists and ankles. She craned her neck upward, trying to see the bands that held her legs, but she could only see her stomach, rising upward like the domed Caldera of Sunder Keep. She let her head drop back and took a breath. The domed ceiling of the Uemn chamber stretched above her, and she suddenly felt very small. Light from the Soel streamed in from dozens of slotted windows, shaped in the same graceful arches as the front doors.

Ser Kreid stood over her with a short knife in his hand. Elysen closed her eyes and whispered to her baby.

"Forgive me for coming here. Forgive me for being so stubborn, so stupid."

Tears slid from the corners of her eyes. The sounds of the gathering around her faded, and she found her mind focused inward. A wave of silence enfolded her. Her body relaxed and she listened. Deep within the silence, she heard a small voice, like the wind at dusk, rippling through fields of wheat. Soft, full of breath, full of life. The sounds rose and fell. The burning in her heart subsided, and she could feel her body melting into the stone slab like wax from a burning candle. The moment broke, and her body reacted with a startled jump. Ser Kreid spoke to the crowd.

"Tribes of the Uemn," he said. His voice carried throughout the room, echoing off the high ceiling like an accompanying ghost. "We are here today to witness a great moment in our history. The transfer of the great Addiss of Consilium Jenus, to the One that will lead us to victory over the tribes of the high plains, that we may return to the lands of abundance."

He paused and let the Uemn shout and shake their fists for a moment. Then he held up his hand and continued.

"The Addiss of Consilium Jenus is ready. The Consilium is feeble now, and will return to the darkness from which we all came, and to which we shall all return."

He turned and poised his knife over the Consilium's chest.

"This life is all we have, Consilium Jenus," he said. "Go now. From nothing you arose, to nothing I now return you." He brought the blade down with both hands on the hilt and plunged it into the Consilium's chest. The Consilium's body arched, held that position rigid, then relaxed. The shadow of the Addiss slipped away from the Consilium's body and drifted across the ground like a dark liquid, hovering beneath the dais where Elysen lay, her heart pounding. The Addiss reached upward with a dark tentacle. It touched Elysen's arm along her bare skin and she shivered.

"So cold," she gasped.

Another tentacle touched her. Caressed her. She shivered again. It began to embrace her, wrapping itself around her, entering her like a lover. She gasped again, arched her back, tried to wriggle free, but it engulfed her like ice water, enveloping her. She began to cry, tossed her head back and forth. She screamed. Ser Kreid knelt down next to her and touched a cup of liquid to her lips. She spit it out, sputtered. He dabbed her lips again.

She saw the spells again, drifting like fluttering birds through the blue, icy water. The ancient runes spoke to her. She heard them, felt their power, but she could not grasp the meaning. The voice of the spell came to her softly, like the voice of Raes as a child gazing at the summer sky. Her heart longed to be near him again.

She felt the cup near her mouth. Swallowed.

She felt Raes there with her. His arms were strong and hard like the steel blades that Rodan forged in the fires of Asaka. She felt the ice melting from her feet and arms, and she relaxed onto a comfortable pile of soft pillows as she watched the bladesmith hammer the soft, red metal. He folded it over and over. The sound of the hammer rang in her ears as the cup touched her mouth once more. She reached up and took it with her hands.

She took more.

It filled her mouth with spice and fire, charging her body with strength. Riding at full gallop, with both arms pumping, she spun her swords like feathers, slicing through skin and bone, spraying blood across the plains. Yergen's eyes were full of fear as she ran him down, stood over him, and plunged her cold steel through his belly, over and over, sliding it in and out as she stood over him with her legs spread apart, laughing, her head thrown back and long, white hair billowing in the breeze.

She drank wildly.

Her body burned.

She knew the Shad'ya. Felt it within her. The maker of the law. All of the power and the glory of the universe became hers to command. She screamed with delight.

Twenty-eight

Elysen awoke in the dark, shivering, with her back on the cold stone. She turned her head and saw the body of Jenus on the slab next to her. Her bindings were gone. She curled up into a ball and moaned as a sharp pain stabbed through her head. As she slid off the altar and onto the floor, a hot fluid welled up from inside her, surging through her throat and nose and spilling onto the stones. She hung her head forward and tried to spit the taste of spoiled meat from her mouth. A string of thick mucous hung from her lips like raw egg. In the dim light, she could see the cracks between the stones, running along the floor like veins. She crawled forward, stood, staggered, vomited again. Her body cramped again, and she stumbled forward, blindly following some instinctual drive, like a drowning person struggling for the surface.

Her legs hit a stone bench. She used her hands to guide her body around it, and then rammed her toe into a crack with the very next step. She snarled and staggered forward again.

A blinding stab of white light flicked through the chamber, and she glimpsed bodies, scattered among the benches. Just in front of where she stood, a man and a woman sprawled naked on the floor between two benches. A peal of thunder pounded the desert just before another blast of lightning carved a glimpse of the chamber on her eyes with its intensity. Another clap of thunder. The sour smell of the hot air made her retch again. Her stomach heaved and convulsed, but nothing came up her throat. She stumbled through the hallways, feeling her way along the cool walls, and finally found herself outside. Another stab of lightning took away her vision, followed closely by thunder so loud she held her ears and cried out. A spatter of rain hit her forehead. The large drops fell suddenly in torrents, straight down, cold, like a waterfall from which there was no escape.

Elysen staggered in a circle, searching for anything familiar. Fear clutched her throat again and she ran, her thin clothes soaked. Lightning struck again, so close that she could feel her skin prickle. She found a slope and headed upward, clambering over piles of boulders, slipping along a steep grade of sharp talus, ducking and dodging the claps of thunder that took the breath from her chest. She climbed upward now, struggling to keep her balance as her large stomach bumped against the rock walls. She came to a narrow cleft in the rocks, scrambled into it, her feet skidding and sliding in the loose gravel. She kept going up, crying and sobbing as the thunder and the heavy rain pummeled her body. She came to a high point. She paused, panting, and then cried out again as another spasm hit her in the belly. She fell to the ground and curled into a ball.

She rolled onto her back and shook her fists at the sky.

"Why are you doing this to me?" she shouted.

Another cramp rolled her into a ball again. She pounded on the ground with her fists, tears streaming from her eyes. In the next flash of light, she glimpsed the black tendrils of her Addiss, lashing out into the air around her, stroking her, whipping against her like shadows. Thunder shook the air around her again. The rain slowed, stopped. She crawled up to her hands and knees, her head hanging, her breath coming in ragged gulps. More lightning revealed a rocky pillar that stuck out beyond the rest of the cliffs. It leaned precariously as if about to fall into the canyon below. Thunder pounded against her again, and she cried out in pain as her body convulsed.

The next strike of lightening split a pine tree below her and the thunder shook the cliffs at the same instant. The broken pine burst into a flare of flames and steam, the heat of the dry inner wood burning rendering the superficial wetness of the branches impotent. The shattered remains of the conifer tipped slowly, falling against a brother tree, sending a cascade of sparks and burning debris across the ground and into the brush. Elysen's body cramped again, her face contorting into a silent scream of agony and fear. As she rolled onto her back, the dark clouds above her parted, and she could see the stars watching silently above her. A hot wind arose, like a blast from the furnaces of Asaka, coursing around her body, drying her clothes, wrapping her in unwelcome warmth. The wind swept off the cliffs and into the pine trees below, fanning the fire like a giant bellows. Elysen cried out again, an unintelligible sound of pain and hunger and confusion. She curled into a ball and sobbed.

The wind blew the fire westward, first from the broken tree to its brother, then to the next, and into the brush, and then to the next and the next, until the giant sticks of flame became a wall of fire, and the wall of fire began to move across the valley, spreading as it jumped from tree to tree. Another flash, from farther away, and a peal of thunder. The wind shifted, swirled, swept back to the west again, and the fire erupted in response. From high on the cliff where Elysen lay huddled in a ball, the heat and light were like the breath of demons, rising against the wind to torment her. She crawled to the edge and looked out across a world gone mad, covered with flames that were now eating away at the structures, crawling along wooden beams, eating away framework, even crumbling the adobe itself, working against the straw and wood fibers that were baked into the bricks, scouring the valley clean of the Uemn dwellings, one by one, relentless, unstoppable. The wall of fire first dried the land before it, and then consumed it.

In the orange light, through the white and black smoke, Elysen saw people running toward the far cliffs, running to escape the monster that had invaded the sanctity of their valley. The winds stiffened, and the monster took on new life, now swirling and stomping through fresh trees and homes. Horses screamed, dogs barked frantically, people shouted and ran. Elysen's body cramped again and she screamed. As she lay on the warm stones above the orgy of fire and wind, she found herself in a warm, wet pool of water. She struggled to her feet, confused, pulling herself into a half-standing position by holding onto a gnarled tree, its back stripped by years of abrasion from sand and wind. She hugged it like a lover, and found the feel of it strangely familiar.

Almost standing, she cried out and bent over, dropped to a squat, and screamed. She gasped for breath, screamed again, and then grimaced with pain and fierce determination. Her eyes opened and she took a series of quick breaths. She felt a calmness seep over her as her pain subsided. She relaxed and took a deep breath of the smoky air. She gagged and coughed for a moment, and then rubbed tears from her eyes. She sat down and took another breath.

The wind whipped the ground around her into a dusty froth. Suddenly the convulsions consumed her again. She threw her head back and crawled over to ancient tree, grabbing its trunk with both hands. She sobbed, stopped, rested, and then cried out again. Below her, the fire raged on, and the night became a relentless succession of agony and exhaustion for Elysen. The cramps that sent her into screaming fits of rage came closer and closer, more and more intense, and the fire billowed and screamed as if too were giving birth, and suddenly, the first of the armender wagons exploded with a fury to match the thunder from the sky, and Elysen screamed in joy and terror as another and another and another of the wagons ripped apart the night, and her contractions became one with the thunder and the explosions, as a terrible rhythm of destruction and hate and fire and lightning and wind and rain pummeled the hillsides, until, suddenly, the baby crowned, then slipped free, and somehow, as if by instinct alone, she caught the baby and held it in her arms as she slid to the ground. For Elysen, at that moment, the night became still and calm again. Around her, the storm and the fire raged, but where she lay, sobbing, spent, bloody and trembling.

Elysen took a shuddering breath. With one hand, she stripped her clothes from her body. She pressed the baby against her bare chest, and the small, wet child came to her breast and suckled there as the warm wind blew across their naked bodies. Elysen's eyes closed, and she collapsed in the dirt, next to the pile of tattered white cloth that had once been her clothes.

Corde found her in the morning, sleeping with the baby held against her chest and the bloody afterbirth languishing in a pile between her legs. Corde took his short knife and cut the leathery umbilical. He tied it in a knot and then took his shirt and wrapped it around Elysen's shoulders as he gently moved her. The feel of his hands woke her. She came to groggy and weak.

"How did you find me?" she asked quietly.

"I asked the refugees, someone said they thought that you caused the fire and the storm, that you stood here on the cliffs and shook your fist and cursed the valley with destruction. I fear that some of the survivors may be hunting you down to sacrifice you to the Addiss."

Elysen's eyes opened briefly. "I dreamed I was coupled."

"I don't think it was a dream," Corde said. He quickly changed the subject. "How do you feel?" he asked.

She shook her head. "I don't know. I feel tired."

She looked down at the tiny creature huddled against her chest, and the baby stirred, his tiny hands opening and closing as if he had been startled. She watched with revulsion as the tentacles of her Addiss wrapped around the boy, and tears came to her eyes.

"It's here," she said. She turned her head away so that she did not have to look into Corde's eyes. He looked sad, distant.

"At least there was one good thing that happened last night," Corde said. He stroked the boy's fine, blonde hair.

"I'm lost to the dark lords," Elysen moaned.

"We need to get you off this cliff," Corde said. He glanced around, and then looked upward. "We should climb to the upper rim," he said. "I think it will be easier than trying to go down. And safer."

Elysen closed her eyes. "I can't go anywhere," she said. "I'm exhausted."

"I know," Corde said. He touched her cheek. "M'lady, you have to somehow find the strength to go on."

She shook her head. "Take the boy," she said. "I am no good to him now anyway. Let the Uemn kill me, or just leave me here to die. Please."

Corde shook his head. "No, m'lady. This is not your time. Come now." He held his jaw tight and pulled on her arm. "Get up," he said. "Or I will carry you."

"You can't carry me," she said.

"I can try."

She looked into his eyes, sighed, and gathered her legs under her body. Corde pulled on her arm while she held the baby in the other.

She stood, and Corde put his arm around her back. It slipped right through the Addiss as if it were no more than a shadow. The Addiss' tentacles reached into Corde's body, exploring him. Elysen closed her eyes so that she did not have to watch. Corde walked slowly.

"What will you name the boy?" Corde asked.

"Is it a boy?" she asked him.

Corde nodded. "Definitely a boy."

Elysen sighed. "I will name him Araden."

"That is a good name," Corde said. His brow wrinkled as he considered it.

"Is it a family name?" he asked.

"Arador was the name of a friend."

As they climbed to the rim, Elysen stopped often to rest, and halfway along the baby began to cry. Elysen broke out in a cold sweat.

"I can't see where I am going," she said. Terror shook her voice.

"It is the Addiss poison," Corde said. "Lack of it clouds your vision."

She could not stop shaking. They sat down on a boulder, and Elysen put the crying child to her breast. He sucked for a long time. She stroked his head and he slept. They climbed again. At the top, a gloved hand reached down and yanked Elysen the final few scrambling steps to safety. Corde followed, on his own, eyeing the Uemn guards that stood above him with suspicion.

"Let him pass," Elysen warned them. They stepped back. Her body shook and she fell to her knees, clutching Araden close to her chest as her mouth filled with a vile liquid from deep within her belly. She spit it out, heaved more upon it. Ser Kreid sat resting in his saddle watching her.

"Is this the way you treat your fellow Addicere?" she asked as she gathered Corde's tattered shirt around her body.

"You are but a vessel for the Addiss," the Consilium said. "It cares not for your physical discomfort. But, I do have what you need." He held up a flask and shook it. The Addiss on Elysen's back flailed wildly, and she doubled over with pain. Ser Veldon rode up and stopped next to the Consilium.

"She is a pitiful sight," he said.

The Consilium shook the flask again, and Elysen's arm reached for it. She felt the baby slipping from her other arm. The Consilium dismounted and helped her drink the dark, foul smelling liquid. It dripped down her chin and onto her white chest, running across the ancient runes and touching Araden's tiny fingers. Corde approached her carefully, still watching the Uemn with fear in his eyes. He reached down and took Araden from Elysen. She drank greedily, and then collapsed. Lost in the world of the Addiss.

"Get her on a horse," the Consilium said. "And get her some clothes."

Corde kept his eyes on the ground and Araden clasped to his chest. "I have her horse and gear with the wagons that we saved from the fire last night, m'lord."

"Very well then," he said. "You brought her this far. Carry her to the wagons and get her dressed. When she is presentable, bring her to me."

Corde bowed and nodded, and rushed over to where Elysen laid, her mouth open, the dark hydria staining her lips. A drop slithered down toward her ear. Corde slipped his free arm under her body as the horses turned and thundered away. He stood slowly, Araden cradled in one arm, awake now and crying, and Elysen over his shoulder. He staggered under her weight. He held them like that, standing in the early heat of the morning Soel, breathing heavily. Then he started walking. One step. Then two. He followed the cloud of dust left by the infantry, heading for the far side of the pit.

Below them, still smoking and burning, the fires of Kardesh burned steadily, sending a plume of white ash into the sky, driven away by the wind into a hazy cloud that covered the world. Corde walked for a long time, Elysen dangling across his shoulder as if she were dead, a glazed look in her eyes, her mouth open. The baby wailed and Elysen's Addiss coiled about him, moving through his body like a cold shiver.

The Soel rose high as he staggered to the supply area. The servants looked unhappily at Corde as he carried Elysen and the screaming child to one of the small wagons. He placed Elysen inside and then turned his attention to the baby, whispering to it. An old woman came to him, frowning. She handed him a soft leather bag full of a warm liquid.

She spoke abruptly. "Goat's milk," she said.

She walked away. Corde watched her go. "Thank you," he said.

He took an awl from a nearby tool pouch and punched a small hole in the bag. The baby sucked and drank hungrily, and Corde smiled. Elysen slept on. A sentry came by at dusk.

"Be ready to move at first light," he commanded.

Corde nodded, but the sentry rode away before he had even ended his mandate. Corde made a small fire and roasted a piece of rabbit. Araden took more goats milk. Elysen woke up and joined them at the fire. She hesitated when Corde offered her the baby, and then took him gingerly.

"Thank you, Corde," she said.

He nodded, poked the fire.

"What is that potion they gave me?" she asked.

"That is the hydria. The Addiss thrive on it. You must have it now, or you will go mad."

"It's foul, and it takes away my will to live. Takes away my care for my child. I hate it."

"And yet you lay in rapture under its spell."

She nodded. "It was as if I was the most powerful, important being in the universe. Strong, wise beyond all knowledge. I thought that I was the one power."

"And now?"

"Now I'm hollow, empty. Disgusted." She hung her head and shook it. "My life becomes more and more meaningless every day." She looked up at Corde. "At the edge of the world, there was ice and cold all around me. And death. And I looked out over a world that I had been told all my life did not exist. I looked out and thought, everything I have ever known was a lie, and it was as if all of my will to live drained out of me at that moment. Since then, I have known nothing but death and cold and heat and torture, and yet my body goes on and on like a mindless turtle crawling across a dry pond, with no hope of reaching the other side, no hope of water, no hope of life. Just some ridiculous inner drive that causes the body to go on when the spirit has departed."

"Life in you is strong, Lady Elysen."

"I'm too weak to end it."

"Only the weak end their own lives. The strong go on no matter what."

"I owe you much, Corde," she said. "If you were to slit my throat during the night, you would do me one last favor."

"I could never do that, m'lady."

"How could you be so fond of a creature like this? A colorless abomination, drawn upon with strange black markings all up and down my body, possessed by a demon shadow, unable to care for my own son. I'm a wreck and a failure. It would have been far better if I had burned in the fires that fill our skies with smoke, than to live like this."

Corde stirred the fire with a stick. "All these things shall pass," Corde said. "In their own time."

Elysen shook her head and stared at her sleeping child. He pursed his tiny lips, as if some deep thought occupied his dreams.

"He knows nothing of our troubles," Elysen said.

Corde smiled. "Yet he knows everything."

Elysen looked at Corde. "Do we know everything when we are born?"

Corde shrugged. "Some say we do. Some say that we forget as we grow, as we become accustomed to the world that we see and hear and feel and smell and taste. But that there is a deeper understanding of the world that we keep in our spirit." Corde pointed at Araden with the smoldering stick he held in his hand. "He is as yet unaware of this surface world around us. All he knows is love and peace. His is the world I wish I knew."

"Perhaps that is the world we will pass on to when our spirits leave our bodies," Elysen mused.

"Perhaps."

"His namesake called it J'Halla."

Corde nodded. "I have heard of this J'Halla."

"I yearn for such a place," Elysen said.

Corde reached out and touched her arm. "Stay here with us for a while longer," he said. He withdrew his hand as the shadow creature that wrapped around her brushed against his outstretched arm.

Elysen sighed, touched her baby, and closed her eyes.

Twenty-nine

They traveled again toward Asaka through the land of never ending summer, with no seasons to gauge the passage of time, only the endless heat and Turoc's shifting gaze, his giant eye changing from full and round to sliver to nothing and back again, as ageless and unchanging as the mountains and the desert, doomed to repeat itself. Elysen marked the passage of time by Turoc's slow movement, staring at it during the night, glancing at it during the bright days. During the second cycle since the destruction of Kardesh, the army stopped at the edge of a river, bounded by green elms and maples and bushes of blue, ripe berries. They waited at the oasis, gathering supplies from a nearby village, and waiting for something.

"Clean my clothes," Elysen said to Corde one morning. "I will go to see Consilium Ser Kreid today. And send word to him that I am coming."

Corde nodded. "Araden smiled today," he said.

Elysen gazed at the baby that Corde held gently in his arms.

"My clothes," she said. Corde nodded, but stood his ground.

"Will you watch him while I clean them by the river?" he asked. "I fear for the baby's safety."

"You seem to manage," she said.

"He needs his mother."

"I can't," she said. The boy made a small sound, a gurgling coo, soft, like a dove's sigh. Elysen turned her head. "Please take him away." Corde left.

He returned later with her white clothes cleaned as best they could be in the dusty country that they traversed. Elysen dressed fully for the first time since the coupling, and slung her weapons across her back. As she unrolled the heavy, steel studded cloak, Rodan's crossbow fell from the folds, so small yet so deadly. She strapped it to her wrist, but did not load it. She buckled the cloak across her chest and walked through the encampment, passing by piles of gear and restless horses, through the ranks of the Regular guard, through the ranks of the Addicere, a thousand strong, more men gathered together than she had even seen. She walked purposefully, yet casually, unhurried yet tense. She found the Consilium in his tent. His Addicere guards admitted her without question.

"Lady Elysen," he said. He stood up. Veldon stood as well. One of the Regulars, a scout, dirty and covered with dust, stopped his report in the middle of a word and came to attention. Veldon nodded at him and he scurried out the door.

"What hails from the servant's quarters?" The Consilium chuckled as he finished speaking, and Veldon joined him with a smile.

"Your flanks are flabby and slow," she said. Veldon's smile faded, but the Consilium took her joke in stride.

"Please, sit," he said. "I thank you for joining us. This has been a difficult time for you."

"Yes," she said.

She remained standing with her arms folded under her cloak as Ser Veldon and the Consilium sat down at the wooden table. Elysen glanced around at the tent, taking in the table, chairs, crates of armor and clothing, and the washbasin of hammered bronze. An entire empty wagon sat outside, loaded and unloaded each day, just to provide these quarters for the Consilium. He spoke to her as if they were old friends conspiring on some childish prank.

"The news from Asaka is good. Your man Tobias has finished the sailing ship. Our men have gained much knowledge in the building of such a ship, and they are now on their way to the Sud de Mer to create an armada. A fleet of twenty such ships that will carry the Addicere to the far western shores."

"Or off the ends of the world," Veldon added.

"We will not fall off the world," Elysen said.

The Consilium Ser Kreid continued. "We have a task for you. A test of your loyalty."

"Am I not Addicere now?" she said. "Do you test the loyalty of your masters?"

"No," he replied. "Just of you. You shirk our companionship. You are sullen and withdrawn. We are not sure of your ability to host the Addiss. And you drink far more than your share of the precious hydria."

"I'm fine."

"Nevertheless, we will send you on an errand to see for ourselves."

"I need to stay with my baby."

"We know that your man Corde cares for your baby while you sit and sulk."

The Consilium leaned back and smiled.

"There is a man who has escaped into the desert bottom of the Great Rift. His name is Rodan. Do you know of him?"

"You know that I do."

"Ah, yes. He made those fine blades you wear. You spent some time with him?"

She stood motionless

"This man is a traitor to the Addiss. He must be eliminated. You will track him into the desert and kill him. Do you understand?"

"And if I refuse?"

Ser Veldon leaned forward suddenly. "Do you see what I mean?" he said. "She is dangerous, insubordinate and disobedient. She may be an Addicere, but she is an abomination. It was a mistake to couple her."

"Nonsense," the Consilium said casually. "It was the will of the Addiss. Will you go?" he said to Elysen.

"Answer my question. If I refuse?"

"You die right here. And your baby. And your friends."

She glanced at the Ser Veldon and then returned her gaze to the Consilium.

"I'll go," she said. "Rodan was a great bladesmith. His loss is regrettable."

"Go then. Go now. You will return to us at Lands End at the Sud de Mer. Ser Veldon will accompany you, as a guide."

Ser Veldon glared at the Consilium.

"Do you have a problem with this assignment?" the Consilium asked.

"Of course not," he said.

"What of my baby?" Ser Elysen asked.

"He'll be fine."

"Don't let anything happen to him while I am gone," she said.

The Consilium waved at her as if she was an annoying fly. "Nothing will happen to the boy while you are gone. You take care to fulfill your duty, and I give my word that your baby will be fine."

"Your word," she said.

"I give you my word. I will have your man and the baby guarded day and night. Go now."

Elysen turned to go, but the Consilium's voice stopped her.

"If you fail, the same fate as if you refuse."

She stood with her back toward him.

"Do you understand?" he asked.

Elysen nodded once. She stepped out of the hot, stuffy tent and into the bright light of day. She winced, put on her visor, and walked away.

Thirty

Elysen rode the slow but tireless mare she had named Serena, a name that reflected the paint's demeanor, an attitude so far opposite from her beloved Temper. Veldon brought two of the Regulars with him. They packed light and headed for Asaka early in the morning.

"I am leading this expedition," Elysen said. "So you will follow me without question, do you understand?"

Veldon showed his disapproval on his face. The Regulars were solemn and distant as they rode through the heat of the day. Elysen did her best to hide her pain and exhaustion. The Soel set in a brilliant show of red that splashed across the entire smoke-filled sky. That night, Turoc came out, full and bright, circled by an orange ring. They rode on until Turoc disappeared below the horizon, and then stopped for the night. Elysen dropped her saddle on the hard ground and leaned against it. Veldon watched her warily as she slept. In the morning, he woke before she did. They mounted their horses and rode westward again. Her horse stumbled twice, so Elysen dismounted and led her, battling through her own exhaustion as well. They continued on this way until they came to Asaka.

At the edge of the cliff, they stopped and gazed down at the brilliant lake, riffled by a light breeze. Below them, a mighty ship sat high in the water. Twenty oars rested idly on each side. A single, tall mast, robbed of its sail, stood like a lonely tree, towering above the deck.

"It must be able to hold fifty men," Veldon marveled.

Elysen led Serena down the steep trail to the commune below. They stopped only long enough to commandeer packs and provisions before they struck out.

From the basin of Asaka, a small stream flowed toward the far away Mortain. Elysen followed the stream to the edge of a bluff that looked over the Great Rift. Below her stretched more dust and rock, so hot and dry that even the sage did not find it friendly.

"He's out there, somewhere," Elysen said.

"The horses won't be able to stand the heat," Veldon said.

"Then stay here and wait for me," she said.

"I thought that you didn't like the heat," Veldon said as they began to descend the steep slopes toward the flatlands below.

"I cannot even begin to tolerate it," she said. "My blood boils and my lungs breathe only fire. My body was not made for heat. It was made for the cold."

"You seem to handle it as well as anyone."

"It only seems that way to you."

Their attention turned to the downward climb, and their voices fell silent. The slope became more gradual and they weaved in and out of boulders and rocks, finding their way along a dusty trail sprinkled with tufts of dry grass.

"How will you find him out here?" Veldon asked. "This is a vast country within which to find such a small man."

"He'll stay near the river," Elysen said.

"Even so, we may never catch up to him."

"Did you come along for moral support?" Elysen asked. "Your confidence and trust in me is overwhelming."

The Soel set quickly, casting a long shadow that slid across the desert toward them, while the sky remained blue above them, and then, as if a candle were slowly snuffed out, the night came. They camped next to the stream, foraging firewood from ugly, dry bushes. They cooked a lizard that dripped an oily substance into the fire and smoked badly. Elysen refused to eat and curled into a ball as far from the fire as she could. She awoke in the darkness, screaming.

Veldon jumped up in an instant, standing in the dim light of the dying fire with his sword drawn. Elysen's entire body shook.

"I need more hydria," she whispered.

"You take too much already," Veldon said. "You are like a pig, drinking more than you need, leaving little for me."

"It is the only thing that makes the heat tolerable." She grabbed the goatskin bag from his hand and drank deeply. Veldon grabbed it back and drank as well, tipping it up far into the air in an attempt to get the last of it.

"We are out," he said.

Elysen laughed. Veldon stood up slowly and threw an armload of dry wood on the fire. The flames reached toward the sky. He drew his sword and began to wave it slowly back and forth.

"Witch," he said, sneering. "I have no reason to spare you any longer."

"You should have killed me long ago," she said. "Before I took more than my share of your precious elixir."

"You're right," he said.

He swung his blade in a long, slow arc aimed at her throat. The Addiss on his back followed his movements, mimicking him. Elysen dropped to the ground and rolled away from the crackling fire. She found her saddle and pulled Soul-Reaver from its sheath just in time to block a descending blow.

"I will give you a lesson in swordplay," Veldon said.

The two Regulars stood up and grabbed their weapons. Elysen faced the three of them with her blade held in front of her body. The Regulars began to spread out, but Veldon stopped them.

"Leave her to me," he said. "Go back to bed. I am giving the witch a lesson, that's all."

The faces of the Regulars, barely visible in the dim firelight, filled with confusion and disbelief. They slowly lowered their weapons and stepped back a few paces. Veldon came forward, toward Elysen. He waved his sword back and forth.

"Just you and me now, little girl," he said.

He swung. She countered. His blows were heavy, merciless, and as they moved around the small fire, their feet shuffling in the sand, he rained blow upon blow at her. She blocked, parried, blocked again. Her breath came hard now and her skin glistened with sweat. Veldon's eyes turned into bottomless pools of black water that reflected the red and orange flickers around which he stalked steadily, like a bored cat playing with a terrified mouse before killing it. The muscles in his arms bulged as he swung, again and again, smiling, laughing. Elysen's smile turned into a grimace, and it took all the strength she had left to lift her sword against Veldon's vicious blows.

"When I am done with you, I will return to Land's End and I will finish my work by killing your son. Then the world will be free from your curse, and I will be hailed as a hero. There will be stories told of my adventures, and songs sung, for all time."

"You will not return home, and no one will kill my baby," she said. She swung her blade, catching him off guard with her sudden burst of energy. Yet he deflected her blow easily. She swung again. Again he deflected her sword.

"There is life left in you yet," he said, smiling.

Elysen lunged, swung again, her feet slipping in the soft sand, the Addiss holding her tightly as if protecting her, loving her. She began a long series of arcing blows, driving Veldon back towards the fire. He laughed, his eyes full of glee. He let his arm drop, Elysen reacted instantly, but Veldon caught her arm under his and trapped her against his body. He dropped his sword on the ground and tore her blouse off her chest, and she drove him to the ground with a lunge. He rolled on top of her and she wrapped her legs around him.

"And now we will make a little brother for your bastard child," he hissed.

Morning. Elysen awoke, naked, lying next to her attacker in the warm sand. She glanced at him, moaned, and rolled over. The Regulars were cooking breakfast over the small fire, just a few paces away. Elysen looked again at Veldon, his naked body, his smirking smile, even in sleep. She turned her head and retched, spitting up nothing.

"What have I come to?" she whispered.

She gathered her clothes together and sat near the horses, using them to shelter her from the eyes of the Regulars as she dressed. She saddled her horse and mounted before she noticed the crouching figure of a man, perched on a dune just beyond their encampment. He wore a robe the color of the sand, with the hood drawn over his face. The first light of the Soel spilled over the far eastern wall, turning the shadow morning into a glaring yellow that would hound them for the rest of the day. Elysen held her position and watched the man. He carried a wooden staff, straight and tall, the tip plunged into the sand next to him. He watched, like the wolves on the tundra watched their prey. He sat motionless for a long time, finally revealing himself by sliding his hood from the top of his smooth head.

"Rodan," she said, under her breath. Then, loud enough so he could hear, "How long have you been there?"

"All night," he said.

"Then you saw everything."

"I did."

"I can't explain."

"The hydria. Takes away our will power. Makes us slaves to the darkness. We become stupid. Defenseless."

"I'm sick," she said with desperation in her voice.

He nodded.

"Do you know why I am here?"

He nodded again. "To kill me, no doubt."

It was her turn to nod. "That is why I was sent here."

"And if you do not?"

"They will kill my baby."

He smiled. "The baby. How is he?"

"Fine," Her eyes filled with pain.

"I told you, did I not? That the fine blade that I made for you would be the one to take my life."

"I won't kill you," she said. "I'll find some other way."

Veldon's voice came from behind her.

"I knew you were a traitor," he said.

Elysen turned. Veldon had donned his armor, the early morning Soel shining behind him like an aura. The two Regulars, attired in lighter leather fighting gear, scrambled up the hill, one on either side of Rodan. Rather than retreat, he stood and walked down the slope toward Elysen. Veldon stepped forward and Elysen slipped from the saddle with a blade in each hand. The Regulars rushed toward Elysen and Veldon charged Rodan. Rodan slipped from Veldon's thrust and hit him squarely in the chest with his stout wooden staff, knocking Veldon to the ground. Elysen intercepted the first Regular, deflecting a thrust that sent her tired body staggering. The second Regular lunged at her, but she spun and slipped Soul-Stealer's short blade up through the soft skin of his belly, deep into his chest. He died with a sigh, and Elysen's dagger left the wound as quickly as it had entered. The other Regular stopped and gaped at his fallen comrade.

Veldon recovered and scrambled to his feet, more wary now of Rodan's staff. He circled around the older man, and then lunged, but Rodan evaded again, this time bringing the staff smartly against the side of Veldon's head.

Veldon staggered and fell sideways, touched his temple, looked at the blood, and snarled. With a glance, Elysen noted that Rodan managed his own defense, and so she turned her back to the duel and concentrated on the remaining Regular.

He attacked bravely, but cautiously. Striking with his sword, stepping away, lunging again. Elysen met his blows, but her arms showed the weariness of the night, and the guardsman took advantage, delivering a series of hard blows that sent her stumbling slowly sideways. She paused, panting, her sword tip buried in the sand, her other hand, holding the short sword, propping her up as she knelt. She relaxed, let her head hang, and closed her eyes, waiting for the blow that would free her from her wretched life.

A thudding sound next to her brought her head up and she opened her eyes to find herself looking into the questioning, fearful eyes of the Regular as he lay in the sand, blood leaking from his neck. She looked up. Rodan stood with his staff pointed at the man as he held his hands on his gushing throat. The tip of the staff came to an iron point, bladed and barbed more for wild animals than for fighting. Even so, it had done the job of killing. Behind Rodan, Veldon struggled to his feet and slogged up the sandy slope.

"Rodan, watch out," Elysen shouted. She reached under the sleeve of her robe and cocked the small crossbow, sliding a bolt into the slot as Veldon came closer, his face twisted in rage.

Rodan put the tip of his spear on the ground and smiled.

"Hold there," Elysen ordered, pointing her arm at Veldon. He stopped for a moment, and then his eyes narrowed.

"Your pitiful life ends here," he said. "And you have as good as killed your baby boy. So ends the prophecy."

"What happens to the Addiss when we die, alone out here?" Elysen asked.

Veldon continued sneering as he replied. "They never die. They will simply wait here, in the ground. Waiting for someone to come by. Just as they waited so long for us to uncover them."

"So there will be one less Addiss in this world," she said.

Veldon laughed. "The Addiss never end. There will be two less human hosts though," he said.

He moved forward. Elysen tensed her arm and the bolt shot home, silent, deadly, punching a small, square hole in Veldon's breastplate. His face showed surprise, then pain, then the vacant look of a spirit leaving the body.

He fell to his knees, and then his face hit the sand. The Addiss on his back slid free. It sat on the sand, tentacles feeling the ground around it, close enough to touch first Rodan, then Elysen. Then it began to seep into the ground, as if it were a puddle of water. In a moment, it was gone. Rodan stared at Veldon's body, and the empty sand around it.

"The Addiss will wait here until some human passes by," Rodan said. "Then it will couple with a new host."

"I hope that it rots out here forever," Elysen said.

Rodan took a breath and winced.

"What will you do now, m'lady?" he asked.

She studied the carnage around her. "I have to go back and take my baby away from them," she said. "Or they will kill him."

"It will be very difficult," he said.

"I'll manage somehow."

"If you fail, all of our hopes die with you."

"Nonsense," she said. "No one's hopes die with me. Not even my own."

"I don't believe that," Rodan said. "You have to take my head back to the Consilium, as proof that you have fulfilled your task. Then he will let you both live. You can claim that I killed these men, for my soul can be harmed no more."

"I can't take your head back," she said. Her eyes were full of shock and surprise. "I just saved your life. I'm not going to take it now."

"You have to."

She shook her head and threw her swords in the sand.

"I am dead already," Rodan said. "Look." He opened the front of his cloak. A bloody stain spread slowly across the dark fabric, just below his ribs. "Veldon has stuck me with the point of his sword in a place that I know will cost me my life."

"It is not that bad," Elysen said. She stood up and touched the wet blood. "I have survived worse. You can heal."

He shook his head. "Not this time," he said. "I have spent most of my life studying blades and teaching how to kill. This was a well-placed blow. I will not die today. But tomorrow is another matter. My blood drains into the cavities in my body. I won't last long."

"You have to rest then," she said.

"We can't rest," he said. "There is a baby that needs a mother, and I am just an old man. My life does not matter now."

"I won't take your life, no matter what," Elysen said.

Pain crossed Rodan's face, but it did not take away the resolve in his eyes.

"Come with me." he said. He took her with both hands. "I have done much wandering in these haunted desert lands, and I have also done much meditation. Come, let me show you where I have fasted for the past forty days and nights."

"Why?"

He smiled. "Because, I think you are supposed to see this place. For some reason, I knew you were coming, and that I was supposed to lead you to this secret place. Come now. And bring your horse," he said. "And all the things you need to survive. I don't think that you will want to pass this way again."

Elysen walked with Rodan, leading her horse. She looked back at the sandy marsh where Veldon's body lay, along with the two guardsmen. Blowing sand already covered their bodies, and small vultures perched on the corpses as if they were staking out their meals, waiting for them to soften in the heat of the Soel so that they could peck them apart. Elysen shuddered and returned her attention to the desert before her.

They walked away from the river, towards the north. The high canyon walls towered in the distance on either side of them. Elysen felt like an insignificant speck in a world that seemed unimaginably vast.

"Are you feeling ill?" Rodan asked.

Elysen nodded.

"It is the effect of the Addiss poison."

"There is none left. We consumed all that we brought."

Rodan laughed. "It is the downfall of the Uemn armies. The reason they always turn back from total victory. They believe the Addiss give them great powers, when in fact it is all just an illusion. The Addiss are clever. Unable to communicate directly, they affect our thinking, making us believe that they are helping us. In return, we feed them with the poisonous hydria. The truth is that they are nothing more than pests. Clever pests, but pests nonetheless."

"Like the morgred," Elysen said.

"I don't know the morgred," he responded.

"It is a fungus. It grows in the northern plains, infects the alder trees, and sucks the life from them. It feeds on them, eventually killing them."

Rodan smiled. "Yes. The Addiss are something like that. Yet much more subtle. And, of course, we are not trees. We imagine ourselves to be much smarter."

"Maybe we are not," Elysen mused.

"Maybe our human minds trick us, even without the Addiss. Look, here we are."

They had come to an outcropping of rock, where a giant plate of solid gray material tipped up, protruding from the desert floor. Rodan led her to the far side, and they stepped into its cool shadow. The taste and smell of musty ice hung in the air. Elysen almost fainted. Rodan caught her and she struggled to her feet again.

"Ice," she said. "How did you find such a blessing in this arid land?"

He smiled again, but his ruddy complexion faded. "The coldness comes from deep within this cave. But it is not the cold that I brought you here to experience."

She frowned. "What could be more blessed to me than this coldness?"

"Come and see."

They moved slowly forward, letting their eyes adjust to the darkness. Within the confines of the ever widenening, ever deepening cavern, the daylight from without seeped in, casting dim shadows along the eerie rocks.

"I found this place by accident," Rodan said. "And, like you, came here to escape the heat. I rested here for quite a time before I began to explore this deeply." He paused and bent his knees slightly, almost losing his balance. "Help me crouch down here," he said.

Elysen helped him. He touched a smooth white stone. Elysen knelt next to him and squinted to get a better look.

"A strange formation," she said. "So smooth."

"Touch it," he urged. She reached out slowly. Her hand stopped just a breath away from the strange object. She touched it, lightly.

"It is cold," she said.

"It is from the time before."

"Time before what?"

"The time before us. From before Thorsen."

"Are you sure?"

Rodan nodded. "Look closely at this. It is not a stone at all. It is some kind of unnatural formation. A cooking pot perhaps. Or more likely, a creation for some use the likes of which we cannot even imagine."

Elysen leaned closer and brushed away some of the debris around the object. She ran her hands along the smoothly curved surface.

"Man could not have made this," she said. "It must be some strange fluke of nature, like me."

Rodan laughed. "Not like you. Although there is a kind of beauty in its perfection."

"Maybe some wandering tribe left this here," she said.

"Perhaps. That is what I first thought too. But come deeper. Here, help me stand."

They stood and moved deeper into the cave. The cold became intense, refreshing, as if they were once again in the far north, feeling the winds blow off the glacial ice. Dim light sifted in from the opening above them.

"I believe this cave is a glimpse into the past," Rodan said. "I came here to ponder our place in this world, why we're here, what we're fighting about. I found only more questions."

He guided her hand downward toward another object, embedded in the sand. Elysen gasped as her fingers recognized a shape that felt like human skull in shape, but slick like oil, despite the grit around it. She could feel runes etched into the otherwise smooth surface, the same runes etched on her body. She withdrew her hand and stood. Rodan held on to her for support.

"If you keep exploring, you will find more strange objects. I think they come from a time before history." He paused. "We are not the first people to walk this world."

Elysen shook her head.

"We are but visitors here," Rodan said. "We are but shadows, as these people were but shadows."

Elysen stepped backwards and tripped over something. She fell backwards, kicking up sand with her feet and embedding her hands in the sand. She brushed the sand away and found more of the strange skulls underneath her. She scrambled backwards, brushing frantically at her legs, as if something were reaching up to grab her. Her foot hit one of the skulls, tipping it backwards. A dark, glistening face emerged from the sand like a living thing. She jumped up, stumbled and fell, and then stood and ran outside, into the glaring heat of the desert. She stood with her hands on her knees breathing quickly. As she caught her breath, she wondered why she had reacted so strongly.

The Addiss is afraid, she realized.

Rodan came to her. He sat down in the hot sand.

"What is that thing?" she asked.

Rodan shook his head.

"There are thousands of them. Shining black heads on shining black bodies. Hard, like metal, but different. All dead."

"Statues?" she asked between gasping breaths.

"No. They move, but only when moved, like empty suits of armor."

"Why did you show them to me?"

"Because," he said. "I wanted you to see what I have seen." He leaned against the rocks, fidgeting to get comfortable. He held his hand against his waist and his face contorted with pain.

"We need to get you back to Asaka. We can get help there."

He laughed and grimaced at the same time.

"I wish to die here," he said.

"But why?"

Rodan sighed. "I stayed here for many days, just sitting here, as you sit now. I watched the Soel rise and set again, and my mind went blank. But, as I sat, I began to feel clear, and I began to hear my thoughts again."

"Perhaps you have just lost you mind," Elysen said.

He smiled and shook his head. "No. I was able to quiet my mind, to focus it. I began to ask questions. What were these things I had found in this cave? What did they mean? And what was I to do with this discovery?"

"And did you get an answer?"

"Not at first. But I think I began to realize that the Addiss was trying to answer me. And with that realization came the realization that the Addiss is not our master, it is our servant. They control us only because we let them. Their desire for the hydria is so great that it fills our minds with that same desire. I overcame their influence through sheer will power, but I freed myself from the Addiss entirely by just letting go. Then, I found that the Addiss was my servant, not my master. And, if I listened carefully, I found that it would answer me."

"And what good is that?"

He nodded. "The Addiss are ancient. They were here before us, maybe they have always been here. But they know of the time before. The time of the things in this cave."

"And what did they tell you?" Elysen asked.

He pulled his lips tight and shook his head. "I couldn't understand what they tried to tell me. Their voices are but vague whispers in my mind. I see visions that I don't understand, and I can't always tell what is real and what are lies. But they do know of something more powerful and much older then our lords. And they cower in fear at the very thought of it."

"The one power?" Elysen asked.

Rodan nodded. "I felt the truth of it," he said.

"Perhaps they believed in the one power and it was their downfall."

He shook his head. "I think not. My mind is clear on this if on nothing else. We are wrong. Our race lives in constant fear and war because we refuse to believe in something greater than ourselves."

Elysen glanced back into the cave. "Then what happened to them?"

Rodan shrugged. "The things in this cave are beyond my ability to understand."

They sat in silence for a while, facing west. The Soel began to slip beyond the edge of the world, into the unknown, casting a red glow along the high cliffs of the horizon. Somewhere, up on the far plateau, Sunder Keep kept a silent watch over the plains.

"Why do the Uemn want Sunder Keep so badly?"

"The Addiss," Rodan said. "They believe that all the knowledge of the old world is locked within." He leaned forward and lowered his voice. "They believe that there is knowledge there that can raise the dead."

Elysen stared at him. Her eyes searched his.

"I have seen this knowledge," she said.

Rodan's eyes narrowed slightly. "Then it's true," he said.

She nodded. "I think so."

Rodan leaned back. "We can't let the Addiss have access to the knowledge," he said.

"I'll ride to the western rim," Elysen said. "I'll climb the wall and make my way to the Keep and warn the people of the Vyr."

"You'll be killed before you ever have a chance to warn them," Rodan said.

"Better to be killed by Yergen than to let the Addiss have what they want."

Rodan grunted. "Rest here with me tonight," he said. "Be calm. Be serene. Tomorrow you have to go back and find your son. But tonight you have to rest here in the cool shade of this strange place."

She sat in the opening of the cave, staring at the stars all night, watching as the Arm of Thorsen moved across the sky so slowly that it seemed not to move at all. And yet, as the night passed, it moved from one side of the sky to the other, under some unknown, mysterious force.

During the night, she dreamed of a marching army of shining metal men. She held Araden in her arms and ran, but the army surrounded her. She fell to her knees and shut her eyes, covering Araden with her body. She awoke with a start, her heart pounding. The dark mouth of the cave loomed over her. She moved out into the open desert and squirmed into the sand to get comfortable. As the effects of the hydria wore off, she found herself yearning for Araden's soft touch.

In the morning, she knelt next to Rodan and tried to rouse him. His pale face reminded her of a corpse, but he awoke, groggy, tired, a sickly look in his eyes. He stood slowly, carefully, and walked into the cave, using the walls for support. Inside, he had stowed some food. He brought out a small grouse and roasted it and they ate the leaves of a small, spiny bush that Elysen had seen often, but had never thought to eat. Rodan ate very little. After breakfast, he tried to help Elysen saddle Serena and pack her gear, but she made him sit down again. She came to where he sat and squatted next to him. Rodan sat back and sighed.

"Help me stand," he said. She helped him to his feet and they stood facing each other. Rodan straightened his shoulders and smiled with half his mouth. Half of his face hung limp, as if made of tallow that melted under the relentless stare of the Soel.

"I am dying," he said. "But too slowly. Make it quick and clean, right here." He used his finger to indicate a line along his neck.

"I can't," Elysen said. "I have had enough killing to last a lifetime."

"You have to," he said. "For my sake and for the sake of the boy Araden, you must."

"I'll find another way."

"My time here is done."

"No," she said.

He shook his head slowly, staring at the ground, but he had a calm, almost pleased look on his face.

"I have done much in my life," he said. "Most of it was wasted, making tools of war. But here, this time that we are in now, I am asking you to do the right thing."

"No, you are not. This is a mistake as well."

"You have to cut off my head, and drag it back to the Consilium. He will reward you, and then you must follow your heart. But above all, you must find your son and love him."

She shook her head. "You ask too much of me. I have abandoned my son. He hardly even knows me. He cries when I am near. He has been raised on goat's milk. I have failed him." She dropped to her knees. Rodan reached under her arms and picked her up.

"It is not too late," he said. "Now, do what you must do, and do it quickly, before I lose my resolve."

He pulled her sword from its sheath behind her back and examined it closely. "Ah, Soul-Reaver. I remember you well."

He stepped out into the Soel and spun the blade several times, letting it catch the early rays. The reflection bounced off Elysen's body, flashed through the ice cave behind her and then shimmered on the rock above her.

"Tell me of Araden," he said.

Elysen stared at the old man as he danced a silent kata with the light blade, swiping it quickly through a series of moves that made it almost invisible.

"His hair is the color of straw," she said. "And his eyes turn more blue every day." She paused to watch Rodan for a moment. "He smiles now. And laughs. His smile is like a flower blooming in spring, full of wonder and life. And he is strong. Very strong for his age. His eyes are bright and quick. He watches everything."

"You have to get home to him," Rodan said.

He stopped dancing, slid the blade across the palm of his hand and nodded. He came back into the shade where Elysen waited and presented the sword to her, much as he had done that evening so long ago when she first took it. Her hands took the blade as if they could do nothing else. She held it with her right hand wrapped around the black grip. A far away sadness filled her green eyes.

Rodan stood in front of her. "You have to do this. Do it now."

"I can't," she said.

"You must."

"There must be another way."

"There is not." He stared into the sky, baring his neck to her. Elysen gripped Soul-Reaver with both hands, but her arms dropped limply in front of her and the tip of the sword touched the ground.

"Please, don't make me do this," she begged.

"I will meet you in J'Halla," he said.

She shook her head. "I will never reach J'Halla," she said.

"Yes, you will," Rodan said. "There is a place in you that knows. Now, let us delay no longer. Do it. Do it now."

Elysen sensed urgency in his voice, but she could not move.

"Your child suffers greatly without you," Rodan said. "You have to get back to him now. If you have any love for him at all, do this thing now." Rodan held his hands clenched at his sides, the tendons in his neck standing out like ropes.

"Now," he shouted.

Elysen jumped, and her arms swung despite the piercing cry of pain and sorrow that sprang from her lips as her half-hearted blow failed to sever Rodan's head and he choked and fell to his knees, grabbing the gaping wound with his hands as he dropped to his knees. Elysen gagged and spit up a foul concoction of wild game and cactus juice as Rodan fell to all fours, blood pouring from the open wound. Elysen staggered around him, circling his body as if she herself were dying. She paused for a moment, then let out a wail so pitiful and full of anger and sorrow that the very desert seemed to cry as she finished the stroke. Rodan's head rolled in the sand, and Elysen fell to the ground, sobbing, her body shaking uncontrollably.

"What has led me to such a place?" she whispered to the ground. "Why has my life become such a nightmare? Spirits of the lords, if you have any mercy at all, help me now. Forgive me for all that I have done. Help me, please, help me." She collapsed, and lay there, next to the pool of blood that soaked quickly into the desert dust.

Thirty-one

Elysen gently placed Rodan's head in a burlap salt bag that he had left with his meager pile of belongings. The inside of the bag was half full of brownish-gray salt. The bag was large, but even so, Rodan's head fit tightly. Elysen packed it as best she could, and then hung it on her saddle. She left his other belongings in the desert sand. A small knife, a piece of rope, a comb made of bone.

The bag thumped and bumped against Serena's flank as they rode slowly eastward, toward the far cliffs, toward Asaka. At the commune, she restocked her supplies but said nothing. The giant sailing ship sat motionless in the center of the lake, abandoned. She stayed one night then rode south, toward Land's End at the Sud de Mer.

The army camped along the shore. She first saw it as she topped a rise. She stopped and sat above the rolling, turf covered dunes, looking down at white dots of sheep that grazed along the downs, digging deep pits through the grass and burrowing into the sand below to stay cool during the day and warm at night. The Soel burned high above her head, and a cool breeze blew into her face, carrying the feel of brine and the sour, stinging smell of thousands of white, gangly birds that circled above the camp, diving at scraps of food.

The sea stretched out vast, disappearing over the horizon, green in the distance, blue nearer the shore, breaking into white capped waves that crashed like thunder, over and over, relentless, tireless, yet unable to keep their tenuous grip, sliding ever backwards into the body from which they had emerged.

Where the army camped, the waves broke against a jetty of sharp rocks, sending foaming spray into the air. The beach below her curved like a half moon, protected by the jetty that kept the water within the bay calm. The corps that camped there had constructed a pier out of logs and planks. Already, the hulls of two sturdy ships floated, roped to the pier, and one more stood on the dock, a skeleton of ribs. Elysen stopped and stared for a long time before she gently tapped Serena in the ribs, urging her down the path. They wound down through the trees and emerged onto the beach, where Tobias ran to meet her.

"We heard you were coming," he said, panting as he placed his hand on Serena's bridle. "The lookouts have been watching you for a few days now."

"Your ships are wonderful," she said.

He smiled, almost bouncing up and down. "You should see them sail. We barely had room to test the one at Asaka. No room, barely any wind. But look at this place, feel this wind? It's simply amazing."

She sighed. "I have to see the Consilium." Tobias looked at her, then his eyes became wide as if he had just noticed the lethargic, undulating Addiss that curled around her body. He nodded, and then wrinkled his nose.

"What is that terrible smell?"

She ignored him, riding with her eyes on the camp, searching for the large tent that carried the mark of the Consilium. She found it and rode away from Tobias, leaving him standing with his hand in the air as if he still held the bridle. He watched her go with a pained look on his face.

Elysen dismounted outside the Consilium's tent, grabbed the sack with Rodan's head and stepped past the guards and through the flap before they even reacted. They followed her in. The Consilium sat at his table, eating. She threw his trophy on the table. Blood had seeped through the inner layers of salt, making a hard, brown crust on the outside of the bag.

"What is that horrible smell?" he said.

"You know that smell as well as I do," she said. "It is the smell of rotted flesh. The smell of death. This is the head of Rodan. I have done as you asked. Now I will see my son." Her heart pounded as she feared the worst. The guards stood behind her, hesitating. The Consilium motioned to one, and he took the bloody bag from the table.

"Where is Veldon?" the Consilium asked.

"Dead," she said. "He betrayed us, and I killed him."

The Consilium stopped eating, and stared at her.

"And the two guards?" he asked.

"They attacked me as well. I defended myself. They are of no consequence. Here is the head of Rodan, as you requested. That was my task. I have completed it. Now, where is my son?"

"I can not believe that Veldon betrayed me."

Elysen stood silently, waiting. The Consilium looked doubtful as he continued.

"And I have a hard time believing that you defeated Veldon in a fair fight."

"Don't underestimate me," she said. "Veldon and I faced each other squarely. His body rots in the desert now, as does the traitor Rodan. I have come to see my son. Is he here?"

The Consilium leaned back in his chair and wiped his mouth. The Addiss that peered over his shoulder waved back and forth, as if agitated and nervous. The Consilium spoke slowly, examining Elysen through tired eyes.

"We are preparing for the journey to the far side of the mountains, and to Sunder Keep," he said. "You have earned your place with us. You will lead us."

"We will need to replace the armenders. All of them," she said.

He smiled at her. "And how do you know of our armenders."

"There is not much secret left in them after the fire at Kardesh," she reminded him.

He nodded. "We will do our best. It takes time to make them."

"You will have to do better than your best," she said. "We will need as many as you had at Kardesh if you wish to enter the Keep."

His eyes narrowed. "Do not think that you have the right to order me," he said. "I am the leader. You are simply a guide on this mission."

Elysen cocked her head to one side. "You will need those armenders. All you can carry. I tell you this as your guide."

The Consilium nodded. "I will see to it," he said.

They waited, staring at each other, for several moments.

"Will you share some hydria with me?" the Consilium asked. "You must be needful after your long journey."

"No, thank you. I will see my son now."

The Consilium sighed and waved her away with the back of his hand. "He is here. Still with your man. They are fine. Safe and sound. You may go now. I will have my guard place Rodan's head on a pike outside this camp. That is all."

Elysen turned and slid out of the tent. She mounted Serena and began a slow patrol of the camp. On the far edge, she heard a baby crying. She followed the sound to a small tent pitched well away from the rest. She rode near and dismounted, approaching the shelter cautiously. She looked inside and saw Corde holding a child, rocking him back and forth, whispering soothing words, a worried look on his face.

"Corde," Elysen said quietly. He jumped and the baby cried louder.

"M'lady," he said.

"May I come in?"

"Of course." She could barely hear his voice over the wailing of the child.

She came over and crouched down next to him. Araden clenched his tiny fists and kicked his feet. Tears slid from the corners of his tightly shut eyes.

"What's wrong?" Elysen asked.

"He's ill," Corde said. "He doesn't eat. He cries day and night, sleeps fitfully. I don't know what to do."

Corde looked tired and the creases in his forehead seemed deeper. He gazed down at Araden and shook his head. "If he does not eat or drink soon, I am afraid he might not survive."

"Don't we have a healer in this camp?" she asked.

Corde shook his head. "Only the army healer, but he is not sympathetic. He would rather see the boy die than help him, and besides, his experience is with healing the wounded and dying, not sick children."

"Give him to me," Elysen said.

Corde looked at her as if he had misheard her. Elysen reached out, and Corde slipped Araden into her arms. Feeling a new presence around him, the baby stopped crying for a moment, his cries turning to sobs as he opened his eyes long enough to study her face. Then he began to cry again, shrieking even louder than before. Elysen sat cross-legged on the floor and rocked back and forth. She began to hum a song.

"What is that tune?" Corde asked.

Elysen frowned. "I don't know. Perhaps something that my mother used to sing to me."

She continued humming and rocking. Araden's cries turned to sobs again, and then he clutched her and slept.

"He is burning with fever," she said. "Fetch me a clean cloth and some fresh water."

Corde did as she asked. Elysen soaked the soft cloth in water and let Araden suck on the wet rag. She stayed with him through the day and night, tending to him, resting with him. Corde curled up in the corner of the tent and slept, fetched water and milk, which Araden could not keep down, and brought food for Elysen. She stroked the boy's soft hair, matted with sweat, and hummed her soft tune to him for hours on end. Tobias came by to see them, but stayed for only a few moments, unsure of what to do, what to say. After several days, Araden drank milk again, tiny amounts at first, and then more and more. His fits of crying stopped and his time awake lengthened. He spent time studying Elysen, touching the markings on her face, and snuggled against her chest as he slept, touching her ear with his tiny fingers.

"I will never leave this boy again," she said to Corde one morning as the Soel began to sift into the tent.

"He gave us a bit of a scare," Corde said. He sat down and gazed at Elysen. "Tell me, what happened in the desert?"

She shook her head. "I can't." She drove back the memory of Rodan's head rolling in the sand. She paused. "Corde, you have been so good to us. But you need not serve us any longer. I will exercise my authority as an Addicere to send you back to Asaka. From there, gather your things and go home. Go back to the northlands and live out your days in the coolness of the Cevante. I want you to be a free man again."

Corde smiled. "Lady Elysen," he said. "I am free. And I love you and your boy. My home is here with you now. I would stay, if you would have me."

She touched his cheek with her white fingers and noticed for the first time how tight and thin her skin appeared over the bones of her hand, and how the black runes looked like empty spaces burned through her body.

"Everyone that has ever cared for me has met with a terrible death," she said. "I am cursed. You have to go. If you do love me, then please go."

He shook his head. "M'lady, you are not the cause of pain and suffering in this world. Not mine, nor anyone else's. And you are not cursed." He paused. "M'lady, if I may be so bold." He bowed his head. "I am an old man, and my years of playfulness are behind me, so please forgive me for what I am about to say, but with all honesty and love, I am honored to serve you, m'lady. I have truly fallen in love with you, as a father loves a daughter. I would no more abandon you then I would my own child."

"Oh, Corde. I surely don't feel as if I am worthy of your love."

"But you are, m'lady. You are as worthy of any love as that small boy is worthy of your love. You have simply forgotten."

She sighed and stroked Araden's head.

"I had much time for thought and reflection as I rode through the desert," she said. "I have spent my life running, Corde. Running away from my dreams, my thoughts, my destiny. But as I rode, I found that my dreams and thoughts followed me. I can't run from myself, Corde."

He nodded. "We all have a destiny to fulfill. Sometimes it feels like it's far away. But we can't avoid it."

"I have tried to avoid my destiny. All I found was pain and suffering."

"Perhaps that is the price of avoidance."

They sat in silence for a while, watching Araden sleep.

"What will you do now?" Corde asked.

Elysen took a deep breath and let it out slowly. "We will take the Addiss to Sunder Keep, and they will establish their reign of darkness. Then we will find a way to protect Araden from the Uemn and all who would harm him out of ignorance and fear. Come. Let's find Tobias. We have to make a pact amongst ourselves to keep our faith together."

Corde smiled. "Yes, m'lady. We will be like family again."

She held his hand and squeezed it gently. "I'll never be able to repay you for caring for Araden for so long, while I was lost."

"My love for you never faltered, m'lady. And neither did his."

Elysen let her mind wander, enjoying the presence of Corde and Araden. Even in the midst of the chaos of preparing for war and the painful memories of her life, she felt peace come over her. She felt the sand between her toes, smelled the briny ocean, tasted salt in the cool air, heard the waves crashing. The walls of the tent glowed as the Soel rose. She noticed Veger's viewing scope hanging from a pole. She stared at it, remembering the tiny ball of blue and brown, and the shadow of Turoc over the Vyr. It made sense, and suddenly she felt a another presence in the room, something larger, as if the sand and the ocean and the salt and the Soel were all part of something she could sense but not see, a power that lived in Araden and Corde and the Uemn and the people of the Vyr and Yergen and Vollen and Raes and even the Addiss. In her mind, Turoc's shadow again passed over the Vyr and she heard Veger's words again.

There is a power here that speaks to you.

Elysen's brow furrowed for a moment. She felt the Addiss reading her thoughts.

It will never work, it said.

Another voice came to her. A quiet voice, deeper, like a current that through her heart.

Yes, it said.

Her eyes opened wide. "Corde," she said. Her heart pounded.

"Yes?"

"This information that you have gathered for us from the slaves, how good is this system of communication?"

"It is very informal, m'lady. Much like the gossiping of the dojen back in the Vyr. The slaves chatter like birds. But the information is dependable."

"Can you get information out, as well as collect it?"

Corde shrugged. "Perhaps."

Elysen leaned forward. "I have an idea."

Corde raised his eyebrows.

Elysen continued. "Next time you are mingling with the slaves, can you let slip from your waggling tongue, in a very subtle and offhanded way, the notion that I am the first child of Vollen of the Vyr, and then say something like 'oh, by the way, I think that she is also the granddaughter of Stratus, since he sired Aephia, who was her mother, and what would that make her to the Uemn?' And then keep your ears open for any signs of their old beliefs that some kind of ruler would emerge from the desert, especially remembering the storms that ensued that night that Araden was born." She paused. "Are you following me?"

Corde bit his lip and shook his head.

"Listen then. In your nonsensical way, try to get the slaves to consider the fact that Aephia was born from Stratus, who was born before Jenus, father of Kreid. That makes her the elder, right?"

Corde nodded.

"And I am the only daughter of Aephia."

Corde began to stare into the air past Elysen. "Then Araden is the grandson of the elder child of Stratus."

"Then I am in line as Consilium of the Uemn before Kreid."

Corde's jaw dropped and his mouth hung open.

"Can you sow the seeds of this, without being too obvious?" Elysen asked.

"To what purpose?" he asked.

"Do you remember our old game of bones?" she replied.

Corde nodded.

"This is the bone, which we may play at a later date," she said. "The details of this plan are not yet wholly in my head, and yet I have a sense of where I am going."

"As I recall," Corde said with a worried look in his eyes, "you were never very good at the bluffing part of playing bones."

"Not as good as my teacher," she said, winking at Corde.

He took a deep breath and held it.

"Trust me," she said. Her eyes sparkled in the bright light.

Corde smiled and let his lungs relax. "All you have ever needed to say to me are those two words, and I would follow you anywhere."

"You really are a fool then."

He nodded again. "I can do this. By the time we reach the Vyr, there will be a current of doubt running throughout the Uemn. They will be watching you, wondering if you might really be the Shad'ya."

I am not the Shad'ya, she thought. *But let them think so, for now.*

"Irritate them," Elysen said, wrinkling her nose. "Prod them with this revelation, although gently, like a shepherd prods his lambs. Use your best wiles. Wink at them, and nudge them with your elbow, and then laugh as if it is a silly notion."

"I will prod them and poke them and worry them."

"I feel the old Corde returning to me."

Corde's smiled widened. "And I feel my Elysen returning to me."

Elysen grabbed his shoulders, and they stood that way for a moment before they fell into a hug. Corde patted her on the back with the palm of his hand.

Thirty-two

A thousand Uemn toiled ceaselessly as Araden played in the sand and slept and ate. His sickness behind him, he grew healthy and strong again. The winter season of the southern coast brought gusty winds and bursts of rain that were gone as suddenly as they appeared, followed by clear nights and days of bright Soel. At night, Elysen held Araden close to her body to keep him warm, but by day he crawled naked among the grasses and reeds that covered the rolling dunes.

As the season of the Proste began to fade into the season of new growth, Consilium Ser Kreid called a gathering, and included Tobias.

"We are ready to depart," he announced. "We will sail west, toward the barrens of the far side. Our armies under Commander Grayson will lay siege to the southern Vyr while we make our way north. We must depart these shores now, so that we can cross the Oken Mountains as the snow melts." He paused for a moment and made eye contact with his best men. He smiled.

"By the hottest days, we will be marching down the backsides of the Vyr army. While Grayson keeps them occupied, we will thrust." He swung his fist upward in an obscene gesture and the men laughed. Elysen held her face still, annoyed with his rude theatrics. Ser Kreid continued.

"Our master shipbuilder, Tobias, will take the lead ship, which he has named Kaliameade. He will be followed by Lady Addicere Elysen in the Odyessia. I will take the Nassisia, and Ser Keantt will lead the second group in the Amandaye. Ser Rothe and Ser Sendal will bring up the rear in the Stottard and the Rheem. We will stay within sight of the shoreline, sailing westward to the far side of the mountains. Once there, we will shuttle ashore in the smaller boats and gather our army there. If we are separated, travel north to the tallest peak, easily spotted for its broken top, covered with snow even in the heat."

"And what if there is no land beyond the mountains?" Ser Rothe asked with a snarl on his lips. "What if the Norgarden witch tricks us, leading us to our deaths in the black emptiness beyond the edge?"

"Then she dies with us," the Consilium said.

"She does not feed her Addiss," Rothe said. "She is a traitor and an unbeliever."

The Consilium put up his hand. Elysen stared straight ahead.

"That may be so," the Consilium said. "We will deal with her at Sunder Keep. Until then, she seems to be cooperating. Her relationship with the Addiss is…" he paused, as if unable to find the right words. "Her relationship with the Addiss is being questioned. You don't need to worry yourself with such things. You may concentrate on your own duties. Get your men ready to sail tomorrow. Make sure all is in readiness. We sail for Sunder Keep." He struck the table with his fist. "And may the Vyr Lord rue this day forever more."

After the council, Elysen found Corde washing clothes for Araden.

"How goes it with your subversion?" she asked.

"The Uemn are a suspicious breed," he said. "But the rumors have awakened in them a new curiosity about you. There are mixed feelings. By and large though, I see that there is a new respect developing for you."

"But not in everyone."

"No. There are still some who doubt you."

Elysen walked quickly through the camp, searching. She stopped at a small group of men. They stopped talking and stood at attention.

"I am looking for Commander Grayson," she said.

One of the men pointed toward a large tent nearby. Elysen nodded and left them. She strode to the tent. The guards stared straight ahead as she ducked inside. A familiar soldier sat at a table, sharpening his sword.

"Commander?" she asked.

He stood up and nodded. She approached him carefully.

"You are looking well."

He nodded. Elysen glanced at his back and noted the absence of an Addiss.

"We are leaving tomorrow," she said.

He nodded.

"It will be hot in the swamps when we approach the Keep from the north."

He nodded again.

"You will be leading the armies from the south."

He kept his nod short and curt this time.

Elysen looked straight into his eyes. "We have come a long way since those days on the ice," she said.

"Yes, m'lady."

"You seem to be showing me more respect these days," she noted.

"You are an Addicere now," he replied.

"Is that it then? You bow to the Addiss?"

He pursed his lips. "To do otherwise would be bad for my career," he said.

Elysen smiled at him. "I do not bow to them," she said. "I bow to no one."

He watched her carefully as she wandered deeper into his tent, examining the steel armor that hung from the side beams. She ran her finger along the polished metal.

He frowned. "I don't understand," he said.

"You and your men, do you tire of death?"

"We fight until we die," he said. "That is our lot."

"No," Elysen said. "It is not. Your men have families, don't they?"

Grayson nodded. Elysen walked over to his simple cot and sat down. She bounced up and down, testing it. "How about you?" she asked. "Do you have a family?"

He nodded.

"A wife?"

He nodded again. He looked confused.

"Children?"

"Two girls."

Elysen smiled. "Are they beautiful?"

Grayson's face broke into a smile. "Very much so."

"They deserve a father that lives. Not one who dies in battle."

Grayson's face became stern again. "We fight until the enemy is dead, or until we are."

"And who is this enemy? The people of the Vyr? The Norgarden? Who is it that drags you from your homes and families?"

Grayson swallowed visibly and glanced around the confines of the tent. "You are drawing me into slanderous conversation."

Elysen stood up and walked over to him. She stood close, her eyes exploring his. "I am the master," she said. "I am the Shad'ya."

She waited, allowing him to absorb her words.

"You knew it when you led me from the mountains of Oken to the lands of ice," she said. "I am the one. I will bring a thousand years of peace. Our people will join as one, and we will defeat the dark lords."

"Or destroy the world," he said.

Elysen shook her head. "I will save it."

"There are rumors about you," he said.

"I came here to ask you a favor," she said, ignoring his comment.

He frowned and shook his head. "I can't betray the Addiss."

She held his arms and looked into his eyes. "Don't be afraid," she said. She clapped his shoulders with her hands. "You are Uemn. Fearless. Strong. We stand at a turning point here, you and me." She opened her arms, palms facing upward. "Here in this little tent, at the end of the world." She smiled and took in the surroundings.

Grayson still looked worried.

She gazed into his eyes again and grabbed his arms. "Grayson, I fought the Lord's Guard with you. I slept with you on the ice and kept you warm. I pulled your lifeless body from the Cevante."

He turned his head away from her, avoiding her gaze. She moved her face so that he looking into her eyes again. "You are here for a purpose," she said. "At least listen to my proposal."

He swallowed again, paused, and then nodded slowly.

"First of all," she said, "let me ask you this. How many Kaanites did you see in the hills above the Vyr?"

He shrugged. "It varied from day to day. They seemed to slip in and out of the camps."

"But you must have some idea about how many there are?"

He thought for a moment. "There are thousands," he admitted. "They live everywhere though, not just in the hills. The Kaanites are a faction, not a tribe."

Elysen smiled and her eyes sparkled. “Here is my proposal to you,” she said. “Send a whisper through your camps. Tell your men that Shad’ya came to you in a dream. Tell them that in your dream, a cold, black night consumed the Soel, and that the armies of the Vyr put down their weapons and the war ended as if it had never been. And tell them that when the darkness passed, the people of the Vyr and the Uemn came together like brothers in the stroke of a single burst of light from the Soel.”

His confused look deepened. “I don’t understand,” he said.

Elysen locked her eyes onto his, tipping her head forward just a bit. Her smiled faded and her face became as serious as death.

“I am the Shad’ya,” she said. “When I am in position to take the Keep from the Black Lord Yergen, I will darken the Soel. That will be the sign that the rule of the Addiss and the Vyr Lords is over. All fighting will stop, or I will plunge the Soel into darkness.”

He shook his head. “How could you do such a thing?”

Elysen grabbed his shoulders and shook him gently. “That is not for you to know,” she said. She searched his eyes with hers. Grayson pursed his lips.

“I am not a fool,” he said.

“I know that,” Elysen said. She continued quietly, slowly. “I can make this happen, but not without your help.” She paused. “Do you love your men and your people?”

He nodded.

“Then all you have to do is tell them about your dream.”

He considered her for a moment, staring into her eyes as if he were seeking an answer to some question. “I will mention this to my men,” he said slowly.

“Don’t say anything to the Consilium. Leave this as myst, as it should be.”

“If the people of the Vyr pick up their weapons to fight on that morning, we shall not hold back our men,” he said.

“The people of the Vyr will back down. I only need your promise that you will allow them safe passage to their homes. You will then bring the beast Yergen and his dage Raes to me.”

Grayson nodded. Elysen let him go.

“Speak to no one of this meeting,” she said. She touched his face and his eyes softened.

“Why did you save me?” he asked.

She smiled and put her hands on his shoulders. She let her forehead come rest against his, and she stared into his eyes.

"Because," she said. "Deep in my heart, I saw you as a good man, just protecting his home, and his people. Just like me. And I could not fault you for that."

Elysen released him. He bowed his head and Elysen slipped out the door.

The next morning, twenty men pulled as many oars on each side of the narrow ships, propelling them out into the open sea. Tobias had trained the men well, and the six ships opened their sails almost as one. A stiff ocean breeze filled the sails and the ships began to lean, gradually at first, before settling into a steady cant that made walking the decks difficult and treacherous. Elysen carried Araden in a backpack Corde had made to be buoyant enough to keep him afloat if they fell overboard. The first days were steady, as they followed the Kaliameade, coming about in rapid succession as they planed across the swelling seas. The coastline shimmered on the northern horizon, visible only to the men perched high on the masts, above clapping white sails stretched tight against their halyards. At night, they could see a faint glow from giant bonfires lit by the troops that fought bravely in the southern swamps against Lord Yergen's crossbows. The fires were comforting, like distant friends beckoning them home. The glow appeared as they rode high upon a swelling wave, and then disappeared again as they dropped down into a dark trough.

Some of the men became ill, unable to hold down their meager rations as the boat lurched and swayed. The boats that had seemed so large in the sheltered bay now appeared small and insignificant against the immense ocean. Elysen stood near the bow, holding onto a rope with one hand, tiny Araden, wide-eyed and silent on her back, nestled into the shadow of the Addiss that flicked its tentacles carelessly to and fro.

Corde's voice came from the darkness behind her.

"Do you ever crave the hydria?" he asked.

"All the time," she said.

"How do you resist it?"

She shrugged. "I just do."

"I tried it once," Corde said. She turned in surprise. She could barely see his face in the dim moonlight.

"You did?"

"Yes. Out of curiosity."

"What did you think?"

"It made me sick. Made me stupid. I hated it. Can't see why the Uemn like it so much."

"It's not the Uemn. It's the Addiss. They crave it for their own reasons. It is a need for them."

"Yet it kills the host."

"Eventually."

"It does not make sense."

"No. It doesn't."

"Where do you think we are?" he asked.

Elysen gazed upward, toward the stars.

"Look at this," she said. "The endless night above us. Endless ocean around us."

He nodded. Elysen continued to stare upward.

"We are insignificant out here," she said. "We are less than specks of sand against this blanket of water, under this tent of sky."

"The stars seem close enough to touch," Corde said.

Elysen reached up, her fingers like dainty wisps of white smoke. Araden's eyes followed her hand, and he reached for her arm.

"I wonder what they would feel like," Elysen said.

Elysen lowered her arm. Araden put his arms around her neck, and she smiled. His little foot caught on something and she reached down. Her hand found Raes' knife in its sheath and she slipped it from her belt.

"What do you have there?" Corde asked.

"Something from my past," she said. She handed the knife to Corde. He turned it in his hands, examining it, then handed it back.

"Do you still love him?"

"He has hurt me terribly. Like this knife, he has wounded me."

"Wounds heal."

Elysen looked at the knife for a moment, shrouded in its black leather scabbard.

"Some wounds don't," she said. She pulled her arm back, ready to throw it into the sea. Corde touched her arm and held her back.

"Keep it for a while longer," Corde said.

Clouds covered the Soel the next day, and a cold wind began to blow from the east. The Kaliameade let loose her giant spinnaker crafted of dusty yellow silk, and Elysen ordered the Odyessia to follow suit. Soon, all six ships were running with the new wind, and the agonizingly slow passage that had marked their voyage so far became a race into the unknown. At the far front of the armada, Tobias stood on the bow of the Kaliameade, shouting, holding his arms wide with the wind against his back, as if he himself were the force propelling the massive vessel forward. The bow rose and fell, casting a spray of water over his shoulders. He turned his face up to the sky.

Elysen watched with amusement for a while before she broke formation and dropped in behind the Kaliameade. The other ships followed behind the Odyessia, all except for the Nassisia, which kept close beside Elysen's ship. The Consilium stood on the deck, watching from the helm. Elysen glanced at him, and then turned her attention back to the other ships, sailing like a grand caravan with billowing sails puffed out like proud chests. She smiled and waved at Tobias, but he was too far away to see her.

"I miss that boy," she said to Corde.

"The wind is cold," he said. "We should get young Araden inside."

Elysen nodded and they went aft to the cabins. As night began to fall, the wind became stronger. Elysen left Araden with Corde and went above. The spinnaker strained with the force of the gale, but off in the distance, the Kaliameade and its followers still held true. She glanced over at the Nassisia. The Consilium waved at her. She saw his men pulling in the big sail, rolling it carefully, struggling with it in the stout wind, as if it refused to be stowed. She glanced again at the distant fleet, then closed her eyes and gave the order. The men wrestled the big sail into the hold, and they trimmed the mainsail so that it stretched tight and wide against the wind. The boat slowed, almost feeling as if it had stopped. The clouds became dark, and the seas filled with huge, frothing waves. Elysen's fingers clutched the railings as she made her way down into the belly of the ship.

"Perhaps man was not meant to sail these seas," Corde said.

"Your face is as white as mine," Elysen replied.

She took Araden in her arms and settled into a corner bunk, bracing her legs against the rocking of the ship. She held the baby close as the tossing became more and more severe. Corde joined her, unable to stand any longer.

"You're trembling," Elysen said.

He nodded, no mirth in his face.

"How sturdy are these ships that we built?" he asked.

Elysen shook her head, keeping her lips pressed tightly together. She closed her eyes and put one arm around the old man as she held Araden with the other. They stayed there as the ship lurched and crashed hard against the ocean as if it were rock, tossing them back and forth, angry at their impertinence. Day became night, and the weather worsened. Night became day, but no light accompanied the change. Thunder and lightning filled the sky, and the wind howled. Elysen and Corde crouched in the corner, seeing no one. On the third day, the seas calmed, and the air became unbearably still. The deathly quiet arose in a single moment, between breaths, between heartbeats. Elysen blinked. She looked at Corde, handed him the sleeping child and made her way above decks. The men were scattered and confused, but they had held on through the storm.

"How many lost to the sea?" Elysen asked.

She glanced around. The storm hovered all around them, yet their tiny ship rested under a clear blue sky made hot by the Soel, without even a breeze to bend the wisps of steam that rose off everything.

"Only a few," one of the men responded. His hair and clothes dripped with seawater and his eyes drooped. Elysen glanced upward. The sail had torn down the middle, a clean cut. The soldier followed her gaze. "We could not get it down, it was the only way. We saw the Nassisia rend her sail like that. We followed their lead."

"Very well," she said. "We will repair it as soon as we can." She glanced around again. Rolling black clouds filled the skies around them. "What do you make of this, soldier?" she asked.

He rubbed the stubble on his cheek. "I fear that we will have to weather more storms before we are done." He looked down nervously.

"What is it?"

"The men want to turn back," he said. "They believe that we are nearing the end of the world, and that this storm does not end."

"Tell them to continue west. If they do not, the Consilium will have them put to death."

"They don't fear death as much as they fear the end of the world," he said.

Elysen looked upward, into the clear sky above them. "This is not the end of the world," she said. "It's just a storm. Nothing more. Tell them to keep going."

"We don't even know which way we are heading," he said.

"When night falls, I will read the stars," she said. "We will navigate by the Arm of Thorsen. Until then, have the men rest and renew themselves." She started to walk away, and then turned again. "Any sign of the other ships?"

"No, m'lady. None."

She nodded and walked to the upper deck. She stood there in the midst of the steam and dripping ropes, and watched the men moving slowly as they repaired what damage they could. Evening came, and then night, and Elysen ordered the men to the oars. She guided the ship back to a westerly course, showed the helmsman how to stay true, and went below.

"Is it over?" Corde asked.

She shook her head. "I fear not."

Corde sighed and collapsed on the bunk. "I can't take any more of this. My heart has already stuck itself into my throat. I can't eat. Can't sleep. Not even the great fire of the Kardesh drove so much fear into my body. I feel as if I will shake apart."

"Have faith, my friend," she said. "The one power did not take us this far to leave us here."

"How can you be so sure?"

She shrugged. "Even if we die here, at least we die together."

"Small consolation," he said. "Araden is too young to die here."

"Then you have to take care of him during the coming storm. I'll go on deck and help the men. Let us hope and pray that Tobias has built us stout ships for our voyage. If not, then we shall all meet in J'Halla for a rest."

Corde nodded. Elysen smiled at him and took her place on deck. Almost all the men were below decks, rowing, as Elysen turned the ship into the storm and stood with a rope wrapped around each arm, her teeth bared against the wall of rain and wind.

Thirty-three

The storm passed. The crew of the Odyessia, once numbering fifty, now counted a mere twenty men. As they traversed a strange shoreline of white sand under the hot Soel, they came upon wreckage, washed up along the beach.

"We will go ashore here," Elysen said. "Stow the sails and use the oars to get us as close as possible. We will use the longboats to go ashore."

As they approached the shore, they were greeted by shouts and waving arms. They joined the Consilium Ser Kreid and about ten of his men. They stood around the wreckage of the Nassisia.

"Thirty men left of over one hundred fifty," he said.

The soldiers watched him, waiting patiently for their orders.

"We march north from here," Elysen said. "We can salvage enough armor and horses from the Odyessia to outfit everyone here. We will leave markers for the others to follow once they arrive."

"If they arrive," the Consilium said.

"They are led by Tobias. If we made it, so can they."

The Consilium's face showed his doubt, but he gave the order with the confidence of command. "Make it so," he said. He pointed to several men. "You and you and you, bring the gear ashore from the Odyessia. We will camp here tonight and gather our wits and our strength. Then we will march to Sunder Keep, to face our destiny there." He came close to Elysen and spoke in a low voice that only she could hear.

"This is not what I expected," he said. "With one hundred fifty men, we were outnumbered a hundred to one. Now we have only thirty."

"If you quit here, you will surely fail."

"I could kill you and your bastard child right here and return to my people by following the southern shoreline, and we could renew our attacks in the swamps and fields of the southlands, and I would be rid of you and your cursed kind forever."

"You have been fighting in the southlands for generations. This is your chance to cut straight into the heart of the Vyr Lord. Pass this up, and you will never know victory. Take the chance, and you will be remembered in song and story for all time."

"I don't know why I listen to you," he said.

"Because," she said. "You hope I am right."

"Maybe it is because I am stupid."

She shrugged. "Maybe that, too."

He frowned at her. His lips were tight, but there was a glimmer in his eye, and he suddenly smiled and then laughed.

"You are a brave and impertinent spirit," he said. He shook his head. "You would have made a great Uemn."

"I am Uemn, remember?"

He smiled at her, and then glanced around at the men attending to the tasks around him.

"Thirty Uemn against the armies of the Vyr. It will be quite a story, no matter how it turns out."

Elysen smiled and nodded. They looked at each other for a moment, warily, then Elysen turned toward the sound of Araden's laughter. She took one last look into the Consilium's eyes and then walked away, towards Corde and her son.

Thirty-four

They salvaged fifty horses and five wagons of armenders from the Odyessia, as well as provisions for a hundred men. From the rocky coast, they traveled northward. Breathing came hard, as if the winds of life could not reach them, and at the top of each barren rise, endless rolling hills of dead soil greeted them. For days on end, they followed the eastern slopes of the Oken Mountains, keeping the craggy peaks in sight as they mounted each hill. Each night, Turoc became thinner and thinner, until he was no more than a mere sliver hovering low on the southern horizon. Each morning repeated the previous; the Soel burned bright but the days remained cold, as if this part of the world could hold no heat. On the darkest night, when Turoc faded to nothing, the sky clouded over and a light rain began to fall.

Morning appeared as just a lighter shade of dark, and afternoon drifted to evening, black replacing gray. Without wood for fire, and with nothing dry to burn, the soldiers huddled together under their canvas tents. Words seldom passed, replaced mostly by sullen scowls. Time passed with nothing to mark one day from the next, until the rain broke one afternoon, late in the day. That night, the clouds broke and the next day Elysen woke to find the soldiers standing around camp, staring at the looming figure of Broken Top. It stood towering into the blue sky, white and gray and pointed, with a frosty cloud clinging to the top like a fragile banner.

"Broken Top," Elysen said. "Where Thorsen and Kaan fought their final battle, destroying all that was good, and leaving only suffering."

"How do we cross?" Ser Kreid asked, gazing upward.

"Carefully," Elysen said. "And slowly. Come on."

They picked their way along the gray rock, day after day, leading their horses. They made steady progress, and yet the mountain never seemed to be closer. They stopped to camp in silence at the bottom of an ice pack that fanned out across the rocky land.

"There is no way over this giant," Ser Kreid complained. Elysen stared at him for a moment, and then she walked away.

"Where are you going?" he demanded.

"I need to be alone," she said.

As the Soel began to slip below the horizon, turning the mountain into an orange pinnacle of fire, Elysen walked up onto the ice mass until she found herself well away from the Uemn. She let her robe fall to the ice and walked a few more paces before she stripped her clothes off and sat down. She crossed her bare legs and let the cold seep upward through her body. She placed her hands on her knees and closed her eyes. A light breeze slipped around her naked body, and her mind began to clear.

She could hear a voice, wafting across the ice, as if it had been waiting here for her from some long ago time. She smiled and felt a sense of peace descend upon her shoulders like a cloak.

Emptiness.

She opened her eyes and gazed out at the barrens. The brown, rolling hills stretched to the western horizon, where the Soel rested, a red ball of flame, now only half-visible. She felt energy pouring toward her, and she felt as if she could hold the entire Vyr in her hands. She turned her palms upward and tipped her head back.

She took a deep breath and concentrated on the mountains, and the plains beyond. She could see Lake Orman, at the base of two giant rock sentries, and Broken Top rising beyond. She felt the Kaanites, amassing in the hills, and the Gennissaries, tired and broken, seeking shelter from the oncoming horde of Uemn. In the valley below, she sensed the resigned disbelief of the seasoned warriors that had followed her this far. The voice continued to speak to her.

The world emerged from nothing, fueled by some power. And that power was nothing more than a word. A thought. For thought becomes movement, and movement becomes creation. And the word peopled the earth, and created the rocks and the sky and the clouds and the trees and the birds and all living things, and all of these things came from one and are still one.

As Elysen sat there, listening to the strange winds, Yergen's face emerged from the darkness and she felt pain. Yet, it was his pain, not hers. And she felt Kreid as he suffered from the hydria and from the lack of it. She sensed a desperate plea from the Vyr, from the world itself, but she could not understand its need. She turned her thoughts back to Yergen. He diminished. She smiled at him and nodded, and in her mind he gazed at her, confused, impotent.

She raised her arms to the universe and spoke to the voice that gently urged her.

"I come here to heal," she said. She shook her head. "I don't know how this will all work out, but I ask you, whoever you are out there, that if what I am doing is right, that you lead me onward to whatever waits for me, and if what I am doing is wrong, that you show me the right way."

The ice lifted her and propelled her toward the dark blue sky, and she felt a great emptiness rushing toward her.

Follow, the voice said.

It came as a whisper, a thought, almost like a stone sinking silently through deep water.

"Thank you," she said. "For whatever happens, for all that has happened, thank you for bringing me here."

She lowered her chin to her chest and took another deep breath. Darkness crept along the ice, reaching for her, but she remained reluctant to move for fear that she would lose the power of the moment.

"I will bring peace, won't I?" she asked.

The voice did not answer. She stood up and gathered her robe. She slipped it on as she walked back to camp. Kreid waited for her as darkness descended. She spoke to him as she walked past.

"Tomorrow we will cross the mountains," she said. "I suggest that everyone sleep well tonight."

The next day, Elysen led them up the ice slope toward a small cleft in the rock. They dismounted and led their horses along narrow ridges and rubbled slopes, camping in a windy ravine that night. The next day they scrambled along the rocks again. Kreid made his way to Elysen, pushing his way past his sweating men as they struggled with the animals and the carts.

"We will never make it over this mountain," Kreid shouted. He pointed upward, toward the rocky slopes. "It's impossible."

Elysen smiled at him and then looked in the direction he pointed.

"If you think it is impossible, then it is. For you. But not for me." She nodded at him. "You can go back if you like. Wait for the other ships. I will push onward."

Kreid put his hands on his hips and glared at her, breathing heavily. His chest quivered a bit as he struggled for air. He turned and looked at his men. They gazed back at him, and then looked at Elysen.

"We push on," she yelled back at them. "Any man who doesn't think we can make it can rot in the barrens forever."

Kreid glared at her as his men pushed past him. He followed, still fuming.

They kept climbing all that day and the next, even though the winds cut through their clothes like knives of ice. On the third day, they came to a small plateau and Elysen stood with her hands on her hips, smiling. A twisted tree appeared in front of her, a strange, lonely thing, stripped of bark by the gritty wind. Yet it held on somehow. Elysen recognized it and smiled.

You and I are much the same, she thought.

She turned and soaked in the view. The army filed onto the bench one by one, pushing and shoving at the heavy carts of armenders. Kreid brought up the rear followed by Corde and Araden. The four of them stood gazing out across the empty lands of the east.

"This was all green and beautiful once," Elysen said.

"Why do you say that?" Ser Kreid murmured. His eyes were sunken and surrounded by dark circles, and the Addiss on his back flailed weakly.

Elysen turned her eyes away from him and looked out across the brown hills again.

"Because it doesn't make sense that the world is that empty. It should be full of life."

"Well then," Kreid said. "What happened?"

Elysen shook her head. "We may never know," she said. She turned and touched the tree, remembering a morning long ago when she had first sat here and stared out at the bigger world. The first sense of a universe, of a power greater than Thorsen, bigger than the Vyr. She smiled and waved her hand.

"Come on," she said. "We have a world to conquer."

They crossed the summit and she found the cave where she had sat with

Joryn and Rachael and Petyr and Joli. She rode into the ravine alone, searched the ground, but found nothing. No bones, no remnants of any kind. They camped there that night, and then descended to Lake Orman the next morning, clad in full fighting gear. They stopped on the ridge above the lake and watched the smoke from a few small cooking fires drift upward into the blue sky.

Elysen raised her hand. "Stay here," she said.

She buckled her armored cape around her chest and slipped her bone visor over her eyes. The handles of her twin swords jutted over her shoulders. Her horse lurched as it clambered down the slope to the lake. As she entered the clearing, a few men and women stood up from their fires and watched the white warrior approach. She stopped in the middle of the rugged compound and waited. No one moved.

The people exchanged worried looks, but no one spoke. Finally, a man came forward, moving very slowly and peering at Elysen as if trying to see within her cloaked armor.

"Lady Elysen?" he asked. She looked more closely at the man, and then she smiled and slipped off her horse. She stepped up to him and embraced him.

"Jaramis," she said. She clapped him on the shoulders. "It's good to see you again." Her thoughts shifted to Arador and her smile faded. "How goes it in the Vyr?" she asked.

Jaramis shook his head and looked at the ground. "Not good," he said. "Yergen has conscripted every man that can fight, and he kills those like us that run to the hills to be with our families. The Uemn are pushing deeper and deeper into the Vyr. And we have no crops. We're starving, we're hunted." He looked at her again and his eyes fixed on the strange markings on her chin and cheeks.

"Much has happened since I saw you last," he said. Elysen nodded and removed her visor. The other refugees stared at her. Men and women hugged their children close, protecting them against their legs.

"I have come to take my place as Lord," she said. "I am the Shad'ya, born of ice and fire, rightful ruler of the Vyr and the deserts. I have an army of Uemn with me. We are marching to Sunder Keep."

Jaramis' eyes opened wide as he listened. He blinked once and then just gaped at her.

"I want you to do something for me," she said.

He stammered for a moment, and then nodded. "Yes," he said.

"I want you to send out word to the Kaanites that I am back, and that they are to report to me. Here. Now."

He nodded.

"And Jaramis," she said.

"Yes, my Lord."

"I want you to let yourself be captured. Let Yergen's guards conscript you. And then I want you to find a man named Tell who serves me as a spy in Yergen's army. He is to report here to me as soon as possible."

Jaramis looked at her with a skeptical eye. "I know of the man named Tell. A master of the dage. He is ruthless and cruel."

"Do as I ask," she said.

He hesitated for a moment, and then turned away. He gathered the people together and began to converse quietly with them. Elysen motioned for the Uemn to enter the camp, and they rode in two by two. Corde followed at the very rear. Ser Kreid rode to the side of the column, his expression hidden under his gruesome faceplate.

The Kaanites began to show up within a few days as news of Elysen's return spread. Tell came before the turn of Turoc and Elysen embraced him. The big man picked Araden up off the floor of the tent and Corde inhaled sharply. Elysen ignored him and smiled as Araden giggled. Tell set the boy back down and turned to Elysen.

"I have done as you asked," he said. "The army awaits you. Yergen is mad. He kills his own men. And we are dying in useless battles with a superior army."

Elysen took his arm and led him to the side of the tent.

"Tell, I want you to go back and inform your men that the Shad'ya has arrived, and that I am now in command. I will send a dark beast to swallow the Soel, and when I do, they are to lay down their arms and surrender to the Uemn. If they do not, I will destroy the fire that gives life to the Vyr, and the deserts, and I will plunge the world into ice."

"The Uemn will cut our heads off," Tell protested.

Elysen shook her head.

"Commander Grayson, who leads the Uemn Regulars, is also loyal to me. His men will lay down their arms during the darkening as well."

"And if they don't?"

"You must have faith," she said. She pulled him close. "Be brave. Make the first move. We are going to change the world. No more fighting. No more killing. But we have to make the first move. We have to take the stand."

"And what about Yergen?"

"I will deal with Yergen," she said. She stayed quiet for a moment as she pondered the dangerous game she now played. She closed her eyes and expelled her breath slowly. "Have you seen Raes?" she asked.

Tell nodded. "He is laying a trap for the Uemn, in the western foothills. We are to draw them into an ambush."

Raes, she thought. *My heart aches for you, and yet there is still a part of me that can never forgive you.*

Elysen sighed, remembering the plan that Raes had laid out so long ago in the Caldera of the Keep. She opened her arms and held her palms up.

"Everything is as it should be," she said. "Go now. Join the army and spread the word. I will see you here again when all this is done."

Tell shook his head and walked out slowly. Elysen stuck her head out of the tent and watched him ride away. She gazed up into the sky at the Soel and bit her lower lip. She closed the flap of the tent and grabbed her cloak and saddle. She gave Corde a serious look.

"It's time for me to go," she said. "Stay here with Araden till I get back."

"And what if you don't come back?" he asked.

"Trust me," she replied.

She led her thirty Uemn and Ser Kreid, plus a hundred and fifty Kaanites armed with recurves and crossbows, down the Ryn Gladde to the hills of Lack Rolan, and then into the northern plains. They saw very little game, few birds, and no people. Along the way, more Kaanites joined them, and by the time they reached the rim of Turoc's Cauldron, they counted more than five hundred strong. They overran the outlying posts easily, stripping the guards of their wooden armor. They crested the ridge and Elysen led the Uemn across the slender causeway and into the Keep. There were very few guards, and they offered little resistance.

"Now what?" Ser Kreid asked as they sat on their horses in the courtyard.

"Are these all of the Addicere?" she asked.

"All that remain," Ser Kreid said.

"Then you wait here," she said.

He pulled his helmet off. "And what about you?" he asked. His face looked drawn and tight, as if he were close to death.

"You have what you want now. You have the Keep."

He looked around. "It's falling apart," he said.

She laughed and nodded. "You wanted it," she said. Her horse danced in a circle. "I'll be back," she said. "Wait for me, and if you are good, I might bring you some hydria."

Kreid's eyes gleamed and a tiny stream of saliva dripped from his lip. Elysen smiled again and shook her head as she turned to go. Ser Kreid called after her.

"And what about the armenders? You said that we would need all that we could carry."

Elysen stopped and glanced back over her shoulder. The Addicere guard dismounted and stood together in the main courtyard. Their eyes spoke of weariness and lack of precious hydria.

"We do," she said. "Our task is not yet over. I will take the armenders with me. You must wait here."

Ser Kreid watched her go for a moment before he waved at his loyal Addicere who turned the heavy wagons around, following Elysen out across the narrow causeway. She galloped on ahead, leaving them to lumber along after her. At the bridge over the Skell, she stopped and addressed the Kaanite guards.

"All Uemn who wear the mark of this shadow creature will be entombed here," she said. She showed them her back, and they scowled at the writhing shadow.

"If any are found outside this Keep, slay them but do not touch the bodies or go near them. Surround anyplace where such have fallen with crosses and warnings, because the Addiss will take any passerby who comes too close."

Elysen reached over and took a bow and arrow from one of the guards. She wrapped a length of grease cloth around the end of the arrow and touched the cloth to a flaming torch. The Addicere guards bringing along the wagons of armenders saw what she intended and froze. Elysen drew the flaming arrow and released, placing it with a precision that only a practiced archer could achieve. The Addicere abandoned their horses and ran toward Elysen. The arrow arched slowly across the sky and touched the first of the two wagons. It bounced once, spinning end for end before it came to rest on top of the canvas the covered the cargo. The canvas caught fire, and the Addicere turned for just a moment, too scared to stop running, too curious to avoid looking back. The first few armenders exploded with a fury that suddenly turned into a fire from hell, as the first wagon became a giant ball of fire, clapping like thunder, and consuming the second wagon, doubling the fire. The fire rushed at the running Addicere, consuming them, throwing them forward like autumn leaves in a thunderstorm. They tumbled and rolled as the arched causeway beneath them began to slope away. Where the wagons had been, the causeway crumbled into the once clear water, filling it with stones and mortar and debris. Between two of the arches, only a single buttress remained. After untold years of patient service, it released itself from duty, tipping slowly toward the island. As it fell against the next support, knocking yet another arched section into the water, Elysen could see Ser Kreid and the other Addicere running through the gate just below Thorsen's watch. They gathered along the front wall of the Keep and watched as two more sections of the bridge collapsed. A foul, black smoke drifted toward the island and its prisoners. Elysen waited until the destruction was complete and then nodded at the Kaanites that stood gawking at the empty waterway between the mainland and the island, where for so many lifetimes the bridge of the Skell had stood.

"Let no one ever again travel to that island or set foot in that Keep," Elysen said. "Throw any demon with an Addiss into the cold waters of Turoc's Cauldron to drown. Above all else, let no one ever again leave that place."

The guards nodded. Elysen kicked her horse and it bolted away. At the top of the ridge, she took one last look at her home. Far across the frigid water, at the gate of the Keep, the Addicere and Ser Kreid still stood, their arms hanging limp at their sides.

"May you rot in that place," she said.

She rode down the other side and kept going, traveling through empty towns and barren fields, day and night. She rode along the lesser trails and roads until she came to an open field just north of Thane's Peak. From there, she followed the fresh rut marks of heavy wagons and horses to an encampment of Gennissaries perched high on the northern slope of the peak. She put on her visor and rode past untrained guards who hailed her but did not stop her. She recognized Yergen's horse and his tent and she pulled into the center of the circle of small tents and jumped off her horse. She could hear the quiet voices of the conscripted men as they recognized her white armor.

"The Shad'ya," they said. She slipped off her heavy robe.

Yergen emerged from his tent and stared at her.

"So," he said. "It's true."

"I have come to claim the Vyr," she said.

Yergen reached behind his back and unsheathed the steel blade that Rodan had named Griever. He held it in front of his body with both hands, waving the tip back and forth at Elysen. She reached up with both hands and her blades flashed out, cutting through the thin air with a sound like the forlorn whistle of a widgeon on a misty pond.

"You have lost, Yergen," she said. "It is time for you to lay down your weapon."

Elysen smiled. She could feel a change coming on. It prickled along the backs of her black and white arms. Under her hood, her bare scalp tingled. Yergen took a step forward and circled to her left. Elysen held both blades toward him, moving cautiously but easily so that she faced him. He put the Soel to his back, and Elysen grinned.

From behind her, she heard Raes' voice call out to her. "Drop your weapons."

She took a glance over her shoulder just as he motioned to the men on either side of him. "Take her," he said. They glanced at him, and then looked at Elysen. They took a step back. Their eyes were wide and full of fear. Raes turned and glared at them.

"Take her," he yelled. They backed away another step.

"She is the Shad'ya," one of them said.

"She's just a girl," Raes hissed.

Elysen turned sideways so that Soul-Reaver pointed toward Yergen, and the smaller Soul-Stealer toward Raes. He glared at the cowering Gennissaries and brought his own bow up. He nocked an arrow and licked his lips, but he did not release it. Yergen charged at her. Elysen turned toward Yergen and slipped from under his blow, pushing Griever away from her with her own thin blade, the metal screaming like a wounded animal as it scraped against its foe. Yergen came around quickly, slicing through the air with his arms extended, but Elysen had already moved out of reach. The Gennissaries surrounded the Lords in a circle, gaping. Raes stepped forward, but Yergen held up his hand.

"I'll take her," he said. "Just like I took her father."

Raes lowered his bow as Yergen's words sunk in. Elysen's eyes narrowed.

"He was weak, and pathetic," Yergen said. "The Vyr is better off without him. And it will be better off without you."

The tip of Raes's arrow touched the ground. He stared blankly into the mountains beyond the camp.

Yergen lunged. Elysen's blade deflected the blow with a flick of her wrist.

"You've practiced since we last met," Yergen said.

Elysen nodded.

"So have I," Yergen said.

He stepped forward quickly, sweeping the blade upward, catching Elysen off guard, but she managed to spin around and take a glancing blow across the back of her light armor. She ran a few steps and then planted her feet wide and faced Yergen with her knees bent. The crowd of soldiers moved and opened, allowing them to take whatever space they needed. Raes turned, watching them now with a frown on his face. Yergen attacked Elysen with a barrage of hacking blows, and she fended them off with concentrated precision. Her blades flashed like lightning in the late afternoon light. Rodan had made Griever heavy and stiff, and Yergen's relentless blows began to push Elysen back. The ground sloped away from her, and she found herself at a disadvantage. Yergen stood taller, with longer arms, and he now had slightly higher ground. Elysen tried to change her position, but Yergen became even more frantic and furious. He ended his flurry with a growling yell and then he staggered in a circle, catching his breath, while Elysen panted. A drop of sweat dripped into her eye and she tried to wipe it away, but her visor blocked her hand.

"I don't want to kill you, Yergen," she said.

He faced her again, his arms relaxed, the tip of his stolen blade almost touching the dry grass.

"Oh, no," he said. "Of course you don't." His knee lifted and he lunged forward again, hacking and hacking like a madman. Elysen reeled backward and tripped on the uneven ground, but managed to keep her feet under her. Yergen brought his blade around and Elysen dodged sideways just enough to miss most of the blow, but it knocked her visor from her face and sent it spinning through the air. Yergen laughed.

"Oh," he said. "Look at you now, Shad'ya." He smirked and walked around her so that the Soel shone on his back again. Elysen tried to catch her breath. Yergen held out his hand as if presenting her to his army for the first time.

"Here is your Shad'ya," he shouted. "Look at her. She has no power."

He spun around and Elysen barely deflected the roundhouse blow. It tipped her to her side and she rolled across the grass before she scrambled back to her feet. Yergen strutted along, trailing after her like a cat playing with a vole. He came to her again, hacking and swinging with all his might, the cords in his neck standing out and his eyes bulging. Elysen warded off blow after blow. The sound of singing blades, of metal striking metal, over and over, resounded off the hills around them. Elysen stumbled again and fell, dropping her short blade as she scrambled backwards. Yergen stepped forward and scooped up Soul-Stealer with his free hand. He took a long stride, almost a leap, and kicked her. He stretched his arms out with the points of the two blades pointing toward the Soel.

"You are not the Shad'ya," he said. "You are an abomination. A mistake." Yergen puffed up his chest and shouted to the crowd of men that circled around them. "Vollen broke the law," he yelled. "And I am here to correct the mistake."

He turned around and shoved Soul-Stealer into his waistband. Elysen stared into his eyes as he brought Griever above his head with both hands on the hilt. She pushed into a half-sitting position, propped up on her elbows, gasping for breath. As they stared at each other, pausing for a moment, the air rippled with a soft sound like a bird fluttering. Yergen whipped his shoulders around and arched his back. Raes' arrow glanced off Yergen's arm, and the Lord's eyes flared with pain and hate. Raes pulled another arrow from his quiver. Yergen slipped Soul-Stealer from his belt and hurled it with a backhanded flick. The thin blade hit Raes in the chest just as he drew the arrow back. Elysen cried out softly as Raes' mahogany breastplate split with a sharp cracking sound. The dage staggered backwards, holding onto the hilt of the knife.

Yergen turned back toward Elysen and glared down at her. She growled at him and ground her teeth together.

"Now I will kill you," she said.

Yergen bent his knees slightly, and then stretched up into the air and brought Griever down with all his might. Elysen rolled and brought Soul-Reaver across her body. Yergen's blow caught her forearm and shoulder and she heard a bone snap as the metal plates buckled. Yergen fell to his knees and Elysen heard a sucking sound as another arrow sliced through the air. From the corner of her eye, she saw Raes on his knees, holding his bow in front of his body. The arrow snuck in just below the plate that covered Yergen's upper arm and plunged deep into his muscle. Yergen cursed and turned toward his new attacker, swinging Griever in a wide arc as he ran forward.

Elysen surged to her feet and fell forward again just as Yergen swung at Raes. The dage tried to use his bow to fend off the blow, but Griever sliced through the wood as if it were water. Yergen turned slightly and brought the hilt of the sword backwards against Raes' face, knocking the smaller man back.

Elysen shouted at Yergen, voicing his name within the roar of a wild animal. Yergen turned and faced her with a wicked smile.

"You are weak," he said. "And your friends cannot protect you. Now come to me, and we will finish what we started so long ago. Our dance of courtship is almost over."

Elysen lurched to her feet. She kept her head tilted down, but fixed her burning eyes on Yergen. He came forward quickly, swinging Griever across his body. Elysen grabbed Soul-Reaver with both hands and brought it around like an ax. The steel wailed through the air, and then the two blades crashed together, again and again. Hate and fury blinded Elysen, and as her pent up emotions exploded from her body, Soul-Reaver became a living thing, driving Yergen backwards. His eyes began to widen, the intensity replaced with a strange sense of awe, and then fear. Elysen sensed the moment when doubt entered his mind, and she spun around quickly, changing from roundhouse blows to a low lunge that caught Yergen off guard. Her blade slid under his chest plate. She felt the tip of it strike hard against the inside of the wooden armor that protected his back, and then she withdrew it quickly.

Yergen's wide eyes were blank and his mouth hung open. He took one step forward, looking past Elysen into the hills beyond. Elysen felt the strength leave her arms and legs, and she dropped to her knees. Yergen fell forward, landing on top of Elysen and dropping Griever on the ground. His face pressed against hers as they toppled into the grass like clumsy lovers.

They rolled, and Elysen felt Yergen's arms moving, his stone knife scraping against her armor as he searched for an opening. He found it, and she felt a hot stab of pain as he slipped the small blade between her ribs. She cried out and the bright sky became dark. Yergen's body floated above her. She sighed and a deep sense of peace came over her as she relaxed into the darkness.

"My time is over," she whispered.

I can finally rest.

A face hovered over her, and she turned her head to the side. Raes knelt down next to her with his hand behind her head. He helped her to sit up, and she gazed out across a land shrouded in a strange, gray darkness.

"Are you still living?" she asked Raes. He nodded. Elysen turned her head a bit. Yergen lay on the ground next to her, staring at the sky.

"He's dead," Raes said. He cringed and pulled his head away a bit as Elysen's Addiss reached for him.

"What about me?" Elysen asked.

Raes shook his head. "Not yet. But the Soel has been consumed by the darkness."

Elysen looked up toward a ball of blackness, surrounded by a ring of flames. She put her hand on Raes' shoulder and he helped her stand. She clutched her broken arm against her body, and nearly doubled over with pain as the wound in her side seeped blood.

They stood for a moment in the mid-day twilight, watching, as a horse thundered up the hill. The rider jumped off and crouched on one knee in front of Raes. The messenger glanced at Yergen's body as Raes spoke to him.

"What news?" Raes asked. The messenger looked back and forth between Raes and Elysen and Yergen and tried to speak, but no words came out.

"Speak man," Elysen hissed.

"The Lord is dead," he stammered, staring at Yergen's body.

"Yergen is dead, and Soel of Thorsen is consumed by my dark power. We don't need you to tell us these things. Now I am Lord here," Elysen said. "So tell us why you have left the field of battle."

He dropped to his knees and lowered his head. "The Uemn ride into the valley. The trap is set. We await your orders.

"Order your men to lay down their arms," Elysen said. Her voice was no more than a whisper. Raes stared at her.

"We have the Uemn trapped," he said. "We can end this war now."

She shook her head and struggled out of her body armor. It fell to the ground and landed in a heap. Her chest moved, but no breath came to her.

"The shadow of death is here," she said. "Tell them to lay down their weapons."

Raes looked at the men that gathered around them. Farmers, millwrights, carpenters. They were dirty, and their eyes were tired. They watched with apprehension, straining to see in the darkness. Raes stripped his bow from his shoulder and threw it on the ground.

"Tell the men to disarm," Raes said to the herald. "It is the order of the Lord."

Raes turned his head slightly so that he could see Elysen's face. Her eyes fluttered shut and her knees buckled. He held her close, supporting her with his hip.

"Go," he shouted at the messenger.

The man jumped back onto his horse and galloped away. Elysen heard the heavy beating of hooves on the ground. She felt Raes' arm around her waist as the blood pooled in her body. Raes' voice whispered in her ear.

"Cheat death again, my Lady."

Epilogue

Elysen woke to the sound of a child's laughter. She rolled to her side and grimaced with pain. A wooden splint bound her arm and she was naked except for a cotton binding that wrapped around her torso. A stain of blood showed where Yergen's knife had slid into her body. She coughed and moaned with pain. A cool hand touched her forehead and she opened her eyes. Corde gazed back at her.

"One again you prove too hard to kill," he said.

She managed a weak smile. "How is Araden?" she asked.

Corde glanced over his shoulder and turned back to Elysen with a smile. "He grows bolder and bolder each day. More and more like his mother. Today he was eating rocks and dirt."

Her smiled deepened a bit, wrinkling the corners of her eyes and the sides of her mouth.

"And what about the war?" she asked.

Corde pursed his lips. "The Uemn army occupies the Vyr, but it was a bloodless battle. The Gennissaries laid down their arms, and the Uemn have marched to the Keep and have relieved the Kaanite guards you set there. Commander Grayson has taken charge in your absence."

"And the Addiss?"

"Still imprisoned in the Keep. The Uemn surround the rim with rotations of guards and the Kaanites now scour the lands for any remaining Addiss, by your order. When they find one, they butcher the poor Addicere and place crosses around the area so that no unwary traveler might be taken by the Addiss."

Elysen relaxed back onto the soft bed and stared at a canvas ceiling.

"The Addiss got what they came for," she said. "They have the Keep."

"It will do them no good," he said. "Their hosts will starve and die from exhaustion, and they will be nothing but disembodied spirits again, trapped forever in their crumbling fortress."

"We must never let anyone set foot on that island again," she said.

"M'lady," Corde said. His voice held quiet concern.

She did not have the strength to reply, but Corde saw that her eyes were still open, so he went on.

"The Kaanites will kill you when they find you. You carry the Addiss on your back, and they will post you no quarter from the law you have set."

She closed her eyes and rested for a moment, but when she awoke, the tent was empty. She tried to sit up, crying out in pain as she collapsed back onto the bed. Raes came running in. He stopped when he saw that her eyes were open.

"Where are we?" she asked. Her voice was soft but hoarse.

"We are at Lake Orman, m'lady," he said.

She reached out to him and he knelt down by the bed but did not take her hand. She let her arm fall back to the ground.

"Thank you," she said.

Raes turned his eyes toward the floor and let his head hang forward.

"Why are we here?" Elysen asked him.

"There are still factions that want you dead," he said. "The Kaanites, Uemn, even people of the Vyr. For their own reasons. Some fear change, some want change so badly that they want the last of Thorsen's bloodline wiped from the world."

"Maybe my time is past anyway," she said. "Everyone dies."

Raes took a deep breath and locked his eyes on hers. Her heart jumped in her chest and she tried to sit up again. "Araden," she hissed.

Raes pushed her down gently and smiled. "Araden is fine," he said. His smiled faded to a look of concern. "But there was an attempt. We foiled it, but everyone is afraid now. We guard him day and night."

Elysen took a shuddering breath and then closed her eyes.

"We can't protect him here," Raes said.

"I know," she replied.

The hot days ended as the season of the Proste approached. The leaves around Lake Orman turned gold and yellow and orange and red. Elysen healed slowly. Raes and his men guarded the camp constantly, but the dage did not visit Elysen again.

On a crisp morning, when the leaves were just beginning to drift to the ground, Elysen walked down to the shore. Corde knelt in the cold water, rubbing a tattered shirt against itself, frowning at a stain that refused to come clean. She crouched down on the embankment and watched him.

"I've been thinking," Corde said. "Maybe we could find a village somewhere on the outskirts of the Vyr where we could raise Araden in peace."

Elysen gazed at him for a moment and then smiled. "You don't even see it anymore, do you?" she asked.

"See what?"

Elysen stood up and held her arms open with her palms facing the sky. "The runes, the spells, the white skin and hairless head, the scars and wounds, the darkness of the Addiss. To you, I am just a sweet little girl, normal as any other."

Corde's withered old face broke into a smile.

"I have something for you," she said, changing the subject. She took his hand and led him back up the hill.

"Close your eyes," she said. She helped him sit down on his favorite log. Araden played in the dirt. A smear of mud crossed his face like war paint. Elysen kissed the top of his head and he reached out and grabbed at the sullen Addiss that clung to her back. She pulled away from him and sighed. He laughed and grasped at the air with his tiny hand, playing with the dark beast. A sad expression crossed Elysen's face, but she took a deep breath and shook it off. She walked over to the fire and returned with a bowl. She placed it in Corde's hands. He opened his eyes.

"What is this?" he asked, with some surprise.

"Potato and leek soup," she said. "I made it myself. For you."

Corde's eyes slowly filled with tears, and then a tear rolled down Elysen's cheek.

"I have done some calculations," she said. "And I have determined that you have prepared almost seven thousand evening meals for me, and never once have I prepared a meal for you."

Corde held the bowl carefully. "This is a great honor," he said.

Elysen knelt down next to him. "The honor is mine," she said. "Until I did this, I never knew how much you honored me by such a simple task, done day after day after day, even when I did not deserve it."

Corde balanced the bowl of soup on his knee and touched Elysen's cheek.

"I love you, old man," she said.

"And I love you too," he said.

Elysen dipped a bowl for herself and they sat and ate together in silence. When Corde finished, Elysen offered him more. He shook his head.

"I thank you," he said. "But this old body does not need much sustenance anymore."

Elysen stared into her bowl. "We can't stay in the Vyr," she said.

Corde sighed. "I know."

"And we can't take Araden with us. I will be hunted wherever I go. And I can hardly hide."

Corde stared at the ground and nodded.

Elysen tipped her bowl back and forth, watching the broth flow back and forth like the tide in the rocky pools of the Sud De Mer where Araden had once played.

"The women of the camp have all left," she said.

Corde nodded.

Elysen took a deep breath before she spoke again.

"They would have nothing to do with my son."

"They are worse for their mistake," Corde said. "Araden is a spirit of joy."

Elysen shook her head.

"I fear some great harm will come to him," she said.

"Nonsense," Corde replied. "Our world is at peace now. Your trials are done, and your son shall grow up to be a man and a Lord."

Elysen's eyes blazed with a hot fire that Corde had not seen for many months.

"He must never be Lord," she said.

"You cannot prevent it," Corde said. "The people will expect him to rule. It is his destiny."

Elysen stopped him by raising her palm and glaring.

"No," she said. "The Uemn rule now. My hope for Araden is a life of simple peace."

"Our hopes matter little in this world," Corde reminded her. His soft voice relaxed her chest and she put her arm down. Her hand settled on her knee and she stared at the dark runes that coursed along the ridges and blue lines under her white skin.

"I have sent Tell to look for a man," she said. "I am hoping that this man will agree to take Araden and raise him like a son."

"Do I know this man?" Corde asked.

She shook her head.

"Can you trust him?"

"As much as I can trust anyone."

They sat in silence again for a while.

"It will break my heart to leave him," Elysen whispered.

"We can go north," Corde said. "We can hide in the ice lands."

She hung her head and shook it. "He will always be in danger, as long as he is with me."

"He needs his mother," Corde said.

"I can't trust myself," she said. "I never know when the Addiss may take control of me. I'll always be looking over my shoulder, dreading the day the Uemn or Kaanites come for him." She shook her head again. "I have thought about this long and hard. This is the only way."

Corde nodded and stared into his empty bowl. Elysen left him there and wandered toward the edge of the clearing where Raes stood, staring into the woods, leaning on the broadsword that he had taken from the field at Thane's Peak.

"I am going to leave," she told him.

He nodded.

"And what about you?" she asked.

He turned and looked at her. "When you are gone, my duty to the Vyr is over. I think I may travel. Maybe north, to the source of the winds of life, or west, across the barrens to see if there is anything beyond it."

"I'll miss you," she said.

Raes looked down at the ground and dug the tip of his sword into the tough grassy soil. "I wish that our lives had turned out differently," he said.

Elysen reached out and touched his cheek. He pulled his head back, away from her hand.

"Good-bye, old friend," she said. "May we meet in J'Halla someday."

Elysen stared into his eyes, searching, until Raes finally turned away. Elysen let her eyes fall to the ground, and found that her fists were clenched. She let her hands relax, began to lift them toward his back, longing to simply hold him, and to be held by him, but something stopped her. She took a step backwards, and then another and another. At some distance, it became easier to turn, and so she did.

Raes stared into the woods again as Elysen walked away.

As the days rolled on, Raes kept his distance, camping along the edge of the forest, prowling the woods during the day, sitting up at night. Elysen would often watch the glow of his fire from the door of her tent. Just when the first dusting of frosty snow touched the ground around the lake, Tell returned with Jaramis. The elder man rode a shaggy donkey and looked tired and worn. Corde fetched Elysen and she ran to Jaramis. She helped him down and they hugged until Tell cleared his throat.

"We've come a long way, m'lady," Tell said.

"Of course," Elysen said. She stepped back and looked Jaramis up and down. "Seeing you reminds me of young Arador."

Jaramis smiled.

"I hear that you have a small package of your own now," he said.

Elysen nodded.

"Did Tell..."

She choked on her own words.

"He told me of your plans," Jaramis said.

"Now that you are here, I will tarry no longer," Elysen said.

Jaramis grabbed Elysen's arm and kept her from turning away.

"I fear that I am not up to this task, m'lord," he said.

Elysen held him with her eyes. Her lips parted slightly but no sound came forth. Jaramis let go of her arm and let his gaze drift to the ground. Elysen stepped close to him and put both her hands on his shoulders. She leaned over a bit so that she could see into his eyes again, and he raised his head to face her.

"In my heart, I know that you are the keeper of this precious child," Elysen said. "Even though I do not know why."

Tell touched Jaramis on the shoulder and Elysen let go of the old man.

"Come," Tell said. "We have ridden for many days, and we need rest and food."

They ate together that night in Tell's tent, and afterwards, Jaramis and Elysen took a walk along the shore of the lake. The air felt fresh and cold and alive. Jaramis noticed the campfire in the distance near the edge of the woods. He pointed toward it.

"Who camps there?" he asked.

"My old friend, Raes."

"Why doesn't he join us?" Jaramis asked.

Elysen slipped her arm around Jaramis' elbow and pulled him close as they walked carefully along, placing their feet gently on the frosty earth.

"He is full of sorrow and remorse and needless worry. He feels that he wronged me and that he has been wronged by me, and that has wounded him."

"And yet he stays close," Jaramis noted.

"Yes."

They circled back around and Jaramis led Elysen to her tent. She let go of him and stepped back, into the doorway. She hovered at the threshold for a moment. Jaramis looked deep into her eyes.

"Is there any way I can talk you out of this?" he asked.

She shook her head.

"Tomorrow, as the sun comes up, I will leave you."

Jaramis pressed his hands together and stared at Elysen's boots. They seemed so fragile and small, cast in soft brown leather more befitting a simple farmer than the Shad'ya.

"M'lady," he said. "I fear that I will fail in this task you give me. This boy needs a mother, not an old man like me."

Jaramis lowered his head even further and Elysen touched his cheek. She let her fingers drift to his chin and then she leaned forward and pulled his face to hers. She kissed him, gently, like a mother kissing a baby. Jaramis looked at her with pleading eyes.

"You will do what needs to be done," she said. "And Araden will follow the path he must follow. As must I."

Elysen smiled and slipped out of the tent.

Morning came. Corde packed some food on the back of a mule and saddled a small horse as Elysen carried her sleeping baby over to Tell's tent. Tell and

Jaramis sat just outside the door, in front of a smoky fire, sipping green tea.

"Will you have something to eat before you go?" Tell asked. Elysen knelt down next to Jaramis and slipped Araden into his arms. The Soel crested the rise above the lake, and the orange light seemed to resonate off the boy's face, as if Araden created the morning light. Elysen touched his cheek and then stood.

"Where will you go?" Tell asked Elysen.

"It's best that you don't know," she said.

Tell just nodded. Jaramis stared at the boy in his arms. Araden coughed and squirmed, and then let out a loud yelp. Jaramis settled the child onto his shoulder and patted him on the back.

"And what of you, Jaramis?" Tell asked.

"We will lose ourselves in the Vyr like nomads, stopping here and there only long enough to leave our message and then to move on. We will be as hard to find as the wind."

Elysen turned her head. A tear slipped down her cheek, moving from white to black like a snake across the baked desert. She took her pouch from her belt and handed it to Jaramis.

"This is for Araden," she said. Jaramis opened the small bag and peered inside. Strands of hair, brown and white, wrapped around a sharp fragment of stone, and a wooden ball tied to a stick. He frowned, but closed it again and nodded.

"And in my tent, you will find my armor and my swords. Please keep them for my boy, and pray that he will never have to use them."

Jaramis nodded again. Elysen touched the red stone blade sheathed at her waist and gazed into the fire for a while.

"You will need to give him a new name," she said. Her words almost caught in her throat.

"We should call him something majestic," Jaramis said.

Elysen shook her head. "Call him something very plain," she said.

They all sat in silence as the morning sky grew light. The Soel hit Elysen's back and she drank the last of her broth.

"We have to go now," she said. She stood up. Corde stood slowly. He gazed at Araden, snuggled against Jaramis' shoulder.

Elysen walked away with Corde close behind.

"It is better for him this way," Elysen said. She mounted her horse in a flowing jump as Corde struggled to get a leg over his short mule.

"Jaramis seems like a good man," Corde said. The words choked him.

"He will be a good father," Elysen said. "I know this in my heart."

They stopped on a low rise, framed by the orange glow of the Soel. Below them, morning campfires dotted the shore of the lake. Elysen watched the plumes of smoke for a moment, and then pulled on the reins and thundered off toward the north. She dropped below the top of the ridge without glancing back. Corde held his spot for a moment longer, his mouth open wide and only a soft wail escaping from his chest. A tear slipped from his eye as he closed them tight, and then he too turned north, into the winds, toward the ice, toward home.

Joe Cooke takes his inspiration from the verdant plains, majestic mountains and rugged canyons of his native Pacific Northwest, where he lives with his wife and children.

Please feel free to contact him via www.joecooke.info.